THE NATURE OF MIDDLE-EARTH

J.R.R. TOLKIEN

The Nature
of Middle-earth

*Late Writings on the Lands, Inhabitants,
and Metaphysics of Middle-earth*

Edited by
Carl F. Hostetter

HOUGHTON MIFFLIN HARCOURT

Boston   New York

First US edition 2021
First published by HarperCollins*Publishers* 2021

For information about how to reproduce selections from this book,
write to trade.permissions@hmhco.com or to Permissions,
Houghton Mifflin Harcourt Publishing Company, 3 Park Avenue,
19th Floor, New York, New York 10016.

hmhbooks.com
tolkienestate.com

ISBN 978-0-358-45460-1

1 2021
4500830768

CONTENTS

PART TWO: BODY, MIND AND SPIRIT

PART THREE: THE WORLD, ITS LANDS, AND ITS INHABITANTS

APPENDICES

FOREWORD

In his own foreword to *Morgoth's Ring* (vol. X of *The History of Middle-earth*), Christopher Tolkien writes of his father that, at the end of the 1950s, and following the publication of *The Lord of the Rings*:

Meditating long on the world that he had brought into being and was now in part unveiled, he had become absorbed in analytic speculation concerning its underlying postulates. Before he could prepare a new and final *Silmarillion* he must satisfy the requirements of a coherent theological and metaphysical system, rendered now more complex in its presentation by the supposition of obscure and conflicting elements in its roots and its tradition.

Among the chief "structural" conceptions of the mythology that he pondered in those years were the myth of Light; the nature of Aman; the immortality (and death) of the Elves; the mode of their reincarnation; the Fall of Men and the length of their early history; the origin of the Orcs; and above all, the power and significance of Melkor-Morgoth, which was enlarged to become the ground and source of the corruption of Arda.

Christopher published a sizeable selection of and from Tolkien's long meditation on his sub-created world in *Morgoth's Ring* and the subsequent two volumes of *The History of Middle-earth*, but by no means all. The texts in this volume constitute a significant part and a fuller record of his "analytic speculation concerning its underlying postulates". They comprise the "writings about Middle-earth and Aman that are of a primarily philosophic or speculative nature" that were not included in the latter volumes of *The History of Middle-earth*; as well as those of a descriptive and/or historical nature, chiefly concerning the lands and peoples of Númenor and Middle-earth, that were not included in *Unfinished Tales*. These texts and this book are very much of a piece with significant portions of the aforementioned volumes, and will be of greatest interest to those who take particular interest in them.

Like *The Lord of the Rings*, this book has been long in the making. I have in a sense been working on this book – though for long I had no awareness or notion that I was doing so – for nearly 25 years. In 1997, in my capacity as one of the authorized editors of his father's linguistic papers, I received from Christopher Tolkien a bundle of photocopies of various manuscript and typescript materials, which he referred to collectively as "late philological essays". As this designation rightly implies, all of the materials in this bundle are concerned to some degree with linguistic matters; but as is often the case in Tolkien's post-*Lord of the Rings* non-narrative writings, the linguistic matters that occasioned each essay led Tolkien into long (seeming) digressions, either because they explain the historical, cultural, mythological and/or metaphysical situations that various words and phrases reflect; or simply because Tolkien wished to pursue some idea or point that occurred to him at that time. I edited and published three essays from this bundle in the journal *Vinyar Tengwar* first, "*Ósanwe-kenta*", a far-ranging essay on thought-communication, in *VT* 39 in July 1998; "Notes on *Órë*", a consideration of the inner warning and advising faculty of Incarnates, in *VT* 41 in July 2000; and "The Rivers and Beacon-hills of Gondor", a lengthy discussion of the names and characteristics of those geographic features, in *VT* 42 in July 2001. (Christopher had in fact prepared an edition of the latter text for inclusion in *The Peoples of Middle-earth*, but it was cut for lack of space.) A fourth long essay from this bundle, supplemented with related materials found in Tolkien's linguistic papers, was edited by Patrick Wynne and published in three parts as "Eldarin Hands, Fingers, and Numerals" in *VT* 46–49 from February 2005 to June 2007. (The first three texts are published here as chapters IX and X of part two, and chapter XXII of part three, respectively. The fourth, in considerably reduced form, is published as chapter III of part two.)

Following the publication of my editions of "*Ósanwe-kenta*" and "The Rivers and Beacon-hills of Gondor", and knowing of my great interest in these and similar philosophical, historical, and descriptive writings by Tolkien, even apart from their linguistic elements, Christopher asked me to assist French scholar Michaël

Devaux in preparing an edition of the (mostly) unpublished materials concerning Elvish reincarnation that Christopher alludes to in several places in both *Morgoth's Ring* and *The Peoples of Middle-earth*, and which he had sent to Devaux. This edition, together with Devaux's French translation and commentary, was eventually published in the journal *La Feuille de la Compagnie* vol. 3 in 2014. (These writings, in my own edition, are published here as chapter XV of part two and chapter XV of part three.)

This interest also explains why, beginning in the late summer of 2008, Christopher began sending me successive batches of photocopies of a large bundle of late (chiefly) manuscript writings, which had been collected together under the title "Time and Ageing", for my consideration and thoughts on their possible disposition. As will be seen, many of these writings are quite unlike the vast bulk of Tolkien's writings, featuring *inter alia* long tables and calculations regarding the maturation rate and population growth of the Eldar from the time of their awaking, to the time of the Great March, and through their arrival in Beleriand and beyond. Despite this technical and undeniably dry accounting, they nonetheless contain many interesting details of historical and cultural significance – e.g. the fact that Tolkien considered having not only the Vala Oromë instruct and guard the Elves at Cuiviénen, but also the Maia Melian, and those of her fellow Maiar that would later, in incarnate form, come (again?) to Middle-earth in the Third Age as the Istari, the Five Wizards that were sent by the Valar to encourage resistance to Sauron. These materials as a whole also exemplify not only Tolkien's unsuspected (at least by me) mathematical skills and precision (in a time well before electronic calculators became affordable), but also his great concern for coherence and verisimilitude, as seen throughout his later writings.

After long study and pondering of the "Time and Ageing" materials, and thinking of the writings in the "late philological essays" (both published and unpublished), and further of certain likewise philosophical and cultural passages (again both published and unpublished) in Tolkien's linguistic papers, similarly arising from etymological considerations – e.g. the essay I had edited and published as "Fate and Free Will" in *Tolkien Studies* 6 in 2009 (chapter XI of part two), and a long discussion of the nature of spirits according to Elvish thought that was edited and published by Christopher Gilson in issue 17 of his journal *Parma Eldalamberon* in 2007 (see chapter XIII of part two) – I began to discern how all this material might be organized together into a coherent book. This would allow me not only to publish such a substantial amount of material, which could not be accommodated in a journal, but also to bring it all to the wider audience I feel it deserves. Having come to this conclusion, I quickly chose to call this projected book *The Nature of Middle-earth*, as succinctly unifying these materials under the two main senses of the word "nature": both the visible and sensible phenomena of the physical world, including its lands, flora, and fauna; and the metaphysical, innate, and essential qualities and character of the world and its inhabitants.

This book is divided into three broad categorical parts. Part one, "Time and Ageing", is almost entirely composed of materials from the collection of the same name described above, though it is here and there supplemented with material from Tolkien's linguistic papers. Part two, "Body, Mind, and Spirit", and part three, "The World, Its Lands, and Its Inhabitants", are composed of materials from three chief sources: a) the bundle of "late philological essays" sent to me in 1997; b) material drawn from Tolkien's linguistic papers; and c) particularly in part three, material collected by me over the years from the two principal archives of Tolkien manuscripts at the Bodleian in Oxford and at Marquette University in Milwaukee. I have re-edited those materials that have been previously published in specialist journals to make them more accessible to a general audience, chiefly by removing or minimizing passages and commentary that are principally concerned with linguistic details. There is of course inevitably some overlap within particular texts among these three broad categories, but the distribution of texts among them, and the ordering of texts within each part, are what seem most sensible to me.

It is a pleasure to gratefully acknowledge the assistance of many people in the compilation and completion of this book. Catherine McIlwaine, the Tolkien Archivist at the Bodleian Libraries in Oxford, and William Fliss, Archivist of the Special Collections and University Archives at the Raynor Memorial Libraries of Marquette University in Milwaukee, have been extremely helpful and enthusiastic supporters of this book. I am also extremely grateful to Cathleen Blackburn and all the Tolkien Estate, and to Chris Smith, Tolkien editor for HarperCollins, for making publication of this book possible. I am, like all Tolkien scholars and researchers, indebted to Wayne Hammond and Christina Scull for their exacting and exhaustive research and reference works, in particular the indispensable three-volume *J.R.R. Tolkien Companion and Guide*. I was fortunate to be able to avail myself of John Garth's extensive knowledge of Tolkien's military experience, and his thoughtful assistance in locating certain texts in the Bodleian archives, in particular the Númenórean material in this book. Arden Smith and Charles Noad have both applied their formidable proofreading and fact-checking skills to the text (though of course any errors that remain are due solely to me). I am also grateful for the support, friendship, and encouragement of numerous Tolkien scholars and friends from around the world who have heard me read from some of the materials in this book over the years, including: David Bratman, Marjorie Burns, Michelle Markey Butler, Janice Coulter, Chip Crane, Jason Fisher, Matt Fisher, Verlyn Flieger, Christopher Gilson, Melody Green, Peter Grybauskas, Wayne Hammond, Yoko Hemmi, Gary Hunnewell, John Rateliff, Christina Scull, Eleanor Simpson, Arden Smith, Valah Steffen-Wittwer, Paul Thomas, Patrick Wynne, and the late, much-missed Vaughn Howland and Richard West.

Finally, my greatest gratitude is of course to Christopher Tolkien, who directly supplied me with most of the materials that have gone into this book and supported my idea to publish them in this manner. He was able to see and approve my book proposal, with a representative selection of my treatment and presentation of the texts, and my plan for the book as a whole, in the year before his passing. I am above all thankful for the kindness, encouragement, and sympathy he expressed to me in the course of our decades-long correspondence. I had the great good fortune to count him as a friend, and I dedicate this book to his memory.

EDITORIAL PRACTICES

In order to make these texts as readable as possible, with minimal editorial intrusion, I have often silently: expanded abbreviations where their meaning is in no doubt; supplied punctuation, conjunctions, and other minor connecting words where Tolkien writing in greater haste has omitted them; and regularized capitalization and other spelling conventions, where such alterations are insignificant to the text or its meaning. I have however tended not to regularize spelling or, save where necessary for clarity, supplied punctuation or other additions to texts cited in the editorial notes. I have also made no attempt to either note or record where Tolkien has both made and subsequently corrected a mathematical error.

With the exception of more or less brief introductions, describing the manuscript or typescript of each text and providing a date (as nearly as possible) and other relevant context, all editorial commentary – chiefly detailing authorial and/or editorial alterations of any significance, citing significant differences among variant versions of a text, and cross-references to Tolkien's other writings – has been placed in numbered end-notes to each text (or group of related texts), and need not be consulted by those not interested in such textual matters. Where editorial comments must be made within Tolkien's own texts, they are distinguished as such by being set in a smaller type and indented from the textual margins.

Tolkien is inconsistent throughout in his use of single-quotes (inverted commas) and double-quotes. I have adopted the practice of using double-quotes for all quotations and phrases (except for quotes and phrases within quotes, for which single-quotes are used), and single-quotes for all glosses (actual or apparent): e.g. *fëa* 'spirit', *hröa* 'body'.

Wherever practicable I have given Tolkien's own footnotes and interpolated notes (frequent in his later writings) as footnotes on the page of the note's referent. Where it is necessary to provide editorial end-notes to these footnotes (which my text editor does not permit) I place the end-note mark in square brackets next to the footnote mark: e.g., *[1], and indicate in the end-note upon which word or passage or matter in the footnote I am commenting.

I have supplied a brief discussion of various metaphysical and theological concepts and themes encountered in these texts, as Appendix I, linked to key points of relevance in the texts. A glossary and index of forms from Tolkien's invented languages that are important to clarifying the meaning of various not-specifically-linguistic passages encountered in the texts in this book, and that can be used for further topical cross-referencing, are included in the editorial Glossary and Index of Quenya Terms as Appendix II.

Familiarity with at least *The Silmarillion* as published in 1977 is assumed. Ready access to *Unfinished Tales* and volumes X–XII of *The History of Middle-earth* will further aid in understanding the texts included here.

ABBREVIATIONS & CONVENTIONS

AUTHORIAL

AY	Awakening Year(s) (i.e., *löar* since the Awakening of the Elves)
Bel.	Year(s) of Beleriand (i.e., since the arrival of the Exiles in Middle-earth)
DB	Days of Bliss
FA	First Age
4A	Fourth Age
Gen(s).	Generation(s)
GY	Growth Year(s) (i.e., multiples of 12 *löar* between the birth and maturity of the Elves)
LY	Life Year(s)
MY	Middle-earth/Mortal Year(s) (= 1 *löa*)
NB	*Nota Bene* ('note well')
SA	Second Age
SY	Sun Year (i.e. *löa*)
TA	Third Age
TY	*The Tale of Years* (cf. X:49)
VY	Valian Year(s) (variously = 100 or 144 *löar*)
YS	Year(s) of the Sun
YT	Year(s) of the Trees (approximately 10 *löar*)

Bibliographic

AAm   *The Annals of Aman* (in *Morgoth's Ring* pp. 47–138) of c. 1951–2, with revisions in 1958

DN   *A Description of the Island of Númenor* (in *Unfinished Tales* pp. 165–72) of c. 1965.

GA   *The Grey Annals* (in *War of the Jewels* pp. 3–170) of c. 1951–2, with revisions in 1958

HoMe   *The History of Middle-earth* (in 12 vols.)

I–XII   Individual volumes of *HoMe*, esp. V: *The Lost Road and Other Writings*, IX: *Sauron Defeated*; X: *Morgoth's Ring*; XI: *The War of the Jewels*; XII: *The Peoples of Middle-earth*

L   *The Letters of J.R.R. Tolkien*

LR   *The Lord of the Rings*

LRRC   *The Lord of the Rings: A Reader's Companion*, by Hammond and Scull, 2014.

OED   *The Oxford English Dictionary*

PE   *Parma Eldalamberon* (journal)

RotK   *The Return of the King*

S   *The Silmarillion*

TCG   *The J.R.R. Tolkien Companion and Guide*, vols. I, II, III. Ed. Scull and Hammond, 2017.

UT   *Unfinished Tales*

VT   *Vinyar Tengwar* (journal)

Editorial

[...]   Editorial insertion/addition (except where otherwise noted)

[?...]   Uncertain reading

{...}   Deleted by Tolkien

>>   Changed by Tolkien to

App.   Appendix

chap(s).   Chapter(s)

esp.   Especially

fn.   Footnote

MS(S)   Manuscript(s)

n.   Note

TS   Typescript

LANGUAGES

C.E.   Common Eldarin

P.E.   Primitive Eldarin

Q.   Quenya

S.   Sindarin

T.   Telerin

LINGUISTICS

√   Root/stem form

*   Primitive or reconstructed form

<   Arose by phonological development from

>   Became by phonological development

†   Poetic

fem.   Feminine

intr.   Intransitive

lit.   Literally

n.   Noun

pa.t.   Past tense

pl.   Plural

tr.   Transitive

PART ONE

TIME AND AGEING

INTRODUCTION

Among the large collection of (mostly) manuscript pages that Christopher Tolkien dubbed the "Time and Ageing" file are two half-sheets of Merton College stationery, on which two related but distinct texts – presented here as chap. I, "The Valian Year" – were written some six years apart. These two texts conveniently demonstrate that, sometime between 1951 and 1957, Tolkien made two decisions that would have far-reaching effects on his *legendarium*. While the first of these decisions – namely, to make the Sun and Moon coëval with Arda, the inhabited world – and its ramifications in and for Tolkien's subsequent writings and revisions have already been documented and considered by Christopher Tolkien in the final three volumes of his monumental *History of Middle-earth* (and particularly in the section titled "Myths Transformed" in volume X, *Morgoth's Ring*), the second transformative decision and its ramifications have not before been presented.

As the second of these two texts shows, Tolkien had by 1957 decided that the number of sun-years (SY) in a Year of the Trees, or Valian Year (VY), should be greatly increased, from the previous rate of 10 SY = 1 VY to a new rate of 144 SY = 1 VY, and thus vastly expanded the length of time in sun-years of the events recorded in the Annals of Valinor and subsequent chronologies dated in Valian Years. Much of the "Time and Ageing" file, whose texts are presented here, is concerned with working out the (perhaps surprisingly) complex ramifications of this decision, not only for the chronology of the First Age – in particular for the Awakening of the Elves (including even just who were the First Elves to awaken), the Great March, and the return of both Morgoth and the Exiles to Middle-earth – but also for the periods

of time occupied by the begetting, growth, maturity, and ageing of
Elves.

Tolkien's preoccupation with some of these matters in the late
1950s, particularly Elvish begetting, maturation, and ageing
relative to Men, has already been glimpsed, in the opening of the c.
1958 text known as *Laws and Customs among the Eldar* (X:209–10):

The Eldar grew in bodily form slower than Men, but in mind more
swiftly. They learned to speak before they were one year old; and in
the same time they learned to walk and to dance, for their wills came
soon to the mastery of their bodies. Nonetheless there was less difference between the two Kindreds, Elves and Men, in early youth;
and a man who watched elf-children at play might well have
believed that they were the children of Men, of some fair and happy
people. ...

This same watcher might indeed have wondered at the small limbs
and stature of these children, judging their age by their skill in words
and grace in motion. For at the end of the third year mortal children
began to outstrip the Elves, hastening on to a full stature while the
Elves lingered in the first spring of childhood. Children of Men might
reach their full height while Eldar of the same age were still in body
like to mortals of no more than seven years. Not until the fiftieth year
did the Eldar attain the stature and shape in which their lives would
afterwards endure, and for some a hundred years would pass before
they were full-grown.

The Eldar wedded for the most part in their youth and soon after
their fiftieth year. They had few children, but these were very dear to
them. Their families, or houses, were held together by love and a deep
feeling for kinship in mind and body; and the children needed little
governing or teaching. There were seldom more than four children in
any house, and the number grew less as ages passed; but even in days
of old, while the Eldar were still few and eager to increase their kind,
Fëanor was renowned as the father of seven sons, and the histories
record none that surpassed him.

And further (X:212–13):

As for the begetting and bearing of children: a year passes between
the begetting and the birth of an elf-child, so that the days of both are
the same or nearly so, and it is the day of begetting that is remembered year by year. For the most part these days come in the Spring.
It might be thought that, since the Eldar do not (as Men deem) grow

old in body, they may bring forth children at any time in the ages of their lives. But this is not so. For the Eldar do indeed grow older, even if slowly: the limit of their lives is the life of Arda, which though long beyond the reckoning of Men is not endless, and ages also. Moreover their body and spirit are not separated but coherent. As the weight of the years, with all their changes of desire and thought, gathers upon the spirit of the Eldar, so do the impulses and moods of their bodies change. This the Eldar mean when they speak of their spirits consuming them; and they say that ere Arda ends the Eldalië on earth will have become as spirits invisible to mortal eyes, unless they will to be seen by some among Men into whose minds they may enter directly.

Also the Eldar say that in the begetting, and still more in the bearing of children, greater share and strength of their being, in mind and in body, goes forth than in the making of mortal children. For these reasons it came to pass that the Eldar brought forth few children; and also that their time of generation was in their youth or earlier life, unless strange and hard fates befell them. But at whatever age they married, their children were born within a short space of years after their wedding. (Short as the Eldar reckoned time. In mortal count there was often a long interval between the wedding and the first child-birth, and even longer between child and child.) For with regard to generation the power and the will are not among the Eldar distinguishable. Doubtless they would retain for many ages the power of generation, if the will and desire were not satisfied; but with the exercise of the power the desire soon ceases, and the mind turns to other things. The union of love is indeed to them great delight and joy, and the 'days of the children', as they call them, remain in their memory as the most merry in life; but they have many other powers of body and mind which their nature urges them to fulfil.

It is evident that the bulk of the texts in the "Time and Ageing" file are later than *Laws and Customs*, as shown by the use of the Quenya word *hröa* for 'body' (nearly) everywhere in these texts, *ab initio* – while in *Laws and Customs* as first written/typed, the form was *hrondo*, before subsequent correction to *hröa*. It will thus be seen that the extensive "Time and Ageing" file is a series of elaborations and reconsiderations of the matters of Elvish gestation, maturation, and ageing raised in *Laws and Customs*, and related matters, in light of the great increase in time spanned by the tally of Valian Years.

On the subject of dating the individual "Time and Ageing" texts, most of which are clearly of a piece, in order to reduce repetition in justifying a probable date for most of them, if I simply flatly state that a text is "c. 1959" without further evidence, then the date is based on one or more of the following considerations:

1. The text uses the Quenya word *hröa* (plural *hröar*), meaning 'body' *ab initio*. There is no independent evidence that that word was in use until after the typescript text B of *Laws and Customs among the Eldar* was made in c. 1958 (see X:141–3, 209, 304).

2. The text employs the name *Ingar* for the people of Ingwë, which otherwise occurs only in Text A of *Laws and Customs among the Eldar* (cf. X:230 n.22) and in Text 2 of *Of Finwë and Míriel* (cf. X:265 n.10), both of which belong to what Christopher Tolkien identifies as the "second phase" in the development of *The Later Quenta Silmarillion*, which he in turn dates to "the late 1950s" (cf. X:199, 300).

3. The manuscript in appearance and the text in character and content is consistent with most of the other writings in the "Time and Ageing" file, including those that can be dated more certainly to c. 1959 by other internal or external evidence.

The texts presented here for the most part fall into one of three stages, based on an apparent conceptional progression in the period of Elvish gestation in the womb: the first, in which Elves gestate for 8 or (more usually) 9 *löar* (as the solar year is called in Quenya); the second, in which they gestate for 1 *löa*; and the third and last, in which they gestate for 3 *löar*. The first two of these stages are exhibited in texts that either firmly or most likely date from c. 1959 or 1960; the third is found in a single document that dates from 1965.

Finally, while I provide a glossary of terms in App. II, there are certain Quenya words that occur in "Time and Ageing" so frequently that I gloss them here as well for ease of reference for the reader:

hröa, pl. *hröar* 'body'.
fëa, pl. *fëar* 'spirit'
löa, pl. *löar* 'year (of the Sun)', lit. 'growth'.
yên, pl *yéni* 'long-year' = 144 *löar*.

I

THE VALIAN YEAR

These two brief texts are written in black nib-pen on two torn half-sheets of two (different) Merton College weekly battels bills. Tolkien was the Merton Professor of English Language and Literature from 1945 until his retirement in 1959. The portion of the bill bearing the first text does not have the date field, but that bearing the second text does, and is dated 27 June 1957.

The first (very hastily written) text shows that when he wrote it, Tolkien had decided that the world must be round and coëval with the Sun and Moon, and so it must post-date the "Round World" version (C*) of the *Ainulindalë* that Tolkien made in 1948 (X:3). It most likely precedes, however, the revisions to the c. 1951 version of the *Annals of Aman* by which the length of a Valian Year was reduced from exactly 10 sun-years (as in the first text) to 9.582 sun-years (X:50, and see X:57–8 n.17 and 59–60 §§5–10).

Text 1

The *yên*, which is merely a mode of reckoning, has nothing to do with the life of the Elves. In Aman this depended on the years of the Trees, or really on the *days* of the Trees; in Middle-earth on the cycles of growth, Spring to Spring, or *löar*. In Middle-earth, one *löa* aged an Elf as much as a year of the Trees, but these were in fact 10 times as long.

A Year of the Trees had 1,000 days of 12 hours = 12,000 [Tree] hours. A year of 365.250 days of 24 hours has 8,766 hours.

Tree-years have 87,660. If 12,000 [Tree] hours = 10 Middle-earth years each Tree-hour = about 7.3 Sun-hours = 7 hours 18 secs.[1]

How are we to arrange for the *Sun* and *Moon*?

Elves do not know how Arda was established or the companions of *Anar* made or their [?companies]. For it is to the life of *Arda* (*not* Eä) which they are bound, and all their *love* is for Arda. Though [?of Lore] they may consider [?the matter] and having amazing sight they can see in the heavens things we cannot [?for need of] instruments.

TEXT 2

Time

There are twelve Tree-hours in each Valian Day, 144 Days in each Valian Year. But each Valian Year = 144 Mortal Years; therefore 1 Valian Day = 1 mortal year, and 1 Tree-hour = approximately 1 mortal month. Time is recorded (for Mortal purposes) during the days of the Trees thus: VY 100 V.Day 136 V.Hour 9 = the 9th month of the 136th [sun-]year of the 100th Valian Year.[2]

In Middle-earth originally the Quendi appreciated and aged in 144 MY (or *yên*) as [mortals] in 1 MY. Therefore when they went to Aman they felt no change – but those who remained soon felt the necessary rate of "mortality" in ageing. After the death of the Trees and the ruin of Beleriand the rate was about 12 years = 1 MY.

The Elves awoke in VY 1050 and reached Aman in 1133 after 83 VY, which felt as 83 years to them but was 11,952 MY. Men awoke in VY 1150 or 100 VY later = 14,400 MY.[3]

It can be seen then that by c. 1957 Tolkien had introduced a new correspondence of 1 Valian Year = 144 sun-years (the length of the Elvish *yên* or 'long year'), and so vastly expanded the length of time in sun-years of the events recorded in the *Annals of Valinor* and subsequent chronologies dated in Valian Years.

NOTES

1 In the c. 1937 *Annals of Valinor*, the Valian Year is implied to be, as here, exactly the same as 10 sun-years: "The First Ages are reckoned as 30,000 [sun-]years, or 3,000 years of the Valar" (V:118). This was also the case in the first version of the c. 1951 *Annals of Aman* (X:50, and see X:57–8 n.17).

2 Tolkien here actually wrote: "of the 14,400[th] Valian Year", an obvious slip of the pen.

3 In the c. 1951 *Annals of Aman* the Elves awoke (as here) in VY 1050 and arrived in Aman in VY 1132 (X:71, 84) and in VY 1500 the Sun and the Moon were fashioned and first rose (X:131); and with that first sunrise Men awoke (X:130). At the time that Tolkien was (first) working on the *AAm* the Valian Year was still just 10 sun-years, and so Men awoke $1500 - 1050 = 450 \times 10 = 4,500$ years after the Elves. Here, with the VY = 144 SY, Men awoke $1150 - 1050 = 100 \times 144 = 14,400$: a more than three-fold increase in time.

It may further be noted that, since, by the time he wrote text 2, Tolkien had decided that the Sun and the Moon were coëval with Arda, the awakening of Men no longer has any chronological correspondence with either the return of the Exiles to Middle-earth or the first rising of the Sun, and so there is no mention of them.

II

VALINORIAN TIME-DIVISIONS

This text occupies eight sides of four sheets of unlined paper. It is written in a clear hand in black nib-pen, with additions and some revisions made in blue ball-point pen. The versos of most sheets are filled with attendant calculations, not represented here. It dates to c. 1959.

In a revised scheme – in which the Sun and Moon are a primeval part of Arda, established before Arda was inhabitable – the *basic time*, even in Aman, must be the *Sun-year*, since this governs all growth, be it slow, normal, or quick. But the sun-day need not be observed, since Valinor was domed over.[1]

Hence the *basic equivalent* of Valian Time and Middle-earth Time (VT and MT) will be:

1 Valian Day (or Tree-day) = 1 Sun-year

All multiplications or divisions of this were by 12. Hence the Valian Month had 12 Valian Days = 12 years, the Valian Year (a *yén*) had 12 Valian Months = 144 years.

These equivalences are exact; since the Valian Day was maintained always at the length of the Elvish *löa* or Sun-year (whether that varied or lengthened or not).*

---

* But since the light of Valinor was quite independent of earth-rotation, and depended on the length of the light of the Trees – which from the opening of

In the Days of the Trees: The Valian Day was divided into 12 Valian Hours, which were arranged evidently to occupy exactly $\frac{1}{12}$ each of whatever was the length of the Sun-year. (This is held to have varied and to have lengthened.) At present Sun-year length a Valian Hour is therefore approximately 1 month of 30 (or nearly 30½) days.*

Since the Valar and Eldar only grow or age slowly, but do not live, act, go, or perceive slowly (on the contrary) for local use in Aman the Valian Hour was further subdivided in repetitive 12s.

A Solar Year contains 365d. 5h. 48m. 46s. = 365d. 20,926 secs. or 365.242199074 days.

1 day has 86,400 secs. ¼ day therefore has 21,600 secs. The Year is thus 674 secs. (11m. 14secs) short of 365¼ days.

Valian Day = Sun-year

12	hours	
144	primes	
1,728	seconds	
20,736	terces	Solar year has 31,556,926 secs.
248,832	quarts	
2,985,984	quints	
35,831,808	minims	Therefore the Valian Minim is 0.88069589 of a second.

Or very nearly. At true value this would be 35,831,807.9581... minims in a year.

Tolkien then wrote "actual value" and calculated the fractional part of the relation of a minim to solar seconds to approximately 360 decimal places, noting where values started to repeat. On the next page he adds a sext before the minim, thus shortening the minim by a further 12th.

Telperion to the closing of Laurelin occupied 1 Day or Sun-year exactly – all smaller fractions of time were reckoned in descending twelfths. These were, of course, exact and accurate for Valinorian purposes, but owing to the inexactitude of the Sun-year in relation to earth-rotations, were complicated if stated in relation to Middle-earth times (in days, hours, seconds).

* 30 days 10h 29m $3\frac{5}{6}$s.

1 Valian Day exactly equalled 1 *löa* or Sun-year. This was divided into 12 Hours of the Trees. Each of these therefore equalled $\frac{1}{12}$ Year. All subsequent subdivisions of the Valian Hour were also by 12, and ran from Prime through Second, Terce, Quart, Quint, Sext (or first, second, etc. subdivision of the Hour) to the Minim, which was $\frac{1}{12}$[7] part of the Valian Hour and approximately $\frac{1}{14}$ of our seconds.

At the present rate of 365 days 5 hrs. 48 mins. 46 secs. to 1 year:

Valian Division	Days	Hours	Minutes	Seconds	Minims [60th of a second]
Hour	30	10	29	3	50
Prime	2	12	52	25	$19\frac{2}{12}$
Second		5	4	22	$6\frac{7}{12}$ approx.
Terce			25	21	$50\frac{1}{2}$ approx.
Quart			2	6	49 approx.
Quint				10	38 approx.
Sext					$53\frac{2}{12}$ approx.
Minim					$4\frac{31}{72}$ approx.

The nearest approximate equivalents are thus:

Valian Division	Equivalent
Hour	1 month ($30\frac{1}{2}$ days)
Prime	2½ days
Second	5 hours
Terce	25 mins.
Quart	2 mins. ($2\frac{1}{10}$)
Quint	10 secs.
Sext	1 sec. ($\frac{10}{12}$)
Minim	$\frac{1}{14}$ sec.

In the narrative time lengths of less than the Valian Second are seldom mentioned; and less than the Valian Quart (2 mins.) practically never.

NOTES

1 Regarding the "domes of Varda" in the "Round World" version of the mythology, see X:369–72, 375–8, 385–90.

III

OF TIME IN ARDA

While I have not felt obliged to retain the precise order of texts as found in the "Time and Ageing" file, I have done so for the first five texts that follow, because Tolkien appears to have selected, re-labelled, and (in the case of the first three) assigned them Roman numerals, in such a way as to indicate a plan to assemble a larger work from them, to be titled "Of Time in Arda".

In the case of the first text, originally called "Time-scales", Tolkien assigned it a number and a new title:

I. The *Quendi* compared with Men

The second text, originally called "Youth of the Quendi", was likewise assigned a number and a new title:

III. Natural Youth and Growth of the Quendi

(If there ever was a text II, it appears no longer to reside in the "Time and Ageing" folder.) The third text was simply assigned a number, otherwise retaining its original title:

IV. Summary of the Eldarin traditions concerning the "Awakening" and of the *Legend of the Cuivië* (*Cuivienyarna*)

Additionally, all the sides of these texts (that had not previously been struck through) were then renumbered continuously from 1–15.

All these modifications were made in red ball-point pen, which may
be significant to the titles supplied in the top margins of the sides of
the subsequent two texts, likewise in red ball-point pen (though
they were not assigned a number nor were their sides renumbered
continuously with the first three texts). Thus:

Awaking of the Quendi

was written in the top margins of the sides of both versions of the
fourth text, and:

March

was written in the top margins of the sides of both versions of the
fifth text, which originally had the title of just "*Quendi*".

Apparently subsequent to the selection and modifications of the first
three texts, Tolkien began a new typescript version of the assembled
texts (though in the event only getting part-way through the newly
renamed first text), which thus now serves as a sort of cover sheet
for them. This typescript occupies two sheets, with the text ending at
the bottom of the second sheet. All Elvish terms are typed with a red
ribbon, as is the extensive footnote on Quenya terms for "love". As
far as it goes, this typescript closely follows the manuscript version,
presented here as chap. IV, "Time-scales", below, but with enough
differences in detail that I give it here in full.

OF TIME IN ARDA

I
The Quendi compared with Men

The Valar having entered Arda, and being therefore confined within
its life, must also suffer its slow ageing, perceiving it as a growing
weight upon them, since they are to the total *erma* of Arda in many
ways similar to the *fëar* within the corporeal *hröar* of the Incarnate
(*hröambari*).[1]

The Quendi, being immortal within Arda, also aged with Arda as
regards their *hröar*; but since, unlike the Valar whose true life was not
corporeal and who assumed bodily forms at their own will as raiment, the being of the Quendi was incarnate, and consisted naturally

of the union of a *fëa* and a *hröa*, this ageing was felt chiefly in the *hröa*.

This, as the Eldar say, was slowly "consumed" by the *fëa*, until instead of dying and being discarded to dissolution it became absorbed, and eventually became no more than the memory of its habitation of old which the *fëa* retained; thus they have become now usually invisible to human eyes. But this has taken long ages to come about. In the beginning the *hröar* of the Elves, being supported and nourished by the great strength of their *fëar*, were vigorous, resisting hurts, and healing such as they suffered swiftly from within. Their ageing was therefore extremely slow by the measure of Men, though they were in their earlier days as "physical" as Men, or even more so: more strong, energetic, and swift in body, and taking greater delight in all bodily pleasures and exercises.

If we disregard the *actual time*, measured in the sun-years of Middle-earth, but use "years" merely as units of measurement in the growth from birth to maturity proper to each kind, it will be observed that the Elves closely resembled Men in this process. They reached maturity (of the body) at about the age of 20, and remained in full physical vigour till about the age of 60. After that the *fëa* and its interests began to dominate them. At the age of about 100 one of the Quendi had reached a stage similar to that of a Mortal of full age and wisdom. The normal period, therefore, for marriage and the begetting and bearing of children and their nurture (which were among the greatest delights of the Quendi in Arda) was between about the ages of 20 and 60.

The Quendi differed, however, from Men in several important aspects, if we speak only of them in the early ages of their life in Arda.

1. Their *fëar* never reached maturity in the sense that they ceased to be able to grow, by further increase of knowledge and wisdom; but they did reach a stage when *memory* (of thought and labour, and of the events of history, general and to each one particular) began to be a burden, or at least began more and more to occupy their minds and emotions. This development, however, which marks the true "ageing" of the Elves, did not concern the Elder Days, and first became evident during the Second Age, increasing rapidly during the Third Age when the Dominion of Men was finally achieved.

2. Individuals were more variable even than among Men. This may be ascribed to the variability of the Elvish *fëar* in native force and talents (greater than any variation seen among Men), and the more powerful influence which these *fëar* exerted upon their bodies. The

ages, therefore, defined above: 20, 60, 100: are only general and approximate. After maturity their minds and wills had far more control than is the case with Men over the events of the body, and over the direction and serial ordering of the uses of the body's powers. For instance, at maturity one of the Quendi could marry and at once enter into the *Onnarië* or 'Time of the Children'. But they could postpone marriage; or within marriage postpone the *Onnarië* (by absence or abstinence): either because they were otherwise occupied in pursuits that absorbed their attention; or because they had not yet found one whom they wished to marry, or as Men say "fallen in love";* [2] or for reasons of prudence or necessity, as in times of trouble, wandering, or exile.

Postponement of the fulfilment of marriage affected the time in which the *hröa* remained in full vigour; for the use of these bodily powers absorbed, relatively to Men, more of the vitality of the Quendi, and more also (though in less degree) of the youth of the *fëa*. So that in certain cases marriage might take place between Quendi of the age of 60 or even more years.

---

* Or as the Eldar said "met love". In this matter the Elven tongues make distinctions. To speak of Quenya: "love", which Men might rather call "friendship" or even "liking" (but for the greater warmth, strength, and permanency with which it was felt by the Quendi) was represented by words derived from √*mel*. *Emel* (or *melmë*, a particular case) was primarily a motion or inclination of the *fëa*, and therefore could occur between those of the same or of difference sexes. In itself it included no sexual (or rather procreative) desire; though naturally in Incarnates a difference of sex altered the emotion, since sex is held by the Eldar to belong also to the *fëa*, and not solely to the *hröa*, and is not therefore wholly included in procreation. Sexual desire (for marriage and procreation) was represented by the term *yermë*; but since this did not occur normally without *melmë* on both sides the relations of lovers before marriage, or of husbands and wives, were often described also by *melmë*.

Two other groups of words also referred to feelings that we should often call "love": those related to √*ndil* and to √*ndur*. √*ndil* may be compared with the Greek element *phil*, occurring in such words as *Anglophile* and *bibliophile*, or in such as *philosophy*. It expressed a deep concern for or interest in things or objects of thought, rather than in individuals or persons, and so was equivalent to the arts and sciences of Men, though it surpassed them in intensity and in the element of affection. Thus *eärendil* 'a lover of the sea', or *ornendil* 'a lover of trees'. It was often found in names, such as *Elendil* (< *eledndil*) 'Ælfwine, lover of the Elves', *Valandil* 'Oswine, lover of the Valar'. √*ndil* (*nilmë*) may be called "love", because while its mainspring was a concern for things other than self for their own sakes, it included a personal satisfaction in that the inclination was part of the "lover's" native character, and study or service of the things loved were necessary to their fulfilment.

NOTES

1 The full significance of this statement will become clearer in part two of this book, esp. in chap. XV, "Elvish Reincarnation"; and cf. my introduction to part two. What it means, in short, is that the Valar give material form to the basic, undifferentiated prime matter (Q. *erma*) of Arda, in accordance with the Music of the *Ainulindalë* and the Vision of Arda shown to them by Eru prior to its physical creation; and so are, in a sense, its spirit.

2 *"Elendil* (< *eledndil*)":* The TS here actually reads: "(< *eld-ndil*)", but this seems a likely typographical error; cf. the form derivation *"Eled-ndil > Elendil"* in the preceding MS version. With the citation of Quenya/Old English pairings here of the names Valandil/Oswine ('lover of the Valar' and 'God-friend', respectively) and Elendil/Ælfwine ('lover of the Elves' and 'Elf-friend', respectively), see the significant paired use of these same names in the c. 1937 *The Lost Road* (V:7 ff.), the c. 1945 *Notion Club Papers* (esp. Part II, IX: 222 ff.), and the subsequent *Drowning of Anadûnê* (IX:331 ff.).

   The typescript ends with this lengthy note, at the bottom of a page, with only: "√*ndur*" following (indicating the intent to begin a discussion of the stem √*ndur* as in the manuscript version; but apparently never taken up).

IV

TIME-SCALES

This text is (for the most part) a clear manuscript written in black nib-pen in a mostly careful hand, on ten sides of five sheets of unlined paper. Tolkien's often lengthy, interpolated notes (here given as footnotes) are in a smaller and italic hand, but likewise careful. It was later supplied with some marginal notes (here given as footnotes) and additions in red ball-point pen. The text dates to c. 1959.

Time-scales

The Valar having entered Arda, and being therein confined within its life, must also suffer (while therein and being as it were its spirit, as the *fëa* is to the *hröa* of the Incarnate) its slow ageing.[1] The Quendi being immortal within Arda also aged with Arda as regards their *hröar*; but since, unlike the Valar, whose true life was not corporeal and who assumed bodily forms at will as raiment, their being was incarnate and consisted naturally of the union of a *fëa* and a *hröa*, this ageing was felt chiefly in the *hröa*.[2] This, as the Eldar say, was slowly "consumed" by the *fëa*, until instead of dying and being discarded to dissolution it became absorbed and eventually became no more than the memory of its habitation of old which the *fëa* retained: thus they became or have now become mostly invisible to human eyes.[3] But this has taken long ages to come about. In the beginning the *hröar* of the Elves, being supported and nourished by the great strength of their *fëar*, were vigorous, resisting hurts, and healing such as they suffered swiftly from within. Their ageing was, therefore, *extremely slow* by mortal standards, though they were in their early days as "physical" as Men, or even more so, more strong, vigorous, and swift in body, and taking greater delight in all bodily pleasures and exercises.

If we disregard the actual time, measured in the sun-years of Middle-earth, but use "years" merely as the units of measurement in the growth from birth to maturity proper to each kind, it will be observed that the Quendi resembled the Atani in this process. Their *fëar* never reached maturity in the sense of ceasing to be capable of further increase of knowledge and wisdom; but they did reach a stage when memory, both of thought and labour (as well as of the events of history, general and to each one particular), began to be a burden, or began more and more to occupy their thought and emotion. But this development, which marks the "ageing" of the Quendi, did not concern the Elder Days, and first became evident during the Second Age, increasing rapidly during the Third Age when the Dominion of Men was finally achieved.

The *hröar* of the Quendi had, however, a definite rhythm and process similar to that of Men. They reached maturity at about the age of 20,* and remained in full physical vigour till about the age of 60, after which the *fëa* and its interests began to assume command. After about the age of 90–96 one of the Quendi had reached a stage similar to that of a vigorous and hale Mortal of high age and wisdom.[4] The normal period, therefore, for marriage and the begetting and bearing of children and their nurture (which were one of the greatest delights of the Quendi in Arda), was between about the ages of 20 and 60.

The Quendi differed, however, from Men in the following important aspects, if we speak only of them in the earlier ages of their life in Arda. Individuals were more variable, so that the ages defined above (of 20, 60, 90) are only general and approximate.[5] After maturity (at about 20) their minds and wills had far more control over the events of the body and over the direction of the uses, and the serial ordering of the uses, of the body's powers and functions. For instance, after maturity one of the Quendi could marry and at once enter into the "Time of the Children". But they could postpone marriage; or within marriage postpone the "Time of the Children". Either because they were otherwise occupied in pursuits that absorbed them; or because they had not found a "desired spouse" (or as Men say "fallen in

---

* Elf-men 24, women c. 18.

love");*[6] or for reasons of prudence or necessity imposed by circumstances, as in times of trouble, wandering, and exile.

Postponement of the fulfilment of marriage affected the length of time in which the *hröa* remained in full vigour of maturity. For the

---

* In this matter the Elven-tongues make distinctions. To speak of Quenya: *Love*, which Men might call "friendship" (but for the greater strength and warmth and permanency with which it was felt by the Quendi) was represented by √*mel*. This was primarily a motion or inclination of the *fëa*, and therefore could occur between persons of the same sex or different sexes. It included no sexual or *procreative* desire, though naturally in Incarnates the difference of sex altered the emotion, since "sex" is held by the Eldar to belong also to the *fëa* and not solely to the *hröa*, and is therefore not wholly included in procreation. Such persons were often called *melotorni* 'love-brothers' and *meletheldi* 'love-sisters'.

The 'desire' for marriage and bodily union was represented by √*yer*; but this never in the uncorrupted occurred without 'love' √*mel*, nor without the desire for children. This element was therefore seldom used except to describe occasions of its dominance in the process of courting and marriage. The feelings of lovers desiring marriage, and of husband and wife, were usually described by √*mel*. This 'love' remained, of course, permanent after the satisfaction of √*yer* in the "Time of the Children"; but was strengthened by this satisfaction and the memory of it to a normally unbreakable bond (of feeling, not here to speak of "law").

Two other stems were also concerned with feelings that we should often call 'love': √*ndil* and √*ndur*. These generally did not concern individuals or persons, and were unconnected with *sex* (in either *fëa* or *hröa*).

√*ndil* is best compared with English –*phile*, in *Anglophile*, *bibliophile*, etc., or especially with *phil(o)* as in *philosophy* or *philology*. It expressed a feeling of special concern with, care for, or interest in things (such as metals), or lower creatures (as birds or trees), or processes of thought and enquiry (as history), or arts (as poetry), or in groups of persons (as Elves or Dwarves). Thus *Eledndil > Elendil* 'lover of the Eldar' or *Elen-ndil* 'of the Stars'; *Eärendil* 'lover of the Sea', *Valandil* 'lover of the Valar'. It may be called 'love' because while its mainspring was a concern with things other than self for their own sakes, it included a personal satisfaction in that the inclination was part of the "lover's" inherent character, and study or service of the things loved were necessary to his or her fulfilment.

√*ndur* seems originally to have referred to devotions and interests of a less personal kind: to fidelity and devotion in service, produced by circumstances rather than inherent character. Thus an *ornendil* was one who 'loved' trees, and who (in addition no doubt to studying to "understand" them) took an especial delight in them; but an *ornendur* was a tree-keep, a forester, a 'woodsman', a man concerned with trees as we might say "professionally". But since (certainly among the free Eldar) √*ndur* was normally accompanied by √*ndil* or personal interest (and even by √*mel*, for the Eldar held that this emotion can rightly be felt by Incarnates for other than persons, since they are "akin" to all things in Arda, through their *hröar* and through the interest of their *fëar*, each in its own *hröa* and so in all substances of Arda) the distinction between –*ndil* and –*ndur* (especially in later Quenya names as used by Elves or Men) became obscured. In ordinary words the distinction was roughly that between "amateur" and "professional" – though not including any question of remuneration.

use of these bodily powers absorbed, relatively to Men, more of the corporeal vigour of the Quendi, and more also (though in less degree) of the "youth" of the *fëa*.* So that in certain cases marriage might take place between Quendi of the age of 60 or even (rarely) of greater age.

It may also be noted that in each Elvish life there was normally only one period of begetting or bearing children, whenever begun; and that the length of this period was variable, as were the number of children produced. It might occupy from 12 to about 60 years (occasionally more).[7] The children numbered usually 2, 3, or 4. One was exceptional, and could be due to different causes: for instance, the separation of the spouses, as in the case of Idril, daughter and sole child of Turgon of Gondolin whose wife Anairë of the Vanyar would not go with the Ñoldor into exile, but remained with Indis (also of the Vanyar) widow of Finwë.[8] In other cases the spouses (one or both) might not desire more than one child. This was rare, and in the histories of the Elder Days occurred only when some child of exceedingly great qualities was born which (as the Eldar say) demanded far more of the vigour and life of the parents than a normal child. The most eminent case was that of Míriel mother of the most gifted of all the Ñoldor, Feänor. Another case was that of Lúthien, daughter of Elwë and Melyanna (Elu Thingol and Melian);[9] though this case was also unique in that Melyanna was not an Elf but of the race of the Valar, a Maia.† [10]

A greater number than *four* was rare, though in the early days of the full vigour of the Eldar *five* or *six* children are recorded to have been born to one pair of spouses.‡ *Seven* was wholly exceptional, and indeed among the High-elves only the case of Feänor is recorded. He

---

* Their "youth" the Quendi call that part of their life-time in which the body is still dominant.

† That is, a divine spirit, coëval with the great Valar, but of less power and authority than the Valar, whom they served. Melian assumed (as the Valar and Maiar could) "the raiment of the Children", the Incarnates, out of love for them. Only one of the greatest of the Eldar in their early vigour could have supported a union of that sort (unique in all known tales). But Melian, having in woman-form borne a child after the manner of the Incarnate, desired to do this no more: by the birth of Lúthien she became enmeshed in "incarnation", unable to lay it aside while husband and child remained in Arda alive, and her powers of mind (especially foresight) became clouded by the body through which it must now always work. To have borne more children would still further have chained her and trammeled her. In the event, her daughter became mortal and eventually died, and her husband was slain; and she then cast off her "raiment" and left Middle-earth.

‡ Especially in the "Youth-time" before the Great March.

had *seven* sons. The last two were twins: Amrod and Amras. Twins were very rare, and this is the only case recorded of the Eldar in the ancient histories, except for the twin sons, Eldún and Elrún, of Dior Eluchil, but he was half-elven. In later times (Third Age) Elrond had twin sons.[11]

It must be remembered, however, in considering the records and legends of the past, that these (especially those made by or handed down through Men) often only mention or name persons who play a recorded part in the events, or were the direct ancestors of such chief actors. It cannot therefore be concluded from silence alone, whether in narrative or in genealogy, that any given person had no children, or no more than are named.

An elven-child was borne in its mother's womb for about the same (relative) time as a mortal child, that is for about ¾ of a "youth-year" = ¾ of 12 *löar* = 9 *löar*;* though in the Quendi this period was more variable, often being less, and on rare occasions being more.[12] It is said that Feänor remained in the womb for one growth-year (12 *löar*).[13]

The *onnalúmë*, or 'Time of the Children', was in normal lives a continuous series, occupying some 12 to 60 years.[14] The interval between the birth of a child and the next birth was usually one "growth-year" = 12 *löar*; but was often more, and in a continuous series tended to become longer (more rest being needed) between each birth. Thus 12 *löar* before the 2nd birth, 24 before the 3rd, 36 before the 4th, 42 before the 5th, and 48 before the 6th. But the intervals could be *longer* and not necessarily in exact twelves.[15]

But in comparing Quendi with Men it must be observed that the *unit* (called a "year") was of quite different actual length in the case of the Quendi. Similar differences occur in comparing other "kinds" of growing creatures, or even other varieties of similar kinds. (Thus animals "age" at different rates measured by Years of Middle-earth – MY or sun-years – and so do different varieties of Men; so did even different varieties of the Quendi: the Eldar grew to maturity less quickly than did the Avari.)[16]

In their beginning the Quendi grew at a rate in which the "unit" was the *yên* or Elven-year, which was 144 MY. If then an elf-child grew to a maiden and a young woman in about 20 "years", wedded at 25 and bore her first child at 26, her age in mortal terms would be 2,880 at maturity, 3,600 at wedding, and 3,744 at childbirth.

---

* Actually, a length of time = Mortal 96 months or 8 years.

This speed of growth and rate of ageing had nothing to do with the *perception of time*. As the Eldar say of themselves (and this may in some degree also be true of Men) when persons (in whole being *fëa* and *hröa*) are fully occupied with things of deep natural concern and of delight to them, and are in great bliss and health, Time seems to *pass quickly* and not the reverse. The minute enjoyment and appreciation of events and thoughts in the time-series does not, as might be supposed, make Time seem longer, as might a road or path that was minutely inspected. For that inspection could only be carried out by slowing the rate of normal travel. But the rate of normal progress through Time cannot be slowed; but the speed of thought and action can be quickened so as to achieve more in a given space of time.[17]

Thus the Quendi did not and do not "live slowly", moving ponderously like tortoises, while Time flickers past them and their sluggish thoughts! Indeed, they move and think swifter than Men, and achieve more than a Man in any given length of time.* But they have a far greater native vitality and energy to draw upon, so that it takes and will take a very great length of time to expend it.

Thus we may observe that all matters of *growth and development*, which belong to the separate nature of the *hröa*, engaged in its own process of achieving its complete and mature form, and which are not under the will or conscious control of the *fëa*, proceed far slower among the Quendi than among Men. Gestation, therefore, proceeds according to the growth and ageing scale of the Quendi, and occupies ¾ *yên*, or 108 MY.[18]

During all this time the parents are aware of the growth of the unborn child, and live in much longer and more deeply-felt joy and expectation; for childbirth is not among the Eldar accompanied by pain.[19] It is nonetheless not an easy or light matter, for it is achieved by a much greater expense of the vigour of *hröa* and *fëa* (of "youth" as the Eldar say) than is usual among Men; and is followed after the begetting by a time of quiescence and withdrawal.[20] The Elf-women also are usually quiescent and withdrawn before and after birth. For these reasons, the Eldar did not (if they could avoid it) enter into the "Time of the Children" in times of trouble, or wandering. There were thus no marriages or births during the Great March; nor again

---

* But not on a wholly different time-scale. Thus to a Man Elves appear to speak rapidly but clearly (unless they retard their speech for Men's sake), to move quickly and featly (unless they are in urgency, or much moved, when the movement of their hands, for example, may become too swift for human eyes to follow closely), and only their thought, perception, and reasoning seem normally beyond human speed.

during the journey of the Ñoldor from Aman to Beleriand, and births were few during all the War against Morgoth. For the same cause, Men who had dealings with the Eldar often saw far less of the Elf-women, and might even be unaware that some Elven-king or lord had a wife. For the withdrawal and quiescence of the wife might occupy the whole time of his sojourn among the Eldar, or indeed much of his whole mortal life-time. For this "withdrawal", occupying from three to four "months" or twelfths of a "year", that is one quarter to one third of a *yên*, would in mortal terms endure for about 36 to 48 years.*

On the other hand the act of procreation, being of a will and desire shared and indeed controlled by the *fëa*, was achieved at the speed of other conscious and willful acts of delight or of making. It was one of the acts of chief delight, in process and in memory, in an Elvish life, but its intensity alone provided its importance, not its time or length: it could not have been endured for a great length of time, without disastrous "expense".[21]

> The text ends here, about two-thirds down the page. At a later point Tolkien wrote in pencil in the bottom margin:

This will not fit the narrative in the Silmarillion. What of Maeglin?

> On this matter, see the texts presented here as chaps. X, "Difficulties in Chronology", XI, "Ageing of Elves", and XVI, "Note on the Youth and Growth of the Quendi".

NOTES

1 Cf. X:401: "The Valar 'fade' and become more impotent, precisely in proportion as the shape and constitution of things becomes more defined and settled."

2 On the natural unity of *hröa* (body) and *fëa* (spirit) in Incarnates, see BODY AND SPIRIT in App. I.

3 Cf. X:427: "Then an Elf would begin ... to 'fade', until the *fëa* as it were consumed the *hröa* until it remained only in the love and memory of the spirit that had inhabited it."

---

* But in Middle-earth where Men and Elves met, the rate was already quickened to 100 = 1. Therefore, here we should have 25 or 33.

4 The age-range "90–96" was a later alteration of original "100". Note that the corresponding passage in the typescript text (chap. III, "Of Time in Arda", above) has "100" in both this case and that in the next endnote.

5 The age "90" here was likewise a later alteration of original "100".

6 In this long footnote the C.E. root "√yer-", at both occurrences, is a replacement of a previous form, heavily struck through, but possibly "√ūyer-". On love as "primarily a motion or inclination of the fëa," cf. X:233. On the dual ends of marriage – unity and procreation – see the discussion of MARRIAGE in App. I. On the "kinship" of Incarnates "to all things in Arda, through their hröar" see chap. II, "Primal Impulse", in part three of this volume. With "a normally unbreakable bond (of feeling, not here to speak of 'law')" see Tolkien's Laws and Customs among the Eldar (X:207 ff.) for a closely contemporary, thematically related, and expansive discussion of marriage among the Elves.

7 The ages "12" and "60" here are later replacements for original "10" and "50", respectively.

8 In chap. X, "Difficulties in Chronology", below, Anairë is said to have been the mother of Idril and to have "refused the Exile". In all other published sources that name her, Anairë is the wife of Fingolfin and thus Idril's grandmother, not mother (cf. XI:323, XII:363).

9 "Elwë" and "Melyanna" are the Quenya forms of the Sindarin names "Elu" and "Melian", respectively.

10 On the increased fixing of soul and body together with increased usage among those not naturally incarnate, see chap. IX, "Ósanwe-kenta" in part two of this book; and BODY AND SPIRIT in App. I.

11 With Eldún and Elrún as the twin sons of Dior, cf. XI:257, 300 n. 16, and 349–50. These names were in Tolkien's last writings replaced with Eluréd and Elurín (cf. XII:369, 372 n.8).

12 As first written, the gestation period was given as "9 months or ¾ of a löa". The alteration was made in red ball-point pen. The correction to "96 months or 8 years" entered as a marginal note in pencil.

13 As first written, this sentence ended: "for one year". The alteration was made in red ball-point pen.

14 As first written, the range of years was given as "10 to 50 years". The alteration was made in red ball-point pen.

15 As first written, this paragraph ended: "the next birth was usually from 3 to 9 years; but it might range from 2 years (very rarely less) to 12 years (seldom more)". The alteration was made in red ball-point pen. An earlier version of this paragraph (heavily struck through) as first written has:

Gestation taking about 1 year, the days of begetting and of birth being normally the same (or nearly so). The "Time of the Children" (ontalúmë or onnalúmë) was in normal lives a continuous series occupying 10–50 years. The interval between children was [?sometimes] less than 2 [?or as much as] 12 years.

Cf. X:212: "As for the begetting and bearing of children: a year passes between the begetting and the birth of an elf-child, so that the days of both are the same or nearly so, and it is the day of begetting that is remembered year by year."

This paragraph was subsequently altered in black nib-pen to read:

Gestation occupied (on the average) about the same time period as among Mortals, though it was perhaps more variable, often being speedier, and on occasion longer – Feänor was borne in the womb for a whole year! The "Time of the Children" (*ontalúmë* or *onnalúmë*) was in normal lives a continuous series occupying 10–50 years. The interval between children was between 3 and 9 years; but might be from 2 (rarely less) to 12 years (rarely more).

The whole was then struck through in black nib-pen.

16 As first written, this paragraph ended: "the Ñoldor grew to maturity less quickly than did Sindar". The alteration was made in broad nib-pen in the act of writing.

17 Regarding the perception of time, see chaps. XII, "Concerning the Quendi in Their Mode of Life and Growth" and XX, "Time and its Perception", below.

18 As first written, this paragraph ended: "occupies a whole *yén*, or 144 MY". Tolkien placed an "X" next to this paragraph, apparently considering it for change/deletion, but did not in the event actually strike it through. The changes to the time occupied by gestation were made in red ball-point pen.

19 On the lack of pain during childbirth among the Eldar, see THE FALL OF MAN in App. I.

20 With this "greater expense of the vigour of *hröa* and *fëa* (of 'youth' as the Eldar say) than is usual among Men" in the begetting of children, cf. X:212.

21 An earlier and increasingly hastier and difficult version of this concluding section, subsequently struck through, reads:

Thus the Quendi do not "live slowly", achieving in 144 years only what a mortal could in 1 year; they are not like tortoises moving ponderously while Time flickers past them. Actually, they move and think rather swifter than Men and get more into any given length of time than any Man could. But they have a much greater natural *vitality and energy* to draw upon, so that it takes very much longer to expend it all.

The procreative act and "gestation" thus take place quickly, at more or less mortal speed, not taking 144 times as long! In fact, the act of union does take longer and gestation a little longer – it [gestation] occupies a *löa* or sun-year in Middle-earth.

But the production of children expends a very great amount of physical and spiritual energy; the desire for the next act is therefore at the Elvish rate, and when we speak of a 3 year interval we thus mean 432 years.

All matters of *growth* which are not directly controlled by the conscious *fëa* are slow in Quendi. Gestation therefore takes a very long while – about 144 MY, during all of which time husband and wife are conscious of the growth of the child, and experience a much longer joy and expectation. For Elvish childbirth is *not* accompanied by fear or pain – but there is a great expense of vigour followed by quiescence and weariness in both of them. But the act of procreation not being one of *growth* until the union of the seed and being under full control of the will does not take long – though it is longer and of more intense delight in Elves than in Men: too intense to be long endured.

V

NATURAL YOUTH AND GROWTH OF THE QUENDI

This text is written in black nib-pen in a rather ornate hand on the four sides of two sheets of unlined paper. It dates from c. 1959.

The text itself, until it reaches the table of mortal equivalences of Elvish ages, closely follows the beginning of the text presented here as chap. XII, "Concerning the Quendi in Their Mode of Life and Growth", below.

Youth of the Quendi

When the Quendi were very "young in Arda" (approximately their first *six* generations in the first 96 Valian years of their existence) they were far more like Men (unfallen).[1] Their *hröar* were in great vigour, and dominant; and the delights of the body of all kinds were their chief concern. Their *fëar* were only beginning to wake fully and to grow and discover their powers and interests. Thus (as was indeed at first necessary, and so ordained for them) they were far more concerned with love and the begetting of children than was so later.*

It was not, however, their natural span of growth and life that was different (at least not until many ages had passed); but they used it differently. The natural life of the Quendi was to grow rapidly (for them) to puberty, and then to endure in full vigour for a great length

---

* The begetting of children also was less exhausting to their "youth" in the earliest generations.

of years, until the interests of their *fëar* became pre-eminent, and their *hröar* began to wane.

The "ages" of Quendi are usually given in terms equated with human life; but not all lengths of years had the same ageing effect upon the Quendi. The Eldar distinguished between *growth* and *life* (or *life-endurance*). The former was 12 times as rapid (in ageing effect) as the latter.

Now as for *growth*: this affected the Elvish *hröa* from *conception* until *maturity* (or *puberty*). The *life-endurance* rate of the Quendi was as 1 *yên* is to 1 *löa* or "sun-year": that is, 144 : Human 1. The *growth-rate* was 12 times as rapid: i.e., was only in proportion 12 *löar* = 1 [Human] *löa* or sun-year. Thus from *conception to birth* they lay in the womb 9 *löar*. *When born* they continued to *grow* at the same rate, until puberty. With Elf-males this was reached at "age" 24; but with Elf-females at age 18.*[2] That is for males 24 × 12 after birth, or 288 *löar*; for females 18 × 12 or 216 *löar*. In early ages this "coming of Age" was a matter of ceremony, at which an Elf's *essekilmë* or personal 'chosen-name' was announced.[3]

But except in the *first three generations* the begetting of children by *Elf-men* did not usually follow immediately on attaining "age 24" (though "betrothal" often did, or even "marriage"). It was by degrees postponed, until soon "age 48" became regarded as the optimum age for the beginning of fatherhood, though it was often delayed until 60 (sc. 24 years of growth + 36 life-years).[4] Of course, begetting of further children could happen later than this. It *could* occur up to about a male age of 96 – later than this age (96) a *first*-begetting seldom occurred.[5]

In the case of *Elf-women*: marriage and child-bearing took place earlier, their first child being born before they were of age 20.†[6] Later indeed some postponement was usual so that marriage at 21 was the most usual time; though any age up to 36 (18 + 18) was not uncommon.[7] In days of trouble, or of travel and unsettled life, the begetting of children was naturally avoided or postponed; and *since the postponement especially of the first child-bearing or begetting* prolonged the "youth" or physical vigour of the Quendi, this might occur up to a female age of about 72 (18 + 54) – but a *first child-bearing* seldom occurred after this age (72).[8]

These dates in early ages at any rate (with which we are concerned)

---

* Concerning this difference the Eldar speak in the legend which they call "The Awaking" (*i·Cuivië*).

† In the earliest generations.

were not so much matters of physical impossibility *as of will or desire*. As soon as they were full-grown, and with increasing rapidity after age 48 (Elf-men) and 36 (Elf-women), the *fëa* and its interests began to gain the upper hand. An Elf who had not become married, or at least found one desired as spouse,[9] by these dates was likely (in normal circumstances) to remain single – though, naturally, in troublous times, when lovers or spouses might be long separated, marriage might well occur much later; or childbearing be long postponed.

The *number* of children produced by a married pair was naturally partly affected by the character of the persons concerned (mental and physical); and partly by various accidents of life. But it was also much affected by the age at which marriage began. Even in the earliest times, after the "First Elves", more than *six* children was very rare, and four soon became the normal average. But six was never attained by those marrying after 48/36. In later marriages two was more usual.

For chronological purposes and comparison of Elves and Men these dates may be exhibited so:

[Elf-years]	[Mortal-years]
An Elf-child conceived was born 9 *löar* later. Elvish "growth" age about 9 months. Actual time:	9 years
The "growth age" of 12:1 (in comparison with mortal years) was maintained until an Elf-man reached "age 24". Actual time:	288 years
In case of women it usually ceased at 18 though it was sometimes continued, especially in Aman, to 21. Actual time:	216 years (or 252)
At "age 48" therefore, an Elf-man was 288 *löar* + 24 *yên* (288 + 3456).[10]	3,744 years
At "age 96" therefore, an Elf-man was 288 *löar* + 72 *yên*	10,656
At "age 192" therefore, an Elf-man was 288 *löar* + 168 *yên*	24,480
At "age 21" therefore, an Elf-woman was 216 *löar* + 3 *yên* (216 + 432)	648
At "age 36" therefore, an Elf-woman was 216 *löar* + 18 *yên*	2,808
At "age 72" therefore, an Elf-woman was 216 *löar* + 54 *yên*	7,992
At "age 144" therefore, an Elf-woman was 216 *löar* + 126 *yên*	18,360

At all times, unless circumstances interfered and separation were forced upon spouses by wars or exile, the Quendi desired to dwell in company with husband or wife during the bearing of a child and its early growth. Also as a rule, they preferred to arrange their lives so as to have a consecutive "Time of the Children" in which all of their children were born – but this of course often, especially in the troubled early years, proved impossible.[11] After a birth, even if a consecutive *Onnalúmë* or 'Time of Children' was achieved, a rest was naturally always taken. This was governed by "growth-time", and so was usually not less than 12 *löar* (= 1 growth-year); but it might be much more; and usually was increased progressively between each birth for consecutive series: as 12 : 24 : 36 : 48 etc.

NOTES

1 Tolkien replaced the original "1000 VY" with "96 Valian years" in the act of writing. With the unfallen state of Elves, cf. chaps. VI, "The Awaking of the Quendi", and XII, "Concerning the Quendi in Their Mode of Life and Growth", below. See also THE FALL OF MAN in App. I.

2 With "The Awaking" cf. chap. VIII, "Eldarin Traditions Concerning the 'Awakening'", below.

3 For more on the *essekilmë* 'chosen-name' (or 'name-choosing', also spelt *essecilmë*) and its attendant ceremony, see X:214 ff.

4 This sentence originally ended at "fatherhood", but was extended by a marginal insertion in black nib-pen. This insertion originally ended: "It was seldom if ever delayed beyond age", before it was struck through. A later insertion, in red ballpoint – above "until soon age 48 became regarded as" – and subsequently struck through, appears to read: "not by life-year but by growth-year, [?by] 12, 24, 48". The idea is perhaps that the postponement resulted from an increase in the number of "growth-years" in the Eldar.

5 As first written, this sentence began: "It *could* occur up to about a male age of 192, though it did not usually occur much after age 96". Next, the figure "192" was crossed through, and calculations added in the line above that read: "24 + 144 (168 year period) 18 + 144 (162)". Subsequently, these calculations and everything between "192" through "after age" were heavily struck through. The sentence originally ended: "seldom if ever occurred".

6 As first written, this sentence ended: "not seldom before they were of age 20". The words "not seldom" were heavily deleted, and replaced with "sometimes", which was also then struck through.

7 This sentence is given as first written, despite subsequent cross-throughs and additions, because the alterations do not seem to have been carried through to

VI

THE AWAKING OF THE QUENDI

This text, a discussion of the issues presented by the chronology of the awaking of the Quendi with respect to "The Silmarillion" as it then stood, is extant in two versions. The first version, which bears the title "*The Awaking of the Quendi* & position of Ingwë/Finwë/Elwë etc.", dates (according to an explicit statement in it) from 1960, and occupies the four sides of two sheets which Tolkien has lettered α–δ. The second version, which appears to be closely contemporary, is a considerable expansion of the first. It occupies six sides of three sheets numbered by Tolkien 1–6. Both texts are written in black nib-pen and (for the most part) more-or-less clearly; and the numberings of both texts, various later notes, and the main title and two section titles of the second version, were added in red ball-point pen. I give here first the second version (B), followed by the significantly variant portions of the first version (A).

Text B

I. Preliminary discussion

At this point: the Story has not been thought out, and the chronology, so far devised, is impossible.

The "Tale of Years" (TY) makes the Quendi awake in VY 1050; but in VY 1085 Oromë finds already a considerable people.[1] Now TY was devised with a scale VY = (about) 10 Sun-years (*löar*).[2] So it is plain that the Quendi must have been created from the first in large numbers (since only 350 *löar* have passed).

Also, since Ingwë, Finwë, and Elwë were first brought to Valinor in VY 1102, at that time only 520 *löar* had elapsed since the Awaking.[3] No scale of Quendian "growth" or "ageing" is devised, but in Valinor events seem to show that they lived at about the rate of 1 VY = 1 year of Elvish life. This fits events in Valinor, for which it was arranged, but makes all the Eldar far too old in later narrative, unless we suppose that they remained unchanged, after maturity, for an indefinite time.

The *actual dates* of the TY need not be regarded, since (being on the wrong scale) they will have to be revised. But, since a mass-creation of the Quendi is poor narrative and mythology, some sort of "legend" of the arising of the Elves and of their increase and fortunes must be devised, and evidently a much longer time than 350 *löar* must elapse between the "Awaking" and the "Finding", and much longer also than 480 *löar* (VY 1085 to VY 1133) between the "Finding" and the arrival of the Ñoldor in Valinor.[4] The whole matter of the "Great March" must be considered.

But: increasing the length of time between the "Awaking" and the "Finding" (which is useful in allowing more time for Melkor to interfere with them) must inevitably lay some blame on the Valar. As is probably just.[5]

The Valar had, of course, no *precise* knowledge of the time of that "Awaking". Not if – *as seems essential* – the Vision (subsequent to the Music) stopped short of the actual "Coming of the Children".[6] The Ainur were vouchsafed a Vision of the Children, but not of their exact place in the sequence. Later Eru deliberately did *not* inform Manwë of the approach of the time: for He did not intend them to be dominated, and the function of the Valar was to prepare and govern the *place* of their habitation. Even so the Valar should have kept better watch, and not have allowed Melkor peace in which to establish himself. They were, of course, very anxious, but neglected the matter until they feared to ruin Arda in a war, which would involve the Children in misery or destruction. (One may object that this could not be – but *all* the operations of Melkor, to those now in Time, appeared to be in defiance of Eru, and to have power to upset or spoil the design; so that if these were permitted by Eru (or could not be hindered!) there was no knowing how far they would proceed.)

It seems clear that the *rescue of the Quendi* must be secret (as far as possible), and *before the assault upon Utumno* – otherwise this very peril would have occurred. The *Great March* must occur behind a screen of investment, and before any violent assault had begun!

But Melkor had, of course, since he largely controlled Middle-earth, and had hosts of spies and servants, soon discovered the Quendi, and he had time to frighten them, fill their minds with dark imaginings and fears, beside (probably) capturing some of them, and even corrupting or seducing some – hence the taint in some degree of "the Shadow" which lay even upon the Eldar.[7]

With regard to Men: see under *Sauron: Arising and Fall of Men*.[8] The arising and fall took place during the "Captivity of Melkor", and was achieved not by Melkor in person, but by Sauron. It occurred about 100 VY after the "Awaking of the Quendi", sc. 14,400 *löar* later. In that case if Men arose in VY 1100, it would explain the "neglect" of the Valar, since they had now done their duty and removed Melkor. If the End of Valian reckoning with the Death of the Trees occurred in VY 1495 (as in TY and so far assumed), by 310 in Beleriand Men would have existed 395 VY + 310 *löar* = 57,190 years (*löar*).[9] Which is adequate (if not scientifically long enough).

The TY is here quite impossible. It makes Men first awake with the first Rising of the Sun, which is VY 1500, after which dates are given in *löar*.[10] But the first Men appear in *Beleriand* – already partly civilized, deeply sundered in appearance and language, and leaving a long history behind them – and many other varieties of "unrepentant" Men, in the East – in SY 310. All that in 310 years![11]

To take any date to begin with: Let Quendi awake in VY 1000. Then some date *before* the Arising of Men would be best, but not very long (in Elvish terms) before, for the Finding. At that time, though fairly numerous (? some thousands), they had not spread far abroad – ? fear of Melkor, Sauron, &c.; and do not seem ever to have met Men (though they had almost certainly heard lies about them from emissaries of Melkor).

The "Finding" should evidently be about VY 1090, or 90 VYs after the "Awaking" (12,960 *löar*): this would give them time, even at Elvish rates, for multiplication from small beginnings. *Also, which is important,* time to invent the beginnings of the *Primitive Quendian language*: to discover something about Arda, and of their own powers and talents.[12] (*Language* we must suppose was a specifically Elvish gift, not possessed by the Valar even until they found the Quendi; a gift of Eru inherent in their nature, so that from their Awaking they immediately began to try to communicate *in speech* with one another.[13] *Men* had a similar gift, but less marked and less *skilled*, as they were less skilled in all *artistic* matter: *language being the primary art*; hence their ruder tongues were much improved by contact, later, with

Quendi; and the general similarity – apart from loan-words – of *Western* speeches of Men with Quendian.)[14]

Quendi, it must be assumed, had from the beginning a natural rate of "growth" and "life", which was not in the early ages much altered anywhere: thus from the beginning we can reckon with a 12 : 1 rate (as compared with Men) of "growth", and a subsequent 144 : 1, or Valian, rate of "ageing".

Their *first generation*, or "First Elves", awoke at the time of first maturity – *see later Legend*;[15] and they began at once to increase with great rapidity in the *first three generations*, though this afterwards slowed down.

The Quendi never "fell" in the sense that Men did.[16] Being "tainted" with the Shadow (as perhaps even the Valar in some degree were, with all things in "Arda Marred") they could *do wrong*. But they *never rejected Eru*, or worshipped Melkor (or Sauron) either individually,* or in groups, or as a whole people. Their lives, therefore, came under no general curse or diminishment, and their "life-span", coextensive with the remainder of the life of Arda, was unaltered – except only insofar as, with the very ageing of Arda itself, their *primitive vigour of body* steadily waned. But the "waning" does not yet appreciably affect the periods dealt with in the Silmarillion.

The "lives" of the Quendi cannot be supposed to be affected by living in Middle-earth "under the Sun" – NOT IF as now seems certain the Sun is made part of the original structure of Arda, and not devised only after the Death of the Trees – since they were *devised to live* in Middle-earth and "under the Sun".[17] Any alteration (if any!) would occur under the "artificial" conditions of Aman. But since the Quendian rate of "ageing" was already that of the Valar (144 : 1) the alteration would only concern the *growth rate* (12 : 1) : this might well be slowed to 36 : 1 or 72 : 1 or even 144 : 1.[18]

When therefore Oromë found the Quendi in, say, VY 1090, the *increase* can be approximately calculated. According to the "legend" and the theory set out below: the Quendi in about VY 1100 would have numbered over 32,000.[19] This is probably adequate IF we allow the begetting of Children on the Great March: as shown also in what follows.

By "what follows" Tolkien means the subsequent texts in the "Time and Ageing" bundle.

---

* Though it is possible that in the remote past some Quendi had been daunted or corrupted by Melkor! If so, they left the Quendian community. The Eldar certainly never, even individually, rejected Eru in word, or belief.

II. Note on Angband and Utumno[20]

In the *Tale of Years* Morgoth has *insufficient time* for the building and organization of Angband. He thus escapes in VY 1495 and only 20 *löar* later (VY 1497) is already assailing Beleriand (before the making of the Sun!).*[21]

Plainly EITHER Angband must be *on the same site* as Utumno, which being actually partially destroyed, and its depths never plumbed, was quickly restored; OR Angband must in some form have already existed.

The latter is greatly to be preferred. A fort far West and not far from the Sea would be a natural strategic device by Melkor for preventing the Valar coming in force against him, or for delaying their advance if they tried to assail him.

This is the probable story ☞. As soon as he discovered the Quendi (if not indeed far sooner, and well before the time of their awaking, which Melkor guessed more shrewdly than the Valar) Melkor constructed Angband. One of its chief functions was not only to defend the Western Shores, but to *shroud them.* The prime function of (originally volcanic) Thangorodrim was to produce *smokes, vapours, and darkness.* All the Northwest shores were covered and the Sun largely excluded for hundreds of years before Melkor was made captive. Sauron had a chief part in this; and when the Valar at last came to Middle-earth he (under Melkor's orders) made a strong feint of resistance, while Melkor retreated and gathered nearly all his forces in Utumno. (Thus passage of the Quendi was made feasible.) Angband was in the event very largely destroyed – though the Valar, passing on to Utumno, which was apparently the real centre of Melkor's power – made no attempt to demolish it completely. But when Melkor feigned submission to Manwë, Sauron was ordered to reconstruct it (as *secretly* as possible: therefore largely in extending its underground mansions) against Melkor's escape and return. *There were no more fumes* until Melkor returned: but when he did in 1495, Angband was almost ready. Melkor then made it his chief seat of power, for strategic reasons, and because of the coming of the Eldar. Had he been successful he would perhaps have returned to Utumno, but *not* until the Eldar were vanquished or destroyed.

---

* Morgoth's flight could be made to precede the Exile by a longer period, but this is not necessary if Angband already existed.

Text A

The second version greatly expanded upon the much-compressed first version, except where the matters of the awaking of Men and of the position and nature of Angband with respect to Utumno are concerned, and of both of these matters with respect to the time of the death of the Two Trees, of Melkor's flight, and of the Exile of the Noldor. On these matters the first version, which shows much more of Tolkien's deliberative process concerning them, reads:

Men must "awake" *before the Captivity of Melkor*.* [22] *It is too* late after the return to Angband; *for there is not enough time*: The Atani already partly civilized reach Beleriand c. 310. That is only about 310 Sun Years after Morgoth's return!† [23]

In any case Morgoth has precious little time in which to build Angband. He escapes in 1495 and only 20 [sun-]years later (TY 1497) is already assailing Beleriand.[24]

Plainly Utumno and Angband must be in the *same place* and, only partially destroyed, was quickly restored.[25] Or, Angband must also have existed.[26] A *fort far west* would be a good device for keeping the Valar out, and ill-informed of what was going on. Thus Melkor *as soon as Elves awoke* must have constructed Angband in the West as a further device – *and he covered all northwest shores and the hinterland with darkness, obscuring the Sun.*

But Angband was chiefly a place for making *smoke and dark*, and not yet very big. When all the Valar came against him, Melkor made only a feint of defending Angband, and then retreated to Utumno. This in the event was pretty well destroyed, but was inhabited by Balrogs. These were *secretly* (though Morgoth feigned submission) instructed to regain and extend Angband (quietly and [?within] fume) against his escape. Angband was therefore almost ready in 1495!‡ [27]

If (as in the *Tale of Years*) the Valar came forth in VY 1090 and Utumno was besieged in 1092 and destroyed in 1100, then Men *must* awake before VY 1090.[28]

If they awoke in VY 1050 that would give 40 VYs, or 5,760 Sun

---

* *But see later.* Men were probably corrupted by Sauron after the Captivity (100 VYs later).

† Or at best 454 years! But Morgoth's flight could take place *some time before* Exile. The Slaying of the Trees could take place in VY 1494, the Exile in 1495, and the arrival in Beleriand in 1496.

‡ *See later*. it was Sauron who controlled things in Morgoth's absence.

Years in which Melkor could have dealings with them and corrupt them, before his captivity. The Atani entered Beleriand in 310 Bel. That is in the 22nd Sun-year of VY 1498. Men had then existed for 448 VYs + 22 SYs: i.e., 64,534 Sun Years,[29] which, though doubtless insufficient scientifically (since that is only – we being in 1960 of the 7th Age – 16,000 years ago: total about 80,000), is adequate for purposes of the *Silmarillion*, etc.[30]

But Elves when discovered in 1085 were already a people, though appear *never yet* to have met Men, who awoke much further east. ☞ *Cuiviénen* must be *fairly far west* (near centre of Endor?).

We may suppose Elves awoke at least 50 VYs sooner than Men (sc. 7,200 mortal years). This is about sufficient.[31] But it would be better to reduce the time of Melkor's dealing with Men, since the damage could be done in much less than 5,760 years of mortal life.

Let Melkor discover Men 1,440 years (that is, 10 VYs) before the Valar open attack in VY 1090. Men will therefore "awake" – the exact process will *not* be disclosed or discussed in the *Silmarillion* – some (little) time before VY 1080; say, 1079/1075.[32]

The Quendi should then awake at least soon enough for the first generation to be full-grown when Oromë finds them; but also long enough for Melkor to affect them seriously.[33]

If Elves from the beginning grew at later rates: the *first generation* would be "maturing" between 216 and 288 years after "awakening", but they would not have reached *prime* (in early days, at age 100) for another 76–82 Elven years = same number of VYs (or SYs 10,944–11,808).[34] When therefore they were found by Oromë they must have existed at least 11,000 years, or (say) 80 VYs. Oromë found them in 1085. They therefore almost certainly began to be c. VY 1000.

Quendi awake VY 1000.

Men awake VY 1075 (and are hidden from other contacts by Melkor)? But Eru independently of Manwë sends messages and *messengers* to them (and the Elves). That is about 10,800 Sun-years after Elves [awoke] and 15 VYs (or 2,160 SYs) before the attack of the Valar. The Valar *do not discover Men* (whose centre was far south of Utumno),[35] and think the removal of Melkor probably sufficient protection: they are not supposed to "meddle" with Men, but only guard them so that they can develop as they should. But they are *anxious*, especially after they discover that Melkor had already affected the Quendi; and are aware that by no means all of Melkor's evil associates and forces had been destroyed or captured. They are therefore always sending out emissaries and explorers to Middle-earth during the Captivity of Melkor.

NOTES

1 Christopher Tolkien notes (X:49) that: "*The Tale of Years*, a chronological list of the same sort as that in Appendix B to *The Lord of the Rings*, exists in different forms, associated with the earlier and later *Annals*; the later form, closely associated with [the *Annals of Aman*] and its companion the *Grey Annals (Annals of Beleriand)*, is perhaps the most complex and difficult text of all that my father left behind him." As such, the text, considered as a complex of layers and developments, has only been partially edited and published (see X:56–7, XI:342–54). The dates cited from the "Tale of Years" here, however, agree with those in the c. 1951 *Annals of Aman* (or at any rate, with their final forms; see X:47–8) in which (X:71) the Quendi awake in VY 1050, and in which (X:72) Oromë finds them in VY 1085 (there said to be 335 of "our years", i.e. *löar*, after they awoke = 9.57 VY). Nor is there any indication given by Christopher Tolkien in his editorial notes on *The Tale of Years* that these dates were any different in that text as originally written.

2 See X:50, §7: "each Year [of the Valar] ... is somewhat more than are *nine and one half* of our years (nine and one half and eight hundredths and yet a little)" (the parenthetical words being, however, omitted in *The Tale of Years*, X:57 n.11); also X:59, §§5–10.

3 The date VY 1102 again agrees precisely with *AAm* (X:81).

4 *AAm* (X:84) gives VY 1133 as the date of the coming of the Noldor to Aman.

5 For other discussions of the possible failings of the Valar, see *Notes on motives in the Silmarillion* (X:394–408), and chap. IX, "*Ósanwe-kenta*", in part two of this book.

6 Tolkien marked this paragraph as a crucial point with a large "★" in the margin against it. The "Vision", as an intervening stage between the Music of the Ainur and the world being spoken into existence by Eru, arose in the c. 1948 text C of the *Ainulindalë* (cf. X:11, §§12, 13; X:14, §22; X:25–6).

7 The corresponding part of version A of this text has here: "Hence latent tendency to *wickedness* even among the Quendi".

8 Tolkien marked this paragraph as a crucial point with a large "★★" in the margin against it. With "screen of investment" cf. *OED* "Investment", sense 2: "An outer covering of any kind; an envelope; a coating"; also sense 4: "The surrounding or hemming in of a town or fort by a hostile force so as to cut off all communication with the outside; beleaguerment; blockade", and the quote illustrating this sense: "Secrecy and speed are secured, in the investment of an inland fortress, by the use of an advanced force of cavalry and horse artillery, which conceals the march of the main body." If any such text as referred to here ever existed, there is, alas, now no extant remnant of it known to me.

9 *AAm* likewise gives the date VY 1495 for the Death of the Two Trees (X:98 ff.). Tolkien actually wrote "57,334" here as the length of the existence

of Men in Bel. 310, but that is a mathematical error. 395 VY × 144 = 56,880 + 310 = 57,190.

10 Cf. XI:30–1.

11 Tolkien marked this paragraph as a crucial point with a large "★" in the margin against it.

12 Tolkien marked this passage regarding language as a crucial point with a large "★" in the margin against it.

13 Tolkien marked this passage as a crucial point with a manicule (☞) in the left margin against it.

14 Tolkien marked the passage regarding the artistic primacy of language as a crucial point with a large "★" against it. On the similarity of "Western speeches of Men" with Quendian, cf. The Lhammas, §10 (V:179).

15 This would appear to be a reference to chap. VIII, "Eldarin Traditions Concerning the 'Awakening'", below.

16 Tolkien marked this passage as a crucial point with a manicule (☞) in the left margin against it. With the fallen nature of Men, in Elvish and Mannish thought, see the Athrabeth Finrod ah Andreth in Morgoth's Ring, and chaps. XII, "Concerning the Quendi in Their Mode of Life and Growth", below, and X, "Notes on Órë", in part two of this book. See also THE FALL OF MAN in App. I.

17 For the potentially far-reaching (and greatly disruptive) decision (or at any rate considered option) by Tolkien to make the Sun and the Moon coëval with Arda (and not the last fruits of the Two Trees), and for the consequent "artificial" situation in Aman, see X:369–90.

18 The various possible rates, being all multiples of 12, evidence what Tolkien elsewhere refers to as the "duodecimal system" of ratios.

19 Tolkien replaced an earlier number, apparently 59,000, with 32,000 in the act of writing. The latter figure matches that calculated for the Eldar at the Finding in "Scheme 2" of text 2 of chap. XVII. "Generational Schemes", below; but see also the similar calculations in chap. XV, "A Generational Scheme", below.

20 The title is original, but the text numbering "II" is a later addition in red ballpoint. See XI:344: "My father pencilled on the typescript (referring to the interval since Morgoth's return from Valinor in 1495): 'Too small a time for Morgoth to build Angband', and also 'Time too small, should be 10 at least or 20 Valian Years'. This would have required substantial modification of the chronology; and it seems conceivable that this consideration was a factor in the emergence of the later story that Utumno and Angband were distinct fortresses in different regions, both built by Morgoth in ancient days (X:156, §12)."

21 AAm (X:98) agrees with the Tale of Years in giving VY 1495 as the date of Melkor's escape, and also lists 1497 (X:118) as the date of the return of the exiled Noldor to Middle-earth.

22 Tolkien marked this passage as a crucial point with a manicule (☞) in the left margin against it. Sometime later, in red ball-point pen, he added the note

beginning *"But see later"*, which agrees with the date (VY 1100) and agent (Sauron) of the corruption of Men set forth in the second version.

In apparently contemporary writing amongst Tolkien linguistic papers is a rejected sheet that, in addition to some Elvish etymologies, has this note:

☞ The Disquiet of the Ñoldor must last a *long while* (the Fëanoröans can dwell in the North of Aman a long while). *A long time must* be allowed (a) for Men to appear and *diverge*, and (b) for Melkor to corrupt them? They should "awake" just at his return to Middle-earth – on an island. (Reason for his returning was his guessing of the Time.)

The whole Time in Beleriand must be extended to at least 1000 years *unless* Men awake before the captivity of Melkor. Thus Fingolfin should dwell *long* in Arvalin [?south] of Valinor.

Fingolfin is nowhere else depicted as having lived in Arvalin, which is otherwise known only as a shadowy land south of Valinor, where Ungoliant dwelt.

Against the first paragraph, in the margin, Tolkien wrote in ball-point pen:

No, *corruption* of Men must occur before captivity.

23 These comments were added later in red ball-point pen. Cf. the similar later note Tolkien made to the corresponding passage in the second version (B) of this text.

24 See XI:14–15.

25 Tolkien preceded this passage with a large "★", indicating its importance as a decision.

26 The statement about Angband's prior existence entered as a marginal note in the course of writing. The sense is that it must be either that Angband arose in the same place, and on the only-partially destroyed foundations of Utumno; or that Angband existed in a separate place before the destruction of Utumno. The latter solution is that described as "greatly to be preferred" in the "Note on Angband and Utumno" in the second version (B) of this text.

27 This note entered as a later marginal note in red ball-point pen.

28 Against this passage, or at least against the statement that "Men must awake before VY 1090", Tolkien subsequently wrote "no" in red ball-point pen.

29 Tolkien actually wrote here "64,434", but I have corrected this calculation error.

30 The parenthetical comment in this last sentence entered as a contemporary marginal note. For the significance of the statement that Tolkien is writing in the year 1960 "of the 7th Age", see AGES OF THE WORLD in App. I.

Earlier, in a letter of 1958, Tolkien had said of the time between the Fall of Barad-dûr and "our days" that: "I imagine the gap to be about 6000 years: that is we are now at the end of the Fifth Age, if the Ages were of about the same length as S.A. and T.A. But they have, I think, quickened; and I imagine we are actually at the end of the Sixth Age, or in the Seventh" (L:283, fn).

Therefore, if Men entered Beleriand in Bel. 310, and the First Age ended c. Bel. 600 (cf. XI:346), then that entrance occurred 290 + SA 3441 + TA 3021 = 6,752 years before the end of the Third Age. Assuming three additional ages, plus 1,960 years of the 7th Age as here, as having occurred about 16,000 years prior, would yield an average duration of the 4th through 6th Ages of: 16,000 − 1,960 − 6,752 = 7,288 ÷ 3 = c. 2,430 years.

31 As first written, this sentence read: "But this is not in fact sufficient".

32 Tolkien has marked the statement that the "the exact process [of the awaking of Men] will *not* be disclosed or discussed in the *Silmarillion*" as crucial by bracketing it in large asterisks. The alternate year "1075" appears to have been a later addition, but in black nib-pen; it agrees with the date given in B for the awaking of Men.

33 As first written, this sentence began: "The Quendi should then awake at least [1000 >>] 10 VYs sooner: say, [?950 >>] 1050, soon enough", before all between "at least" and "soon" was heavily struck through.

34 These figures reflect a "maturing" rate of 12 SYs to 1 Elven-year, and a rate from maturity to "prime" of 144 SYs to 1 Elven-year. Hence, at maturity, Elves would be between 18 and 24 Elven-years (i.e., 216 ÷ 12 = 18 Elven-years to 288 ÷ 12 = 24 Elven-years).

35 Far south and, presumably, far east of Utumno. At one point Tolkien baldly stated that: "The Great Central Land, Europe and Asia, was first inhabited. Men awoke in Mesopotamia" (IX:410).

VII

THE MARCH OF THE QUENDI

The text presented here occupies twelve sides of seven sheets of unlined paper, which Tolkien lettered A–M. It is for the most part written in black nib-pen in a fairly clear hand, but was subsequently given a new title, "March", and revised and added to in places, in red ball-point pen. It dates from c. 1959. I give the text here as emended.

Quendi

If we take VY 1000 as the probable date of the "Awakening" and 1085 of the "Finding" (by Oromë); 1090: beginning of the Assault of the Valar; 1102: Ingwë, Finwë, and Elwë brought to Valinor; 1105: beginning of the Great March; 1115: separation of the Nandor; 1125: Eldar reach Beleriand; 1130: Thingol lost; 1133: Vanyar and Ñoldor land in Aman; then we must consider the matter of the Eldar, and the ages and position of Ingwë, etc.

In 1085 Oromë found already a considerable people (who had already had dealings with emissaries of Melkor).

According to Eldarin tradition: The Quendi "awoke" in maturity of body, and had "slept" during the making of their *hröar* "in the womb or Arda"; but when they awoke they were in *12 pairs*, elf-man and elf-woman lying side-by-side each with a "predestined" mate. After 1 *löa* they begat children; so that in "Awakening [Year] 10" the First-begotten or so-called 1st generation began to appear. The Quendi were at first eager to increase their kind; *on the average* they begat children, at the age of 40, and at average intervals of 24 years.

In the first three generations the number of children born to each pair was 6. In the next three generations the average number was 5; in subsequent generations up to the Great March the average number was 4. (During the Great March very few children were begotten, and there were no new marriages.) The number of males and females was at first equal (for about three generations) but more variable later, when males tended to be slightly more numerous.

		Total Population
1st gen. appears VY 1000/10 AY 10	In AY 10, 12 children were born. Total population then became 36 (24 + 12).	36
[1st gen. complete] VY 1000/130 AY 130	More children followed at intervals of 24 years until each pair produced 6 children: The "First Elves" then ceased to beget. Thus in 5 × 24 + 10 = AY 130 the "First Generation" was complete: it was 72. Total population was now 24 + 72 = 96.	96
2nd gen. appears VY 1018/19 [AY 2611]	The "First Generation" began to beget children when "40 years old": that is, the *first* 6 pairs of the 36 pairs of the 1st gen. began in AY 10 + 288 (= 24 GY) + 2,304 (= 16 VY): sc. in 18 VY + 10 *löar* after the Awakening. So allowing for approximately 9 years of gestation: the first 6 of the 2nd gen. would appear in 18 VY + 19 *löar* after the Awakening.	
2nd gen. complete VY 1018/139 [AY 2731]	The last six (the last children of the youngest of the 1st gen.) would appear in 18 VY + 10 *löar* + (5 × 24) *löar* + 9 *löar* = 18 VY + 139 *löar*. The population increase would be 6 × 36 = 216.	312
3rd gen. appears VY 1036/28 [AY 5212]	The 2nd gen. would begin to produce the next gen. in 40 age-years after the appearance of the 2nd gen.[1] There were 216 of the 2nd gen., or 108 pairs. The time of generation-completion from first birth to last birth would be *as before* 120 *löar* (5 × 24).	

The 3rd gen. would thus begin to appear in VY
1018/19 + 18 VY/9 *löar*.

3rd gen. complete	The last of the 3rd gen. would appear in	960
VY 1037/14	VY 1018/19 + 18 VY/139 *löar*, or VY 1037/14.	
[AY 5342]	The increase was 6 × 108 = 648.	

The number of children per pair now drops to five, and pairing is
not exact. The interval between children also increased to about 30,
so total time to produce the 4th generation was the same, 120 *löar*.

4th gen. appears	The 3rd gen. begins to produce the 4th gen. in
VY 1054/37	VY 1036/28 + VY 18, and the first of the 4th gen.
[AY 7813]	would appear in VY 1036/28 + VY 18/9
	= VY 1054/37.

[4th gen. complete	The 4th gen. would be complete in 120 *löar*	1,710
VY 1055/13	later = VY 1054/37 + AY 120 = VY 1054/157 =	
AY 7933]	VY 1055/13. The population increase was	
	5 × 150 = 750.	

5th gen. appears	In VY 1054/37 + VY 18/9 the 5th gen. began to	
VY 1072/46	appear: VY 1072/46. There were 750 in the 4th	
[AY 10414]	gen., of which about 700, or 350 pairs, mated.	

[5th gen. complete	The generation was complete in VY 1072/46	3,460
VY 1073/22	+ 120 *löar* = VY 1073/22.[2] Increase: 5 × 350 =	
AY 10534]	1,750.	

6th [gen. appears]	In VY 1072/46 + VY 18/9 the 6th gen. appear	
VY 1090/55	= VY 1090/55. There were 1,750 in the 5th gen.	
[AY 13015]	of which about 800 pairs mated.	

[6th gen. complete	The generation was complete in VY 1090/55	7,460
VY 1091/31	+ 120 *löar* = VY 1091/31. Increase: 5 × 800 =	
AY 13135]	4,000. The total in 1090, or *about the time of the*	
	Assault [on Melkor], about 7,000.[3] At time of the	
	Finding by Oromë in 1085 only 3,460.	

The number of children per pair now drops to four, but the
completion of a generation takes about 100 *löar*.

7th [gen. appears]	The 7th gen. begins to appear in VY 1090/55	
VY 1108/64	+ VY 18/9 = VY 1108/64. Of the 4,000	
[AY 15616]	members of the 6th gen., about 1,900 pairs	
	beget 4 children each.	

[7th gen. complete]	The generation is complete in VY 1108/64	15,060
VY 1109/20	+ 100 *löar* = 1109/20. Increase: 4 × 1900	
[AY 15716]	= 7,600.	

The youngest of the 7th generation would be active and able to march in some 10 growth-years = 120 *löar*; sc. VY 1109/140, or say VY 1110.

The dates for the March etc. given in the *Tale of Years* are devised to fit scale 10 *löar* = 1 VY; but even so are too long? The Eldar take 20 VY = 200 [sun-]years to reach Beleriand. But we must imagine many *long halts* and waverings. Also the Eldar *still desired children*, and no doubt *begot many on the March*. But they would *halt* for this purpose. Halts would occupy at least 10 [sun-]years (gestation 9 + mother's rest) + 10 growth-years (120 [SY]) = 130 [*löar*] for youngest children to grow to marching age.[4] They would then march on during an interval of about 30 [sun-]years; and halt 130 [*löar*] again.[5] Let us say the March began in VY 1110, when the total number of Quendi was about 15,000.

Suppose 10,000 marched (Eldar), and 5,000 Avari remained: Ingar 1,000, Noldor 3,500, Teleri 5,500 (*later* Lindar – Sindar – Nandor).[6]

Distance? Beleriand was about 550 miles broad from Eglarest to the Mountains of Lune. From the Mountains of Lune to the Sea of Rhûn is, according to the LR map over 1,250 miles: [total] 1,750 miles. How far east or southeast of the Sea of Rhûn was Cuiviénen?[7] If we say in ancient days that Cuiviénen was 2,000 miles as the crow flies from the coast of ancient Beleriand this will be approximately right.

Let 10,000 Eldar set out at the beginning of VY 1110. The begetting of the 8th generation is due to begin in VY 1108/64 + VY 18/9 = VY 1126/73. But then 16 VY = 2,304 [sun-]years will have elapsed! (It *could* begin in VY 1108/64 + 2 VY = VY 1110/64 when the 7th generation would be 24 [growth-] years [= 288 *löar*] old.)[8]

Clearly *either* no more children are begotten before reaching Valinor, *or* the March must have been delayed.

8th [gen. appears]	The 8th gen. begins in VY 1126/73. The 7th	
VY 1126/73	gen. contained 7,600 persons: of these, let	
[AY 18217]	3,500 pairs marry.	

[8th gen. complete]	The gen. will be complete in 1126/73 + 100	29,060
VY 1127/29	löar = VY 1127/29. The increase will be	
[AY 18317]	3,500 × 4 = 14,000.	

Let the March begin when the youngest of the 8th gen. are at least 10 [growth-]years old (= 120 solar years), so in VY 1127/29 + 120. This is in VY 1128/5 or *early* in 1129. Let 20,000 march (leaving 9,060 or about 9,000 Avari). Ingar 2,000, Ñoldor 7,000, Teleri 11,000. No more begetting of the 9th gen. will occur regularly until VY 1126/73 + 18/9 = VY 1142/82. But it can begin in 1126/73 + 2 VY = 1128.[9] Of these 20,000, 14,000 × $\frac{2}{3}$ will be above 11/10 [growth-]years old, 7,600 × $\frac{2}{3}$ will be 81, 1750 × $\frac{2}{3}$ will be 120 etc. So:

		["Age"]
over 9,000	young children	[GY] 11/10
over 5,600	young adults	40+
over 2,700	full grown	80+
over 1,200	prime	120+
over 500	prime	160+
over 400	prime	200+
144	prime	240+
48	prime	300+
24		340+

19,616
9,000 children +
11,000 adults

Too many children, so probably *delay march* until maturity (288 [sun-]years) after the birth of the youngest of the 8th gen. If 1127/29 + 2 VY (= 288 [sun-]years) = 1129/29 or early 1129. The youngest marchers will be 24 [growth-years] (288 [sun-]years) old, the oldest 168 löar or 1VY/24 older. But begetting of a 9th generation would now be possible for, say, 4,000 pairs of the 8th generation.

[Generation, year, and progress toward Sea]		[Population of Marchers]

[8th gen.]
VY 1129/29
[AY 18605]
450 miles

The March begins in VY 1129/*löa* 29. The great host of 20,000 goes very slowly (2,000 miles to go);[10] it has to provide food, clothing, etc. *en-route*, though it had the help of the Valar via Oromë.* It proceeds mainly in the late spring to early autumn: April to September. The general process is to make a period of marching and then to halt for repairs, cloth-making or fur-curing, and rest. The March began about April 1 of *löa* 29 of VY 1129. Thus well provided to start. It goes about 200 miles by the end of April, halts, then goes on again from June 20 to July 20 with 200 more miles (total 400). It is now near the east side of the Sea of Rhûn, then a very pleasant place. After some debate, it moves to the shores of the Sea of Rhûn (total 450 miles) and there stops during the rest of *löa* 29 and does not move on again, because many are for the time being content, and desire to beget children.

20,000

[9th gen. begins]
VY 1129/39
[AY 18615]

Of the available 4,500 8th-gen. pairs, 2,000 beget children in the spring of *löa* 30. They (2,000) are born in the spring of *löa* 39 (VY 1129/39). The host therefore does not move again for 10 growth-years more = 120 *löar*. VY 1129/159 = VY 1130/15. It is now combined with 2,000 young children (of about GY 11/11 age).

22,000

VY 1130/15
[AY 18735]
650 miles

In spring and summer of VY 1130/15 it only moves 200 miles (650 total). It camps in what are the wide grasslands before Mirkwood is reached, and full of grain and food. The Elves taught by Oromë sow grain that autumn, and reap in summer of 1130/16. They do this three times till 1130/19 and do not move on till spring 1130/20.

---

* [A marginal note apparently referring to the other Valar reads:] Others occupied with war?

VY 1130/20
[AY 18740]
800 miles

That year they reach the Great Forest, another
200 miles. This looks a lovely place, but they find
it contains lurking evils. Possibly Sauron is aware
of the March? Anyway many of Melkor's evils are
abroad. Some Eldar are lost; the rest are afraid.
They retire back into the grasslands 50 miles
(850 − 50 = 800) and await help from Oromë.
Oromë comes in 1130/25 and drives off the evils
and encourages the Eldar.

VY 1130/26
[AY 18746]
1,050 miles

The Ingar and the Ñoldor following Nahar pass
through the Great Forest (rich in fruit and berries?)
at its southern end (which was farther south than
in the Third Age) during 1130/26. They come out
into the Anduin Vale and are delighted with it.
Their chieftains cannot get them to proceed further
at that time. Their general thought is "why not dwell
here, and let the Valar guard us? This is where Quendi
should dwell, between wood and water!" Only the
Chiefs who had seen Aman are not content.

    The Lindar here begin to straggle. Not all had
reached the east side of the Forest when the Ingar
and Ñoldor went through. None have yet followed
Oromë.

VY 1130/36
[AY 18756]

The Ingar and Ñoldor settle on the east bank
of the Anduin (the region of later Lórien). They
rest till spring 1130/27. Then a new begetting of
children begins. Available pairs of the Ingar and
Ñoldor are about 4,000. (The total 8th gen. =
14,000 − but $\frac{1}{3}$ are Avari, leaving about 9,000 Eldar,
$\frac{9}{20}$ of which = 450 × 9 = 4,050 available pairs. 2,000
pairs beget children (1,000 first time, 1,000 second
time) who are born in spring of 1130/36. The Eldar
like their life there: the presence of the Máyar drives
off evil, and the place is rich in flowers and food.[11]
In spite of the Chiefs they are unwilling to move.

24,000

VY 1130/79
[AY 18799]

They linger till 1130/70 and then begin new
begetting (2,000 pairs); further [?births] of the
9th generation appear in spring 1130/79. The Teleri
now begin to appear: they left the grasslands and

26,000

came round south of the Forest. They like the new home and are now eager for more children.

VY 1130/89 [AY 18809]	About 2,000 pairs (of the available Telerin 8th gen. of 4,950) beget children in spring 1130/80. The Chiefs and Oromë are disturbed. No move can be made until the latest children are above 10 [GY]: sc. in 1130/89 + 120 = 1130/209 = 1131/65.	28,000

[VY 1130/90] [AY 18810]   Either by chance, machinations of Sauron, and/or because Oromë withdraws protection (hoping to make the Eldar less content with their new Home (*Atyamar*),[12] winters are hard and the weather worsens. The host is now burdened with many young born between 1129/39 and 1130/89. The oldest are those [that] (in 1131/65) [will be] VY 2/26 years old = 314 *löar*,[13] the youngest about 10 [GY]. The total of these is 8,000 in the total host of 28,000.

The Chiefs order an advance across the Anduin for spring 1130/91. The Teleri already show a love of water and boats, and begin a great boat-building. They are ready with rafts and boats in the course of 1130/90. But a large part of the Teleri later fought this, in the winter of 1130/90–91. The Anduin is wild and flooded and great snowstorms fall in the Misty Mountains – then much taller – which last far into the spring. The total Telerin host is 13,000 now; more than 3,000 refuse to leave Atyamar. These are the *Nandor*.* [14]

[VY 1130/91] [AY 18811] 1,150 miles	The host, now 25,000 strong, moves across the Anduin, but finds the *Hithaeglir* impassible. Some are lost in the attempt. Eventually they wander south through woods into the plain of later Rohan (Calenardhon).[15] The Teleri lag again.	25,000

---

* It is said that many remained here for thousands of years but others migrated – some eventually going south down the Anduin and settling on the shores south of the White Mountains, especially in later Belfalas. Others went on along the coasts until a number, and Denethor, came up into southeast Beleriand.

VY 1130/95 [AY 18815] 1,850 miles	The Ingar and Ñoldor settle at last about the Isen (near later Isengard). The wandering has taken about four *löar* (1130/95). The main host halts for a long while. The Teleri straggle in.[16] NB: All the coast south of the Haradwaith originally extended much farther west (before the ruin of Beleriand and later Númenor) so that they are still very far from the Sea, which they do not see or hear about.	
VY 1130/109 [AY 18829]	A new begetting of children begins in 1130/100. (Some are concluding the 9th gen., some being 4th or Telerin 2nd children.) New [?occasions] of 9th gen. appear in 1130/109. Available 8th gen. pairs 6,000 (less 900 Nandor). About 3,500 pairs beget children.[17]	28,500
VY 1131/5 [AY 18869]	A new begetting began in 1130/140, but not so many produce children. Some have already produced four. Also, women are getting [?unruly] because of difficulties of children and many are eager now to go on. 2,000 pairs produce 2,000 children in 1130/149 = 1131/5.[18] Oromë is impatient. They wait nonetheless until the youngest children are 12 [GY], that is, 144 [sun-]years = 1 VY = VY 1132/5.	30,500
VY 1132/9 [AY 19017] 2,110 miles	The Eldar scheme to beget no more children till Beleriand. The host of the Ingar and Ñoldor move west till it comes to Gwathló (about 260 miles) at the end of 1132/9.	
VY 1132/11 [AY 19019] 2,310 miles	Here they wait for the first of the lagging Teleri who come up in 1132/10 and help the Ingar and Ñoldor across. Olwë and rest come slowly on behind. The Ingar and Ñoldor reach the Baranduin in 1132/11. They are now near the southern end of the Ered Luin.[19]	
VY 1132/17 [AY 19025] 3,111 miles	They are led in 1132/12 to eastern Beleriand "which is safe". In the next few years they accomplish about 800 miles by [?drawing] about to the area of Western Doriath. Say about 1132/17 they reach the coast of Beleriand.[20] The March is over.	

VY1132/20	The Lindar (Teleri) are eager for the Sea and	30,000
[AY 19028]	push west to the Falas or Nevrast. The Ñoldor	
	and Ingar chiefly inhabit the area about Sirion.	
	About 1132/20, all the Eldar of the main host are	
	in Beleriand, and total 30,000.	

Now begins negotiation for transport

Having at last brought the Host of the Great March to the coast of Beleriand, and having detailed the time it took and their population increase along the way, Tolkien goes on to compare this new scheme with that of the scheme of the *Tale of Years* (see X:49, 56–7), and to consider its implications, particularly as arising from Finwë's abstaining from wedding before reaching Aman:

In the "Tale of Years" the Eldar reach the coast in VY 1125 (only 20 VY = 200 [sun-]years on the March).[21] Ulmo takes the Ingar and Ñoldor in 1132; they arrive in Aman in 1133. The Teleri leave in 1150. VY here [i.e., in the "Tale of Years"] = 10 sun-years. The Eldar (Ingar and Ñoldor) only abide in Beleriand $7 \times 10 = 70$ sun-years. It only takes 10 sun-years to cross the Great Sea. The Teleri depart 180 sun-years later. Except for passage of the Great Sea, these lengths [of time] are sufficient?

In the above scheme the Eldar reach the coast in 1132/17. The March began in 1129/29: they were nearly 3 VY in migration = 420 sun-years. They should abide 1 VY (1133/17) before the Ingar and Ñoldor depart. Transit [across the Great Sea] = 12 [sun-]years. The Teleri now go to the shores and are befriended by Ossë. Part of the Teleri and Olwë are taken off in 1134.

In the "Tale of Years" Finwë begets Fëanor in 1160 and he is born in VY 1169.[22] This is (according to TY scale) 27 VY = 270 [sun-]years after Finwë's arrival in Valinor.[23]

Where in the present scheme did the chieftains come in? Ingwë, Finwë, Elwë (Olwë)? If "First Elves" they awoke in VY 1000, being approximately 24 age-years old. In VY 1133/29 they reach Valinor. They are then 24 + 133/29 VY old = 24 +133 = 157 age-years; actually 288 + 19,152 = 19,440 [sun-years].

Clearly *Finwë cannot wed in Aman* unless the arrangement of Elvish lives is *altered*. It could be altered satisfactorily in this way:

1. The Eldar, especially in the early ages, do not wed or beget until late, and maybe at least 200 years old.

2. They do not necessarily beget in consecutive Times of the Children; but may beget in any suitable or peaceful time, at will. But they do not beget when past *hröa*-prime, which was in the Elder Days about 200 age-years (but this dwindled: in the Second Age it was 150, in Third Age 100).

Ingwë, Finwë etc. could postpone wedding till arrival (and probably did not expect to be so long on the road). If so, however, it might be a good thing to have few weddings on the March –: but Ingwë, Finwë, and Elwë being special cases (as the only ones who had yet seen Aman, and so desired the children to be born there), they could be among the few who abstained [i.e. from wedding before and during the March]. If there are few weddings on the March, then *either* Elves must awake longer than 82 VY before their finding *or* far more must be "created": 144 (72 pairs), or 144 pairs?

But in any case – how would Ingwë etc. or any "First Elf" know of what was going to happen, so as to postpone marriage? How could Elwë/Olwë/Elmo be "brothers"? Fairly clearly then Ingwë etc. are *not* "First Elves". What then became of older generations?

This can be got over. The Quendi at first (to 3 gens.?) were very *philoprogenitive*. They mated almost at once with their predestined mates. It was not for *some time*, when their young, inexperienced *fëar* began to take command, that their other faculties demanded fulfilment, and they began to be absorbed in the study of Arda.[24] The *younger generations* therefore progressed rapidly in strength, nobility, and intellectuality of character, and made natural leaders. The first few generations (expending much vigour in begetting) were least adventurous and were nearly all Avari in the event.

Secondly, *in any case*: Elvish lords or Kings (as Númenóreans later) tended to hand on lordship and affairs to their descendants if they could or were engrossed in some pursuit. Often (though we don't see it in Beleriand, since the War occupied so short a span of Elvish-time, and lords and Kings were so often slain), after passing 200 age-years they would resign. It would thus be *young, eager Quendi* of some later generations (whose fathers or grandfathers were lords) who were chosen and/or willing to go as ambassadors to Aman – after which they would be preeminent and obvious leaders of the March. "The light of Aman was in their faces", and the other Elves were in awe of them.

Against this paragraph Tolkien placed a large "*" and added a note:

This is better than making the Ambassadors different from the later leaders.

> He also drew vertical lines against the last two paragraphs on this page, and in the upper left-hand corner he further added the word: "Important", indicating his enthusiasm for these solutions. Important, indeed, as these solutions to the problems – of 1) reducing the number of weddings (and thus begettings) of the Eldar on the March, while 2) still having sufficient numbers of Elves to believably populate both Aman and Beleriand, and 3) allowing Finwë to still be of marriageable and begetting age when he arrives in Aman within the "age-year" scheme laid out in these papers – turn out to have been the germ of "The Legend of the Awaking of the Quendi (*Cuivienyarna*)" given at XI:420–4. For on the pages that immediately follow this discussion are the germ and the rough working-out of the mechanics of that legend, beginning:

The "First Elves" awaking in VY 1000 should be 144: 72 pairs of *destined spouses*. But they did not all wake at once from sleep "in the womb of Arda". There were *three first Elves* known in later legend as Imin, Tata, and Enel (from whom the Eldar said the words for 1, 2, and 3 were made: but the reverse was probably the historical fact).

> It is apparently here that the names and figures of Imin, Tata, and Enel, as the first three male Elves to awake, first arose. For the continuation of the development of this legend, see the next chapter.

NOTES

1 This sentence continues in the MS with: "that is, in VY 1018 + 19 *löar*"; but this is impossible, since the 2nd generation itself appeared in that year.

2 Tolkien here actually wrote: "VY 1073/24", which is a calculation error (since $46 + 120 - 144 = 22$).

3 Tolkien marked this as a crucial point with a large "★".

4 As first written, this sentence concluded: "at least 10 years (gestation 9 + mother's rest), more likely 20". There followed: "[?Or] If a whole generation or Time of Children", struck through in the act of writing.

5 As first written, this sentence ended: "and halt 20 again".

6 That is, these Teleri and their descendants later became the Lindar, Sindar, and Nandor of Beleriand. For the name *Ingar*, the "People of Ingwë" (i.e., the *Vanyar*), see the introduction to this part of the book.

7 Tolkien here actually wrote: "How far W or SW of Sea of Rhûn was Cuivié-nen?", but this must be a slip, since in no account of the Awakening was Cuiviénen ever west of the Sea of Rhûn and, as will be seen, the Eldar here too reach the shores of the Sea of Rhûn from the east.

8 This last sentence, represented here as a parenthetical comment, was a late addition in red ball-point pen.

9 This final sentence entered as a later, faint addition in red ball-point pen.

10 That is, 2,000 miles "as the crow flies", as previously stipulated. The actual course of the journey, as will be seen, is much longer than this.

11 "Máyar" is a seldom-used form of the name "Maiar" that appears to have arisen in linguistic notes dating from 1957 (PE17:124, 149 s.v. √AYA-N, and cf. 145 s.v. ADA for the date). The Máyar in question are not here named, but see the entry for DB 866/13 in chap. XIII, "Key Dates", below.

12 "*Atyamar*" in Quenya is literally 'second-home'.

13 Tolkien here actually wrote: "2/26 years old = 166 *löar* = 13 *löar* 10 [?months]", but this is irreconcilable with the record and the mathematics.

14 "Denethor": cf. S:54, 94–6, X:93, XI:13.

15 Here a curious element enters the new scheme of the Great March: sc., that *none* of the Eldar crossed the Misty Mountains (*Hithaeglir*) into Eriador after crossing the Anduin, but instead the whole host (save some 3,000 Nandor) turned south down the Anduin. In contrast, *The Silmarillion* recounts (S:54, and cf. X:82–3 entry for YT 1115):

> Now the Teleri abode long on the east bank of that river [the Anduin] and wished to remain there, but the Vanyar and the Noldor passed over it, and Oromë led them into the passes of the mountains [the Hithaeglir].

and further that the Teleri too eventually passed over the mountains (S:54):

> And the host of the Teleri passed over the Misty Mountains, and crossed the wide lands of Eriador.

16 Originally, this sentence continued (before being struck through):

> but many go down to the Sea, at Isenmouth. Oromë eventually gets them to go – saying that they can dwell by the Sea long at their journeys' end, and that the Valar want them to go north-wards to

"Isenmouth" here must refer to the mouth of the River Isen/Angren (and not the Carach Angren 'Jaws of Iron'/Isenmouthe of later Mordor; see LR:920, 927–8). If so, this original continuation implies that in the First Age the River Isen emptied into the Belegaer at or about the same latitude and longitude that it does in the Third Age, despite the submergence of vast amounts of the western lands of Beleriand in the War of Wrath at the end of the First Age. The realization of this implication of the passage no doubt occasioned its deletion in the act of writing and the note that immediately follows.

17 The last two sentences are additions in red ball-point pen, and roughly written. The number of available 8th generation pairs appears to have originally been 8,000, and the number of begetting pairs 4,000.

18 Tolkien actually wrote "1131/9" here, but that is an error.

19 Here again, in consequence of the southerly route the host takes to avoid crossing the Misty Mountains and its subsequent passing through the (later-named) gap of Rohan at the southern end of the mountains, the host enters Beleriand below the southern end of the Ered Luin; whereas in *The Silmarillion* the various bodies of the whole host cross over the Ered Luin (at different times) at a much more northerly point (S:54, and cf. X:83 entry for YT 1125):

At length the Vanyar and the Noldor came over Ered Luin, the Blue Mountains, between Eriador and the westernmost land of Middle-earth, which the Elves after named Beleriand; and the foremost companies passed over the Vale of Sirion and came down to the shores of the Great Sea between Drengist and the Bay of Balar....

Thus after many years the Teleri also came at last over Ered Luin into the eastern regions of Beleriand.

Accounts of the Great March prior to this give the impression that it proceeded more-or-less straight from east to west at about the mid-latitude of the Misty Mountains, and so much closer to the latitude of Doriath. Given this new, more circuitous and much more southerly route, it seems difficult to understand why, after entering Beleriand at the southern end of the Ered Luin, the host would deviate so far north as to reach the area of Doriath? As Oromë at least must have known, the Bay of Balar directly to their west was much closer than the Falas or Nevrast, and in the event became their point of departure from Middle-earth to Valinor.

20 Tolkien here actually wrote: "Say about 1132/17 they are in Beleriand"; but since the (main) host entered Beleriand in VY 1132/12, and since Tolkien next writes: "March is over", and then writes further below that "Eldar reach coast in 1132/17", I have used the latter to clarify what seems to be the actual intent here.

21 Cf. X:81–3, where the Great Journey starts in YT 1105 and ends in 1125. As Tolkien notes, in the scheme of the earlier "Tale of Years", 20 VY = 200 sun-years, not 2880 as here.

22 Cf. X:101 n.1.

23 Cf. X:84 §67, which assigns 1133 as the year when the Vanyar and Noldor arrived in Aman. This is indeed 27 VY before the begetting of Fëanor by Finwë and Míriel (but 36 VY before his birth), and so appears to be what Tolkien is referring to here by "this".

24 Draft material for this passage reads:

When Quendi were very "young in Arda", they were far more
like Men (unfallen), or indeed grown-up children. Their *hröar*
(and the delights of the body of all kinds) were dominant, and
full of vigour; and their *fëar* only beginning to grow and wake
and discover their powers. So they were far more progenitive and
less exhausted by the production of children.

Cf. the opening paragraph of the text presented in chap. V, "Natural Youth and
Growth of the Quendi", above. On the unfallen nature of the Quendi, see THE
FALL OF MAN in App. I.

VIII

ELDARIN TRADITIONS
CONCERNING THE "AWAKENING"

This text is written in black nib-pen on five sides of four sheets of unlined paper. It dates from c. 1959.

As was seen at the end of the previous chapter, the legend of Imin, Tata, and Enel arose in the context of Tolkien's desire to reduce the number of weddings (and thus begettings) of the Eldar on the March, while still having sufficient numbers of Elves to believably populate both Aman and Beleriand, and yet allow Finwë to still be of marriageable age when he arrives in Aman.

While the subsequent typescript version of this text, published in *The War of the Jewels*, follows this manuscript (as emended) quite closely (see *The legend of the Awaking of the Quendi (Cuivienyarna)*; XI:420–4), there are enough differences of details and textual development to warrant giving the full manuscript version here, in the context in which the legend first arose.

Summary of the Eldarin
traditions concerning the "Awakening" and of the
Legend of the Cuivië (Cuivienyarna)

During the waking of their first *hröar* from the "flesh of Arda" the Quendi slept "in the womb of Arda", beneath the green sward, and "awoke" when they were full-grown. But the "First Elves" (also called the *Unbegotten*, or the *Eru-begotten*) did not all wake together. Eru had so ordained that each should lie beside his or her "destined spouse".[1] But three Elves awoke first of all; and they were elf-men, for elf-men are more strong in *hröa* and more eager and adventurous in strange places.[2] These three are named in the oldest traditions: *Imin, Tata,* and *Enel.* They awoke in that order, but with little time between each; and from them, say the Eldar, the words for 1, 2, and 3 were made: the oldest of all numerals.* [3]

Imin, Tata, and *Enel* awoke before their spouses, and the first thing that they saw was the stars, for they woke in the early twilight before dawn. And the next thing they saw was their destined spouse lying asleep on the green sward beside them.[4] Then they were so enamoured of their beauty that their desire for speech was immediately quickened and they began "to think of words" to speak and sing in. And being impatient they could not wait but woke up their spouses. Thus (say the Eldar) elf-women ever after reached maturity sooner than elf-men; for it had been intended that they should wake later than their spouses.[5]

But after a time, when they had dwelt together a little and had devised many words, Imin and Iminyë, Tata and Tatië, Enel and Enelyë walked together, and left the green dell of their waking, and they came soon to another dell and found there *six* pairs of Quendi, and the stars were again shining in the morrow-dim and the elf-men were just waking.[6]

Then Imin claimed to be the eldest and to have the right of first choice; and he said, "I choose these twelve to be my companions". And the elf-men woke their spouses, and when the eighteen Elves had dwelt together a little and had learned many words and devised more, they walked on together, and soon in another even deeper and wider hollow they found *nine* pairs of Quendi, and the elf-men had just waked in the starlight.

Then Tata claimed the right of second choice, and he said: "I choose these eighteen to be my companions". Then again the elf-men woke their spouses, and they dwelt and spoke together, and devised many new sounds and new and longer words;[7] and then the thirty-six walked abroad together, until they came to a grove of birches by a stream, and there they found *twelve* pairs of Quendi, and the elf-men likewise were just standing up, and looking at the stars through the birch boughs.

Then Enel claimed the right of third choice, and he said:

---

* The Eldarin words referred to are *Min, Atta* (or *Tata*), *Nel-de.* The reverse is probably historical. The *Three* had no names until they had developed language, and were given (or took) names after they had devised numerals (or at least the first 12).

"I choose these twenty-four to be my companions". Again the elf-men woke their spouses; and for many days the sixty Elves dwelt by the stream, and soon they began to make verse and song to the music of the water.

At length they all set out together again. But Imin noticed that each time they had found more Quendi than before, and he thought to himself: "I have only twelve companions (although I am the eldest); I will take a later choice". Soon they came to a sweet-smelling firwood on a hill-side, and there they found *eighteen* pairs of Quendi, and all were still sleeping. It was still night and clouds were in the sky. But before dawn a wind came, and roused the elf-men, and they woke and were amazed at the stars; for all the clouds were blown away and the stars were bright from east to west. And for a long time the eighteen new Quendi took no heed of the others, but looked at the light of *Menel*. But when at last they turned their eyes back to earth they beheld their spouses and woke them to look at the stars, crying to them *elen, elen!*[8] And so the stars got their name.

Now Imin said: "I will not choose again yet"; and Tata, therefore, chose these thirty-six to be his own companions; and they were tall and dark-haired and strong like the fir-trees, and from them most of the Ñoldor later were sprung.

And the ninety-six Quendi now spoke together, and the newly-waked devised many new and beautiful words, and many cunning artifices of speech; and they laughed, and danced upon the hill-side, until at last they desired to find more companions. Then they all set out again together, until they came to a lake dark in the twilight, and there was a great cliff above it upon the east side, and a waterfall came down from the height, and the stars glittered on the foam. But the elf-men were already bathing in the waterfall, and they had waked their spouses. There were *twenty-four* pairs; but as yet they had no formed speech, though they sang sweetly and their voices echoed in the stone, mingling with the rush of the falls.

But again Imin withheld his choice, thinking "next time it will be a great company". Therefore Enel said: "I have the choice, and I choose these forty-eight to be my companions". And the hundred and forty-four Quendi dwelt long together by the lake, until they all became of one mind and speech, and were glad.[9]

At length Imin said: "It is time now that we should go on and seek more companions". But most of the others were content. So Imin and Iminyë and their twelve companions set out, and they walked long by day and by twilight in all the country about the Lake, near which all the Quendi had awakened – for which reason it is called

Cuiviénen.[10] But they never found any more companions: for the tale of the First Elves was complete.

And so it was that the Quendi ever after reckoned in *twelves*, and that 144 was for long their highest number, so that in none of their later tongues was there any common name for greater numbers.[11] And so also it came about that the "Companions of Imin" or the Eldest Company (of whom came the Ingar)* were nonetheless only 14 in all; and the smallest company; and the "Companions of Tata" (of whom came the Ñoldor) were 56 in all; but the "Companions of Enel" although the Youngest Company were the largest. From them came the Teleri (or Lindar), and they were in the beginning 74 in all.[12]

Now the Quendi loved all of Arda that they had yet seen, and green things that grow, and the sun of summer, were their delight; but nonetheless they were ever moved most in heart by the Stars, and the hours of twilight, at "morrow-dim" and "even-dim" in clear weather were the times of their greatest joy.[13] For in those hours in the spring of the year they had first awakened to life in Arda. But the Lindar, above all the other Quendi, from their beginning were most in love with water, and sang before they could speak.

NOTES

1 As first written, this read: "pre-destined spouse".

2 The qualifier "elf" in "elf-man" was a later insertion.

3 For other Eldarin traditions concerning the numerals, see "Eldarin Hands, Fingers, and Numerals" in chap. III in part two of this book.

4 As first written, what became these two sentences read: "the first thing that each saw was his destined spouse lying asleep on the green sward".

5 As first written, this sentence originally ended: "sooner than Elf-men; and were usually wedded to Elf-men a little older than themselves".

6 The words "the stars were again shining in the morrow-dim, and" were a marginal insertion in black nib-pen. As first written, the last phrase of the sentence began: "*six* pairs of Quendi, still asleep, but".

7 As first written, this phrase read: "devised many new words and artifices of speech".

---

* Vanyar.

8 The end of this sentence, "crying to them" etc., entered as a marginal insertion, apparently not long after the original composition.

9 As first written, this paragraph ended with the partial sentence: "But though they loved all that they yet had seen", before this was struck out.

10 As first written, this read: "for which reason it was called *Cuiviénen*".

11 As first written, this sentence began: "And so it came about".

12 As first written, the text continued with: "And the Lindar from the beginning were most in love with water (by which they awakened); but all the Quendi, although they loved [?A]", ending abruptly there, before this passage was struck through.

13 As first written, this sentence began: "Now the Quendi, although they loved all of Arda that they had yet seen, and green things that grow were their delight".

IX

TIME-SCALES AND RATES
OF GROWTH

This is a clear manuscript written for the most part in black nib-pen on six sides of three unlined sheets that Tolkien lettered, in red ball-point pen, a–f, and clipped together. Some corrections and additions were made by Tolkien in red and blue ball-point pen and in pencil. It dates from c. 1959.

For similar applications of the greatly increased rate of Sun-years to Valian Years of 144 : 1 to specific characters in the *legendarium*, see the texts presented here as chaps. X, "Difficulties in Chronology"; XI, "Ageing of Elves"; and XVIII, "Elvish Ages & Númenórean".

Time-scales and "rates of growth"

	Valian Year of Ageing	Mortal Men
	1	144
Original Quendian	1	144
Later	25/36	100

The Quendian rate originally corresponded to the Valian and it so remained in Aman. But by each act or choice which as it were allied the Quendi, or any group of them, more closely with "Arda Marred", the rate of "growth" became quicker (for the tendency towards physical decay was increased).

It is said that the Avari quickened to 100 : 1 as soon as the Eldar had departed; that the Nandor did likewise as soon as they forsook the

March; that the Sindar did so also when they chose to remain on the Western Shores; and that finally the exiled Noldor were quickened in the same way as soon as they left Aman, or rather as soon as the Doom of Mandos was spoken and they persisted in their rebellion.[1]

In all the earlier legends, therefore, the rate 100 : 1 can be used to determine approximately the age of any of the Eldar in human terms (except while they were in Aman where it is 144 : 1).

It is said that after the fall of Sauron, and the beginning of the Fourth Age and the Dominion of Men, those of the Elves who still lingered in Middle-earth were again "quickened" to a rate of about 72 : 1, or in these latter days to 48 : 1.[2]

Some calculations

It will be seen that the dates given in the "Lord of the Rings" fit well with these rates, *save in two points*.

The rate of the *Half-elven* that chose to join the Quendi was evidently in Middle-earth 100 : 1. (For those who joined Men a special rate of growth was established, approximately 3 : 1, though this diminished, but was in Aragorn almost restored: he was 5 : 2).[3]

Elrond. He was born 58 [sun-]years before the end of the First Age in the overthrow of Morgoth;[4] but he was born in Middle-earth and so inherited from the beginning the rate 100 : 1. He lived then through the Second Age of Middle-earth: 3,441 years. He wedded Celebrían in TA 100 (it is said),[5] and left Middle-earth at the end of the Third Age (3021). He said that in the Last Alliance (SA 3430) he was "the herald of Gil-galad".[6]

We see therefore that when he left Middle-earth he was 58 + 3,441 + 3,021 years old = 6,520. He was then in human terms just over 65 and still in full vigour.[7]

At the Last Alliance he was 58 + 3,430 = 3,488 ÷ 100 = nearly 35. At his wedding he was 58 + 3,441 + 100 = 3,599 ÷ 100 = 36.

Celebrían was born (it seems) early in the Second Age, when Galadriel refused to return to Eressëa, and passed over the Mountains. Probably SA 300. At her wedding with Elrond therefore she would be 3,441 − 300 + 100 = 3,241 years old, or 32. A reasonable age, and further to be explained by the fact that her marriage was postponed by the War of the Last Alliance, and the preceding troubles in Eriador. At her departure from Middle-earth in TA 2509 she was 3,141 + 2,509 = 5,650 years old, or 56.[8]

Arwen. She was born (according to LR) in TA 241. She was married to Aragorn in TA 3019. She was then 2,778 years old, or in human terms nearly 28. This in elvish terms is a very suitable age. Her wedding was in any case inevitably postponed by the War of the Ring and the preceding troubles. Also, in 2951, when Aragorn first met her, she was 2,710, or 27, whereas he was then 20: he had yet to overtake her, which in this case was desirable, since she was to become mortal in his degree. In 2980 when they plighted their troth in Lórien she was very little older, but he was 49.[9]

Now *Aragorn* was born in TA 2931, but lived until 4A 100, and was then of full age, but not yet becoming senile. His years were then 190.[10] He was the "last of the Númenóreans", and his span was equal to the Kings of Men of old (as is said): thrice that of ordinary Men. Actually, his rate was probably rather 5 : 2 than 3 : 1: so that he was at his wedding in TA 3019 in years 88, in age 35; and at death in years 190, in age 75. (The full Númenórean rate would make him 29 at his wedding and 63 at death.)[11]

It would appear that the "grace" accorded to the Númenóreans was like that of Aman: it did *not* alter the human rate of growth to maturity, but postponed the decay of old age after that for a long while – until one knew inwardly (by a motion of the *fëa*) that the time had come to relinquish life in this world *voluntarily*.[12] If one did not do so, but clung to life, senility would soon arise. If Aragorn had yielded to Arwen's entreaties, he would have become decrepit, at least in body, very soon.

Galadriel. She was born in Aman. At the exile she was young and eager, just at or upon the threshold of maturity: probably in age about 20. She must therefore have been in years about $20 \times 144 = 2,880$. She became acquainted with Celeborn (a Sindarin prince, and kinsman of Thingol) in Beleriand. But there were few marriages or child-births among the Eldar during the War with Angband, which though it occupied 590 years,[13] was to the Eldar in "ageing time" only a matter of some *six* year-equivalents. She probably married Celeborn soon after the overthrow of Morgoth, and when she (it appears, because of love for Celeborn, who would not leave Middle-earth yet) declined to return West to Eressëa,* they passed together over the "Mountains of Lune" into Eriador.[14] She was then about 26 in age, for the years in

---

* There may have been also an element of pride in her decision; for she was a princess of the Noldor, who had lived in Aman itself. Eressëa seemed only a "second best".

Beleriand had been at the ageing-rate of 100 : 1. In SA 300 or thereabout (3 [life-]years later) she bore Celebrían in Eriador. She was then about 29. She lived through all the remainder of the Second Age to SA 3441, and left Middle-earth in TA 3021. She was thus at that time in [life-]years $20 + \frac{3441 + 3021}{100} = 20 + 70.5$, or 90 and a half years in age;[15] and thus in elven-terms, according to the time in which the "fading" of the Quendi was approaching, now passing the prime of her *hröa*.

As can be seen, these calculations show that the events and dates (of LR) are well-fitted to Elvish nature, and are evidently in the main correctly reported. But there are *two points* in which *error* appears: probably of scribal origin.

It is stated in the *Tale of Years* that Elrond married Celebrían in TA 100, and that his twin sons (Elladan and Elrohir) were born in TA 139, and Arwen in TA 241. This must be erroneous: for in TA 139 only 39 years, or in "ageing terms" of the Eldar and the Half-elven, 2/5 of a year had passed since Elrond's wedding. This was impossible.[16]

Also, in TA 241 only 102 years had passed since the birth of the twins, which is not much more than a year of ageing time, and though not impossible is according to Elvish nature and behaviour, entirely improbable. (Especially after the birth of twins, and in the begetting and bearing of a special child of high excellence.)

It is thus probable that 100 and 241 are errors for 10 and 341: for these are in the circumstances easy errors to make; and it will be observed that if 10 and 341 are substituted the entries [i.e., in the published *Tale of Years* in App. B] are not displaced from their present position.

With these emendations we shall see that Celebrían and Elrond were at their wedding 90 years, or less than 1 [life-year], younger than as stated. This is of no great concern. But the birth of the twins was 129 years later or 1.29 [life-years], which is about a year and four months, which is in elven-terms very probable. The birth of Arwen was then 202 years later again, or about 2 [life-]years. This is possible though sooner than would be expected.*

No more children were born to Elrond, though Celebrían did not leave Middle-earth until 2509, when she was in years about 5,650, or about 56½ [life-years]. This is no doubt related to the birth of twins,

---

* It is thus possible that 241 is an error not for 341, but for 421: an even more likely error to have occurred, except that the next following entry is for 420. In that case about 2.8 [life-]years would have intervened between the births, which is even more probable.

and still more to the fact that Arwen was a "special child" of great powers and beauty.

> In later marginal notes in blue ball-point pen against the two paragraphs beginning at "This must be erroneous", he reconsidered the changes proposed in them:

No. For child-growth (including time in the womb) to maturity was at rate 10 : 1. Gestation took 8 years (= 96 months). [TA] 139 is therefore quite possible. But the resting in ageing time of *parents* was at the 100 : 1 [rate]. So 200 years should intervene. Sc. the conception of Elladan and Elrohir [should be in] 131, born 139. Arwen begotten 333 born 341, after 194 or nearly 2 [life-]years of rest.

> Although Tolkien did later change the birth-year of Elladan and Elrohir to 130 in the second edition (1966) of *LR* App. B, he in the event made no change to that of Arwen.

NOTES

1 Tolkien at some later point wrote in the margin against this paragraph in red ball-point pen: "*no quickening*"; and apparently at the same time wrote in the space between the initial table and the first paragraph: "*All this needs revision to duodecimal*", also in red ball-point pen. This indicates that Tolkien had decided that the Quendian growth-rate ought *not* in fact, as here, generally increase outside of Aman from 144 (duodecimal) to 100 (decimal).

2 There is no indication in the text of just when "these latter days" are meant to be.

3 As will be seen below, at the time of writing Tolkien still regarded Aragorn as having died at age 190, not, as later, 210.

4 In the c. 1951–2 "Tale of Years", as emended, Elrond and Elros are said to have been born in YS 532 (XI:348), which makes him 58, as here, when the First Age ended in YS 590 (XI:346).

5 This is the year given in App. B in the first edition (1955) of *The Return of the King*. This was changed to 109 in the second edition (1966).

6 Cf. LR:243.

7 The words "and still at full vigour" were a later addition in red ball-point pen.

8 Both App. A and B to *The Lord of the Rings* say that while Celebrían was attacked by Orcs and poisoned in TA 2509, she departed over Sea in 2510 (LR:1043, 1087).

9 Tolkien subsequently pencilled in – but did not actually adopt here – alterations of various dates and consequent ages for Arwen (changes that in part anticipate the scheme adopted in chap. XI, "Ageing of Elves", below), thus suggesting that Arwen be born in TA 341 and so 2,678 sun-years old = 27 age-years at her marriage to Aragorn in TA 3019; that she was 2,610 or 26 when she met Aragorn in TA 2951.

10 In the first edition (1955) of *RotK* App. B, Aragorn (born March 1, 2931) was said to have died on March 1, 1521, thus aged (exactly) 190 years, as here. In the second edition (1966) the year was altered to 1541, with Aragorn thus departing precisely at the age of 210 (which, it may be noted, is precisely three times 70; cf. Psalm 89 [90] verse 10: "The days of our life are seventy years, or perhaps eighty, if we are strong").

11 As with Arwen's ages, Tolkien subsequently pencilled in – but did not adopt – suggested changes, in this case to Aragorn's rate of growth and consequent "normal" human equivalent ages (and similarly in part anticipating the scheme adopted in chap. XI, "Ageing of Elves", below) In the margin against this paragraph, Tolkien wrote:

Aragorn grew up [to] adult[hood] in [the] normal rate, he was adult at 20. He then [?endured] at Númenórean rate of 3 : 1. So when 49 in [sun-]years he was $20 + \frac{29}{3}$ = about 30 in [?fact].

Tolkien then calculated Aragorn's ages on this 3 : 1 basis: so that he was $20 + \frac{68}{3}$ = 43 at his wedding in TA 3019, and $20 + \frac{170}{3}$ = 77 at his death in 4A 100.

12 Tolkien elaborates on this matter in chaps. XI, "Lives of the Númenóreans", and XII, "The Ageing of Númenóreans", in part three of this book.

13 In the c. 1950–1 "Grey Annals" the Siege of Angband is said to have begun in YS 60 and to have been broken in YS 455 (XI:39, 52).

14 For the problematic question of the history of Galadriel and Celeborn in Tolkien's writings, before, within, and after the publication of *The Lord of the Rings*, see Christopher Tolkien's summary at UT:228 ff. The situation portrayed here agrees with what little is said of the matter in App. B (LR:1082), though the account here ascribes motives to Galadriel that App. B does not state explicitly: both love and pride.

15 Tolkien has made a mathematical error here: (3441 + 3021) = 6462 ÷ 100 = 64.62 + 20 = 84.62 life-years.

16 Tolkien here is apparently regarding the period of gestation as equal to one life-year in Middle-earth, sc. 100 *löar*. But see the later marginal note presented near the end of this text, it which he corrects this to 8 *löar*. It remains, though, that even after the 1966 revisions to App. B, in which Elrond and Celebrían wed in TA 109 and the twins are born in 130, 21 *löar* elapse between the events.

X

DIFFICULTIES IN CHRONOLOGY

This text is written, in a (mostly) clear hand in black nib-pen, on six sides of three sheets of printed copies of a memo proceeding from a College Meeting that took place on 21 June 1955, during Tolkien's period of office as the Sub-warden of Merton College. There are however several reasons to date this text somewhat later than 1955. First, it uses *ab initio* the Quenya word *hröa* for 'body', but there is no evidence that that word was in use until after the typescript text B of *Laws and Customs among the Eldar* was made in c. 1958 (see X:141–42, 304). Second, it refers to specifics of the differing rates of Elvish ageing in Aman and in Beleriand as though already introduced and adopted ("144 SY in Aman = 1 year of Elf-life, but 100 SY in Beleriand = 1 year"), whereas there is no evidence that this difference was introduced before c. 1959, sc. in the text presented here as chap. IV, "Time-scales", above; and further, it is in that text that Tolkien appears first to have noted the difficulty presented by the birth of Maeglin in Beleriand that is central to this text. Third, near the end of this text it specifically cites Celebrían's age in TA 10, a year that has no significance except that in the c. 1959 text presented in the previous chapter, TA 10 was suggested as a correction for the year that Elrond and Celebrían wed. I therefore think the text in fact dates, like so many others in the "Time and Ageing" file, from c. 1959.

For similar applications of the greatly increased rate of Sun-years to Valian Years of 144 : 1 to specific characters in the *legendarium*, see the texts presented here as chaps. IX, "Times-scales and Rates of Growth"; XI, "Ageing of Elves"; and XVIII, "Elvish Ages & Númenórean".

Grave difficulty will be found in the chronology on the scales 144 SY in Aman = 1 year of Elf-life, but 100 SY in Beleriand = 1 year. For no Elf not born in Aman would be of age to marry (though there might be numerous children), since the whole time (approximately 590 years) of the War against Morgoth was only equivalent to about 6 life-years of the Eldar. Any marriageable Elda would then have to be at least 20 [life-years] and therefore have been born 14 to 20 [Valian] years before VY 1500 when Beleriandic reckoning begins: i.e. [Valian] 11 to 15 years before the Exile began.

It would on whole be best to have *no* Exilic children (born in Beleriand) coming into the tale. But the case of Maeglin cannot be got round. The narrative makes it inevitable that he should have been born *after the occupation of Gondolin* in Bel. 116. At the period of Tuor's coming to Gondolin (Bel. 495) or wedding with Idril (502), he would if born in (say) Bel. 120 be c. 375 or c. 382 years old – but that only = less than 4 [life-]years old.[1]

(Isfin must either stray – *refusing to be married in Gondolin* – or soon depart again, say after 120/125. Best is that she should refuse and be forced, and *soon escape*. So that Maeglin would be born c. Bel. 120.)[2]

Solution 1) Elves *married late* in Aman (usually). They became adult at life-age 20, but that = 20 VY = 2,880; but they remained very young and vigorous (and youthful in mind and interests) so that often they did not wed until they were 200 life-years old or nearly that: sc. when 28,800 Sun-years old!

2) But *under the Sun* (outside Varda's Domes) all the Eldar had quickened *in growth*, though they had not lost (at first) much of their steadfastness in vigour and health at that point. They therefore reached maturity 10 times quicker or became 20 when only *200* [sun-]years old; they then maintained this vigour, ageing only at the rate of 100 years = 1 life-year.

(Note in the "Tale of Years" that 5 VY is allowed for the wanderings of the Exiles, 1495 to 1500,[3] but that was reckoned on a scale of 1 VY = 10 SY, and so was *insufficient*, being only 50 Sun-years. It is now *far too much*, being 720 years! Adequate would be 1 Valian Year = 144 [SY]. Therefore the Crossing of the Ice should be in FA 1496.)

To find the approximate age-equivalence therefore in mortal years: *For those born in Aman* reckon years in Aman as if mortal (or divide real number of Sun-years by 144) up to FA 1496; then divide

Beleriand Years by 100. Thus an Elda born in Aman in 1475 would be 20 at the Exile, 21 at arrival in Middle-earth, $+\frac{590}{100}$ [older] at the fall of Morgoth = about 27.

For those born in Beleriand. Maeglin for example, born in Bel. 120, was in only 200 years (= 20) an adult: sc. he was in life-age 20 in Bel. 320. But in 495, when Tuor came to Gondolin, he was only $\frac{495-320}{100}$ years older: sc. $\frac{175}{100}$ = less than 2 years or about 22. When Maeglin came to Gondolin c. 400 he was thus $20 + \frac{80}{100}$ years old. It was this *disparity of age* (and experience) that made him distasteful to Idril.

   Tuor was born in 472. He came to Gondolin in 495, being then 23. He married *Idril* in 502, being then 30. To look on him with any favour Idril must have been young, about the *equivalent* of 22/23 in 495. To reach 22 in 495 she must (if born in Beleriand) have taken 200 years to become 20 and then 400 years to become 22: sc. 600 years. *She cannot have been born in Beleriand* (in fact she was not, as her mother Anairë refused the Exile, but Idril adhered to her father).[4] If born in Aman her 495 years in Beleriand = about 5 years of her life. She must therefore have been 17 on entry into Beleriand and have been born in VY 1496 − 17 = 1479.

   If born in Aman, it must be remembered that if they were not yet adult, the rate of growth would become 10 = 1 when they set foot in Middle-earth (or probably as soon as the Doom of Mandos was spoken in VY 1495).

   Thus Finduilas is evidently very young in 490 when Túrin comes to Nargothrond; but she had already been (virtually?) betrothed to Gwindor before the Nirnaeth in 472. (Túrin had had a hard life and had commanded men, so at 26 (born 464) he would seem to her a hardened warrior of full maturity.) If we say she was only 20 in 490, she could have reached that age in 200 years and need only have been born in Bel. 290. In 472 she would have been 1–8 years younger: about 18. But she was probably older in 472, say 20 then at least: in which case she could have been born in Bel. 272 and she would not be appreciably older in 490. But she could have been born in Aman in say 1486, being 9 at the Exile, 10 on entry to Beleriand. She would then need 100 years to become 20 in Bel. 100. In 490 she would be nearly 24.

A better solution is 3) The *Rate of Growth* of those *born in Beleriand* was 10 = 1. But of those born in Aman it was 50 = 1 in Beleriand.[5] But it *began* to increase as soon as they left Valinor,[6] say after the

Doom of Mandos. The Valian Year spent in reaching Beleriand via the ice *aged all the Exiles* about 2 years (it took 144 Sun-years) = 72[7] (but Fëanor reached Beleriand in one half the time = Bel. 50 and so only aged 1 year). As soon as they reached Beleriand the rate quickened to 50 = 1. Thus Finduilas, 12 in 1495, was 13 at 1496 and needed 7 years to become 20. This took her $7 \times 50 = 350$ years. She was therefore 20 in Bel. 350. In Bel. 472 she was however only 122 Sun-years older, only just over 21, and in 490 only 140 Sun-years older: nearly 21½.[8] *She was the youngest Exile.*

Galadriel is known to have been "young and eager" at the Exile in 1495. If she was then 20, she would be 22 at the end of 1496, but by Bel. 590 at the destruction of Beleriand only about 6 years older, say 28. She wedded Celeborn about that time and went into Eriador;[9] but they did not beget any children until they had settled (first near to Evendim), that is, about SA 250. She was then 30½. *Celebrían* would be born about SA 260. She would be 20 therefore in SA 460, and at the end of the Second Age would be $20 + \frac{3441-460}{100}$ $(=\frac{2981}{100}) = 50$.

Here the text devolves into a series of rough notes and calculations, among which are:

Gestation of Elves 9 months life-time = in Bel. 900 months.[10]

But should it suffer *law of growth*. All children together in Middle-earth were made to 10 = 1 law … gestation took 96 months (longer than men) = 8 years.

At end of SA 3441 she [Galadriel] was 28 + 34.41 years old = 62. At end of Third Age she was 30.21 years older − 92.62 and so approximately the time of the Prime of the *hröa*.

Celebrían born SA 350. Galadriel did not wed Celeborn till they were settled. [Celebrían] was 20 in 550, in TA 10, 2,901 years later, she was 49.

Eärendil obtained "long youth" for his sons and their immediate descendants.[11] Elrond, an Elf, has 1,000-year youth; he was thus 20 in SA 1000 − 58 = 942. At end of TA he was in years 3,441 + 3,021 + 58 = 6,520 = 5,520 + 20 = 75. In [SA] 1697 [the founding of Rivendell] he was 27.

NOTES

1 The dates given here for the occupation of Gondolin (Bel. 116) and of Tuor's coming to Gondolin (495) agree with those given in the *Grey Annals* of c. 1951 (XI:44, 89, respectively).

2 Regarding the (relatively late) arising (after c. 1951) of the form of the name "Maeglin" (from prior "Meglin" and "Glindûr"), and the still later substitution of "Aredhel" for "Isfin" see XI:48, 122–3 §§119–20, and 316.

3 In the c. 1951 *Annals of Aman*, 5 VY elapse between the death of the Two Trees in VY 1495 (X:98) and the first rising of the moon and sun in VY 1500 (X:131), which coincided with the arrival in Middle-earth of the Exiles that had crossed the Helkaraxë (XI:29–30).

4 In chap. IV, "Time-scales", above (c. 1959), Anairë is said to have been the Vanya wife of Turgon who "would not go with the Ñoldor into exile". In all other published sources that name her, Anairë is the wife of Fingolfin and thus Idril's grandmother, not mother (cf. XI:323, XII:363).

5 As first written the text from "in Aman was 50 = 1" continued thus: "in early years after leaving Valinor: sc. 50 years from 1495 = 1 year of life. Thus Finduilas (cleaving to her father and brother) was the youngest Exile, being only 12 in 1495. She then needed 8 years of life to become 20, that is". These lines were then all struck out in the act of writing and replaced with "in Beleriand".

6 As originally written the rate began to increase for the Exiles as soon as they left "the light of the Trees".

7 I take this to mean that while crossing the Ice the Elvish rate of ageing had increased from 144 = 1 in Aman to 72 = 1, thus adding 2 life-years in the 144 Sun-years it took to cross the ice. Upon arriving in Middle-earth, this rate increased again to 50 = 1.

8 If the rate in Beleriand was 50 = 1, then in the 122 years in Beleriand lived after reaching 20 in Bel. 350, she should have aged in Bel. 472 nearly 2½ life-years and been 22½. Similarly, in 490 she should have aged a further ½ life year and been 23. I cannot explain this discrepancy.

9 In *The Lord of the Rings* it is said that "ere the fall of Nargothrond or Gondolin [Galadriel] passed over the mountains" into Eriador (LR:357). For the much-vexed history of Galadriel and Celeborn, see UT:228ff.

10 As originally written the gestation time was 12 Sun-years.

11 Tolkien elaborates on this point in the next chapter.

XI

AGEING OF ELVES

This is (for the most part) a clear manuscript written in black nib-pen on eight sides of four unlined sheets that Tolkien numbered, in pencil, 1–8. Some corrections and marginal notes were made by Tolkien in red ball-point pen. It dates from c. 1959.

For similar applications of the greatly increased rate of Sun-years to Valian Years of 144 : 1 to specific characters in the *legendarium*, see the texts presented here as chaps. IX, "Times-scales and Rates of Growth"; X, "Difficulties in Chronology"; and XVIII, "Elvish Ages & Númenórean".

Ageing of Elves

Adjustment must be made of these rates to fit the narrative; at least if the story of Maeglin's origin is kept as in the "Annals". For Maeglin is evidently of an age to desire Idril in marriage, *but he was born in Beleriand*. (The date in the Annals is impossible: SY 316. Maeglin would then be about 179 when Tuor came to Gondolin in SY 495; but he would on the 100 : 1 scale be less than 2 years old in life-age!)[1] Gondolin was occupied in SY 116.[2] Isfin therefore cannot have borne Maeglin before, say, 120 – even if she refused entry to Gondolin, not wishing to be "immured", or escaped soon after Turgon compelled her to enter. So that at best Maeglin would only be 375 years old in SY 495.

Thus *either* (a) the story must be altered; *or* (b) scales of growth must be adjusted.

(a) Maeglin must be born at least 20×100 or 25×100 sun-years before SY 495: that is (on present notation with VY reckoning ending at 1496 and MY 1 then beginning) about 2,000 or 2,500 years before MY 495: sc. in 1,500 to 2,000 years before the coming of the Ñoldor in MY 1. That is, since 1 VY = 144 MY, about VY 1484 or 1486. This is difficult or impossible to work with if Isfin = sister of Turgon (as is essential to the tale).

If Isfin was rebellious at the time of the departure of the Eldar over Sea (VY 1132) [3] – as it might be said were a few of the Ñoldor also – then matters might be arranged so:

Eöl was not a "Dark-elf", in the sense of being an Avar (none of these in fact existed in Beleriand, certainly not at so early an age); nor was he of the Teleri. There were a few of the Ñoldor who in heart were "Avari", but marched because all their people did.[4] Eöl was one of these. He did not wish for Aman. *Either* he already knew and desired Isfin, and persuaded her to remain behind, *or* she met him in Beleriand when she too had refused to go at the last minute, and went wandering alone in the land. In that case the birth of Maeglin could be anywhere about VY 1232 to (say) 1400. If born in VY 1232, by VY 1496 Maeglin would have lived 264 VY $\times$ 144 sun-years = 38,016 years! But this is obviously impossible – besides the fact that *Turgon and Isfin were both born in Aman!**

The story must then be entirely altered, and Maeglin must also be born in Aman. His sinister character will then be accounted for by the fact that he (and his mother and father) were specially attracted by Melkor, and grew to dislike Aman, and their kin. They joined the host of Fëanor (this would explain Eöl's skill in smith-craft!) and were estranged from their immediate kin.

Or (b) The age or "growth" scale must be altered. In Aman in the early ages it was very slow. The Eldar then lived at Valian rate: 144 : 1, but also their youth *lasted very long*, and they were engaged in many pursuits of absorbing interest, so that they did not become "mature" or wed until aged over 100 [VY] or even nearly 200. This does not apply of course to the first generation: e.g., Finwë was born in Middle-earth some time before VY 1085 (when Oromë found the Quendi), say about 1050; in 1132 he was therefore already 82 [Valian] years old and wedded Míriel somewhere about 1150 when he was 18 [Valian] years older: sc., was about 100 [VY].

---

* This at Middle-earth's 100 = 1 rate makes him 380! Or at rate 144 = 1 [makes him] 264.

But this slow growth was only maintained in Aman "under the domes of Varda".[5] The rate of growth "under the Sun" soon quickened. For all periods relative to the narrative it may be taken as 10 : 1. That is, from conception to maturity the Elvish *hröa* in Middle-earth only took 10 times the period of Men. But reaching maturity at 20 they *then* remained in long-lasting vigour with little perceptible change: i.e., the ageing rate was 144 : 1, or in Middle-earth 100 : 1. As soon as the Exiles left Valinor their ageing and growing rate increased. Those who had to make way on foot and cross the Ice spent a Valian year (= 144 [sun-years]) on the journey after the doom of Mandos. This dreadful journey aged them all to an extent of about 2 [Valian] years (or 72 : 1). As soon as they stepped on Middle-earth the growth rate leapt to 10 : 1. Thus those who were "mature" at the Exile must add 2 life-years to their age (or 1 if in the company of Fëanor) before reaching Middle-earth; and then proceed at the Middle-earth rate of 100 : 1. Those who were immature (under 20 [VY] must add 2 years, and then complete their maturity (if necessary) in Beleriand at a rate of 10 : 1, before proceeding to live at a 100 : 1 rate. (Since this growth rate affected the *hröa* as soon as conceived, the gestation period was about 9 solar months × 10 = 90 [months].)*

That being so, Maeglin if born c. MY 120 would be 20 in MY 320, but in MY 495 would only have grown $\frac{495-320}{100}$ [life-]years older = 1.75 or less than 2 [life-]years. (He was less than 22 and younger than Idril: among her reasons for not accepting him.)

This will fit the later narrative fairly well, but will make characters such as Galadriel and Elrond rather older in the later ages. It however makes difficulties with Arwen and Aragorn.

Thus Galadriel was just mature, 20 [life-years], at the Exile in [VY] 1495. She was therefore 22 on entry into Beleriand and then lived at a 100 : 1 rate. At the ruin of Beleriand in MY 590 she was therefore about 28.

Now if Celebrían was born no earlier than SA 300 she was "mature" (20 [life-years]) in SA 500. By the end of the Second Age in 3441 she was then $\frac{2,941}{100}$ = 29 [life-]years older = 49. By TA 100 (her wedding with Elrond)[6] she was therefore 50: not impossible, and explicable by the troublous times.[7] If actually born much later, say 850 or so, she was 20 in [SA] 1050 and in TA 100 $\frac{2,491}{100}$ years older = 45.

But Galadriel would be in SA 300 about 31 [life-years] (28 + 3) and in SA 850 about 36½.

---

* 12 × 9 = 108 months therefore 9 years.

If Arwen was born in TA 341 (as a correction)[8] she was 20 [life-years] in 541. Therefore when in 2951 she met Aragorn (then 20) she was $20 + \frac{2,410}{100} = 44$! At her betrothal in 2980 she was $20 + \frac{2,439}{100}$, still about 44. At the wedding in 3019 she was nearly 45. Aragorn was 20 in 2951, 49 in 2980, and at their wedding 88. But it seems probable that Aragorn's life was similarly arranged: thus he grew to maturity as quick as the normal human rate, and then slowed to the Númenórean ageing rate of 3 : 1. He was thus 20 in 2951; but in 2980, $20 + \frac{29}{3} =$ about 30; at wedding $20 + \frac{68}{3} =$ nearly 43 (and so close in age to Arwen); at death he was $190 = 20 + \frac{170}{3} =$ nearly 77.[9] On conceiving Eldarion Arwen joined her husband's rate, and so at Aragorn's death (100 years later) [45 +] 34 = 79, an old woman.[10]

The only way of making Arwen younger at their meeting is this: The Half-elven lived at the human rate.[11] Eärendil was only 39 when he came to Valinor. He was not allowed to return to Middle-earth, but he obtained the grace (from Eru via Manwë) that his children, being half-elven on both sides – descendants of Idril and of Lúthien – should (a) have a choice of which kindred they would belong to, and (b) should in each kind have "a long and fair youth" – sc., should only slowly reach maturity – and that this should extend to the second generation: thus Elrond : Arwen and Elros : Vardamir.[12]

To Elrond it was thus granted that he should return towards the ancient growth-rate: he reached maturity at 20 [life-years] only in 1,000 [sun-]years (rate 50 : 1). He was thus 20 in SA 1000 – 58 = [SA] 942. When sent by Gil-galad to the war in Eregion (SA 1695) he was therefore $20 + \frac{1695-942}{100} = 27\frac{1}{2}$ [life-years], which is suitable. At the end of the Second Age he was $20 + 25 = 45$ [life-years] and at his wedding in TA 100 he was 46, only one year older than Celebrían (see above), which fits well. Elrond at the end of TA 3021 was thus about 75 [life-years], in full Elvish vigour.

If Arwen had the same growth-rate she was born in TA 341 but did not reach maturity (20 [life-years]) until TA 1341. In 2951 she was therefore $20 + \frac{2951-1341}{100} = 20 + 16 = 36$ [life-years]. In 2980 she was still of much the same age: and Aragorn (by above reckoning) 30. In 3019 at their wedding she was nearly 37 [life-years] (but Aragorn 43). She *then* acquired the life-span of her husband after the birth of Eldarion in 4A 1. In 4A 100 therefore she was 33 [Númenórean life] years older or 70.

Eldarion was mortal and was not by promise included in the "grace of Eärendil", but he had in fact a long youth: which took the form of remaining like a young man from maturity at 20 until 60 without change. He then lived another 65 years: making him 125, but in life-age 20 + 65 = 85. His descendants became normal, but long-lived (80–90).[13]

Elros had the Númenórean scale of life, 3 : 1. But the grace of "long youth" took the form of doubling this. He thus should have become "mature" at 60, but in fact became so at 120: he then lived at the Númenórean rate and died at the age of 500 (*voluntarily* and therefore not at very great age. He was therefore actually in life-age 20 + $\frac{500-120}{3}$ = 20 + 127 = 147. Vardamir lived to be 391 and so was little more than normal Númenórean age (300).[14] Succeeding kings lived for about 400 years until Queen Vanimeldë (the 16th ruler): mostly because after maturity they remained "young" for a long time.

With regard to those born in Aman it might prove useful to increase their growth-span. Thus the maturing rate of those born in Aman should be 50 : 1, and this should continue in the second generation (those begotten in Beleriand or Eriador of one or two Aman-born parents). Thus Galadriel would not be affected; but Celebrían, born in SA 850, would not reach 20 [life-age] for 50 × 20 = 1,000 [sun-]years: i.e., not until SA 1850. She would then be a young girl at the time of the ruin of Eregion. In TA 100 she would be only 20 + $\frac{3541-1850}{100}$ = 20 + 17 = 37 [life-years]. If born in SA 350 she would be 20 [life-years] in 1350 and in TA 100, 20 + $\frac{3541-1350}{100}$ = 20 + 22 = 42 [life-years].

Finduilas was about 21 [life-years] when Túrin came to Nargothrond in [FA] 490. If she was 12 in VY 1495 (the youngest Exile) she was 14 in VY 1496. She then needed 6 [life-]years for maturity, or as one born in Aman 6 × 50 = 300 [sun-]years. She was thus 20 in MY 300 and in 490 was 5 years older = 25 [life-years]. This will not work.[15]

There follows a series of rough attempts, much revised, apparently to find a chronology that would make Finduilas younger when Túrin comes to Nargothrond in FA 490.[16] What appears to be Tolkien's final scheme appears in the left margin of the last page of this text:

But note [growth] rates *doubled* in 1496.[17] Finduilas (the youngest Exile) was 12 in 1495. During 1496 she "grew" at a rate of 25 : 1. Therefore in $\frac{144}{25}$ years she grew 6 years. She landed in Beleriand at 16. She then resumed the 50 : 1 growth-rate and needed 4 × 50 − 4 = 196 [sun-years] to complete maturity. She was therefore 20 in MY 196. In MY 502 she had lived 306 more years at 100 : 1 and so was 23.

It is unclear what the significance of First Age 502 is to Finduilas's life. In no version of *The Annals of Aman* or the *Tale of Years*
did Finduilas survive to FA 502, but rather she died no later than
FA 496 (see XI:92). A possible explanation is provided by some
obviously contemporary draft materials, in which it is said of *Idril*
that:

Idril should be rather older [than Maeglin]. When Tuor reached
Gondolin in Bel. 495, he (born in 472) was age 23;[18] but when he
wedded Idril in Bel. 502 he was 30. *Idril should be also about 30 in
Bel. 500.* To be 30 in Bel. 500 *required* 2 [life-]years on journey
[across the Ice from Aman to Middle-earth], 16 [life-]years at
[growth rate] 12 : 1 = 192 [to reach maturity], and then 12 more
[life-years] at 144 : 1.

The journey to Middle-earth [took] 144 [sun-]years but counted
as 2 [life-]years: 144 + 192. We still have to alter the arrangement
during the march from Aman in VY 1496. This occupied 144 sun-
years; but it was so horrible that the mature aged at a double rate 2
[life-]years during that time. The immature should also have aged at
a double rate, at 6 [sun-years] = 1 [growth-year]. Thus an Elda going
into exile in VY 1495 at 12 [growth-years] would, by the end of the
journey, if female, only require another 6 [growth] years for maturity
= 36 [sun-years] and would therefore become 18 in SY 36 of VY
1496.[19] At the end of VY 1496 and arrival in Beleriand she would
have had another 108 years at the 72 : 1 rate = 1½ [life-years] and
therefore be 19½. She would then resume the 144 : 1 rate and in Bel.
502 would be only $\frac{502}{144}$ years older, or about 3½ [life-years]. She
would be 23. This fits fairly well. *If we make Idril* 18 at Exile in 1495,
she was then "mature" and lived rest of [her] life at 144 : 1 save the
year of journey = 2 [life-years]. She was therefore 20 when she
arrived in Beleriand, and in 502 would be 23½. If Idril was 20 at
Exile she will be 25½ in Bel. 502. This makes her a little *older* than
Maeglin (and still vastly older in experience) *which is better for the
narrative, if* the marriage of Turgon can be rearranged.

It would thus seem that Tolkien took the date of Idril's marriage to
Tuor in Bel. 502 here and mistakenly applied it to Finduilas's
chronology.

This is a convenient place to give a further detail found in still
other, very rough but apparently contemporary drafting in red and
blue ball-point pen:

Gilgalad became king in Lindon (under [?Suz[erainty] *or* ?Sway] of Galadriel) about SA 10–20 after departure of Galadriel and Celeborn. He must then have been at least 25 [life-years]. That is, 25 in say Bel. 610. Thus [born] 25 – 6.10 = 18.90 VY before VY 1500 = VY 1481.1.

NOTES

1 In the c. 1951 *Grey Annals*, Eöl "took [Isfin, Maeglin's mother] to wife" in Bel. 316, and Maeglin was born in Bel. 320 (XI:47–8); and (as emended) Tuor came to Gondolin in Bel. 495, as here (XI:91). That would make Maeglin 175 sun-years old at that time.

2 Cf. XI:44.

3 That is, at the departure of the Ñoldor from Beleriand to Aman in VY 1132, as in chap. VII, "The March of the Quendi", above.

4 In red ball-point pen, Tolkien subsequently wrote a vertical line against these two sentences, as well as a check-mark, and the words: "Keep this".

5 Regarding the "domes of Varda" in the "Round World" version of the mythology, see X:369–72, 375–8, 385–90.

6 In the first edition (1955) of *RotK*, App. B gives TA 100 as the year that Elrond wed Celebrían. This was changed to TA 109 in the second edition (1966).

7 In contemporary draft materials it is said that Celebrían:

should be older [at her wedding] than early in maturity, because of the delay of the wedding by the troubles of the end of the Second Age.

8 In *LR* App. B Arwen's birth-year is given as TA 241.

9 In the first edition (1955) of *RotK*, App. B, Aragorn (born March 1, 2931) was said to have died on March 1, 1521, thus aged (exactly) 190 years, as here. In the second edition (1966) the year was altered to 1541, with Aragorn thus departing precisely at the age of 210.

10 This last sentence entered as a marginal note in red ball-point pen.

11 As first written, this passage read:

Eärendil was not allowed to return to Middle-earth. The Half-elven / since their mothers took on mortality at their wedding (or conception) – i.e. then aged at human rate / lived at human rate.

I have taken the slashes to be an indication that Tolkien considered deleting the text between them, and since that passage is moreover an incomplete thought, I have removed it editorially to render the passage grammatical. I have also joined the passage on Eärendil to the discussion that follows.

12 As first written, this passage read:

and that this should extend to the third generation: thus Elrond :
Arwen : Eldarion and Elros : Vardamir : Tar-Amandil.

This appears to be the only suggestion in Tolkien's writings that Vardamir was
like Arwen among the Half-elven and so likewise had a "choice of kindred".

13 As first written, this passage began:

Eldarion was mortal, so that his "long youth" was of modest
scale: He reached "maturity" at 60 and then lived another 65
years ....

14 According to "The Line of Elros", Vardamir lived to be 410 (UT:218).

15 A rough note in red ball-point pen in the top margin of the page apparently
refers to this passage:

These reckonings are defective as they do not realize the growth
rate was double in 1496.

16 Cf. XI:83.

17 Cf. chap. VII, "The March of the Quendi", above.

18 Cf. XI:79 §251.

19 This calculation implies that the doubled growth-rate of 6 : 1 for the immature
Exiles continued for at least six years after reaching Middle-earth.

XII

CONCERNING THE QUENDI
IN THEIR MODE OF LIFE
AND GROWTH

This is a very clear manuscript written in black nib-pen on 16 sides of eight unlined sheets that Tolkien numbered, in red ball-point pen, 1–14, with two unnumbered sides of tables at the end. These sheets were then clipped together with a torn half-sheet as a cover/title-page. Some corrections and highlights were made by Tolkien in red ball-point pen. It dates to c. 1959.

The text closely follows the beginning of the text presented here as chap. V, "Natural Youth and Growth of the Quendi", above, until that text reaches the table of mortal equivalences of Elvish ages.

Concerning the Quendi
in their mode of life and growth
especially as
Compared with Men

I. Youth and Ageing
of the
Quendi

When the Quendi were "young in Arda", during their earliest gener-ations, before the Great March and especially in the first six generations after their Awaking, they were far more like Men. Their *hröar* (bodies) were in great vigour, and dominant; and the delights of the body of all kinds were their chief concern.* [1] Their *fëar* ('spirits') were only beginning to wake fully and to grow in knowledge of their latent powers, and of their pre-eminence.

Thus, as was indeed at first necessary, and so ordained for them, they were in their early generations far more concerned with love and the begetting of children than was so later. Moreover, the engendering of children was then less costly to their vigour or "youth".

It was not that their natural span of growth and life was different; but that in their early days they used it differently. The natural life of the Quendi was to grow quickly (according to their kind) to bodily maturity, and then to endure in full vigour for many years, until the motions and desires of their *fëar* became dominant, and their *hröar* waned.

The Quendian "growth" and "life" may be compared with that of Men, so long as it is remembered that (a) its rate of "expenditure" was far slower than the human, especially after achievement of maturity, and (b) that when the Quendi spoke of their bodies "waning" it did not mean that these became decrepit or that they felt the oncoming of senility or death.

The Eldar distinguished between *olmië* and *coivië*. The former was the period or process of their 'growth' from conception to maturity of body, and was achieved *twelve times* as rapidly as the *coivië*. This latter was the process of 'living' or "enduring in Arda", and of acquiring skill, knowledge, and wisdom.

The *olmië* was achieved at a rate equalling 12 *löar* (or sun-years) to 1 *löa* of human life. An Elvish 'growth-year', or *olmen*, was therefore 12 sun-years. Thus from conception to birth they grew in the womb 9 *löar*. When born they continued to grow at this rate until maturity of body.

The *coivië* then proceeded at a rate 12 times as slow, so that 144 *löar* (or sun-years) may be more or less equated, *so far as change or alteration are concerned,*† [2] with 1 year of human adult life. This length of time was the *yén* or Elvish year, or *coimen* as a measure of age.

Elf-men reached maturity at about 24: that is, after 24 *olmendi* (or

---

* Though they were, from their Awaking, also immediately concerned with linguistic expression – at first in especial of their delight and joy in Arda, and of their love for their spouses.

† This rate of "change" is not concerned at all with the *perception of Time*. The Quendi did not live or perceive or act slowly. On the contrary they perceived more swiftly and minutely, and acted more quickly than Men.

2 *yéni*): 288 *löar*. Elf-women reached maturity normally after 18 *olmendi* (or 1½ *yéni*): 216 *löar*.* [3]

After this, their 'youth' (*vinyarë*), or the time of their full bodily vigour, endured (for both sexes) for about 72 *coimendi* or *yéni* after maturity. That is: it lasted until Elf-men were of "age" 24 + 72 or 96; and Elf-women were of "age" 18 + 72 or 90. But expressed in "years" or *löar* this is 288 + 10,368, or 10,656 years for males; and 216 + 10,368, or 10,584 for females.

The arrival at maturity was recognized at once by individuals, and occurred with little variation. It was (in times of peace) recognized also by the Elvish families and communities and honoured with ceremony, part of which was the announcement of the *essekilmë* or personal "choice of name".[4]

But the beginning of the "waning" at the end of youth was hardly observable, and was also more variable. Its chief mark, indeed, was the ending of any desire for the begetting or bearing of children (but not of the physical potency until many years had passed). Its approach and process was variable for many reasons. It differed naturally according to the vigour and constitution and character of individuals. Also, among the Quendi, it was much influenced by begetting and by child-birth.

In this, say the Eldar, more of their "youth" is expended than is the case with Men; and for Elf-men, they say that each child costs as much as 1 *coimen* or life-year; but for Elf-women as much as, or more than, 2 *coimendi*. So that for the parents of six children the "waning", or passing of youth, might come 6 life-years sooner for the father, but for the mother 12 life-years sooner, or more.

Other special "expenditures", such as grief, long and arduous travel, great craft-labours, and especially the bodily recovery from grave wounds and hurts, might also hasten the waning. It is said that the "dreadful year" (1 *yén*) of the journey of the Exiles from Valinor, over the Grinding Ice, to Beleriand, affected those of the Ñoldor who endured it as greatly as *three* normal life-years.

But these "expenditures" are not (as they are not either in reckoning human ages) taken into account in computing the "age" of any given Elf. As we may say that two men are both "sixty years old", though one may be weaker or more worn than the other, so of the

---

* This rate was in some individuals rather slower and might take up to 21 *olmendi*, or 252 *löar*. Concerning this difference between men and women the Eldar speak in the legend of the Awaking, which they call the *Cuivienyarna*, q.v. [see chap. VIII, "Eldarin Traditions Concerning the 'Awakening'", above].

Quendi we may give their ages in *olmendi* and *coimendi*, and take no account of the chances of their lives.

As for the begetting and bearing of children: This might naturally begin as soon as maturity was achieved. So it was in the beginning of the Quendi; but soon the other commanding interests of their being, as their *fëar* awoke, began to occupy their thoughts even in earliest youth. After the first two generations (that is *three* including the First Elves) the *begetting of children by Elf-men* was postponed beyond the age of 24, little by little; until soon the age of 48* became the most usual for the beginning of fatherhood. Later it was often delayed until the age of 60. It could naturally occur at any time up to the end of "youth" (at about age 96), but later than this a *first* begetting seldom occurred.

In the case of Elf-women, marriage and child-bearing tended always to take place earlier than for Elf-men. (For Elf-women were as a rule more eager for motherhood, and until the "waning" of youth, less distracted or deeply engrossed in other pursuits of mind or in crafts.) In the earliest generations their first child was often born before they were of age 20. Later, indeed, as with Elf-men, the date of the first child-birth was often delayed; and first child-birth often took place at age 36.† It could, of course, take place later. In days of trouble and wandering or of war the producing of children was naturally avoided or postponed. And since this postponement (especially of the first child) prolonged the "youth" of the Quendi, child-birth might in such cases occur up to a female age of 72 (18 *olmendi* + 54 *coimendi*).

These dates – at any rate in the early Ages with which these ancient histories are concerned – were not so much a matter of physical vigour or potency, as of *will* or *desire*. As soon as they were full-grown, and with increasing rapidity after the age of 60‡ in either sex the *fëa* and its interests began to dominate those of the *hröa*. An Elf who had not yet become married, or had at least not found a "desired spouse" by that age (60) was likely, in normal circumstances, to remain unwedded.§

---

* I.e., 24 *olmendi* + 24 *coimendi*.

† I.e., 18 *olmendi* + 18 *coimendi*.

‡ This is, after 36 *coimendi* for Elf-men, 42 for Elf-women.

§ It sometimes happened that a lover failing to find a response in the "desired spouse" would remain unwed, and later, maybe long after, would fall in love again, and wed much later than usual.

The *number of children* produced by a married pair was again naturally affected by the characters (mental and physical) of the persons concerned. But also by various accidents of life; and by the "age" at which the marriage began, especially the age of the Elf-woman.

Even in the earliest generations after the Awaking, more than *six* children was very rare, and the average number soon (as the vigour of *hröar* and *fëar* began more and more to be applied to other "expenditures") was reduced to *four*. Six children were never attained by those wedding after ages 48 for Elf-men and 36 for Elf-women. In the later Ages (Second and Third) *two* children were usual.

In the early generations the Quendi seem to have arranged their lives normally so as to have a continuous 'Time of the Children' (or *Onnalúmë*) until their desires were fulfilled and (as they said) the generation was complete. This was still often the case with married pairs later, if they lived in times of peace and could control their own lives; but it was not always done, and in the later Ages children might be born after long and irregular intervals.

This often depended upon the circumstances of the parents. For at all times the Quendi desired to dwell in company with husband or wife during the bearing of a child, and during its early youth. (For these years were one of chief joy to them, and longest and dearest held in memory.)[5] So that the Quendi did not wed, or if wedded did not engender children, in troublous times or perils (if these could be foreseen).

After a child-birth a "time of repose" was always taken, and this again tended to increase in length.* This time (being concerned mainly with bodily refreshment) was reckoned in growth-years or *olmendi*. It was seldom less than one *olmen* (or 12 *löar*); but it might be much more. And usually (but not necessarily) it was progressively increased after each birth of a continuous *Onnalúmë*, in such series as: *löar* 12/18/24/30/36 or often 12/24/36/48/60; or in the case of smaller families: 12/30/48/66. But these series are only averages, or formulated examples. In practice the intervals were more variable. They normally occupied some exact number of *löar*, since conception (and therefore birth 9 *löar* later) was nearly always in Spring; but they were not necessarily in exact twelves or sixes, nor in regular progression.

A completed "generation" or *Onnalúmë* of *six* children could thus in theory occupy at *minimum* 114 *löar*. That is 6 × 9 gestations + 5 × 12

---

* During this time Elf-women went usually into "retirement" and went abroad little.

intervals. This was naturally rare. At theoretic *maximum* it might occupy the whole time between maturity of the mother (18) to the end of her "youth" (90), or 72 *yéni*: i.e., 10,368 *löar*. But this never occurred. So great an interval (as this average of over 2,060 *löar*) never occurred, and in cases where large families were engendered the intervals were seldom greater than 1 *coimen* or 'life-year' (144 *löar*). Six *coimendi* was in fact the longest interval found in the early histories; except in Aman where "waning" was retarded, and an interval of 12 *coimendi* occasionally recorded.

In the early Ages (before the Great March) an *Onnalúmë* of several children (6, 5, 4) seems usually to have occupied about 1 *coimen* (equivalent to 1 Valian year or 144 *löar*) from first birth to last birth: that is, 144 + 9 *löar* from the beginning of the "generation" with the first conception to the last birth.

The Quendi never "fell" as a race – not in the sense in which they and Men themselves believed that the Second Children had "fallen".[6] Being "tainted" with the Marring (which affected all the "flesh of Arda" from which their *hröar* were derived and were nourished),[7] and having also come under the Shadow of Melkor before their Finding and rescue, they could *individually* do wrong. But they *never* (not even the wrong-doers) rejected Eru, nor worshipped either Melkor or Sauron as a god – neither individually or as a whole people. Their lives, therefore, came under no general curse or diminishment; and their primeval and natural life-span, as a race, by "doom" co-extensive with the remainder of the Life of Arda, remained unchanged in all their varieties.

Of course the Quendi could be terrorized and daunted. In the remote past before the Finding, or in the Dark Years of the Avari after the departure of the Eldar, or in the histories of the *Silmarillion*, they could be deceived; and they could be captured and tormented and enslaved. Then under force and fear they might do the will of Melkor or Sauron, and even commit grave wrongs. But they did so as *slaves* who nonetheless in heart knew and never rejected the truth. (There is no record of any Elf ever doing more than carrying out Melkor's orders under fear or compulsion. None ever called him Master, or Lord, or did any evil act uncommanded to obtain his favour.) Thus, though the carrying out of evil commands, quite apart from the sufferings of slavery and torment, clearly exhausted the "youth" and life-vigour of those unfortunate Elves who came under the power of the Shadow, this evil and diminishment was *not* heritable.

The lives of the Quendi, also, cannot be supposed to have been affected by living "under the Sun", in Middle-earth. *As now is known and recognized in the Histories*, the Sun was part of the original structure of Arda, and not devised only after the Death of the Trees. The Quendi were, therefore, designed in nature to dwell in Middle-earth "under the Sun".

The situation in Aman requires some consideration. It appears that in Aman the Quendi were little affected in their modes of growth (*olmië*) and life (*coivië*). How was that so? In Aman the Valar maintained all things in bliss and health, and corporeal living things (such as plants and beasts) appear to have "aged" or changed no quicker than Arda itself. A year to them was a Valian Year, but even its passage brought them no nearer to death – or not visibly and appreciably: not until the end of Arda itself would the withering appear. Or so it is said. But it seems that there was no general "law" of time governing all things in Aman. Each living thing, individually and not only each kind or variety of living things, was under the care of the Valar and their attendant Máyar.[8] Each was maintained in some form of beauty or use, for the Valar and for one another. This plant might be allowed to ripen to seed, and that plant be maintained in blossom.[9] This beast might walk in the strength and freedom of its youth, another might find a mate and bring up its young.*

Now it is possible (though not certain)† that the Valar could have graced or blessed the Eldar, singly or as a whole, in like manner. But they did not do so. For, though they had (wisely or not) transported them to Aman, to save them from Melkor, they knew that they should not "meddle with the Children", or attempt to change their natures, or dominate them in any way, or wrest their being (in *hröa* or *fëa*) to any other mode than that in which Eru had designed them.

The only effect of residence in Aman upon the Eldar seems to have been this: in the bliss and health of Aman *their bodies remained in vigour*, and were able to support the great growth in knowledge and ardour of their spirits without any appreciable waning (except in very special cases: such as that of Míriel). Those who entered Aman,

---

* And of course, since Aman was limited, some things must pass away, while a perennial balance of the whole was maintained. But this was not confused with "Death".

† That is, it is not certain that they could alter the "constitution" of any creature housing a *fëa*, and having its own independent centre of being, one of the same *status* and relation to Eru as their own being, even if of less might.

from without or by birth, would leave it in the same health and vigour as they had to begin with.

    This slower rate of growth and of ageing natural to the Quendi, as compared with Men, has nothing to do with the *perception or use of Time.* This was primarily of the *fëa*, whereas growth and ageing were of the *hröa*. The Eldar say of themselves (and it may be in some degree true also of Men) that when "persons" – in whole being, *fëa* and *hröa*,[10] are fully occupied with things that are of deep concern to their true natures, and are therefore of great interest and delight to them, Time seems to pass quickly, and not the reverse. That is: the full and minutely divided employment of Time does not make it seem *longer* than the same period passed in less activity or in idleness, but *shorter*. It is not with Time as it might be with a road or path. If this were closely and minutely inspected it would take long to traverse, and would maybe seem to be itself of greater length; for that inspection could only be carried out by slowing the rate of normal travel. But the *fëa* may quicken its speed of thought and action, and achieve more, or attend more minutely to events, in one space of time than in another.

Thus the Quendi did not (and do not) *live* slowly, moving ponderously like tortoises while Time flickers past them and their sluggish limbs and thoughts! Indeed, they move and think swifter than Men, and achieve more than any Man in any given length of time. But they have a far greater native vitality and energy to draw upon, so that it takes, and will take a very great length of years to expend it.

    However, they were from the beginning, and so still remain, close kin of Men, the Second Children, and their actions, desires, and talents are akin, as are their modes of perception and thought. They do not think and act in ways unobservable or actually incomprehensible to Men. To a Man Elves appear to speak rapidly (but with clarity and precision) unless they a little retard their speech for Men's sake; to move quickly and featly, unless in urgency, or much moved, or eager in their work, when the movement of their hands, for instance, become too swift for human eyes to follow closely. Only their perception, and their thought and reasoning, seems normally beyond human rivalry in speed.

    The main text ends here, but on the following (and last) sheet Tolkien drew up two tables for numerical aid. I give the first here in full:

Some tables for reckoning approximate equivalents of Elvish "age" to human terms.

Olmendi 'growth-years' :	1 *olmen*	= 12 *löar* (sun-years)
	12 *olmendi*	= 1 Valian Year
		= 1 *coimen*
		= 1 *yén*
		= 144 *löar*
Coimendi 'life-years'	1 *coimen*	= 12 *olmendi*
		= 144 *löar*
Gestation (*colbamarië*)	¾ *olmen*	= 9 *löar*
Maturity (*quantolië*) achieved		
for males in	24 *olmendi*	= 288 *löar*
for females in	18 *olmendi**	= 216 *löar*

End of "youth" naturally is if not hastened (or more seldom retarded) achieved for both sexes in	72 *coimendi*	= 10,368 löar
	from maturity	

The "end of youth" thus came for an Elf-man after 74 *coimendi* = 10,656 *löar;* for an Elf-woman after 73½ *coimendi* – 10,584 *löar.*

The second table calculates the total number of *löar* for the *coimendi* from 1 to 80: being 144 to 11,520 in 144-year increments. To the end of this table Tolkien appended a note:

☞ An Elf ages from 22 to 24 "life-years" [i.e., 3,168 to 3,456 *löar*] in each Age of Arda.

---

* Sometimes delayed up to 21 *olmendi* = 252 *löar.*

NOTES

1 With this footnote cf. chap. VIII, "Eldarin Traditions Concerning the 'Awakening'", above.

2 Regarding the perception of time, cf. chaps. IV, "Time-scales", above, and XX, "Time and its Perception", below.

3 In this footnote the phrase "between men and women" is a later insertion in red ball-point pen.

4 With the *essekilmë* cf. X:214–15, 217, 229.

5 Cf. X:213.

6 With the unfallen state of Elves, cf. chaps. V, "Natural Youth and Growth of the Quendi" and VI, "The Awaking of the Quendi", above. With the fallen nature of Men, in Elvish and Mannish thought, cf. the *Athrabeth Finrod ah Andreth* in *Morgoth's Ring*, and chap. X, "Notes on *Órë*", in part two of this book. See also THE FALL OF MAN in App. I.

7 With the Marring of Arda and the consequent tainting of the "flesh of Arda", cf. X:399–401.

8 For "Máyar" as a seldom-used form of the name "Maiar" see n.11 to chap. VII, "The March of the Quendi", above.

9 As previously mentioned, the cover/title page of this bundle is a torn half-sheet. This sheet appears to have originally been the same size and nature as the other sheets in this bundle, before being torn roughly in half. The verso of the sheet demonstrates that it was in fact extracted from a prior version of this text, as on it is written, in the same hand and with the same ink and instrument as the rest of the bundle, passages clearly related to this discussion of "the situation in Aman":

[The] Elvish rate of life or 'ageing' (*coivië*) was the same as the Valian, being designed to endure with Arda. No difference, therefore, was discoverable in the process of the *coivië* of the Quendi in Aman.

But Aman had, inevitably, an effect on their *olmië* or process of growth, which would be felt by all those not yet adult or entering it, or later born there. In Aman, by the act of the Valar all living things, such as beasts and plants, with corporeal forms were unaltered in these forms, but used the Valian Year as the equivalent of 1 year in their growth, natural to each kind. Thus a flower whose nature in Middle-earth was to grow from a seed sown in the autumn, to appear in the next spring, and reach its full

The text ends here, mid-sentence, at the bottom of the sheet.

10 See BODY AND SPIRIT in App. I.

XIII

KEY DATES

The texts presented here occupy 16 sides of nine sheets of mixed nature, clipped together by Tolkien, and written in a variety of hands and implements of greatly varying legibility. The characteristics of each are described for the individual texts below. As for a probable date for the bundle as a whole, this is provided by the reuse of two engagement calendar pages, for 8–14 Feb. and 1–7 Mar. 1959, for Text 3.

Text 1

This text occupies sides 1–4 and 15–16 (sheets 1–2 and 9, all unlined paper) of the clipped bundle, in which the other texts are interspersed between sheets 2 and 9. It is written in black nib-pen in what is a mostly clear hand, with some rougher alterations and re-arrangements made subsequently in green ball-point pen.

Of special note in this text is the introduction, or at least sugges-tion, of events and motives not previously found elsewhere, including: the sending of Melian and (at least three of) the later Istari to Cuiviénen for a time as guardians of the Elves; the doubt of the younger Elves at Cuiviénen as to the existence of the Valar, and the prideful sense among these Elves of a "mission" to themselves defeat Melkor and possess Arda; and of the refusal of the 144 First Elves, "the Seniors", to depart on the Great March.

Suggestions for key dates

"Days of Bliss" begin VY 1.

First *löa* of VY 850	First Age 1. Quendi awake in the Spring (144 in number). Melian warned in a dream leaves Valinor and goes to Endor.

VY 854   576.[1] About the time the 12th generation of Quendi first appeared, Melkor (or his agents) first get wind of the Quendi.[2] Quendi originally warned by Eru or emissaries, and forbidden (or *advised*?) not yet to stray far. Adventurous Elves did so, nonetheless, and some were caught?

VY 858   1152.[3] Shadows of fear begin to dim the natural happiness of the Quendi. They hold debate, and it appears that already some hearts are overshadowed. Younger elves (who never personally heard the Voice of Eru) doubt the existence of the Valar (of whom they heard from Melian?). The do not waver in allegiance, but in pride believe that *their mission* is to fight the Dark, and ultimately to possess the world of Arda. This "heresy", though driven under at the Finding, is the seed of the later Fëanorian trouble.

end of VY 864   2016. Oromë finds the Quendi. He dwells with them for 48 years (to 2064).

VY 865/2   2018. Tidings reach Valinor.

VY 865/44   2060. Melkor seeks to attack Oromë. Oromë informs Manwë. Tulkas is sent.

VY 865/48   2064. Leaving guards, Oromë returns to Valinor.

D[ays of] B[liss] VY 865/50   2066. Oromë reports. Council of the Valar. They resolve on behalf of the Quendi to make War on Melkor, and begin to prepare for the great struggle. They debate what is to be done with the Quendi, since they fear Endor will suffer great damage. Most of the Valar think they should remove the Quendi to safety, at least temporarily. Ulmo in chief (also Yavanna?) is against this: It is not Eru's intention that they should reside in such a place; and could not or would not be temporary. He prophesies that once brought thither the Quendi would either have to be sent back to their proper homes *against their will*; or would rebel and do so against the will of the Valar.

DB 865/56   2072. Birth of Ingwë of the House of Imin.[4]

DB 865/104   2120. Birth of Finwë.

DB 865/110   2126. Birth of Elwë.

VY 866/1   2163.[5] Oromë returns to Cuiviénen, with more *mayar*. (Melkor becomes suspicious, and guesses war is purposed against him, because of the Quendi. During Oromë's absence his emissaries were busy, and many lies circulate. The "heresy" awakes in new form: the Valar clearly do exist; but they have abandoned Endor: rightly as the appointed realm of the Quendi. Now they are becoming jealous, and wish to control the Quendi as vassals, and so re-possess themselves of Endor. Finwë, a gallant and adventurous young *quende*, direct descendant of Tata (therefore 25th gen.), is much taken by these ideas; less so his friend Elwë, descendant of Enel.)

DB 866/13   2175. Oromë remains for 12 years, and then is summoned to return for the councils and war-preparations. Manwë has decided that the Quendi should come to Valinor, but on urgent advice of Varda, they are only to be invited, and are to be given free choice.[6] The Valar send five Guardians (great spirits of the Maiar) – with Melian (the only woman, but the chief) these make six. The others were *Tarindor* (later Saruman), *Olórin* (Gandalf), *Hrávandil* (Radagast), *Palacendo*, and *Haimenar*.[7] Tulkas goes back. Oromë remains in Cuiviénen for 3 more years: VY 866/13–16, FA 2175–8.

DB 866/14–24   2176–86. The Valar continue their war-preparation. (Melkor also. Angband is strengthened and Sauron put in command.)

DB 866/49   2211. The preparations and plans are now nearly complete. The Valar decide that the Quendi should now be "invited". But Manwë decrees that first the Quendi should send representatives as ambassadors to Valinor (Ulmo insists this is perilously near to overaweing their free will.) Oromë is sent back to Cuiviénen.

DB 866/50   2212. Oromë sets out from Cuiviénen with the Three Ambassadors. These were elected by the Quendi, one from each of their kindreds. Only the youngest Elves are willing. Ingwë, Finwë, and Elwë are chosen. (Ingwë belonged to the 24th gen., and was then 140 years old; Finwë was of the 25th gen. and 92, Elwë of same and 86.)[8]

DB 866/51   2213. Ingwë, Finwë, and Elwë arrive in Valinor. They are indeed dazzled and overawed. Finwë (with "heretical" leanings) is most converted, and ardent for acceptance. (He has a lover, Míriel, who is devoted to crafts, and he longs for her to have the marvellous chance of learning new skills. Ingwë is already married, and more cool, but desires to dwell in the presence of Varda. Elwë would prefer the "lesser light, and shadows" of Endor, but will follow Finwë his friend.)

DB 866/60   2222. They remain 9 years, for Ingwë and Finwë are reluctant to hurry away.

DB 866/61   2223. The "Ambassadors" return. Great Debate of the Quendi. A few refuse even to attend. Imin, Tata, and Enel are ill-pleased, and regard the affair as a revolt on the part of the youngest Quendi, to escape their authority. None of the First Elves (144) accept the invitation. Hence the Avari called and still call themselves "the Seniors".

Imin makes a speech, claiming that the "Three Fathers" have authority (from Eru, since He woke them first), and should decide. Tata says that each of the Fathers should have authority but only over his own Company. Enel agrees to this, but makes it clear that he is against the move. Imin claims to be "Father of All Quendi", but urges that they should at least in the end all *do the same*, and not break up the Kindred.

The Ambassadors speak. Ingwë speaks with great deference of the Three Fathers, and especially of Imin. He says it was a mistake that Imin, Tata, and Enel did not go themselves, for they could have exerted authority with judgement. But since *they sent* him and his companions *as their representatives*, they should now (in spite of their youth) pay great heed to their reports and opinions. He thinks they have no conception of the riches of beauty[9] in Valinor. He asks Oromë if it is still possible for Imin, Tata, and Enel to go to Valinor? Oromë says "yes, if they will go at once". The Three Fathers are not willing.

Finwë speaks similarly, but lays stress on the riches of knowledge and crafts in Valinor. Also he says that the Quendi have only seen "the skirts of the Shadow", and have no idea of its dreadful power, or of the power of the Valar – and do not realize what the War (which the Valar are about to wage on behalf of the Quendi) will entail to Endor. His speech is very effective, as large numbers of the Quendi who cannot conceive of Valinor's attraction are nonetheless frightened of what may befall them if they remain.

Elwë says: "I will go with my friend, but I do not choose for anyone but myself. Let all my Folk do likewise. I do not see what harm dividing the Kindred will do – and it cannot be avoided, unless some are to be *forced* to do what they do not wish to do (to remain or to go). No doubt (indeed this is guaranteed) we, or any who wish, will be free to return to our homes when the War is over". Also he says, "We are a great company – the most given to wandering afar. Let many of us at least go with the safe conduct of the Lord Oromë and see what Endor is like, and the Sea! We need not pass the shores!" ([?prophetic]!). His great point is the vision of the Sea. This moves the Lindar deeply.

> At this point, apparently dissatisfied with the absence of the Three Fathers from the ambassadorship to Valinor, Tolkien proposes a new scheme:

Alternative. Let Imin, Tata, and Enel be the Ambassadors, and take with them as "representatives" of the Younger Elves Ingwë, Finwë, and Elwë.

Of the Three Fathers Imin and Tata are both impressed by Valinor and desire at least to live there for some time. (Imin loves the beauty and Tata the wisdom of the Valar and their works.) Enel is less moved: there is less "space" in Valinor, and he missed the great heavens, and unexplored lands, and the freedom of plants and beasts.

Imin claims to be the 'Father of All Quendi' (*Ilquendatar*) and to have right of decision. Tata will have it that each has authority only over his own Company; Enel that no one should be overruled to go or stay against his/her will. He proposes that first they should decide by vote of all adults what is the general wish, or which is the majority. Imin says that will inevitably divide the Folk. Tata says that is inevitable anyway without force. Imin says "but how can those decide *by vote* who have not seen the choice?" They must rely on their ambassadors. There then is a clamour for the "young assistants" to speak.

Ingwë speaks with deference of the Three Fathers. His feelings are much the same as Imin's. He was filled with the memory of the beauty of Varda. He makes a moving speech of the loveliness of her and all her works.

Finwë (more rebellious and independent?) speaks with less deference, hinting that even Tata did not employ his time as fully as might be, and has not depicted aright the wealth of the Valar in wisdom and skills, of which a long sojourn could master only a small part. (He has undisclosed thoughts of the enhancement of his lover Míriel's skill.) But his most effective point is (see above) in frightening the Quendi by revealing the power of Melkor and the Valar and the probable ruin of the War in Endor.

Elwë as above – He [?treats] Enel for a free vote and emphasizes freedom of return.

Imin reluctantly agrees to a vote. Not all are present, but about ⅔ are in favour of acceptance, and the Quendi sit long in silence. The stars come out and they are reluctant to go. Dawn comes and many are eager to start. As day wears on they vote: ¾ will go. The stars come out again and many change their minds.[10]

TEXT 2A

These draft texts (2a and 2b), which as will be seen precede text 1, occupy four sides of two sheets of unlined paper. They are written in black ink with a narrow-nib pen, in a hand that differs from the preceding text and from most of the other texts in the "Time and Ageing" bundles, more closely resembling the hand used in chaps. XII, "Concerning the Quendi in Their Mode of Life and Growth", above, and XVI, "Note on the Youth and Growth of the Quendi", below. Some subsequent alterations and notes are made in green ball-point pen and (mostly) in pencil. The four sheets on which these texts and text 3 below are written were inserted between the third and fourth sheets of the preceding text.

New Scheme

Some tentative dates

Days of Bliss. End of Waiting Time. First Age begins.

VY 865/1[11]	Awaking of Quendi (Spring). Melian warned in dream leaves Valinor and goes to Endor.	1
871/1	Oromë finds the Quendi and dwells with them for 48 years.	864–912
871/48	Tidings of the Quendi brought to Valinor. Melkor seeks to attack Oromë. Oromë sends news back to the Valar, and Tulkas comes.	912–960
871 end	Oromë returns to Valinor and reports. Council of the Valar.	960–1007
872/1–10	Oromë returns to Cuiviénen. Valar prepare for War against Melkor. Manwë decides (though ?Varda and Ulmo are against it) that the Quendi should be brought to Valinor before the War – which may be very destructive. But in Varda's urgent advice the Quendi are only *invited* to come.	1008–1018
872/48	Oromë and Tulkas are needed for the War. The Valar send the Five Guardians (Olórin etc.), with special power.	1056
872/50	Oromë and Tulkas return to Valinor, bringing ambassadors or representatives of the Three Companies (young Quendi: Ingwë, Finwë, Elwë, grandsons of Imin, Tata, and Enel).	1058

This chronological scheme ends here, but is accompanied by two marginal notes (left and bottom, respectively) which read:

864 – 872/50 = VY 8/50 = 1,202 years.[12] Ingwë, Finwë, Elwë are about 36 only and *unwed*, or Ingwë is 60 and *wedded*. Finwë is 48 and *betrothed*. Elwë is 36.

Ingwë 60 in 1058, therefore born 998. On the "Quick prolific" scheme = one of the 5th gen. = great-great grandchild [of Imin]. Finwë 48 born 1010. Elwë 36 [born] 1022. *On older scheme*

The note ends here, in the bottom margin of the page. On the verso are somewhat rougher, struck-through notes in ink, the contents of which are clearly preliminary to and were incorporated into the next text, and so are not given here.

TEXT 2B

New Scheme

Old Scheme. "Days of Bliss" last [VY] 1–1050 before "Awaking" = 10,500 [sun-]years.[13] Not long enough. Let "DB" be longer, and Elvish Events packed at end. The intrusion from outside into the "artificial" world of the Valar soon destroys it!

New. The Trees flower for 864 VY before Awaking = 124,416 [sun-]years. Quendi then awake in Spring of [VY] 865 (124,417 [YS]).[14] "DB" still goes on, but Quendi start reckoning of *First Age* with Awaking.

First Age must last *somewhat longer* than SA (= 3,441). Still be more regularly "duodecimal" (as mythological) up to Death of Trees and after! Say, 4,056 years.

Death of Trees is 24 VY (= 3,456 [YS]) after Awaking = VY 888. First Age should then occupy 4,032 years = 28 VY. That is 3,456 (Death of Trees) + 576 [sun-]years (= 4 VY). But actually war last[s until] 600? So FA = 4,056 [YS] = 28[VY +]/24[YS].

Quendi therefore enter Valinor sometime after VY 864. After VY 864 all dates should be given in [sun-]years (as well as VY). Found 864 [sun-]years after awaking = 6 VY. VY 870. (About 12 VY elapse before all settled in Valinor. VY 876.)

The text ends here, about three-fourths down the page. Tolkien subsequently made some alterations to dates in green ball-point pen, changing the year of the Awaking again, to 850, and writing against this change: "Quendi Found in 864"; then changing the relative date of the Death of the Trees to 24 VY after the "Finding"; and finally changing the date at which the Quendi enter Valinor to "after VY 850". Tolkien however did not make the further adjustments to the rest of the text that would be needed to harmonize it with these changes (e.g., recalculating the number of sun-years elapsed at the Awaking in VY 850), so I have left the original figures and wording to stand above. But since the date of the Awaking arising here by final alteration, VY 850, appears *ab initio* in text 1 above, it is evident that these two texts, 2a and 2b, are successive preliminary drafts for the much more expansive text 1.

On the verso of this last sheet are, again, somewhat rougher notes and calculations, mostly in pencil. Of chief note are the two statements Tolkien wrote in black ink in narrow-nib pen, the first at the top of the page:

Time in Valinor must be given in Sun-years (*löar*). In old scheme Trees lasted from VY 1–1495 = nearly 1495 × 10 [sun-]years = 14,950 *löar*. This period is too short.

The second is in the top margin (with which cf. the element in text 1, whereby both Melian and the Istari were sent to the Elves at Cuiviénen as Guardians):

Elves warned by Eru or guards?

TEXT 3

This text was written in increasingly difficult red ball-point pen on the rectos of two pages from an engagement calendar, for the weeks 8–14 Feb. 1959 and 1–7 Mar. 1959, respectively. The Valian-year dates here are considerably later than those of the preceding texts, but those for the Awaking and the Finding by Oromë agree with those in the text presented here as chap. XIV, "Calculation of the Increase of the Quendi", below, as revised.

Tale of Years

VY 1728	Death of Trees
VY 1386/1	Awaking of Quendi. Melian has warning of them in dream and leaves Valinor.
1392/1	Finding by Oromë. 6 VY = 864 [sun-]years
1392/3	Oromë returns to Valinor with tidings. Council of the Valar.
1392/6	Oromë returns to Cuiviénen.
1393	Valar prepare for war. Oromë returns with Ingwë, Finwë, Elwë. Valar issue from Valinor, invest Angband. See [?difficulties].[15]
1394	Oromë sent with Ingwë, Finwë, Elwë to Cuiviénen. Debate

of the Quendi. Long delay, they do not wish to leave
Cuiviénen and [?will not].

1395   Fall of Angband. Valar anxious as war will break out and be
destructive. Delay deploying forces [?all round] Utumno
[?and Oromë heads up coasts]. [?But] Sauron escapes. [? ? ?].

1396   Great March begins. ⅔ follow Young Lords Ingwë, Finwë,
Elwë. ⅓ Avari. [?Mostly proceed by ? ?] of the first born
[?march]. [?] of March. Oromë has often to go back to war.
March [?occupies] 3 VY?

1399   Elves reach Beleriand.

1400   Elwë lost. Vanyar and Ñoldor taken by Island reach Aman.

1402   Teleri depart leaving Sindar.

1402/92+   Eressëa made fast.

NOTES

1   Tolkien altered this year from original "c. 600". The revised year reflects a rate
of 1 Valian Year = 144 sun-years (*löar*), thus FA 576 = VY 854 – VY 850 = VY
4 × 144 SY = SY 576 from FA 1.

2   That the 12th generation first appears in 576 implies an average of 48 sun-
years between the generations.

3   Tolkien altered this date from original "c. 1200", This reflects a calculation of
FA 1152 = VY 858 – VY 850 = VY 8 × 144 SY = SY 1152 from FA 1.

4   This entry and the following two, giving the years of birth of Ingwë, Finwë
and Elwë, are later additions in green ball-point pen.

5   Tolkien subsequently changed this year to 2161 in green ball-point pen, but he
did not carry through the change in subsequent years, so I have left it as first
written.

6   A passage later struck through in green ball-point pen originally followed:

[Ulmo >>] Manwë decrees advice that ambassadors should be
brought to see Valinor and the Valar – though Ulmo thinks this is
perilously like overaweing their wills by sight of splendour.

Cf. the entry below for DB 866/49 = FA 2211.

7   Aside from the name *Olórin* for Gandalf, these Quenya names of (appar-
ently) the Istari are nowhere else recorded. They apparently mean: *Tarindor*
*'High/wise-mind(ed)-one', *Hrávandil* *'Wild-beast-friend', *Palacendo*
*'Far-sight(ed)-one', *Haimenar* *'Far-farer'.

8   The description of the election of the Three Ambassadors was originally the
end of the entry for DB 866/13 = FA 2175, where it was preceded by a sentence stuck through in green ball-point pen:

Oromë (and Tulkas?) return, taking Three Ambassadors.

Tolkien indicated in green ball-point pen that the remainder of the description should be moved to this entry instead, some 37 years later.

9 Tolkien here first wrote "knowledge" (in apparent anticipation of Finwë's response), but replaced it with "beauty" in the act of writing.

10 A deleted final paragraph reads:

Imin looks up at the stars. He says, "I will remain if any of my folk do". Tata and Enel say the same. In the end ⅔ decide to go. The *Imillië* numbered about 2,625; the *Tatalië* 10,500; the *Enellië* 13,875. The greatest population of "Eldar" are from *Tatalië*.

Tolkien first struck through the final sentence, and then bracketed the whole paragraph and struck it through.

11 As first written, this date was "VY 888"; the year was then struck through and replaced with "864", which was itself then altered to "865".

12 That is, 1,202 years since the Awaking of the Quendi in VY 864, and so calculated before the revision of the year to 865.

13 That is, under the former scheme where 1 Valian Year = 10 Sun Years (*löar*). With the Valian year 1050 as that of the Awaking of the Elves under the "old scheme", cf. X:71.

14 Tolkien first wrote that the Quendi awoke in 864/1, but later changed this in blue ball-point pen to 865.

15 As first written, the entry for 1393 began:

Valar prepare for War. Land in NW. Invest Angband. Angband held by Sauron. Melkor retreats to Utumno. They decide that Quendi must be given chance of rescue, since the War will be great and destructive.

XIV

CALCULATION OF THE INCREASE OF THE QUENDI

The two texts presented here are written in a generally clear hand in black nib-pen on nine sides of ten sheets of unlined paper. Subsequent additions and corrections were made in red ball-point pen. There is no clear indication of date, but given its general character and the fact that it evidently precedes the text presented here as chap. XVI, "Note on the Youth and Growth of the Quendi", below – since unlike that text Elves here still have a 9-year gestation period – it can be confidently dated to c. 1959.

Note that the dates of the Finding and Awaking as revised agree with those appearing *ab initio* in text 3 of chap. XIII, "Key Dates", above.

TEXT 1

Calculation of the Increase of the Quendi
from the *Awaking* to the *Beginning of the Great March*[1]

First Elves. Awoke at *maturity*. Population 144. Began at once to engender the second generation. This, therefore, with the first births will begin to appear in VY 1000/9. It will take VY 1/90* years to

---

* Reckoned from the first begetting to the last birth: that is, 6 periods of gestation (9 years) + 5 intervals of an average of 36 years each (times increase: 12/24/36/48/60): $6 \times 9 (= 54) + 5 \times 36 (= 180) = 234$ years = VY 1/90.

complete (i.e. up to date of last births). All 72 pairs of "destined spouses" wed, and the average family is 6 per pair. In VY 1001/90, therefore, the *increase* will be 72 × 6 = 432. Population 576.

After this various things that modify this first process must be considered:

(a) The age at which the new generations begin to beget children will slowly increase by 6 *coimendi* (= 6 VY) *on an average*, until 48 is reached, which will then remain the average age for a very long time: *First Elves* at maturity (24): *2nd gen.* at 30; *3rd gen.* at 36; *4th gen.* at 42; *5th gen.* (and many later generations) at 48.

(b) The length of time in which a generation is completed, sc. *the average intervals between births*, also increases, while becoming (in cases considered individually) more variable. But probably *an average time* for the completion of a generation (from *first begetting* to *latest birth*) for the completing of all generations after the First until the Eldar reach Valinor may be set at 2 VY = 288 *löar*.[2] ☞ This will be irrespective of the actual average number of children produced in each family, since as this number falls, the intervals between births also rise.[3] (This average of VY 2 = 288 *löar* reckons from *the first begetting* to the *last birth*. The period would probably be for 6 children: 294 *löar*; for 5: 285; for 4: 288; for 3: 287; averaging at 288.5.)*

(c) *Average production of children* per pair or family also decreases from 6 by 1st, 2nd, and 3rd generations, to 5 by the 4th gen., to 4 by the 5th gen., to 3 thereafter in the 6th gen. and subsequent generations (at least up to arrival in Valinor).[4]

(d) After the engendering by the First Elves of the 2nd gen. the proportion of males and females varied, not being equal

---

* Thus:

Gestations [of 9 *löar* each]	Interval times	Total [*löar*]
6 = 54	+ 5 intervals of av. 48 = 240	294
5 = 45	+ 4 intervals of av. 60 = 240	285
4 = 36	+ 3 intervals of av. 84 = 252	288
3 = 27	+ 2 intervals of av. 130 = 260	287
		1,154 = 288.5 [average]

(though remaining always near to an equal division). Thus not all could find spouses; already a few did not desire marriage; and there were various ill-chances and losses (especially after Sauron discovered the Quendi). The wedded pairs therefore cannot be found by dividing the numbers of each generation by 2. A proportion, beginning with 1% of the 2nd gen., and increasing (by 1%) in each following generation until 10% is reached, must be deducted from the complete 100s before division by 2.

If these factors are taken into account, it is possible to calculate, with fair accuracy, the *increase* of the Quendi from the date of their *Awaking* until their *Finding* by Oromë 90 VY later, or any other date decided upon.[5]

Gen.	Births	[VYs from the Awaking until] First births and last births	Increase	Pop.[6] 144
2	First: VY 0/9	VY 0/9		
	Last: VY 1/90	VY 1/90		
	Increase: $72 \times 6 =$		432	576
3	First: VY 0/9 + age 30 (= VY 8) + 9 =	VY 8/18		
	Last: VY 1/90 + VY 8/9 + VY 2 =	VY 11/99		
	Increase: $\frac{432-1\%}{2}$ (= 214) $\times 6 =$		1,284	1,860
4	First: VY 8/18 + age 36 (= VY 14) + 9 =	VY 22/27		
	Last: VY 11/99 + VY 14/9 + VY 2 =	VY 27/108		
	Increase: $\frac{1,284-2\%}{2}$ (= 630) $\times 6 =$		3,780	5,640
5	First: VY 22/27 + age 42 (= VY 20) + 9 =	VY 42/36		
	Last: VY 27/108 + VY 20/9 + VY 2 =	VY 49/117		
	Increase: $\frac{3,780-3\%}{2}$ (= 1,834) $\times 5 =$		9,170	14,810
6	First: VY 42/36 + age 48 (= VY 26) + 9 =	VY 68/45		
	Last: VY 49/117 + VY 26/9 + VY 2 =	VY 77/126		
	Increase: $\frac{9,170-4\%}{2}$ (= 4,401) $\times 4 =$		17,604	32,414
7	First: VY 68/45 + age 48 (= VY 26) + 9 =	VY 94/54		
	Last: VY 77/126 + VY 26/9 + VY 2 =	VY 105/135		
	Increase: $\frac{17,604-5\%}{2}$ (= 8,362) $\times 3 =$		25,086	57,500

The number of the Quendi therefore at about 106 Valian years after their Awaking would have been about 57,500.

But if Oromë arrived in VY 1090 that would be *before the first births* of the 7th gen.; and the *youngest* of the 6th gen. would be VY 90 − VY 77/126, or nearly 12 VY "old" = Elf-men VY 2 = 24 + VY 10 = 10 = 34; Elf-women VY 1½ = 18 + VY 10½ = 10½ = 28½. They would all be fully mature and marriageable, and though the beginning of the 7th gen. would in undisturbed circumstances have probably been delayed for another 4 VY (or nearly so) the change of life might alter that.

Also note that the *eldest men* of the 6th gen. would already be over age 43, while the *youngest* women would be over 28 and past the ordinary marrying age. So that from at least the 6th gen. (or indeed the 5th gen.) we have to reckon with marriages *within a generation* and the loss of an unmixed sequence.[7]

On the above calculation: if there were a total of 32,414 Quendi at the end of the 6th gen., this would be the total population when Oromë found them in (say) VY 1090 (90 VY later): the youngest would then be "30" in age.

The "Companies" should be still in approximate proportion of $^{14}/_{144}$, $^{56}/_{144}$, and $^{74}/_{144}$. If we take the actual total to be 32,400, these proportions would be exactly 3,150, 12,600, and 16,650. But many of the Quendi will become Avari. Say ⅓ of total = 10,800. The *Marchers* or Eldar then will number 21,600. $^{1}/_{72}$ of this is 300. Therefore the Vanyar will be 2,100; the Ñoldor 8,400; and the Lindar 11,100.

This suffices (barely?). There will probably be increase on the March, and greater increase in Valinor(?). But *more* would be better. *And the time required is far too great.* 90 VY = 12,960 [sun-]years: this is much too long for the Quendi to be left unguarded and at the mercy of Melkor and Sauron!! (In the original scheme only 85 × 10 = 850 years was allowed.)[8]

But if the time is reduced, the rate of increase must be very greatly raised. The Quendi in their first few generations before the March (or reaching Valinor) must − as is quite reasonable − be made far more eager for love and the begetting and bearing of children. *They must have larger families, at shorter intervals between births.*

The *Valian Years of the Trees* should be duodecimal. Let VY 1728 be the *death of the Trees*. In the older scheme about 400 VY = 4,000 years covered events from the *Finding* to the *Darkening of Valinor*. But Elves now live at a rate 14 times or more as slow. We can allow about 48,000 years, or on present scheme about 333⅓ VY. Say 336 (or 12 × 28) = 48,384 *löar*. (Or 324 = 12 × 27 = 46,656 *löar*).

In that case the Finding should take place about 1728 − 336 = 1392. The Awaking should take place not more than 6 VY (= 864 years) previously, that is in VY 1386. (The entry into Valinor could be later by 12 VY − later allowing for a long sojourn of Oromë and negotiations, and for delays on the March − or perhaps better only 6 VY: sc. early VY 1404 or 1398.) In these 6 VY the Quendi must increase to over 30,000 from 144.

Let the *First Elves awake* in VY 1386 (with the Finding in 1392).

Between VY 1386 and 1388/94, all 72 pairs wed and (at once) produce 12 children each = 72 × 12 = 864. Population = 1,008.

Between VY 1386/9 (first births) + VY 2 (maturity) = 1388/9 and 1388/84 + 2 VY + VY 2/84 = 1393/24, 430 (not 432) pairs wed and produce 12 children each = 5,160.[9] Population = 5,738.[10]

Between VY 1388/9 + 2 VY = 1390/9 and VY 1393/24 + VY 2 + VY 2/84 = 1397/108, 2,500 pairs (not 2,580) and produce 12 children each = 30,000. Population = 35,738.

About this time the Great March begins.

It is not necessary to have quite so many as 35,738 Quendi, and their generation need not be quite so prolific and precipitate![11]

Elves awake VY 1386. Population 144.

The First Elves at once beget children and in their joy and vigour begin at once and beget 12 each pair on average: 12 × 72 = 864. These the first births will take place therefore in 1386/9 and the last after VY 1/96 years. 12 gestations of 9 years (= 108) + 11 intervals of 12 years (= 132) = 240 = VY 1/96. 1387/96. Population = 1,008.

2nd gen. First born 1386/9. Last born 1387/96. First births 1386/9 + VY 2 (maturity) + 9 = 1388/18. Last births 1387/96 + VY 2 + VY2/18 = 1391/114. (VY 2/18 represents rise of interval to 18 years.)[12] 430 pairs × 11 = 4,730. Population = 5,738.

3rd gen. First born 1388/18 + VY 2 + 9 = 1390/27. Last born 1391/114 + VY 2 + VY2/84 = 1395/198 (VY 2/84 represents rise of interval to 24 years.)[13] 2,350 pairs × 10 = 23,500. Population = 29,238.

4th gen. First born 1390/27 + VY 3 + 9 = 1393/36. Last born 1396/54 + VY 3 + VY 2/84 = 1401/138. 11,500 pairs × 9 = 103,500. Population 132,738.[14]

TEXT 2

There remains a curious final scheme – final in the sense that it is now on the recto of the last sheet in this small bundle – but that is in no sense continuous with or a development of the second of the two schemes presented above. In fact, it shares the chronological starting point of the first of those schemes, in which the Quendi awake in VY 1000 and the 2nd generation begins to appear in VY 1000/9, and so conceptually precedes the second scheme, in which the Quendi awake in VY 1386.

As mentioned in the editorial notes, the verso of this last sheet appears to be draft material for the first scheme presented above; moreover, the first line of that first scheme echoes the final line of that draft material. It might be thought then that this scheme is continuous with that drafting: i.e., that it is in fact the first and earliest of the schemes in this bundle. But if so, it adheres less strictly to the contents of that drafting than does the first scheme presented above, in that the intervals between birth and next gestation don't begin to increase until the 5th gen., and neither is there a percentage reduction in wedded pairs until the 5th gen. (where it is 5%, as it is in the 6th gen.).

I cannot therefore with assurance place this scheme chronologically with respect to the preceding schemes. Nonetheless, since Tolkien both retained the sheet and did not strike its recto through, I present it here in its bundle-order.

Thus: the Quendi awake in VY 1000. Number 144. The 2nd gen. appears in VY 1000/9.

Gen.[15]		Increase	Population[16]
2	By VY 1001 the increase is $72 \times 6 =$	432	576
3	By VY 1000/9 + VY 14/9 = 1014/18 the 3rd gen. will begin to appear. It will be complete in VY 1015/18.		
	Increase is $\frac{432}{2}$ (= 216) $\times 6 =$	1,296	1,872
4	By 1014/18 + VY 14/9 = 1028/27 the 4th gen. will begin to appear. It will be completed in 1029/27.		
	Increase is $\frac{1,296}{2}$ (= 648) $\times 6 =$	3,888	5,760
5	By 1028/27 + VY 14/9 = 1042/36 the 5th gen. will begin to appear. It will be completed in 1043/36.		
	Increase is $\frac{3,888}{2}$ (= 1944) $\times 6 =$	11,664	17,424

6	By 1042/36 + VY 26/9 = 1068/45 the 6th gen. will begin to appear. It will be completed in 1070/45.		
	Increase is $\frac{11,664-580\ (5\%)}{2}$ $(=\frac{11,084}{2})$ × 5 =	27,710	45,134
7	By 1068/45 + VY 26/9 = 1094/54 the 7th gen. will begin to appear. It will be completed in 1096/54.		
	Increase is $\frac{27,710-1,385\ (5\%)}{2}$ $(=\frac{26,325}{2})$,		
	say 13,100 × 5 =	65,500	110,634[17]

Before the 7th gen. was produced Oromë arrives in VY 1085.

NOTES

1 Increasingly rough notes and calculations, found on the verso of what is now the last of this small bundle of sheets, and subsequently struck through in red ball-point pen, appear to be draft material for what became the first scheme presented here:

A better calculation. First Elves produce the 2nd gen. at once. It begins therefore to appear in VY 1000/9, and only takes about VY 1/9 to complete. All the 72 original pairs are wedded, and produce an average of 6 children each.

The time at which the succeeding gen. begins to produce the next gen. *steadily increases*: 1st gen. at once (24), 2nd gen. + 6 (30), 3rd gen. + 6 (36) 4th gen. + 6 (42), 5th gen. + 6 (48), 6th gen. + 6 (54). Average product wanes from 6 in first 3 gens. to 5 in gen. 4, to 4 in gen. 5, to 3 thereafter (6 –). Also the proportion of available pairs that actually wed is reduced: 1) the exactitude of proportion of males and females is not maintained, 2) not all can find mates, 3) various accidents. So that after the 1st gen. the pairs will be overestimated if the previous generation is divided by two. A proportion increasing from 1% through to 10% must be deducted in each generation.

Thus: First Elves. 2nd gen. appears in VY 1000/9.

2 As first written, the average was "V2/6 = 294 *löar*".

3 The text originally continued as follows on the verso of the sheet, before the whole side was subsequently struck through in black ink:

This average V2/6 represents 294 *löar*, made up of 6 gestations = 54 *löar* + 240 *löar* representing five intervals of 48 *löar* for 5 births (60 for 4 births, 80 for 3 births, and 120 for 2 births).

1) Average production of children per pair also decreases from 6 in generations 1, 2, 3 > 5 in gen. 4 > 4 in gen. 5 > 3 thereafter in gen. 6 and subsequent gens. (at least up to arrival in Valinor).

2) After the production by the First Elves and their "destined spouses" of 2 generation the proportions of males and females varied (though remaining never v. far from equality). Not all, however, could find spouses; already a few did not desire them; and there were various accidents and losses – increasing when Sauron discovered their dwellings. So that the wedded pairs cannot be found by dividing the number of each generation by 2. A proportion beginning with 1% of 2 gen. and increasing by 1% in each succeeding generation until 10% is reached, must be deducted from the complete 100s of each generation before division by 2.

If these factors are taken into account, we shall be able to calculate with reasonable accuracy the increase of the Quendi from VY 1000 until the Finding by Oromë in V [Tolkien here leaves the date blank, presumably pending further calculation].

The First Generation or First Elves numbered 144. In V1001/90 they had completed the 2 gen. which numbered 72 × 6 = 432. Pop. 576.

The Second Generation began to appear in V1000/9. It began production of 3 gen. after 30 years from that date. In a further V2/6 it had completed the 3 gen. of 6 children per pair in V1000/39 +

The rejected text ends here, at the bottom of the page and mid-sentence. There are however two marginal notes added in red ball-point pen that read:

Time between first and last births of each generation therefore VY 2/6 – 9 = 285 *löar* or VY 1/141.

If VY 2/6 is [?needed] for first birth to last birth for [a] generation this will allow a small margin for [*illegible*].

4 In the event, as will be seen, the first table of generations Tolkien produced following this statement actually shows 6 children per pair for generations 1 through 4, 5 in the 5th gen., 4 in the 6th gen. and 3 in the 7th gen.

5 The clause "or any other date decided upon" is an addition in red ball-point pen, as is the tabular footnote of intervals.

6 The population column was an addition in pencil. Beside the 2nd, 3rd, and 4th gen. entries, in the left margin, Tolkien later wrote in red ball-point: "865/9 866/90", "873/18 876/99", and "887/27 892/108", respectively, apparently the dates of

first and last births of those generations in a revised chronology where the Elves awake in FA 865.

7   This paragraph entered as a marginal note written in red ball-point pen.

8   It is unclear where Tolkien's figure of 850 years comes from. In *The Annals of Aman* of the early 1950s, the Elves awoke at Kuiviénen in VY 1050, and Oromë discovered them there in VY 1085 (X:71–2), which means they were left unguarded for 35 VY, which in the scheme in effect at that time was 350 sun-years. Tolkien may have forgotten that at that time the Elves did not awake in VY 1000.

9   Tolkien here actually wrote "1388/84 + 2 VY + VY 2/84 = 1392/24", but this is an error. The correct total is 1392/168 = 1393/24, which I have provided. Similarly, I have corrected the subsequent calculation from "VY 1392/24 + VY 2 + VY 2/84 = 1396/108".

10 This figure derives from the original number of children Tolkien assigned to each pair, 11, multiplied by the number of pairs, 430, and the corresponding increase of 4,730. Tolkien later changed the number of children to 12 (in accordance with the number born to each pair in the 1st and 3rd generations) and revised the increase to 5,160, but he did not revise the figure for the total population. However, he nonetheless used the new increase of 5,160 to derive the number of pairs in the 3rd gen., sc. 2,580. I have therefore let the mathematical error stand, to show the intended scheme, even though the numbers do not add up.

11 I cannot account for the fact that immediately following this statement (which begins a new page but is not evidently a marginal note), Tolkien presents a new scheme in which the Quendi are in fact much more "prolific and precipitate" in producing offspring.

12 The total gestations + intervals time of VY 2/18 (= 306 years) here is inconsistent with a reduction of the number of children born to each married pair, even with the increase of the individual interval from birth to next conception to 18 years. Since there is an average of 11 offspring of the 3rd gen. for each married 2nd-gen. pair, the total time of gestations should be $11 \times 9 = 99$ years, and the total time of intervals should be $10 \times 18 = 180$ years, for a total span from first conception to last birth of 279 years = VY 1/135. It appears that Tolkien has instead calculated the times as 12 gestations $\times$ 9 (= 108) + 11 intervals $\times$ 18 (= 198) = 306. It may be that Tolkien had not yet settled on the reduced number of children per pair in the 2nd–4th generations when he made these calculations; but there is no indication that the calculations of increase were a later insertion.

13 Similarly, the figure of VY 2/84 (= 372 years) here and in the 4th gen. seems to be a calculation based on 12 gestations $\times$ 9 (= 108) + 11 intervals $\times$ 24 (= 264) = 372.

14 In both cases "VY 3" as the time to maturity was altered by Tolkien from "VY 2", and in the first case the correction was underscored in red ball-point pen.

15 Tolkien here actually started the generations from 1, not 2; but in doing so he must have meant generations after the First Elves (who strictly speaking were not "generated" in the womb). I have altered the generation numbering to accord with that which Tolkien used everywhere else, to avoid confusion.

16 Tolkien miscalculated the total population of the 2nd gen. as 572 (it should be 144 + 432 = 576), and carried this error through the rest of his population tally. I have corrected this error throughout.

17 Tolkien here miscalculated 13,100 × 5 as 75,500, and thus the total as 120,634. I have corrected the error.

XV

A GENERATIONAL SCHEME

This text is written in black ink with a narrow nib-pen on the versos of engagement calendar pages for 22–28 March, 29 March–4 April, 19–25 April, 26 April–2 May, 3–9 May, and 17–23 May, 1959, which Tolkien clipped together.

First Elves. Start with 144. First births: FA 10, 31, 52, 73, 94, 115, 136, 157, 178, 199, 220, 241; each produce 72. 2nd gen. $72 \times 12 = 864$. 240 years from first begetting in year 1 to last birth in 241.

Second Elves: born in 12 groups of 72 each between FA 10 and 241. Of these 36 pairs in each group only an average of 35 pairs wed $= 420$ pairs: each produce $11 = 4,620$. The first group, born at 10, will beget at maturity, $288 = FA$ 298, and their first births will follow in 307; the second group, born in 31, will beget in 319 (births in 328).

The Third Elves will therefore begin to appear in 307. Since Second Elves only produce 11 children, each pair will have an *Onnalúmë* of 219 years ($11 \times 9 = 99 + 10 \times 12 = 120$). The *last births* will therefore be from those born in 241 and mature in 529, sc. in $529 + 219 = FA$ 748.

Thus Second Elves:

Group	Born	Beget [year]	[Years of] First birth–last birth
1	10	298	307–517
2	31	319	328–538
3	52	340	349–559
4	73	361	370–580
5	94	382	391–601
6	115	403	412–622
7	136	424	433–643
8	157	445	454–664
9	178	466	475–685
10	199	487	496–706
11	220	508	517–727
12	241	529	538–748

Births by year

307	35	538	385
328	70	559	350
349	105	580	315
370	140	601	280
391	175	622	245
412	210	643	210
433	245	664	175
454	280	685	140
475	315	706	105
496	350	727	70
517	385	748	35

Thus there will be 4,620 persons born between 307 and 748.

Third Elves: born in 22 groups of varying content, two groups (born 307 and 748) of 35 each, two (328 and 727) of 70 each, and so on. There will obviously already be marriages outside groups and so on. But the average will probably be fairly closely found if 34 is substituted for 35, making two groups of 34, two of 68, etc. Total wedded pairs = 4,488. These produce 10 children each. The 4th gen. therefore = 44,880.

Group	Born	Beget [year]	[Years of] First birth–last birth	Produce
1	307	595	604–793	340
2	328	616	625–814	680
3	349	637	646–835	1,020
4	370	658	667–856	1,360
5	391	679	688–877	1,700
6	412	700	709–898	2,040
7	433	721	730–919	2,380
8	454	742	751–940	2,720
9	475	763	772–961	3,060
10	496	784	793–982	3,400
11	517	805	814–1003	3,740
12	538	826	835–1024	3,740
13	559	847	856–1045	3,400
14	580	868	877–1066	3,060
15	601	889	898–1087	2,720
16	622	910	919–1108	2,380
17	643	931	940–1129	2,040
18	664	952	961–1150	1,700
19	685	973	982–1171	1,360
20	706	994	1003–1192	1,020
21	727	1015	1024–1213	680
22	748	1036	1045–1234	340

[Total] 44,880

Onnalúmë = 198 [sun-years]. Begetting and bearing of 4th gen. from FA 595 to 1234.

At the time of the Finding in FA 864 the first 3 Gens. were complete = 144 + 864 + 4,620 = 5,628. But the 4th gen. began to appear in 604. Its first four groups = 3,400 had appeared. Of the subsequent groups to 864:

Group	[Years of births]	Births
5	688–856	9 × 170 = 1,530
6	709–856	8 × 204 = 1,632
7	730–856	7 × 238 = 1,666
8	751–856	6 × 272 = 1,632
9	772–856	5 × 306 = 1,530
10	793–856	4 × 340 = 1,360

Group (*cont.*)	[Years of births] (*cont.*)	Births (*cont.*)
11	814–856	$3 \times 374 = 1,122$
12	835–856	$2 \times 374 = 748$
13	856	1×340
		[Total] 14,960

The population at the arrival of Oromë therefore was 5,628 older Elves (youngest 116 years old = age $9^8/_{12}$) + 14,960 young Elves (eldest 260 = age $21^5/_{12}$, youngest = 8 years = $^8/_{12}$ or 8 months) = 20,588. (This number will be greatly increased in immediately following years.)

Generation	Age	No. of Children	Average interval	*Onnalúmë*
1	—	12	12	240
2	24 = 288	11	12	219
3	24 = 288	10	12	198
4	27 = 720	9	18	225
5	27 = 720	9	18	225
6	27 = 720	9	18	225
7	30 = 1,152	8	24	240
8	30 = 1,152	8	24	240
9	30 = 1,152	8	24	240
10	36 = 2,016	7	30	243
11	42 = 2,880	6	39	249
12	48 = 3,744	5	48	237
13	48 = 3,744	4	60	216
14	48 = 3,744	3	72	243

After this the average number of children varies. 3 remains frequent (but 2 is also frequent) but the interval varies from 84 to 144.

Note: There was *never* any objection at any time to marriage outside the "generations": in fact it soon becomes inevitable and necessary (though the Quendi always *know* their ancestry and place in the descent from the Three First Elves). *Also*, the Quendi were all one people, and though "the Companies" soon began to dwell and house separately (hence they were called *olië* 'people together' and *ombari* 'dwellers together') there was never any objection to marriage between members of different companies. Though these were natur- ally not frequent (more common among the leaders and chief families). They did not upset the "average" calculations. The *Company of Imin* (*Imillië*) were always more separate (rather proud of being the Eldest), and relations between the *Tatalië* and *Enellië* were closer. It was arranged – for Imin, Tata, and Enel said men [i.e., Elvish males] awoke first, and began the families – that when any woman married one of another Company, she was reckoned to have joined the Company of her husband. The exchange was about equal and does not affect calculations materially. For the same reason, *descent of authority* was reckoned from the immediate father; but women were in no way considered less or unequal, and Quendian genealogy traced both lines of descent with care.

XVI

NOTE ON THE YOUTH AND GROWTH OF THE QUENDI

This text occupies two sides of an unlined sheet, and is written in black ink with a narrow nib-pen. It dates from c. 1959.

In appearance and content it is closely related to the initial schemes of the text presented in the next chapter, and probably closely precedes those, since they uniformly exhibit a gestational period of one sun-year for Elves, whereas prior to this text the period was 9 sun-years.

All the elaborate calculations based on *olmië* 12 : 1 and *coivië* 144 : 1 are both cumbrous, and in *early narrative* (Awaking and Finding, March, etc.) quite unworkable. Also *unlikely*. The difference between Elves and Men is mainly in *longevity* after becoming full-grown: this depends mainly again on the difference in powers of Elvish and Human *fëar*. As far as *hröar* go Elves are "of the flesh of Arda" and quite unlikely to grow at a rate wholly out of keeping with the rest of corporeal or incarnate creatures.

The Elvishness should therefore only appear when their *hröar* reach *prime* (adult) and then do not *for a very long time* show any diminishment of physical youth and vigour. (This will help with Maeglin!)[1]

Elves should grow *from conception* at a rate comparable to Human; but from maturity onward should slow to 144 : 1 rate, diminution appearing (almost imperceptibly at first) at c. age 96.

Let Elves *remain in the womb* for 1 *löa*, Spring to Spring. *Both sexes* reach maturity at 24 *löar*, and then slow. But *puberty* is different: in males reached at about 21, in females at 18. *Nowadays before* [?*these ages*].[2] The First Elves awoke at 21/18. Weddings were immediate. Later weddings in "Early Years" (before the March) usually at 24/21–24.

Olmendi ['growth-years']: 1 *olmen* = 1 *löa*.
Coimendi ['life-years']: 1 *coimen* = 144 *löar*
Colbanavië ['gestation'] = 1 *olmen*

Ontavalië 'puberty': male 21 *olmendi*, female 18 *olmendi*.
Quantolië 'maturity': 24 *olmendi*
Vinimetta: 'end of youth': 96 = 24 *löar* + 72 *coimendi* = 24 + 10,368 = 10,392.

NOTES

1 For the issue of ageing with respect to Maeglin, see chaps. X, "Difficulties in Chronology", and XI, "Ageing of Elves", above.

2 There is nowhere any indication of just when this "nowadays" is meant to be.

XVII

GENERATIONAL SCHEMES

This complex of texts, which were pinned together by Tolkien, dates like most of the "Time and Ageing" file from c. 1959, as indicated by the engagement calendar pages for May, June, and August used for some of them. I characterize the individual texts below.

Note that throughout the gestation period is 1 *löa*, as is the length of a growth-year.

Text 1

The first text is written in a (mostly) clear hand in black ink with a narrow-nib pen, on the backs of two engagement calendar pages for 24–30 May and 31 May–6 June, 1959, respectively; with a few later changes and additions in pencil.

First Elves. Awoke at *ontavalië* ['puberty'] ([males] 21/[females] 18).[1] But they did not turn to marriage until maturity of the elf-man (24), the elf-woman then being 21. These ages were ever after held the earliest *suitable* ages for marriage, though elf-women were some-times married earlier. (As soon as they were 18 they were sought in betrothal – a period which, whenever entered, usually lasted 3 years.)[2] But *marriage* could take place at any time before the "waning of the *hröa*" – the cessation of [?sexual] desire was a mark of its approach.[3] It was, however, naturally seldom entered into after the "End of Youth" – c. age 60 (= [growth] year[s] 24 + *coimendi* 36

= 24 + 5,184 = c. 5,208);*[4] and births after this age are seldom recorded. The *later* the marriage the *fewer* the children.

In the "Early Years", especially before the March, the Quendi tended to concentrate on the *Onnalúmë*, and produce their children in a (for them) quick series, and then satisfied to turn to other things. But this only happened in the days of peace and serenity.

The first two generations of Elves in their vigour are recorded to have produced 6 children for each wedded pair.[5] In all succeeding of "Early Years" generations the *average* declined to 4 at 3rd gen., 2¾ at 4th gen., 1⅚ at 5th.[6]

The intervals between births were at all times very variable; but naturally more regular in early times and in any times of peace (as in Valinor). Even when children were produced long after *maturity* (*quantolië*) the interval was governed by growth-years or *löar*, since it was governed by *physical recuperation* ([?*increasing*]).

The Quendi aver that more vigour (or as they say "of their youth") is used in the production of a child, than is so among Men; at the same time they are far more vigorous in "youth" and especially before age 48 (3,480 years),[7] and their bodies recuperate far swifter and more completely from strains or hurt. The minimum "rest" was 3 *löar* (or 3 times the bearing),[8] depending chiefly on the woman: it was seldom reduced, and often much increased. In later generations it was often much lengthened – naturally in the days of war, exile, and troubles. It might be extended to 2 *coimendi*, or in some cases 3 or even 4.[9]

In larger families the "interval" tended to increase after each birth. This interval was reckoned from birth to begetting of the next child.[10] In the early years the *Onnalúmë*, reckoned from [first] begetting to last birth, averaged at about 108 [sun-]years: 8 intervals of 3, 6, 9, 12, 15, 18, 21, 24 = 108; + 9 [for] gestation[s] = 117 [sun-years].[11]

TEXT 2

The recto of the next sheet (of unlined paper) in the first bundle begins a new text, in black ink in broader nib-pen, with one addition in green ball-point pen.

All this business makes the "remote" legend of origins too recent. In spite of all difficulties I think the Elves must awake *much longer*

---

* But could often be delayed to about 96.

before the Finding, and *therefore* their *propagation* should be *slower*, and their *marriages later*.

If the Trees are destroyed in VY 888, that allows 127,872 *löar* for the "Bliss of Valinor"! If the Awaking were c. 800, say VY 792 (12 × 66), then 96 VY would elapse before the Death of the Trees = 13,824. But the Finding should be not till VY 864 = 72 VY [later] = 10,368 *löar*, leaving 24 VY for the March and the Sojourn of the Ñoldor [in Valinor] = 3,456 [sun-years].[12]

How long before should the Quendi "awake"? Quendi *awake* VY 850 (*löar* 122,400); *found* VY 864 (*löar* 124,416). 2,016 [sun-years] elapse = 14 VY. Only 216 [sun-]years (12 × 18) or 1½ VY elapse before the March.

The First Age begins with the Awaking and ends with the Downfall of Angband. In the Older Scheme the March is about FA 1080.[13] Here it would be about 2016 + 216 = FA 2232 (or 15½ VY after the Awaking). The Embassy set out 20 years before the Great March = 2212.[14]

TEXT 3

This text is a gathered series of seven generational schemes, all but the first labelled and numbered as such. The first two schemes are written in a clear hand in black ink with a narrow-nib pen (the same pen and in the same hand as that employed in text 1 above) and later pencil additions, on the back of engagement calendar pages for 2–8 and 9–15 Aug. 1959, respectively. The remaining five schemes are written in black ink with a broader nib-pen, with additions and corrections made variously in pencil and green or red ball-point pen.

While all exhibit, in the date of the first births after each wave of weddings, a gestational period of 1 *löa*, and share VY 864 as date of the Awaking, these successive schemes exhibit considerable variation in the date of the beginning of the Great March, ranging from VY 878 (FA 2016) to VY 1070. This variability of course provides Tolkien with flexibility in balancing Elvish rates of increase with a desired population size at the March.

Calculation of Quendi: Increase and Population
at Time of Finding and March

[*Scheme 1*]

No. in generation	Pairs	Children per pair	Wedding (age) & date	Date of 1st births
1) 144	72 all	6	3	4
2) 432	216 less 1% = 214	6	(24) 28	29
3) 1,284	642 less 2% = 630	4	(96) 125	126
4) 2,520	1,260 less 3% = 1,220	4	(168) 294	295
5) 4,880	2,440 less 4% = 2,340	3	(240) 535	536
6) 7,020	3,510 less 5% = 3,330	3	(312) 848	849

In the year of the Finding (FA 864) the total population of Quendi therefore was 16,280 (or less allowing for losses) of the first 5 generations. But the 6th gen. was appearing: first births FA 849 (second births FA 934, third FA 1043). We must therefore add 3,330, making a total of 19,610, or over 19,000.

At the March the whole of the 6th gen. had appeared: add again 2 × 3,330 = 6,660, total 26,270. The 7th gen. was not due to appear until FA 1234 (= FA 849 + age of marriage 384 + 1). The 6th gen. was the *end* of the "Early Years". The Age of Marriage tended thereafter to increase towards "Age 48" = 24 [sun-]years + 24 *coimendi* = 24 + 3,456 = 3,480 [sun-years] and often reached "[Age] 60" = 24 [sun-years] + 36 [*coimendi*] = 5,208 [sun-years].

The Average of Children became 2. The percentage of non-pairs rose to 10% by degrees. But in Valinor non-pairs dropped to 1%, the average age of marriage was 36, and the average number of children 6. The Noldor thus increased greatly. But since Quendi did not bear children if possible in war and exile there were few births in

Average interval & "*Onnalúmë*" (since wedding)	Last births	Increase	Pop. 144
36 (186)	189	6 × 72	432
48 (246)	274	6 × 214	1,284
60 (184)	309	4 × 630	2,520
72 (220)	514	4 × 1,220	4,880
84 (171)	706	3 × 2,340	7,020
96 (195)	1043	3 × 3,330	9,990
		[Total]	26,270

Beleriand, thus the average number of children was ½ per pair, and the unwed pairs rose to 30%; so that the Eldar barely replaced losses.

In pencil Tolkien subsequently detailed in each row the sun-years occupied by the intervals in the *onnalúmë* from wedding for each generation:

0–12–24–36–48–60 [= 180]
0–24–36–48–60–72 [= 240]
0–48–60–72 [= 180]
0–60–72–84 [= 216]
0–72–96 [= 168]
0–84–108 [= 192]

In the year of the Finding (FA 864) the population contained all of the 5th gen. = 27,322. The four [intervals of] births of the 6th gen. occurred in FA 849, 934, 1031, and 1140. Therefore at the Finding

Scheme 2

No. in generation	Pairs	Children per pair	Wedding (age) & date	Date of 1st births
1) 144	72 all	6	3	4
2) 432	216 less 1% = 214	6	(24) 28	29
3) 1,284	642 less 2% = 630	5	(96) 125	126
4) 3,150	1,575 less 3% = 1,528	5	(168) 294	295
5) 7,640	3,820 less 4%= 3,668	4	(240) 535	536
6) 14,672	7,336 less 5% = 6,970	4	(312) 848	849

add the first births of the 6th gen. = 6,970. Total population at the Finding (excluding losses) is 27,322 + 6,970 = 34,292. At the March the third births of the 6th gen. (FA 1031) will also have occurred, therefore add 2 × 6,970 = 13,940. Total 48,232.

In pencil Tolkien again subsequently detailed in each row the sun-years occupied by the intervals in the *onnalúmë* from wedding for each generation:

1) 0–12–24–36–48–60 [= 180]
2) 0–24–36–48–60–72 [= 240]
3) 0–42–54–66–78 [= 240]
4) 0–54–66–78–90 [= 288]
5) 0–72–84–96 [= 252]
6) 0–84–96–108 [= 288]

Also in pencil he subsequently added a partial row for the 7th generation in which children per pair is 3, the wedding age and date is (384) 1233, the date of first births is FA 1234, the average interval & length of the *onnalúmë* is 108 (219), and the year of the last births is FA 1452.

Average interval & "*Onnalúmë*"	Last births	Increase	Pop. 144
36 (180)	189	$6 \times 72 = 432$	576
48 (246)	274	$6 \times 214 = 1{,}284$	1,860
60 (245)	370	$5 \times 630 = 3{,}150$	5,010
72 (293)	587	$5 \times 1{,}528 = 7{,}640$	12,650
84 (256)	791	$4 \times 3{,}668 = 14{,}672$	27,322
96 (292)	1140	$4 \times 6{,}970 = 27{,}880$	55,202

What is now the verso of the sheet on which Scheme 3 was written contains a text that, despite being written with the same broader nib-pen as is Scheme 3, agrees with Scheme 2 against Scheme 3 in its details, and moreover specifically references "Scheme 2" in a marginal note; and so I give it here instead:

Let Ingwë, Finwë, Elwë all be young 6th gen. Elves, but each a direct descendant (by eldest son) of Imin, Tata, and Enel [respectively]. (Divergence in dates of birth is due to intrusion of earlier-born daughters.)

Ingwë was in the first births of the 6th gen. The earliest births of this generation were in FA 536. Let Ingwë be born in 536: 328 [sun-years old] at the Finding in FA 864, 534 at the March in FA 1070. The 6th gen. married at [sun-year age] 312. Therefore Ingwë married in FA 848 (just before the Finding). At the March he had three children, born in FA 849, 934, and 1031. The youngest was 39 at the March.

Finwë must have been a later 6th-generation birth. Let Finwë be born in FA 772: 92 at the Finding, 298 at the March. He would have married about FA 1084. He already loved Míriel and postponed marriage till the end of the March.

Elwë was born in FA 792: 72 at the Finding, 278 at the March. He would have been married about FA 1108, but had not yet set his heart on any spouse.

When Oromë asked for Ambassadors, Imin, Tata, and Enel were against the whole business, and refused to go. Ingwë was the eldest son of Ilion, who was in a direct line from Iminyë in the 4th generation (all having been first children and sons); sc. great-great grandson: he was tall, beautiful, beloved by the *Imillië*, more given to thought than the arts. His spouse was Ilwen (born FA 539). His first child was a son, Ingwil, his second a daughter Indis (born FA 934).[15]

> In addition, a small bundle of sheets placed after the seven schemes presented here, but obviously preceding scheme 3, has notes making reference and comparison to the preceding two schemes, written for the most part in the same pen and hand as those schemes, and that motivate certain features seen in the subsequent schemes, and so I give them here as well:

With Scheme 1: Total population at the time of the March would be 26,270. If we say 26,244, allowing for losses and/or miscalculation, then: Avari were recorded as being ⅓ of total. Avari therefore 8,748, Eldar 17,496. Now, the original division was $\frac{14}{144}$, $\frac{56}{144}$, and $\frac{74}{144}$.

Imillië (Vanyar) should have $\frac{7}{72}$, Tatalië (Ñoldor) should have $\frac{28}{72}$, Enellië (Lindar) should have $\frac{37}{72}$. $\frac{17,496}{72} = 243$ therefore Vanyar = 1,701, Ñoldor = 6,804, Lindar = 8,991; say Vanyar = 1,700, Ñoldor = 6,800, Lindar = 8,900; total = 17,400

This allows for the loss of the other 96, or inaccurate division. It is just barely sufficient.

With Scheme 2: Total population at the time of the March would be 48,232 (excluding losses). Avari ⅓ = 16,077, Eldar = 32,154. If we say the total is 48,168 (allowing for 64 future losses), then Avari = 16,056, Eldar = 32,112.

$\frac{32,112}{72} = 446$ therefore Vanyar = 3,122, Ñoldor = 12,488, Lindar = 16,502; say Vanyar = 3,100, Ñoldor = 12,400, Lindar = 16,500; total = 32,000.

This allows a future 122 loss. Losses before March will be 64 + 56 + 112 = 232.

Taking the Great March to have begun c. 1070, the oldest Quendi would then have been 1,070 years old = $24 + \frac{1,046}{144}$ (= 7 VY/38) or 31 plus 38 *löar*. The youngest 1070 – 1031 (third births of the 6th gen.) = 39 years: i.e., 24 and 15 *löar*. None would be old at all; and divergence between the Eldar and Avari could not much have depended on *age* as such. But the eldest of the two elder generations (1, 2) would have lived near Cuiviénen for 1,070 to 1,041 *years*; thus all those born up to FA 300 would have lived then 770 years and more (sc. all gens. 1, 2; first 4 births of gen. 3).

Those who had lived over 600 years at Cuiviénen (sc. were born in or before 470) were:

Gen.	Scheme 1 [increase]	by [year]	Scheme 2 [increase]	by [year]
1)	144	1	144	1
2)	432	189	432	189
3)	1,284	274	1,284	274
4)	2,520	309	3,150	370
5)	3,660 (first 3 births)	430	4,584 (first 3)	419
	8,040		9,594	

If we add births up to year 570:

Scheme 1	[increase]	Scheme 2	[increase]
Last births of gen. 5	1,220	Last births of gen. 5	1,528
First births of gen. 6	2,340	First births of gen. 6	3,668
	3,560		5,196
[+ 8,040 =]	[11,600]	+ 9,594 =	14,790

In Scheme 1 therefore none born after 470 but a few, 660, need go.

In Scheme 2, 1,210 beyond the first births of gen. 6 must go.

But this is a purely abstract calculation. All 1st gen. married at the same time. Therefore in FA 189 all of the 2nd gen. – 432 – was complete. But they were born at *different times*; sc. about:

4   17   42   79   128   189

(The last long after their oldest brothers had married.) Marriages at:

28   41   66   103   152   213

Producing children in series:

29	42	67	104	153	214
54	67	95	129	178	239
91	104	132	166	215	276
140	153	181	215	264	325
201	212	242	276	325	386
274	285	315	349	398	459

So that the last of the 3rd gen. was born while the 4th gen. was well in progress.

These groups of 36 births would marry 96 years later, and begin the 4th gen. 97 years later, sc. in FA 126 to 556.

Scheme 3

No. in generation	Pairs	Children per pair	Wedding (age) & date
1) 144	72 all	4	(4) 4
2) 288	144 all	4	(168) 173
			198
			223
			248
3) 576	(288) 280	3	(312) 486–572
4) 840	(420) 400	3	(456) 942–1027
5) 1,200	(600) 550	2	(600) 1543–1750
6) 1,100	(550) 500	2	(744)

Providing 5 children each is 180 groups!
  1) 26 to 370; 2) 139 to 383; 3) 164 to 408; and so till last
  group 586 to 800.

The last of the 3rd gen. is born in 800, while the 5th gen. was in progress, so that [?] generations would not keep intact. Plainly a child could be born in practically *any year* between 4 and 864 or 1070.

Scheme 3

Quendi awake in DB 850, spring = FA 1 spring. Elves awake at *Ontavalië*, 21/18, and are therefore adult in FA 4 spring. They marry and first births of the 2nd generation are in FA 5 spring. Oromë finds them in DB 864 = FA 2016. The March begins in spring 216 [sun-] years later = FA 2232. There are therefore 2,016 years for propagation.

Let the First Elves, 144, all wed at 24 (men) and produce 4 children in an *onnalúmë* of 24-year intervals = $4 + 3 \times 24 = 76$ years.

Births [dates]				Increase	Pop.
[1	2	3	4]		144
5	30	55	80	$4 \times 72 = 288$	432
174	211	248	285	$4 \times 144 = 576$	1,008
199	236	273	310		
224	261	298	335		
249	286	323	360		
487	536	585		$3 \times 280 = 840$	1,848
573	622	671			
943	1004	1065		$3 \times 400 = 1,200$	3,048
1028	1089	1150			
1544	1617			$2 \times 550 = 1,100$	4,148
1751	1824				

The table ends here, incomplete; but following the scheme through, there would have been a total of just 5,148 Quendi at the end of the 6th generation: far less than Scheme 1's 26,270 and Scheme 2's 55,202.

Scheme 4

No. in gen.	Married (pairs)	Married (age) & dates	Children per pair	Interval (*Onna.*)
1) 144	72 all	(4) 4	6	24 (126)
2) 432	(216) 210	(168) 173–298	4	36 (112)
3) 840	(420) 410	(312) 486–722	4	48 (148)
4) 1,640	(820) 800	(456) 942–1027	4	60 (184)
5) 3,200	(1,600) 1,560	(600) 1543–1750	4	72 (220)
6) 6,240	(3,120) 3,050	(744) 2289–2525	4	84 (256)

Scheme 5

No. in gen.	Married (pairs)	Married (age) & dates	Children per pair	Interval (*Onna.*)
1) 144	72 all	(4) 4	6	24 (126)
2) 432	(216) 210	(96) 101–226	4	36 (112)
3) 840	(420) 410	(168) 270–506	4	48 (148)
4) 1,640	(820) 800	(240) 511–858	4	60 (184)
5) 3,200	(1,600) 1,560	(312) 824–1354	4	72 (220)
6) 6,240	(3,120) 3,050	(360) 1185–1935	4	96 (292)

6th gen. first-born: FA 1186 / 1283 / 1380 / 1477; last-born: FA 1936 / 2033 / 2130 / 2227.

In FA 2016 therefore the 6th gen. would be complete but for the last 3 [intervals of] births. The 5th gen. had 1,536 groups, therefore the last three births = $\frac{3}{1536}$ of the total 12,200 or about 24 children.

		Births	[dates]			Increase	Pop.
[1	2	3	4	5	6]		144
5	30	55	80	105	130	6 × 72 = 432	576
174	199	224	249	274	299	4 × 210 = 840	1,416
211	236	261	286	311	336		
248	273	298	323	348	373		
285	310	335	360	385	410		
487–723						4 × 410 = 1,640	3,056
943–1180						4 × 800 = 3,200	6,256
1545–1781						4 × 1,560 = 6,240	12,496
2290–2526						4 × 3,050 = 12,200	24,696

		Births	[dates]			Increase	Pop.
[1	2	3	4	5	6]		144
5	30	55	80	105	130	6 × 72 = 432	576
102	127	152	177	202	227	4 × 210 = 840	1,416
213	238	263	288	313	338		
First birth 271 Last birth 506 + 112 = 618						4 × 410 = 1,640	3,056
First birth 512 Last birth 858 + 184 = 1042						4 × 800 = 3,200	6,256
First birth 825 Last birth 1354 + 220 = 1574						4 × 1,560 = 6,240	12,496
First birth 1186 Last birth 1935 + 292 = 2227						4 × 3,050 = 12,200	24,696

Subsequently, Tolkien added some notes in red ball-point pen:

Still only 6 generations! Early generations must marry earlier. 1st gen. each 4 [children], next 6 gens. 3, next 6 [gens.] 2.

Tolkien addresses all these concerns in the next scheme:

Scheme 6

No. in gen.	Married (pairs)	Marriage (age) & dates				Children per pair
1) 144	72 all	(4) 4				4
2) 288	(144) 140	(24) 29	42	55	68	3
3) 420	(210) 200	(24) 54 73 92	67 86 105	80 99 118	93 112 131	3
4) 600	(300) 285	(72) 127–254 (182 + 72)				3
5) 855	(427) 404	(72) 200–389 (317 + 72)				3
6) 1,212	(606) 576	(72) 273–536 (464 + 72)				3
7) 1,728	(864) 820	(120) 394–763 (643 + 120)				3
8) 2,460	(1,230) 1,170	(120) 515–982 (862 + 120)				2
9) 2,340	(1,170) 1,148	(120) 636–1164 (1044 + 120)				2
10) 2,296	(1,148) 1,122	(168) 805–1402 (1234 + 168)				2
11) 2,244	(1,122) 1,100	(168) 974–1629 (1461 + 168)				2
12) 2,200	(1,100) 1,078	(168) 1143–1877 (1,709 + 168)				2
13) 2,156	(1,078) 1,056	(216) 1360–2181 (1965 + 216)				2

Interval (*Onna.*)*	Birth dates				Increase	Pop. 144
	[1	2	3	4]		
12 (39)	5	18	31	44	288	432
18 (39)	30 49 68	43 62 81	56 75 94	69 88 107	420	852
24 (50)	First birth 55 Last birth 132 + 50 = 182				600	1,452
30 (62)	First birth 128 Last birth 255 + 62 = 317				855	2,307
36 (74)	First birth 201 Last birth 390 + 74 = 464				1,212	3,519
42 (86)	First birth 274 Last birth 537 + 86 = 623				1,728	5,247
48 (98)	First birth 395 Last birth 764 + 98 = 862				2,460	7,707
60 (61)	First birth 516 Last birth 983 + 61 = 1044				2,340	10,047
72 (73)	First birth 637 Last birth 1161 + 73 = 1234				2,296	12,343
72 (73)	First birth 806 Last birth 1388 + 73 = 1461				2,244	14,587
78 (79)	First birth 975 Last birth 1629 + 79 = 1708				2,200	16,787
84 (85)	First birth 1144 Last birth 1878 + 85 = 1963				2,156	18,943
90 (91)	First birth 1361 Last birth 2182 + 91 = 2273				2,112	21,055

* From first birth to last.

Tolkien subsequently added some rough notes in pencil:

Let "Early Elves" (before the Finding) marry soon after maturity:

1) 4   2) 24   3) 24   4) 36   5) 36   6) 36   7) 48

8) 48   9) 48   10) 60   11) 60   12) 60   13) 72   14) 72   15) 72

(In uncertainty after the Finding they postponed marriages. These were few in the March. In Valinor they had more children, but left greater intervals plus married later.)

Scheme 7

No. in gen.	Married (pairs)	Marriage (age) & dates	Children per pair
1) 144	72 all	(4) 4	4
2) 288	(144) 142	(24) 29 36 43 50	4
3) 568	(284) 282	(24) First m. 54 Last m. 96	3
4) 846	(433) [18] 428	(36) First m. 91 Last m. 147	3
5) 1,284	(642) 636	(36) First m. 128 Last m. 210	2
6) 1,272	(636) 630	(36) First m. 165 Last m. 260	2
7) 1,260	(630) 624	(48) First m. 214 Last m. 322	2
8) 1,248	(624) 618	(48) First m. 263 Last m. 390	2

Average intervals go up with marriage.

These suggestions were taken up in the next and final scheme. Tolkien made subsequent emendations to this scheme in green and red ball-point pen, increasing the number of pairs in each generation and their marriage rates (from about 98% to about 99%), thus resulting in a higher rate of increase in population (and a total in the 29th generation of 30,522 vs. the original total of 23,640). I give here the final version with all emendations adopted.

Interval (*Onna.*)*[16]	Birth dates	Increase	Pop.
	[1 2 3 4]		
6 (22)	5 12 19 26	4 × 72 = 288	432
6 (22)	30 37 44 51 37 44 51 58 44 51 58 65 51 58 65 72	4 × 142 = 568	990[17]
6 (15)	First birth 55 Last birth 111	3 × 282 = 846	1,836
12 (27)	First birth 92 Last birth 174	3 × 428 = 1,284	3,120
12 (14)	First birth 129 Last birth 224	2 × 636 = 1,272	4,392
12 (14)	First birth 166 Last birth 264	1,260	5,652
18 (20)	First birth 215 Last birth 342	1,248	6,900
18 (20)	First birth 264 Last birth 410	1,236	7,136[19]

---

* From first birth to last.

Scheme 7 (cont.)

No. in gen.	Married (pairs)	Marriage (age) & dates	Children per pair
9) 1,236	(618) 612	(48) First m. 312 Last m. 458	2
10) 1,224	(612) 606	(60) First m. 373 Last m. 538	2
11) 1,212	(606) 600	(60) First m. 434 Last m. 624	2
12) 1,200	(600) 594	(60) First m. 495 Last m. 710	2
13) 1,188	(594) 588	(72) First m. 568 Last m. 808	2
14) 1,176	(588) 582	(72) First m. 641 Last m. 912	2
15) 1,164	(582) 576	(72) First m. 714 Last m. 1016	2
16) 1,152	(576) 570	(84) First m. 799 Last m. 1132	2
17) 1,140	(570) 564	(84) First m. 884 Last m. 1254	2
18) 1,128	(564) 558	(84) First m. 969 Last m. 1376	2
19) 1,116	(558) 552	(96) First m. 1066 Last m. 1510	2
20) 1,104	(552) 546	(96) First m. 1163 Last m. 1650	2
21) 1,092	(546) 540	(96) First m. 1160[21] Last m. 1790	2

Interval (*Onna.*)	Birth dates	Increase	Pop.
18 (20)	First birth 313 Last birth 478	1,224	8,360
24 (26)	First birth 374 Last birth 564	1,212	9,572
24 (26)	First birth 435 Last birth 650	1,200	10,772
24 (26)	First birth 496 Last birth 736	1,188	12,160[20]
30 (32)	First birth 569 Last birth 840	1,176	13,336
30 (32)	First birth 642 Last birth 944	1,164	14,500
30 (32)	First birth 715 Last birth 1048	1,152	15,652
36 (38)	First birth 800 Last birth 1170	1,140	16,792
36 (38)	First birth 885 Last birth 1292	1,128	17,920
36 (38)	First birth 970 Last birth 1414	1,116	19,036
42 (44)	First birth 1067 Last birth 1554	1,104	20,140
42 (44)	First birth 1164 Last birth 1694	1,092	21,232
42 (44)	First birth 1161 Last birth 1834	1,080	22,312

Scheme 7 (cont.)

No. in gen.	Married (pairs)	Marriage (age) & dates	Children per pair
22) 1,080	(540) 534	(108) First m. 1269 Last m. 1942	2
23) 1,068	(534) 528	(108) First m. 1378 Last m. 2100	2
24) 1,056	(528) 522	(108) First m. 1487 Last m. 2258	2
25) 1,044	(522) 516	(120) First m. 1608 Last m. 2428	2
26) 1,032	(516) 510	(120) First m. 1729 Last m. 2604	2
27) 1,020	(510) 504	(120) First m. 1850 Last m. 2780	2
28) 1,008	(504) 498	(132) First m. 1983 Last m. 2968	2
29) 996	(498) 493	(132) First m. 2116 Last m. 3162	2

On the verso of the first sheet of Scheme 7, Tolkien wrote (in black nib-pen):

If this Scheme is accepted: At the Great March in FA 2232, some of Generations 25–30 would not yet be born. Of gen. 25, probably 16 births would have occurred from 1488 to c. 2223 (intervals 49);[22] of gen. 26 some 12 births from 1609 to c. 2214 (intervals 55); of gen. 27 some 10 births from 1730 to c. 2225 (int. 55); of gen. 28 some 7 births from 1851 to c. 2181 (int. 55); of gen. 29 some 5 births from 1984 to 2228 (int. 61); of gen. 30 some 2 births from 2117 to 2278 (int. 61). It is not possible to tell how many "birth groups" there

Interval (*Onna.*)	Birth dates	Increase	Pop.
48 (50)	First birth 1270 Last birth 1992	1,068	23,380
48 (50)	First birth 1379 Last birth 2150	1,056	24,436
48 (50)	First birth 1488 Last birth 2308	1,044	25,480
54 (56)	First birth 1609 Last birth 2484	1,032	26,512
54 (56)	First birth 1730 Last birth 2660	1,020	27,532
54 (56)	First birth 1851 Last birth 2836	1,008	28,540
60 (62)	First birth 1984 Last birth 3030	996	29,536
60 (62)	First birth 2117 Last birth 3224	986	30,522

were, or how many on average in each; but taking 18 as the average number: then of gen. 25, $\frac{16}{18}$ were born; of gen. 26, $\frac{12}{18}$; of gen. 27, $\frac{10}{18}$; of gen. 28, $\frac{7}{18}$; of gen. 29, $\frac{5}{18}$; of gen. 30, $\frac{2}{18}$. These proportions of yield in each generation added to the population of gen. 24 (24,436) make a population of between 27,000 and 28,000. Allowing for *losses* (in perils before the Finding), 27,000 should be a safe estimate. This will make: Avari = 9,000, Eldar = 18,000. Therefore, since $\frac{1}{72}$ of 18,000 is 250, at the March, Vanyar were $\frac{7}{72}$ = 1,750; Ñoldor 7,000; and Lindar 9,250. These are very suitable numbers.

When do Ingwë, Finwë, and Elwë come in? If born before the Finding in FA 2016, they should be then adult, and at least 24: sc.

born no later than 1992. Now, this is the date of the last birth of gen. 23; but only gen. 30 is excluded (1992 could be among earliest births of gen. 29). But an Elf born in 1992 would be 240 [sun-]years old at the March, at which time the marriage age was 120; but it is important that neither Finwë nor Elwë should be married. So far in tentative schemes, the Embassy was less than 100 years after the Finding (sc. now before 2116, c. 2110). The three ambassadors should be *young*, *adventurous*, but direct descendants or "heirs" of Imin, Tata, and Enel; but they must be at least about 24 (or older!) at the time of their going to Valinor. If born in (say) 2086, they would be 146 at the March – still too old. The Embassy must be later, not more than 20 years before the March, allowing 10 years of absence and 10 years of preparation: say 2212. Let Ingwë be born in 2072; Finwë in 2120 (48 years later); and Elwë in 2126. Then at the Embassy Ingwë would be 140, Finwë 92, and Elwë 86. At the beginning of the March Ingwë would be 160, Finwë 112, and Elwë 106. Ingwë married about 2072 + 108 = FA 2180; his first child (Indis) was born in 2181 (so 51 at the March), his second in 2230, just before the March. Míriel, also in the 25th gen., was born about 2130?

A marginal note partly in broad nib-pen and partly in green ball-point pen reads:

Finwë and Elwë were friends, very adventurous. Olwë, born 2185, was 27 at the Embassy, 47 at the March (Elmo was born on the March). All three were direct descendants or heirs of the Three First Elves and regarded as chieftains.

Ingwë was 24th gen., his children therefore 25th. Finwë was gen. 25, Elwë gen. 25.

Finally, a note in green ball-point pen on the verso of one of the Scheme 7 sheets reads:

At the Finding in 2016 (spring) the oldest Elves would have been 2,015 years old. But they were 21 at the Awaking, and 24 in FA 4. Therefore at the Finding they were 24 + 2011 in *years*, but 24 + 14 (less 5 years) or practically 38 in age (= vigour and experience!).[23]

NOTES

1 Cf. the previous chapter.

2 A marginal note here, subsequently struck through in pencil, read: "Marriage was soon delayed by 3 *löar* as usually or beyond 24."

3 As first written, this sentence ended: "before the 'waning of the *hröa*' was far advanced". The last three words were struck through in ink. The words that later replaced them were added in pencil.

4 The footnote here entered as a marginal addition in pencil against this paragraph. The main text itself here originally read: "c. age 96 (= year 24 + *coimendi* 72 = 24 + 5,184 = c. 10,392)", with the various figures subsequently being altered in pencil.

5 In this sentence "two generations" was changed in pencil from original "three generations", and "6 children" was changed in pencil from original "9 children".

6 This was altered in pencil from: "the *average* was 6 children". About the 5th generation Tolkien actually wrote "⅗ @ 5[th gen.]", but I interpret this as an error for 1⅗, since the trend appears to be that the average number drops by about one third in generations succeeding the first two.

7 That is, at 24 growth-years (*löar*) + 24 VY = 24 + 24 × 144 *löar* = 24 + 3,456 = 3,480 *löar*.

8 The implication here is that Elves gestate in the womb for one sun-year, as in the previous chapter.

9 As first written, before pencil alterations, this sentence read: "It might be extended to 1 *coimen* or in some cases even more". Here, a *coimen* is 144 sun-years (again cf. the previous chapter).

10 The phrase "birth to begetting" replaced the original "conception to conception" in the act of writing.

11 As first written the final clause read: "+ 1 year at each end for gestation = 110". Further, the text originally, before strike-through in ink and pencil, read:

But the *Onnalúmë* of the First Elves was only 54 [sun-years]: intervals 3, 4, 5, 6, 7, 8, 9, 10 = 52 + 2 = 54. This was the *Onnalúmë* of the First Elves with 9 children, 2nd Elves, Third. The 4th generation produced only 6, and this remained usual average for three generations, before falling successively to 5, 4 where it long remained. *Onnalúmë* of the 6th gen. was intervals of 6, 12, 18, 24, 30 = 90 + 6 = 96. *Onnalúmë* of the 5th gen.: 12, 21, 30, 39 = 102 + 5 = 107. *Onnalúmë* of the 4th gen.: 24, 36, 48 = 108 [+ 4 =] 112.

12 Tolkien actually started this sentence with: "But the Finding should be (as above) not till VY 864", but since the only other texts in the "Time & Ageing" bundle that place the Finding in VY 864 are the generational tables that immediately *follow* this text in the bundle, I have removed the likely confusing direction.

13 It is unclear to what "Older Scheme" Tolkien is here referring. In the *Annals of Aman*, the Eldar do not start on the Great March until VY 1105 (X:81–2). It may be noted however that in text A of chap. VII, "The Awaking of the Quendi", above, Melkor is said to have discovered Men in VY 1080, which was 10 VY before the Valar opened their attack on Melkor.

14 This sentence was a later addition in green ball-point pen.

15 The father of Ingwë is nowhere else named (and is of course not found in *The Silmarillion* because he was there one of the First Elves and so had no parents), nor is his spouse, nor is he elsewhere than this bundle of texts identified as the father of Indis. In other somewhat contemporary sources Indis is said variously to be Ingwë's sister (X:261–2) or niece (XII:343; and cf. XII:365). Also, in other and earlier sources, the son of Ingwë is named *Ingwiel* (cf. V:144, 326).

16 This note is an addition in pencil.

17 990 here is an error for 1000. I have not corrected it, however, because of the additional error introduced in the 4th generation.

18 433 is an error for 423 (846 ÷ 2) and thus the number of married pairs, 428, is higher than it should be (c. 419), but Tolkien did not catch the mistake, and so all succeeding population numbers are higher than they should be (about 1,350 too high at the 29th generation).

19 This is another miscalculation: 6,900 + 1,236 is 8,136, not 7,136; but Tolkien has carried this through the rest of the generations.

20 This is yet another miscalculation: 10,772 + 1,188 is 11,960, not 12,160. This does however balance out the previous miscalculation.

21 Tolkien has here miscalculated the year of first marriage as 1160 (and thus the year of first birth as 1161). The correct number (the year of the first birth of the preceding generation, plus the age at marriage) is 1164 + 96 = 1260. Tolkien has carried this error through all subsequent generations, thus miscalculating all the subsequent years of first marriages and first births. As Tolkien subsequently refers to and makes calculations with these erroneous figures, I have let them stand. The correct years of first marriages and first births for generations 21–29 should be:

21)	First m. 1260	First birth 1261
22)	First m. 1369	First birth 1370
23)	First m. 1478	First birth 1479
24)	First m. 1587	First birth 1588
25)	First m. 1708	First birth 1709
26)	First m. 1829	First birth 1830
27)	First m. 1950	First birth 1951

28)   First m. 2083   First birth 2084
29)   First m. 2216   First birth 2217

22 See the previous editorial note. Tolkien's estimate of pre-March births are too
    high, if strictly determined by dividing the span of each date-range by the
    stated interval: by 2 or perhaps even 3 in generation 25 (intervals of 49), and
    by 1 or 2 in the subsequent generations (intervals of 51 and 61).

23 Tolkien here in fact wrote that "at the Finding they were 24 + 2011 in *age*",
    but I have altered this to avoid the confusion of the two different ages cited in
    this sentence, in which the first refers to age in sun-years but the second to age
    in Elvish life-years.

XVIII

ELVISH AGES & NÚMENÓREAN

This text is, for the most part, written in black nib-pen, on ten sides of engagement calendar pages for various weeks in May through September of 1965, which Tolkien clipped together. The rectos (only) of each page were numbered 1–8 by Tolkien in green ball-point pen. The text itself is dated by Tolkien in red ball-point pen in the top margin of the first page: "15/Aug/1965"; and again in black nib-pen in the body of the text. All footnotes are in red ball-point pen. In the top left margin of the first page Tolkien wrote in red ball-point pen: "This is the scheme followed in LR and Tale of Years".

For similar applications of the greatly increased rate of Sun-years to Valian Years of 144 : 1 to specific characters in the *legendarium*, see the texts presented here as chaps. IX, "Times-scales and Rates of Growth"; X, "Difficulties in Chronology"; and XI, "Ageing of Elves", above.

Elvish Ages
& Númenórean[1]

Elves' ages must be counted in two different stages: growth-years (GY) and life-years (LY). The GYs were relatively swift and in Middle-earth = 3 *löar*. The LYs were very slow and in Middle-earth = 144 *löar*.

Elves were *in womb* 1 GY. They reached "full speech" and intelligence in 2 GY. They reached "full growth" of body in 24 GY.*

They then had 48 LY of youth, and then 48 LY of "full age" or "steadfast body",[2] by which time their knowledge ceased to increase. After that the "fading time" began – of unknown duration (very slow) in which (as they say) the *fëa* slowly consumed the *hröa* until it became merely a "memory".

If we neglect the difference of speed and call each unit a "year", we then see that an elf[†] reached maturity at 24, end of "youth" at 72, and "old age" at 120.

In mortal equivalents the *age* in physical and other characteristics indicated can be found approximately by multiplying by ¾: "full speech" in 18 months, full growth in 18 years, end of youth approximately at 54, and old age approximately at 90.

The Elves thus (in their own scale) were grown up swiftly. They reached "full speech" in 18 months and physical maturity in 18 years. In *actual time*, however, reckoned in *löar* (Sun-years) the figures are these:

In womb: 3 years.
"Full speech" at 6 years old.
Full growth at 72 years old
Years of youth lasted 48 × 144 *löar* = 6,912 years
"Maturity" or standstill was not therefore reached till they were 6,984 years old.[3]
"Fading" began at 13,896 years old.

Thus after 72 years an Elf could be reckoned equal to an 18-year-old Mortal. But he was not 19 years old till he had lived for 216 years. In the "course" of the Second Age the elves (if of full growth when it began) aged only at the equivalent of a little less than 23 years (or in mortal equivalent less than 18). In the course of the Third Age they aged less than 21 years (or in mortal equivalent about 15).

---

* Puberty and full growth coincided (usually). It did not occur earlier, but might be delayed as late as 36 GY.

† There was no marked difference in sex, except that male puberty might be later.

The "resting time" for women* after childbirth was, however, reckoned in GY units: it was seldom less than 1 (= 3 sun-years), usually 2 (= 6 sun-years). An indefinite period could, however, elapse between births, depending only on the length of "youth". In times of peace the Elves usually set apart a *bearing-time* and then had no more children.

It may be noted that Elven women did not in fact usually bear children (never a first child) as late as 72 "end of youth" (mortal equivalent 54). The latest date for a first (and usually last) child was mortal equivalent 48 = 64 elf life-years.[†]

Examples of application to Narrative

Galadriel was born in Aman: "young and eager" at the beginning of the Exile; not yet full-grown: say 20. The March [back to Middle-earth] took a whole life-year of the survivors at whatever rate they were living, sc. to the young [but] "grown" it added 1 growth-year (3 *löar*); to the older and full-grown 1 life-year (144 *löar*). Therefore Galadriel was 21 when she reached Middle-earth. She became full-grown therefore (24) in 9 *löar* after arrival. By the end of the First Age – the overthrow of Thangorodrim and the ruin of Beleriand – she had added $\frac{600-9LY}{144}$ = approximately 4 LY. She was thus about 28 (or in mortal equivalent aged 21). Early in the Second Age she married Celeborn, and dwelt first in Lindon. In TA 1 she had added 23 years and was 51 (mortal equivalent 38). In TA 3021, when she sailed West, she was about 51 + 21 = 72 (mortal equivalent 54) and had just passed her "youth" and entered "maturity". *This fits well.*

Celeborn was older than Galadriel. It is difficult to be sure of any person whose origin goes far back into the First Age. Celeborn was in the 2nd generation of the three Elf-kings that led the March: he was by tradition the son of a younger (2nd) brother of Elwë (Thingol), called Elmo.[4] But the relative ages of the Kings Ingwë, Finwë, and

---

* And men; Elves claimed that both parents gave up or used more "vigour" in begetting and conception than mortals do. For each birth a male was reckoned to give up 1 life-year, and women 2 or more.

† All these are periods of change in physical life and efficiency. They have nothing to do with *rapidity of events*. Thus the "resting time" of 6 years is only 1/24 of an Elvish life-year or about a fortnight!! But it is as effective as a 6-year rest. An Elf did not have to wait 144 years (say) before begetting a second child. Elves spent their lives with *more* deeds and thoughts than men, not less.

Elwë is not known. Elmo *probably* was much younger than Finwë. Galadriel was of the 3rd generation, being the daughter of Finarphin (4th child), the son of Finwë (5th child). However, Galadriel was young at the Exile (which, whatever scale of ageing is assumed for the Elves while dwelling in Aman, means relatively near to the end of the Days of Bliss, and to the Exile). According to Elvish calculations, the period between the arrival of the Eldar in Aman and the end of the First Age in the Overthrow of Morgoth, was 3,100 *löar*. If that is correct,* then Celeborn was of unknown age when he entered Beleriand, but certainly 24 and full-grown, added in 3,100 *löar* nearly 21 life-years and was 45† at the end of the First Age. He married Galadriel shortly after when she was 28 (21 [mortal equivalent]). In TA 3021, when bereft of Galadriel he was 68 + 21 = 89 (66+ [mortal equivalent]) and advanced in "maturity".

Celebrían was born in Lindon at least 1 GY (3 *löar*) after the beginning of the Second Age; but probably (according to Elvish custom) 3 GY or 9 *löar*: say SA 9. Celebrían will be therefore full-grown (24 = 18) in SA 81 (9 + 72). When she weds Elrond (if the date is correct) she will have added life-years $\frac{3,441-81+100}{144} = \frac{3,460}{144} = 24$ and will be 48. Her marriage was delayed by the wars against Sauron.

But if (as seems a probable tale) Amroth was the son of Celeborn:[5] the following calculation is possible.[6] Celeborn and Galadriel were not married (though betrothed) during the dreadful years of the "Battle of Wrath", nor for some while afterwards in the confusions of the Second Age (i.e., not till SA 24).[7] Amroth their first child was born in SA 33: he was full-grown in SA 105, and at the founding of Eregion (SA 750) he was nearly 4½ years older: 29. At the time of the sack of Eregion (1697) he was 35. At the end of the Second Age he was 47+ (47⅙). At the time of the disaster in Moria, and the loss of Nimrodel, TA 1981, he was 60–61: nearing the end of youth, but (in mortal years) about 45. This is possible. The story was probably that Nimrodel would not give her love to the incoming non-Silvan elves, and hid herself in the mountains, not wishing to "go West".

In that case Celebrían could be younger? She was born in Lindon (say) SA 45, and was full-grown in SA 117. She would then be at wedding $\frac{3,441-117+100}{144}$ (= exactly 24) + 24 = 48.[8] Evidently this shift of 37 years makes insignificant difference. In TA 2510 [her departure

---

* It probably was not; it was very likely longer. In that case Celeborn must have been a descendant (not son) of Elmo and born in Beleriand.

† At least (thus = 33–34 [life-years]).

from Middle-earth] she would be $48 + \frac{2,510}{144} (= 17\frac{1}{2}) = 65$ (mortal equivalent 49).

The marriage would however be suitable since Celebrían would be 48 (mortal equivalent = 36) and Elrond (see next) nearly 57 (mortal equivalent = nearly 43). Mortal equivalent 36 was a frequent age in the troublous times for an Elven woman to bear a child.[*]

Elrond. The "Half-elven" should age slower than ordinary Men, before the "doom" of the Valar was spoken.[9] Probably at rate of 1 to 5 as for Elros, the only one who lived his life out as Half-elven. (Full growth being achieved at Elvish rate of 24 but reckoned in normal *löar.*)

Elrond was present (see LR I 256)[10] at the fall of Thangorodrim. Eärendil his father wedded Elwing in FA 525,[11] being then 23. Elrond[†] may have been born about 527–530. He was thus at least 70 at the fall of Thangorodrim in c. FA 600.[12] But this would be the [mortal] equivalent of $24 + 46/5 =$ approximately 33.

He was made Elven soon after, and would then slow down to the Elvish rate of 144 SY = 1 life-year. In SA 3441 he would be 56. In TA 100 he would be nearly 57, but still in youth (= mortal equivalent nearly 43).

The dates of Elrond's wedding (as in LR III 366) and of the births of his children are perfectly possible, but not likely.[13] For the present (Aug. 15, 1965) they are left unchanged, since they cannot be fixed until a decision is taken about the story of Celeborn and Galadriel, and their connexion with Lórien.[14]

The best story seems to be that outlined under "Galadriel",[15] in which they take part in the settlement of Eregion, and later of its defence against Sauron. But another possibility is that hinted at in the proposed emendations to the "Tale of Years" (LR III 366), by which they did not come to Lórien till TA 1060.[16] ☞ NB: alterations of the dates of Elves (including Elrond) only affects their lives at a rate of about 8 months = 100 years!

The case of Arwen. Taking her birth as TA 241, she will then be "full-grown" in TA 313 (241 + 72). In 2951, when she first meets Aragorn, she will be (in Elven Growth- and Life-years) $24 + 18\frac{1}{3}$

---

[*] The only way to make Celebrían effectively younger (e.g. 40 = mortal equivalent 30) would be to shift the wedding of Celeborn and Galadriel or arrange for later birth of Celebrían, but to reduce her to 40 would mean postponing the birth 8 × 144 = 1,152 years.

[†] But dates are confused here.

(nearly); $\frac{2,951-313}{144}$ = 42⅓ = mortal equivalent 31¾. Aragorn was only 20.

In 3019, when they were married, she would have aged very little and would be nearly Elvish 43 (24 + $\frac{3,019-313}{144}$) = mortal equivalent 32–3. But Aragorn would have lived 88 years and 4 months. His "age" would however be about "45". (See the note below on the Númenórean life-scale.)

At marriage Arwen became "mortal": she would then join her husband's scale of "expectation of life". ☞ This would not alter her "age" of 43 = approximate mortal equivalent 32–3. But for the purpose of reckoning her expectation of life (as a mortal), she would count as having lived 81 years (24 + (19 × 3)), and her further "permitted life" would be about 153 years (to total 234). She might have lived on to about Fourth Age 151. Aragorn as 88 at wedding would have a permitted life of 146 more years and could have lived to about 4A 144. When Aragorn "resigned life" in 4A 120 he thus resigned 24 years of life. He had lived 210 years and was already within his "decline".[17] Arwen was reckoned as 203 years at that time and also in the beginning of her decline. Aragorn resigned on the day of his birth, March 1, 4A 120. Arwen apparently "resigned" life and died on Cerin Amroth on March 1 in the following year, at Númenórean age 204 (mortal equivalent = 84). *So she was now and felt.* (Had she remained Elvish she would have been only 3,020 − 241 + 1 + 120 = 2,800 Sun-years old, giving an Elvish age of 24 + $\frac{2,800-72}{144}$ = almost exactly 43 (mortal equivalent about 33).

The Númenórean scale fixed by the Valar (for other than Elros) was for a life in full (if not "resigned" earlier) of thrice that of ordinary men. This was reckoned so: A "Númenórean" reached "full-growth" at 24 (as with Elves; but this was for them reckoned in Sun-years); after that, 70 × 3 = 210 years were "permitted" = total 234. But decline set in (at first slow) at the 210th year (from birth); so that a Númenórean had an expectation of 186 fully active years after reaching physical maturity.

For more on the Númenórean scale of life, see chaps. XI, "Lives of the Númenóreans", and XII, "Ageing of Númenóreans", in part three of this book.

NOTES

1 The title as originally written was added in the top margin in red ball-point pen. The words "& Númenórean" were added to the title, and the pages numbered, in green ball-point pen.

2 The phrase "'full age' or 'steadfast body'" is a replacement in red ball-point pen of original "maturity".

3 "Maturity' or standstill" is a replacement in red ball-point pen for original "old age" and for intermediary "full age" (which was also a replacement in red ball-point pen).

4 In later writing Elmo is the grandfather of Celeborn (not as here his father): cf. UT:233–4; also XI:350.

5 Tolkien would later reject this parentage for Amroth: see UT:240, 244.

6 As first written, before most of it was struck through, this concluding sentence (after the colon) read: "The following calculation is probable. Celeborn's wife [?stole] away and left him with a son, Amroth". In conjunction with this, it appears that the following footnote was supplied:

The Elves did *not* normally marry again, but after the judgement of Míriel they were permitted lawfully to do [so] if one partner deserted the other. This very seldom occurred; but in such a time of divided feelings as [the] end of [the] First Age this could occur.

7 The parenthetical clause "i.e. not till SA 24" was a later insertion in red ball-point pen.

8 In the first (1955) and Ballantine (1965) editions of *RotK*, the Tale of Years (App. B) still gave TA 100 as the year of Celebrían's wedding to Elrond. This was changed in the second revised edition (1966) to TA 109.

9 As first written, the text here continued:

In fact probably at the Númenórean rate of 1 year to 3 Sun-years after "full growth", which was at elvish rate 24 years. One of the Half-elven therefore

The continued text ends here, mid-sentence. However, to the first sentence Tolkien added this note in red ball-point pen:

Which was only the fixing or making more permanent this rate ("natural" [?in these cases]) already operative.

All of this was then struck through in black nib-pen.

10 In the latest trade editions this is LR:243.

11 This date agrees with that in text D of *The Tale of Years* (XI:352). The preceding text C gives the date as 527, emended to 530 (XI:348). The pre-*LR Annals of Beleriand* gave the date as 324, emended to 524 (see V:142–3).

12 The pre-*LR Annals of Beleriand* as emended gives the date of the start of the Great or Terrible Battle, at the culmination of which the fall of Thangorodrim occurred, as FA 550 (see V:144), and says that the war lasted fifty years from Fionwë's landing in 547 (V:143). Fionwë is said there to have departed Middle-earth in 597.

13 As first published (1955) and still in the second edition (1965) App. B gives TA 100 as the date of the wedding of Elrond and Celebrían, and TA 139 as the date of the births of Elladan and Elrohir, their twin sons. In the revised second edition (1966) these dates are changed to TA 109 and TA 130, respectively.

14 For more on this, see chap. XVI, "Galadriel and Celeborn", in part three of this book.

15 This is the text titled *Concerning Galadriel and Celeborn* that Christopher Tolkien describes and retells at UT:233–40.

16 No such change was in the event made to App. B.

17 Prior to the second edition of *LR* (1965), App. B gave the year of Aragorn's death (in the Shire Reckoning) as 1521, at which point he was 190 years old.

XIX

ELVISH LIFE-CYCLES

These two texts, while written with different implements on different types of paper, were clipped together by Tolkien and are closely connected conceptually. The second text, as shown below, can be confidently dated to c. 1969, and there is no reason to think that the first text doesn't date from about that time as well. Regarding Elvish life-cycles, cf. the c. 1968 text "From *The Shibboleth of Fëanor*" (VT41:9): "A note elsewhere in the papers associated with this essay reads: 'Elves did not have beards until they entered their third cycle of life. Nerdanel's father [cf. XII:365–6 n.61] was exceptional, being only early in his second.'" On the matter of Elvish beards, see chap. IV, "Beards", in part two of this book.

TEXT 1

This brief text was written somewhat hastily in black nib-pen, on one side of a sheet of lined paper.

The Elvish lives should go in *cycles*. They achieved longevity by a series of *renewals*. After birth and coming to *maturity* and beginning to *show age*, they began a period of *quiet* in which when possible they "retired" for a while, and issued from it renewed again in physical health to approximately the vigour of early maturity. (Their knowledge and wisdom were however progressively *cumulative*.)

This had not appeared in the periods dealt with (or had only begun towards the end of the Third Age).

The "Fading" was apparent in this way:

1) The periods of activity and full vigour became progressively shorter, and
2) The *renewal* was not so complete: they were a little older at each renewal than at the previous renewal.

TEXT 2

This text was written increasingly hastily in soft pencil on the versos of two sheets of Allen & Unwin publishing calendars for February and March of 1970.

Elves lived in life-cycles? sc. birth, childhood to bodily and mental maturity (as swift as that of Men) and then a period of *parenthood* (marriage, etc.) which could be delayed for a long time after maturity.[1] This "cycle" proceeded until *all* children of the "first period of parenthood" were grown up. Then there was a youth-renewing.

Elves married *in perpetuity* and as long as a first mate was alive and incarnate they had no thought of other marriage. In Aman the only case of a breach was Míriel/Finwë. In Middle-earth, especially in the Elder Days, violent death was frequent; but the slain ([?etc.]) could by the Valar be restored to life.*[2] At their *own* choice. The Valar became more [?gentle] in this matter – and the griefs of the Eldar were often so great before death that being unwilling to return was held pardonable – especially to those having no wife or ungrown children. (Only in one known case, Beren, did the Valar – by special permission of Eru – restore a human body to life and suffer its *fëa* to return.) If a wife was left widowed (or vice versa) forever remarriage was permissible, but seldom occurred.

In lives not marred by death or who enter [it] the "youth-renewing" left the pair young and vigorous, but for awhile *though they dwelt together* they went about their own businesses and [?recovered] in [?] before a second period of parenthood arose. (Some never entered such a new period.) But, though it was long before it was noticed, at each new "cycle" their vigour of the Eldar waned a little. Before the end of the Second Age youth-renewals and the re-Generation of

---

* By healing of the body or its complete rebuilding of one. That the Eldar were ever "reborn" is a fancy of Men. The relation of *fëa* and *hröa* made this impossible. The *fëa* was a gift of Eru and fitted from the beginning and *forever* to its particular body.

children were becoming rare.* The Eldar were "fading": whether this was by the original design of Eru, or a "punishment" for the sins of the Eldar, is not certain. But their "immortality" within the Life of the World was guaranteed, and they could depart to the Blessed Realm if they willed.

NOTES

1 On the permanence of marriage, see the discussion of MARRIAGE in App. I.

2 Tolkien placed a query mark next to this note.

---

* They were not "immortal" in eternity.

XX

TIME AND ITS PERCEPTION

This text occupies six sides of three sheets of unlined paper, which Tolkien has pinned together. It is written in an increasingly hasty hand in black nib-pen, with additions and some revisions made in red ball-point pen. It dates from c. 1959.

The Valar reckoned in *twelves*. During the Days of the Trees:

12 Tree-hours	=	1 Valian Day	VD
144 VD	=	1 Valian Year	VY
144 VY	=	1 Valian Age	VA

But:

1 VY	=	144 Years of Men	MY
1 VD	=	1 MY	
1 VH	=	¹⁄₁₂ MY or one month about 30½ days	

Any (mortal) creature (sc. things appearing inside Eä) in Valinor during the Trees would have aged only with the rate of 1/144 of its *natural* Middle-earth speed (save only the Quendi who were immortal). At the awaking of the Quendi this proportion 1/144 (with regard especially to Men) was natural, and those that came speedily to Aman maintained this. But in spite of "immortality" (within Arda) the ageing of Arda soon affected those who remained in Middle-earth: quickest those who refused the Summons. But the Eldar who remained (or the Sindar) were soon reduced to a rate of 1/100 more or less and that proportion can be used in reckoning the "relative age" of Elves in the Silmarillion. For High Elves it probably remained more or less so until the end of the Third Age and then, for those remaining in Middle-earth, it quickened rapidly.

It must be considered that (disregarding actual length of the time scale) Quendi were similar to Men in these respects: though they *began* quicker they soon slowed down, and reached maturity about 20. Their normal marriage time was therefore approximately between 20 and 60. But in earlier times, before the end of the Third Age, while they were still *physically* vigorous, unlike Men, they *could* postpone the marriageable state. Normally they only had *one* period of child-begetting and bearing lasting 20–40 years or more after marriage. But if they did not *use* this power at the normal time it could be postponed till they were 100 or a little more.

But it must then be considered that in earliest times and in Aman always that meant a "year" was in fact the *yên* or 144 years (and even later, after the Death of the Trees, was 100 years). So that an Elf in earlier times or in Aman matured in mortal terms when about 2,880 years old, and could bring forth children up to the age 8,660, or an exceptional one 14,400. In later times these ages reduced to 2,000, 6,000, and 10,000.

> At some point Tolkien struck through all the above text, but specifically retained the following:

Elves should awake about VY 1050 and reach Beleriand c. 1450 = 400 VY = after 57,600 years. Their West-march began about 1445 and took 144 × 5 MY = 720 years.[1]

Men awake in VY 1500 and reach Beleriand in 1531 = 31 VY × 144 = 4,464 years. (Too little!)

Men must awake *before* Melkor is taken to Valinor, or *after* his escape. In the former case it must be about VY 1050, in the latter much more time must be devised between the Return of Melkor and the arrival of Men in Beleriand.[2] Fleeing Aman, crossing the Ice, sojourn in Arvalin could take a [?great while].[3]

If Men awake in 1050, Elves must awake earlier.[4]

Time in Lórien? See explanation in LR vol. I but adjusted except for Elves. Probably mortals entering had [?their] growth-rate and ageing altered, not to the Elvish rate but much slowed, say to 1 : 7: so the true 30/28 days seemed about 4. Then downstream for a short while.[5]

These rates and calculations are concerned only with growth and ageing, and *not* with the perception or *appreciation* of time as subjectively long or short (except in so far as such perception may be affected by ageing, etc).

The question of "perception of Time" is more difficult to deal with, since it varies with persons, circumstances, and kinds of persons, and it is difficult also to express or communicate, so that when the Eldar conversed with the Atani on such matters neither side was sure that they understood the other's clearly. And again the *fëar* of Elves and of Men are not corporeal or subject [?actually] to Time, and [are] able to move in it in thought and retrospect and so can have divergent views of the subjective length of one and the same time or experience. They may say of [?such] it fleeted by and yet it seemed to endure for ages.

These things however, so far as the Eldar are concerned, seem specially to influence time-perception and/or its recollection. On one side youth (inexperience, vigour) and eagerness; on the other age (experience, failing vigour), dullness. And secondly, *full occupation* in delight, affection, or mutual interest; and on the other side *lack of occupation*, or mutual interest, and absence of delight or a presence of distaste or pain.

The "length of time" that is attributed to *Youth* as against Age is probably chiefly one of *hope* and *expectation*, [?allowed] to inexperience. A child's afternoon seems a boundless vista – but this is chiefly in [?thought] or before it is spent. If it is fully of "occupation" it [?will race by soon] like a flash, and teatime will come before anything but a beginning of the [?plan] is achieved.

The old look forward with hard experience – an afternoon they know will not suffice for much achievement. It seems brief in prospect (as it proves), but whether it *actually during the experiencing of it* seems any briefer than the same actual period in childhood (spent in about the same amount of occupation) may be much doubted.

In Age to Men (and Elves) years seem to go swiftly they say, but that is for various reasons, some really of "reasoning" rather than feeling. They go "swiftly" because of experience: (1) as few new things or none are encountered, there is little to [?save] in a memory already [?stocked]. (The mind is also duller and hardly notes the present.) (2) there is all the same *no desire to come to the end*, or rather *desire not to do so*; the time therefore seems to stop though [?hands] are unable to stay it. As if two travellers went along the same road: the one has never journeyed there before, and he is young and full of hope, maybe eager to reach the end and enter upon other roads; the other has travelled the same way many, many times, and barely notes the things seen or passed, and he is tired maybe, and yet fears to reach the end, having little hope of going on to further journey. To which will that road seem shorter? To the young [?halting (at least in light and ? ?]) barely at all [?] and yet not [?hoarding] the [?moments] it may seem a long and memorable journey in experience and in retrospect. To the older it will hold little of memory to distinguish it from other journeys like it, and yet its end will come too soon. It will seem swift, at least in retrospect.

The older also will in *retrospect* retain the feeling of [?experience here ? ? ?]. As when an old man wonders at the short time in which a babe is born and grows up to run. For this occurs now while [?his mind] is [?] and the days go by quickly, but such things he remembers occurring earlier in his life (or his own childhood) and they *seemed longer*. But he knows they were not.[6] Therefore he says *now* the time seems short in which they occur!

NOTES

1 As first written, the March began in 1400 and took 7,200 years. Tolkien altered the figures in red ball-point pen and placed a large asterisk against it in the same pen.

2 Tolkien placed a large asterisk against this paragraph in black nib-pen.

3 This sentence was written in the right margin in red ball-point pen.

4 This sentence was likewise written in red ball-point pen, in the bottom margin.

5 As first written, the slowed rate was 1 : 15. According to *LR* App. B, the Fellowship entered Lothlórien on Jan. 17 and departed on Feb. 16, so staying there a total of 29 nights. Tolkien subsequently enclosed this and the preceding paragraphs back to that starting with "Elves should awake about VY 1050" in red ball-point pen lines, probably indicating his wish to retain them.

6 Regarding the perception of time in terms of occupation and inspection, see chaps. IV, "Time-scales", and XII, "Concerning the Quendi in their Mode of Life and Growth", above.

XXI

NOTES ON ELVISH
TIME-REFERENCE

The following texts are all derived, not from the "Time and Ageing" file, but rather from Tolkien's late (c. 1968) writings on his invented languages. This seems a convenient place to share Tolkien's further thoughts on the Elvish perspective on time.

TEXT 1

Elvish time.

Our language is confused, using *after* or *before* both (in certain circumstances) of the future. We sometimes think and speak of the future as what lies before us, we look *ahead*, are *pro-vident*, forward-looking, yet our ancestors *preceded* us and are our *fore-*fathers; and any event in time is *before* one that is later. We speak as if events and the succession of human lives were an endless column moving forward into the unknown, and those born later are behind us, will *follow* us; yet also as if though facing the future we were walking backwards or being driven backwards, and our children and heirs (*post*erity!) were ahead of us and will in each generation go further forwards into the future than we. A widow is a *relict*, one left behind, by a husband who goes on.[1]

As far as a single experiencing mind goes, it seems a most natural transference of spatial or linear language to say that the past is *behind* it, and that it *advances* forward into the future; that later events are *before* or in *front* of earlier ones. At the point when the individual ceases the survivors go on further ahead of him. All living creatures are in one mass or column marching on, and falling out individually while others go on. Those who do so are *left behind*. Our ancestors, who fell out earlier, are further behind, behind us for ever.

In Elvish sentiment the *future* was not one of hope or desire, but a decay and retrogression from former bliss and power. Though inevitably it lay *ahead*, as of one on a journey, "looking forward" did not imply anticipation of delight. "I look forward to seeing you again" did not mean or imply "I wish to see you again, and since that is arranged and/or very likely, I am pleased." It meant simply "I expect to see you again with the certainty of foresight (in some circumstances), or regard that as very probable" – it might be with fear or dislike, "foreboding". Their position, as of latter-day sentiment, was as of exiles driven forward (against their will), who were in mind or actual posture ever looking backward.

But in actual language time and place had distinct expressions.

Text 2

The Eldar regarded all that was *past* as behind them, their faces being *towards* the future. With reference to time therefore words with a basic sense "behind, at the back" = "before"; and those originally meaning "in front, ahead" = "after".

Nonetheless in thinking of people and the generations they spoke as if the elders were leaders marching at the head of a line of *followers*. It thus became difficult to speak of "those behind" = "peoples of former days" being followed by later generations. *But* such terms as *leading* and *following* were to them *pictorial* analogies, only used with a definite transfer of sense: as if we were to speak of *looking back* into the dark mists of days *before* our time.

For ordinary purposes, e.g., as what happened before my time, "*behind*" was used, at least originally. In practice, Common Eldarin had developed four distinct prepositional or adverbial bases:

A. (1) before of time (2) behind of place
B. (1) after of time   (2) in front of, ahead of place

TEXT 3

Time reference

The Eldar spoke of people and generations as if the picture before their minds was of a line on the march with the elders *leading* ahead and the later-born *following*. This was no doubt due to the fact that the elder-born so frequently remained among them. It coloured all their speaking of time. They usually imagined themselves *looking* [?*inwardly*] to what has been, that is they *found* the past (and do not call it "looking back") and had their backs to the future and would not call anticipation of it "looking ahead" but "looking back" as looking over the shoulder.

Tolkien struck through this text, and began again:

The Eldar did *not* use a linear-space picture of the time relation, unless they were deliberately constructing an analogical *picture*. That is, they conceived the relation of precedence or consequence in *time* as something different from preceding or following in space.

Of course they could, speaking of a long experience as a journey, as if passing from one year to another were like going from one place to another (though the much decreased speed of time-apprehension ? ? ? was envisioned made this much less usual than with us). Or they could speak of older people as if they were at the *head* of the march, and the later-born as *following*: this was a fairly common "figure of speech", but was much more a *figure* than with us. They did not call elders *ancestors* = preceders.

For one thing (as they said) in space one can turn and look in many directions; in *time* one's position is fixed. Hence the two groups confused in our language were *distinct*:

A. (1) before, earlier of time   (2) before, in front of place
B. (1) after, later of time   (2) after, behind of place

NOTES

1 The word *relict* meaning 'widow' (now considered archaic) is borrowed from Old French *relicte*, '(woman) left behind', itself derived ultimately from the Latin verb *relinquere* 'to leave behind' (whence also English *relinquish*).

XXII

A FRAGMENT FROM
THE ANNALS OF AMAN

This brief typewritten text appears to be a late reworking of part of the chronology of *The Annals of Aman*. (see X:47, and especially X:92–5), and so probably dates from c. 1958.

1260. The last of the Vanyar leave Tirion and go to dwell upon the west-slopes of Taniquetil. Fingon son of Fingolfin awoke.[1]

1300. Thingol (by which name Elwë Singollo was after known in Beleriand) and Melian his Queen begin the building of Menegroth in Doriath, with the help of the Naugrim.
Daeron, minstrel and lore-master of Thingol, contrives his Runes (*i Cirdh Daeron*).
Turgon son of Fingolfin and Inglor son of Finrod awoke in Eldamar.[2]

1320. The Orcs first appear in Beleriand.[3]

1350. The Nandor led by Denethor cross the Mountains of Lindon and come to Ossiriand. They are called the Green-elves.[4]

1362. Isfin, the White Lady of the Ñoldor, is born in Tirion.[5]

1400. Here ended the Captivity of Melkor. Melkor is released from Mandos, and sues for pardon at the feet of Manwë before the assembled Valar.

1410. Melkor is permitted to go free in Valinor. He seeks the friendship of the Ñoldor.

1450. Fëanor makes the SILMARILLI.

NOTES

1 *The Annals of Aman* (*AAm*) gives the year of the departure of the Vanyar from
   Tirion as 1165 (X:87) and the year of Fingolfin's birth as 1190 (X:92).

2 *AAm* gives the following dates: establishment of Menegroth in 1250 (X:93),
   Daeron's invention of his Runes and the birth of Turgon in 1300 (X:106).
   The events for 1300 were a later addition to the *AAm*.

3 *AAm* likewise has an added entry for 1320 giving that as the year Orcs first
   appear in Beleriand (X:106). All subsequent dates agree with *AAm* as given at
   X:93–4.

4 *AAm* has an added entry for 1350 giving that as the year of the entry of the
   Nandor in Ossiriand (X:93, 102 n.8).

5 *AAm* likewise has an added entry for 1362 giving that as the year of Isfin's
   birth (X:102 n.8).

XXIII

A FRAGMENT FROM
THE GREY ANNALS

For reasons that eluded even Christopher Tolkien, a fragment of
what appears to be drafting for the *Grey Annals* (subsequently
struck through) came to be collected into the "Time & Ageing"
bundle. For the most part it is similar to the account given at XI:55
(and more so after numerous pencil emendations), but there are
many differences in detail, and it features an otherwise unpublished poetic version of Fingolfin's challenge of Morgoth to battle
before the gates of Angband (itself clearly deriving from *The Lay
of Leithian* ll. 3552–57, III:285); and so I give the fragment here
in full.

… [all that beheld] his onset fled in amaze, deeming that Oromë
himself was come, for a great madness of ire was upon him. Thus he
came alone even to Angband's gate and smote upon it once again,
and sounded a challenge upon his silver horn, calling upon Morgoth
to come forth to combat, crying:

> "Come forth, thou coward lurking lord
> to fight with thine own hand and sword!
> Thou wielder of hosts of slaves and thrall,
> pit-dweller, shielded by strong walls,
> thou foe of gods and elven-race,
> come forth and show thy craven face!

"Come forth thou coward king, and fight with thine own hand! Thou den-dweller, wielder of thralls, liar and lurker. Come foe of Gods and Elves, for I would see thy craven face!"[1]

Then Morgoth came. For he could not refuse such a challenge before all his folk and captains. But Fingolfin was not daunted by him,[2] though he towered above the Elven-king like a shadow of thunder or a storm above a lonely tree, and his vast black unblazoned shield was like a thundercloud that drowns the stars.[3] Long they fought, and Ringil pierced Morgoth with seven wounds, and his cries were heard in all the northlands.[4] But wearied at last Fingolfin was beaten to the earth by the great hammer that Morgoth wielded as a mace,[5] and Morgoth set his foot upon his neck and crushed him.[6] In his last throe the Elven-king pinned the foot of his Enemy to the ground with Ringil, and the black blood gushed forth.[7]

NOTES

1 After later pencil emendation, Fingolfin's prose challenge ends:

"Den-dweller, wielder of thralls, liar and lurker, foe of gods and Elves, come for I would see thy craven face!"

2 This was subsequently altered in pencil to read: "Fingolfin withstood him".

3 The words "that drowns the stars" were subsequently struck through in pencil.

4 This sentence was subsequently struck out in pencil, and replaced as described below.

5 The words "that Morgoth wielded as a mace" were subsequently struck through in pencil, as redundant following the replacement described below.

6 This sentence was altered in pencil to begin "Fingolfin fell", and the words "that Morgoth wielded as a mace" were struck through (see further below).

7 Beneath this, and also in the top and left margins of the page, Tolkien added some additional textual elements in ink and pencil, with pencil lines indicating (roughly) where each element should be inserted in the text, thus in conjunction with the other changes noted above, bringing it into much closer agreement with the text given at XI:55:

so that his eyes shone like the eyes of the Valar [*to be inserted after* "a great madness of ire was upon him"]

overshadowed the star of Fingolfin [*to be inserted after* "his black unblazoned shield"] before the face of his Captains [*replacing* "before all his folk and captains"]

Morgoth fought with a great hammer, Grond, that he wielded as a mace, and Fingolfin with Ringil. Swift was Fingolfin, and avoiding the strokes of Grond, so that Morgoth smote but the ground (and [at] each stroke a great pit was made), he gave Morgoth seven wounds with his sword, and the cries of Morgoth echoed in the Northlands. [*to be inserted after* "like a thundercloud"]

and filled the pits of Grond. Then Morgoth lifted the body and would cast it to the wolves [*to be inserted at the end of the text*]

There remains one very rough pencil note in the left margin, with no indication that it is to be inserted here (but see XI:56):

Great wolves [?assailed] Rochallor and he escaped only because of his swiftness, and ran to Hithlum and there died.

PART TWO

BODY, MIND, AND SPIRIT

INTRODUCTION

As seen in part one, and further in various texts published in *Morgoth's Ring* (see especially X:217–25), by the late 1950s Tolkien had become greatly interested in the nature and relationship of spirits (in Quenya *fëar*) and bodies (Q. *hröar*) in incarnates – that is, beings like Men and Elves that are by nature a union of a material body and a created, immaterial soul. As will be seen herein, consideration of bodies and spirits, and the closely related matter of minds, continued into the last years of Tolkien's life, and ran in both metaphysical and mundane directions: from the nature of being and identity, the relation of free will to divine foreknowledge, thought-communication, and the manner and mode of Elvish reincarnation; to the finger-games of Elvish children, and the question of which races and characters did or did not have beards.

It will further be seen that the metaphysics of Middle-earth as reflected here is firmly Catholic: that is, it is clearly informed by the metaphysics espoused by St. Thomas Aquinas (itself deeply influenced by Aristotle's metaphysics), which enjoyed a dramatic reaffirmation by the Catholic Church during Tolkien's youth, under Pope Leo XIII (who reigned 1878–1903). As Tolkien famously said, "*The Lord of the Rings* is of course a fundamentally religious and Catholic work" (L:172), a statement that has puzzled many critics, because both *The Lord of the Rings* and Tolkien's wider *legendarium* are all but devoid of references to any religious *cultus* (let alone a Catholic system of rites and worship). As I hope the texts presented here will show, the key word in Tolkien's statement, often ignored as simply emphatic, is *fundamentally*: that is, in its foundations, in its essential nature. In these particular texts, this is most clearly seen in Tolkien's implied commitment to *hylomorphism*: that is, the Aristotelean-Thomistic teaching that all material things are ultimately a union of created but undifferentiated *prime matter* (in Quenya, *erma*) with a God-given *form* (in Tolkien's parlance here, *pattern*, that which gives each portion of *erma* the nature and shape of the thing that it is). It is also reflected in the commitment to the belief that everything, even Morgoth himself, was as created *good*, but that due to the free will possessed by every creature with a rational mind, they could fall: as one Vala and various Maiar, and Men corporately, did; and that even Manwë, had he asserted his own will and judgement over Eru's, would likewise have fallen. Further discussion of these and similar matters is provided for the interested reader in App. I.*

---

* The Thomistic nature of Tolkien's metaphysics has been most fully delineated – though without reference to the materials in this book – by Jonathan S. McIntosh in his important monograph, *The Flame Imperishable: Tolkien, St. Thomas, and the Metaphysics of Faërie* (Angelico Press, 2018).

I

BEAUTY AND GOODNESS

This text comprises a selection from etymological notes by Tolkien, made probably c. 1959–60.

These notes were previously published in slightly different form in *Parma Eldalamberon* 17 (2007), pp. 150, 162.

√*ban.* (related to √*man*?) This appears originally to have referred simply to 'beauty' – but with implication that it was due to *lack of fault*, or *blemish.* Thus Q *Arda Vanya* 'Arda Unmarred', *Arda Úvana* = Arda Marred. *ilvanya, ilvana* 'perfect'.

[Derivatives:] Q *Vána*, name of Valië, the most perfectly 'beautiful' in form and feature (also 'holy' but not august or sublime), representing the natural unmarred perfection of form in living things. *vanya*, beautiful, unmarred, of fair unspoiled form, &c. *vanima* (only of living things, especially Elves or Men) 'beautiful'. *úvano, úvanimo,* a monster, corrupt or evil creature. S *bân* or *bain*, fair, good, wholesome, favourable, *not* dangerous, evil or hostile.

√*man* 'good'. This implies that a person/thing is (relatively or absolutely) "unmarred": that is in Elvish thought unaffected by the disorders introduced into Arda by Morgoth: and therefore is true to its nature and function.[1] If applied to mind/spirit it is more or less equivalent to morally good; but applied to *bodies* it naturally refers to *health* and to absence of *distortions, damages, blemishes*, etc.

Derivatives: *⋆Āmān*: Q *Aman* (aman-), S *Avon* 'Unmarred State', especially applied to the "unmarred" western regions, of which *Valinor* (abode of the Valar) was part. *Manwë* Quenya name of the "Elder King", Lord of the Valar of *Aman. māna*, any good or fortunate thing;

a boon or "blessing", a *grace* (being especially used of some thing/person/event that helps or amends an evil or difficulty). (Cf. a frequent ejaculation on receiving aid in trouble: *yé mána (ma)* = 'what a blessing, what a good thing!') *manya-* 'to bless' (sc. either to afford grace or help or to wish it).

NOTES

1 See EVIL (AS LACK OF PERFECTION) in App. I.

II

GENDER AND SEX

This text, found among Tolkien's linguistic papers, where it is located in a large group of printed Allen & Unwin notices dating from late 1968, is written in a clear hand in black nib-pen.

Gender and Sex

The Elvish languages did not distinguish grammatically between male (masculine) and female (feminine). Thus *se* meant 'he' or 'she'. But there was a distinction made between *animate* and *inanimate*. *Animates* included not only rational creatures ("speaking people"), but all things living and reproducing their kind. To these were applied the pronouns such as *se* 'he/she'. *Inanimates* included not only all physical objects recognized or thought of as distinct things, such as "river, mountain", or substances such as metal, stone, gold, but also parts of bodies or living shapes whether dead, or thought of as analysable parts or organs of a living whole: such as *leg, eye, ear, hand, arm, head, horn, flesh, blood, flower, seed, root, stem, tentacle, skin, leather, hair*, etc. It also included all grammatical abstracts such as *thought, act, deed, colour, shape, feeling, sight, mood, time, place, force, strength*, etc.

NB: It did not include *mind*, or *spirit* when thought or spoken of as an integral thing, and attributed to a rational creature. There were several words in Quenya that bore those senses, but those regarded as only functions or operations of the individual "mind-soul" went with all other "abstracts" into the inanimate class. The organs of the body, such as "heart" were never used for or as the "seat" of thought, wisdom, feeling, or emotion; but this may have been due to later thought and analysis. The physical organ 'heart' had the base *khom* (Q. *hón*, *hom*) and this was not in recorded Quenya used of feelings; but an ancient derivative *khomdō* (Q. *hondo*) was often used as the (seat of the) deepest feelings, such as pity or hate parallel to *ōre* 'innermost mind', and region of deep thought, where also inspiration or "guidance" was received.[1] In *The Lord of the Rings* this was translated 'heart', as in "my heart tells me", etc. Cf. Treebeard's adjective applied to Orcs, *sincahonda* 'flint-hearted'.[2] *hondo* was probably influenced in formation by *indō* (probably < *im-dō* 'self, innermost being' (taken as referring to the centre of "reason")), very similar to *ōre*. (*ōre* was not related to √OR/RO 'up, rise', but was from √GOR 'deep, profound', seen in Q. *orda* 'profound'; cf. S. *gorð* 'deep thought', *gæria* 'ponder'.)

In phrases such as: "A's mind was wise/good, it seldom erred", *it* would be *se* (animate), and it would not matter to the sense if this was translated 'he' and taken to refer to A.

NOTES

1　For more on Q. *óre*, see chap. X, "Notes on *Óre*", below.

2　An apparently contemporary typescript note among Tolkien's linguistic papers reads:

CE *khōn-*, *khond-* was only used of the physical heart, and that was not regarded as or supposed to be a centre of either emotion or thought. Thus when Treebeard uses the adjectives *morimaitë*, *sincahonda* 'black-handed, flint-hearted' of the Orks, these were both physical in reference – as indeed were all the other adjectives, whatever they may have implied with regard to Orkish minds and characters. *Sincahonda* referred to their immense staying power in exertion, marching, running, or climbing, which gave rise to the jesting assertion that their hearts must have been made of some exceedingly hard substance; it did not mean pitiless. The last adjective 'blood-thirsty' (*serkilixa*) was also literal: the Orks actually drank the blood of their victims. A compound of similar kind meaning 'hard-hearted, pitiless', would have been in Quenya *ondórëa*.

III

ELDARIN HANDS, FINGERS, AND NUMERALS

The three texts presented here are excerpted from material published (in slightly differently edited form) as *Eldarin Hands, Fingers and Numerals* in *Vinyar Tengwar* 47–8 (2005).[1]

In this presentation, space between paragraphs indicates where intervening text of a more linguistic or otherwise technical nature has not been included.

Text 1

The first text was composed on a typewriter on the blank sides of printed Allen & Unwin stationery, one sheet of which is a publication notice dated Jan.–Feb. 1968, which provides an approximate date of composition. The typescript consists of nine pages, numbered by Tolkien in ink 1–5, 6A, 6B, 7A, and 7B (pages 6B and 7B are revised versions of 6A and 7A). The typescript itself bears only the title "E. Hands" written in ink at the top of the first page. The full title, "Eldarin Hands, Fingers & Numerals", appears on a piece of cardboard placed before the first page of the typescript, and is adopted here as suitable title for this grouping of texts.

The Words for *Hand*

The Eldar regarded the hand as of great personal importance, second only to the head and face. Common Eldarin had a number of words for this part of the body. The oldest (probably) and the one that retained a general and unspecialized sense – referring to the entire hand (including wrist) in any attitude or function, had probably the primitive Common Eldarin form *maȝa, a stem proper to the sense 'hand' and having no other meaning. It may have been related (though this is naturally merely conjectural) to C.E. MAGA, a stem meaning 'good' – but without moral reference, except by implication: sc. it was not the opposite of 'evil, wicked' but of 'bad (damaged, imperfect, unfit, useless)', and the adjectival stem derived, *magrā, meant 'good for a purpose or function, as required or desired, useful, proper, fit'.

Common Eldarin had a base KWAR 'press together, squeeze, wring'. A derivative was *kwārǎ: Q. quár, T. pār, S. paur. This may be translated 'fist', though its chief use was in reference to the tightly closed hand as in using an implement or a craft-tool rather than to the 'fist' as used in punching. Cf. the name Celebrin-baur > Celebrimbor ['Silver-fist']. This was a Sindarized form of T. Telperimpar (Q. Tyelpinquar). It was a frequent name among the Teleri, who in addition to navigation and ship-building were also renowned as silver-smiths. The famous Celebrimbor, heroic defender of Eregion in the Second-age war against Sauron, was a Teler, one of the three Teleri who accompanied Celeborn into Exile.[2] He was a great silver-smith, and went to Eregion attracted by the rumours of the marvellous metal found in Moria, Moria-silver, to which he gave the name mithril. In the working of this he became a rival of the Dwarves, or rather an equal, for there was great friendship between the Dwarves of Moria and Celebrimbor, and they shared their skills and craft-secrets. In the same way Tegilbor was used for one skilled in calligraphy (tegil was a Sindarized form of Q. tekil 'pen', not known to the Sindar until the coming of the Noldor). In Common Eldarin and the derived languages the *kwāra was also used as a symbol of power and authority.

   Common Eldarin had also a word *palatā, a derivative of Common Eldarin stem PAL, 'extended': palat, palan- 'wide, extended' (originally also with the implication that the area was more or less flat and even, without hindrance to movement, or view). Cf. Q. palan, adv. 'far and wide'; palda 'wide, broad' (< *palnā). *palátā, Q. palta, T. plata, S. plad meant 'the flat of the hand, the hand held upwards or forwards, flat and tensed (with fingers and thumb closed or spread)'. This attitude had various important significances as gestures in Eldarin custom (Q. Mátengwië, 'language of the hands'). One hand palm upwards was a gesture of a recipient, or of someone asking for a gift; both hands so held indicated that one was at the service or command of another person. A hand held palm forwards* towards another was a gesture of prohibition, commanding silence or halting or ceasing from any action; forbidding advance, ordering retreat or departure; rejection of a plea.† The gesture of the Dúnadan, Halbarad (L.R. III 47)[3] was therefore not an Elvish sign, and would have been ill received by them. In such a case their gesture was to open both arms wide, somewhat below shoulder-level, with palms outward: in this case as in the Mannish gesture the open palm signified "no weapon", but the Elvish gesture added "not in either hand".‡ Extension of the fingers modified the significance. The gesture of a receiver or asker, if the fingers and thumb were opened, indicated distress and urgency of need or poverty. The gesture of prohibition in the same way was made more hostile and threatening, indicating that if the command was not immediately obeyed force or weapons would be used.

Left and Right

No distinction was felt between right and left by the Eldar. There was nothing queer, ill-omened (sinister), weak, or inferior about the "left". Nor anything more correct and proper (right), of good omen, or honour about the "right".§ The Eldar were "ambidexters", and the allocation of different habitual services or duties to the right or the left was a purely individual and personal matter, undirected by any general inherited racial habit.[4] An Elda could usually write

---

* Shoulder-high or higher. The raising added emphasis.

† So that a hand was never held up in this way in greeting or welcome. In such a case the hand would be raised with palm backwards, and for emphasis with waving of the fingers towards the signaller. In casual greeting in passing, when no further speech was desired, the hand was held edge forward, with or without movement of the fingers.

‡ Necessarily from their point of view, since the Eldar made no distinction between the hands and their operations: see further below on Left and Right. The gesture of Halbarad was with the right hand.

§ A "nursery" or instructional substitution for the older word Gmc. *tehs-*, *tehswa-* (I.E. *deks-* as in Latin *dexter*), which was preserved only in Gothic and OHG, except precariously in place names such as the island *Texel*: in which the meaning may have been 'south'. This use of 'right' as south is found in Sanskrit, and is usual in Keltic; but is secondary and due to reckoning the compass points from a position facing East (the rising sun). The I.E. *deks-* stem was probably in fact connected with the stem *dek-* 'right, proper, good, fitting', familiar in English borrowings from Latin: *decent, decorous*, etc.

with either hand; if he wrote with the left he began on the right side, if with the right on the left side – because the Eldar found it more convenient that the writing hand should not be liable to cover what had been written immediately before the letter that it was engaged on.* [5]

In making the above-described gestures either hand was used without change in significance. Making them with both was more emphatic, indicating that the gesture expressed a command from a whole community or party, or from a king or authority via a herald or subordinate. The stone images of the Argonath each held up a hand, palm forwards, but it was the left hand (L.R. I 409).[6] It was a Mannish gesture: the left hand was more hostile; and its use allowed the display in the right hand of a weapon: an axe.

> Elsewhere among Tolkien's papers is found this sentence (which he rendered in both Quenya and English) that also elaborates on this concept of Elvish ambidexterity:

The Elves were ambidexters; consequently, the left hand was not to them evil in their imaginations. On the contrary. For if one turned the face westwards as was usual, the left hand pointed away from Melkor (in the North), and if northwards, it pointed towards Aman (the Blessed Land).[7]

The fingers

In Quenya the fingers were called, reckoning from the thumb outwards: *nápo* 'thumb'; *lepetas* 'first or index finger'; *lepenel* or *lepende* 'middle finger'; *lepekan* 'fourth finger'; *lepinka* 'little finger'.

In children's play the names given (to which various stories were attached) were: *atto/atya*; *emme/emya*; *tolyo* or *yonyo*; *nette* or *selye*; *wine* or *winimo*: that is 'daddy', 'mummy', 'sticker-up' or 'big boy', 'girl' ('daughter'), 'baby'. The fingers and toes were called *tille*

---

* But writing was a special case. For economy and clarity it was desirable that each letter should have a standard form. Fëanor had devised his *tengwar* with shapes more convenient to the right hand, and these were regarded as the "correct" forms; consequently the *tengwar* were normally written from the left with the right hand, especially in books and public documents. If written with the left (as often in letters or private records) the *tengwar* were reversed, and were correct in a mirror. In the "runes", of later and more elaborate forms and arrangement, reversal was made significant, and there was no difference in convenience for either hand. They were written (or cut) in either direction, or alternating.

(pl. *tilli*) 'tips, points'; or differentiated as *ortil(li)* 'up-point(s)' and *nútil(li)* 'under-point(s)'. The same play-names *ataryo/taryo* etc. could be given to the toes.

In ordinary language 'toe' was *taltil* (pl. *taltilli*); the big toe was *taltol* or *tolbo*, and the other toes had no special names, but were counted outwards from the big toe.

In the primitive days, before the Great Journey, while the building up of the Common Eldarin language was in the making, play with the hands and naming of the fingers went together with the naming of the numerals (those above 2). The hand was the primitive counting instrument.* In the first stage one hand was used as a group-unit, and names were devised for its separate prominences. Later both hands were laid out with the tips of the thumbs touching.

TEXT 2

> The second text is extracted from a group of manuscript pages written in a fairly clear hand in black nib-pen and placed just after text 3 below. Internal linguistic evidence (not detailed here) shows however that its composition preceded that of text 3.

The stem of the Common Eldarin numeral for 9 was *neter*, which resembles the Quenya play-name for the 4th finger (in Eldarin count): *nette*, which is in 2-handed display, with thumbs inward, the 9th from L or R. The name was old enough to appear in related forms in T. *nette*, *nettica*, S. *netheg*. The resemblance was observed by the earlier loremasters (who quote the Telerin forms otherwise not recorded); but it was rejected as fortuitous, because *nette* had a sense only suitable to the children's hand-plays in which the fingers were represented as a family or two families of neighbours: it meant 'girl', but was a colloquial "family" diminutive of a Common Eldarin base NETH (*not* NET) 'woman'.†[8]

---

* Much later, but before the end of the Common Eldarin period, the Eldar, leaving behind the primitive beginnings with the hand, devised a counting in sixes and twelves which they used in all more elaborate reckonings; but in daily and colloquial use many of the decimal terms remained in use.

† *nette* meant 'girl approaching the adult' (in her "teens": the growth of Elvish children after birth was little if at all slower than that of the children of Men). The Common Eldarin stem *(wen-ed) wendē* 'maiden' applied to all stages up to the fully adult (until marriage).

The primitive handling of the fingers numerically was older than the personalized play-names, though the two were interconnected. In the numerical handling as the numerical list was filled up *nete* would come before 5, or 10: one more beyond the prominent middle-finger. In the primitive play-name series "father" (thumb) and "mother" (index) were certainly the oldest, the others being just "children", though the notable little finger possibly early had a name = "baby". It was here that the resemblance between *net(e)* and *nette* became effective: *nete* 'one more beyond the middle' and before the end of the count became *nette* 'girl/daughter', and so caused *tolya 'prominent' to become masculine, and generated for itself the definite variant *selye* 'daughter', and for *tolyo* the variant *yonyo* 'son': and the family was complete.

TEXT 3

This text is found on three manuscript sides, placed immediately after and closely contemporary with text 1, written in a clear hand in black nib-pen, and numbered (i)–(iii) by Tolkien. Like text 1, the manuscript is found on the blank sides of printed Allen & Unwin stationery, one sheet of which is a publication notice dated Jan.–Feb. 1968.

The fingers. The 5 "fingers" included the *thumb.* Their naming is of considerable interest, since it is connected with the development of the *numerals* 1–10, the basis of the Eldarin decimal system, and also in the "play-names" it gives a glimpse of the Eldarin children which the legends and histories do not provide.

The numbers 1, 2: *one* (alone, or first) and *two* (another, or the next) were probably the oldest and not necessarily originally connected with the fingers: though the *thumb*, larger, differing in shape and function from the others, and capable of being extended sideways, so that it is alone and distinct, while it can also be brought alongside the slenderer fingers and be the first in a series, is eminently suited to the development of two distinct word-stems: (a) one, only, alone and (b) one, first.*

In using the hands as assisting in counting (and in teaching

---

* The actually recorded *names* of *thumb* and *index-finger* have, however, no connexion with the numerals for *one, two.*

counting) they were laid down flat with the thumbs touching. The count, and naming, then proceeded from thumb to little finger (in either direction), and returning to the middle continued from the second thumb. Each name thus occurred twice; and in two-handed reckoning had two numerical places, the second being + 5. Connexion therefore between numerals five apart, for example 3 and 8, would not be surprising – insofar as the numerals can be shown to have etymological relations with the finger-names occurring at the appropriate places.*

The following account is an abbreviation of a curious document, preserved in the archives of Gondor by strange chance (or by many such chances) from the Elder Days, but in a copy apparently made in Númenor not long before its downfall: probably by or at the orders of Elendil himself, when selecting such records as he could hope to store for the journey to Middle-earth. This one no doubt owed its selection and its copying, first to Elendil's own love of the Eldarin tongues and of the works of the loremasters who wrote about their history; but also to the unusual contents of this disquisition in Quenya: *Eldarinwe Leperi are Notessi*: The Elvish Fingers and Numerals. It is attributed, by the copyist, to *Pengoloð* (or *Quendingoldo*) of Gondolin,[†] and he describes the Elvish play-names of the fingers as used by and taught to children.

The fingers. The 5 "fingers" included the *thumb*. The Common Eldarin word for 'finger' was *leper*, pl. *leperī*: Q. T. *leper*, pl. *ī*; S. *leber*, *lebir*.

These were named from thumb (1) to little finger (5): (a) in Quenya 1. *nápo*, 2. *tassa, lepetas*, 3. *lepenel*, 4. *lepente* or *lepekan*, 5. *níke* or *lepinke*; (b) in Telerin 1. *nāpa*, 2. *tassa*, 3. *i nellepe*, 4. *nente*, 5. *nīke*; (c) in Sindarin 1. *nawb*, 2. *tas* or *lebdas*, 3. *lebeneð*, 4. *lebent*, 5. *niged* or *lebig*. In addition there was a dual formation naming thumb and index as a pair: Q. *nápat*, T. *nāpat*, S. *nobad*.

---

* Such a connexion is seen in the case of 3 and 8; while 5 is certainly related to the words for 'finger'.

† Reputed to be the greatest of the *Lambeñgolmor* (linguistic loremasters) before the end of the Elder Days, both by talent and opportunity, since he himself had known Quenya (Vanyarin and Noldorin) and Telerin and preserved in a memory remarkable even among the Eldar the works (especially on etymology) of the earlier loremasters (including Fëanor); but also had as an Exile been able to learn Sindarin in its varieties, and Nandorin, and had some acquaintance with Khuzdûl in its archaic form as used in the habitations of the Dwarves in Ered Lindon.

In the hand-play of children each hand was regarded as a "family" of 5: father, mother, brother, sister, and little-one or baby, about which and their family dealings and also, when two hands were juxtaposed, their relations to the neighbouring family, tales were made-up, some handed on traditionally, and others often improvised. There were more variations in these than in the adult names, but the following were the best known:

1. (thumb) Q. *atto, atya*; 2. *emme, emya*; 3. *tollo* or *hanno*; 4. *nette*; 5. *wine* or *winimo, win(i)ke*.

2. T. *atta(ke)*; 2. *emme(ke)*; 3. *tolle* or *hanna(ke)*; 4. *nette* or *nettike*; 5. *winike* (*winke, pinke*).

3. S. *atheg*; 2. *emig*; 3. *tolch, toleg, honeg*; 4. (*neth*), *nethig*; 5. *niben, gwinig*.

NOTES

1 Cf. also IV:187, where the explanation of Mablung's name as meaning 'with weighted hand' is cited from this material.

2 On the implication here that Celeborn was himself an exiled Teler, see UT:233.

3 I.e. LR:774.

4 Tolkien did not originally conceive of the Elves as ambidexters. The earliest *Qenya* and *Gnomish Lexicons* explicitly portray the left hand as clumsy, the right as skilful: Q. *lenka* 'slow, dull, stiff; left (hand)' and *malenka* 'lefthand, -ed', G. *gôg* 'clumsy; left (hand)'. Predominance of the right hand is still evident in the later *Etymologies*, which includes Q. *formaite* 'righthanded, dexterous'. It is also implicit in the story of Maedhros, who after losing his right hand in his rescue by Fingon from Thangorodrim "lived to wield his sword with left hand more deadly than his right had been" (V:252). Even in the latest version of this story in the *Grey Annals* (written in the early 1950s), which simply notes that "Thereafter Maidros wielded his sword in his left hand" (XI:32), the mere fact that this is mentioned implies that the feat was somehow noteworthy or unusual.

5 Tolkien himself made a few attempts at this practice of writing from right to left in mirror-image *tengwar*. Two examples are reproduced here:

The first reads *Mordor* while the second is *Tindómrl* (i.e., *Tindómerel*). The shakiness of Tolkien's penmanship indicates that he probably wrote these *tengwar* inscriptions with his left hand.

6 I.e. LR:392.

7 Cf. the statement in App. E of *The Lord of the Rings* that the *tengwar* 17 *númen* 'west', 33 *hyarmen* 'south', 25 *rómen* 'east', and 10 *formen* 'north' "commonly indicated the points W, S, E, N even in languages that used quite different terms. They were, in the West-lands, named in this order, beginning with and facing west; *hyarmen* and *formen* indeed meant left-hand region and right-hand region (the opposite to the arrangement in many Mannish languages)" (LR:1123).

8 This note is of interest as showing that the scheme that Tolkien eventually arrived at in the "Time and Ageing" papers, whereby Elves matured only somewhat more slowly than Men, persisted to at least the final years of the 1960s. Cf. chap. XV, "Note on the Youth and Growth of the Quendi", of c. 1959 in part one of this book, where Elvish gestation occupies one sun-year and growth proceeds at the same rate as Men until maturity is reached at 24 sun-years; but cf. also chap. XVIII, "Elvish Ages & Númenórean" of 1965, also in part one, where the gestation is 3 sun-years and growth until maturity occurs at a rate of 3 : 1 sun-years compared to Men.

IV

HAIR

This text is found among notes "in explanation of revised names in genealogy", and is dated by Tolkien "Dec. 1959" (see XII:359 n.26). It is written in a clear hand in black nib-pen. These notes are mostly linguistic and etymological, but one passage, pertaining to words related to "hair", provides certain details that are of relevance here.

Ingwë had curling golden hair. Finwë (and Míriel) had long dark hair, so had Fëanor and all the Noldor, save by intermarriage which did not often take place between clans, except among the chieftains, and then only after settlement in Aman. Only Finwë's second son by Indis had fair hair,[*] and this remained generally characteristic of his descendants, notably Finrod. Elwë and Olwë had very pale hair, almost white. Melian was dark, and so was Lúthien.

This is a convenient place to give a late (1969) typescript note found elsewhere amongst Tolkien's linguistic papers:

Base √ÑAL 'shine, glitter', always with reference to reflected radiance from a bright surface. As in the name *Gil-galad* 'star of radiance' given to Finwain, last High-king of the Eldar, because of the radiance of his silver hair, armour, and shield that, it is said, could even in the moonlight be seen from many leagues afar. The same word occurs in the name *Galadriel* (kinswoman of Finwain), 'lady of the radiant crown', referring to the shining of her golden hair.

---

[*] That is, Finarfin, father of Finrod Felagund.

V

BEARDS

This text is found among the "Last Writings" that Christopher Tolkien dated to the last year of his father's life (see XII:377), thus 1972–3. It occupies two and a half pages and is written in a slightly hasty hand in black nib-pen. Christopher made reference to it in *Unfinished Tales*, with a brief quotation, pp. 247–8.

Beards

An account of these and the fact that the Elvish race had no beards, so that this also became a mark of an Elvish strain in certain kingly families of Númenórean descent.

A note was sent to Patricia Finney (Dec. 9/72), answering a question about *beards*, that mentioned some of the male characters which she and a friend did not imagine as having beards.* [1] I replied that I myself imagined Aragorn, Denethor, Imrahil, Boromir, Faramir as beardless. This, I said, I supposed *not* to be due to any custom of *shaving*, but a racial characteristic. None of the Eldar had any beards, and this was a general racial characteristic of all Elves in my "world".[2] Any element of an Elvish strain in human ancestry was very dominant and lasting (receding only slowly – as might be seen in

---

* When I came to think of it, in my own imagination, beards were not found among Hobbits (as stated in text); nor among the Eldar (not stated). All *male Dwarves* had them. The wizards had them, though Radagast (not stated) had only short, curling, light brown hair on his chin. Men normally had them when full-grown, hence Eomer, Theoden and all others named. But not Denethor, Boromir, Faramir, Aragorn, Isildur, or other Númenórean chieftains.

Númenóreans of royal descent, in the matter of longevity also).[3] The tribes of Men from whom the Númenóreans were descended were normal, and hence the majority of them would have beards. But the royal house was *half-elven*, having two strains of Elvish race in their ancestry through Lúthien of Doriath (royal Sindarin) and Idril of Gondolin (royal Noldorin). The effects were long-lasting: e.g. in a tendency to a stature a little above the average, to a greater (though steadily decreasing) longevity, and probably most lastingly in beard-lessness. Thus none of the Númenórean chieftains of descent from Elros (whether kings or not) would be bearded. It is stated that Elendil was descended from Silmariën, a royal princess.*[4] Hence Aragorn and all his ancestors were beardless.

The matter of Denethor and his sons is not so clear. But I explained this by referring to Gandalf's remarks concerning Denethor: that "by some chance" the Númenórean was nearly "true" in him[5] – meaning that by some event in Denethor's ancestry which Gandalf had not investigated,[6] he had this mark of ultimately "royal" descent. This "chance", I said, was to be seen in the fact that Húrin the First Steward (from whom Denethor was directly descended) must have been a *kinsman* of King Minardil (see L.R. III 319, 332, 333)[7] sc. of ultimately royal descent, though not near enough in kin-ship for him or his descendants to claim the throne. I did not but could have noted the following points. The Kings of Gondor had no doubt had "stewards" from an early time, but these were only minor officials, charged with supervision of the King's halls, houses, and lands. But the appointment of Húrin of Emyn Arnen, a man of high Númenórean race, was different. He was evidently the chief officer under the crown, prime counsellor of the King, and at appointment endowed with the right to assume vice-regal status, and assist in determining the choice of heir to the throne, if this became vacant in his time. These functions all of his descendants inherited. It may also be noted that they had *Quenya* names,†[8] which had long

---

* Who had the law been changed in her time would have become queen, and Elendil would probably have been King of Númenor.

† Notably *Húrin* is not one of these names, but being in origin the name of the most renowned in legend of the House of Hador (from whom on the male side the Kings were descended) it was reckoned of equal worth. Why after Mardil Voronwë the Quenya names were abandoned is not clear; but it was prob-ably simply a part of the ritual "humility" of the Ruling Stewards, like their never sitting on the throne, having no crown or sceptre, and banner without device, and holding office only *"in the name of the King* until he shall return". I say "ritual", because it was impossible that any King should return, unless

been a privilege only of those of proved royal descent.

In the case of Faramir and Boromir another "strain" appears. Their mother was Finduilas (another "Silmarillion" name), daughter of Adrahil of Dol Amroth, and sister of Prince Imrahil. But this line had also a special Elvish strain according to its own legends, as clearly noted in the text (III 148).[9]

The people of Belfalas (Dol Amroth) were mainly Númenórean in origin, descendants of settlers before the division of the people or the armada of Ar-Pharazôn. Hence they often used Númenórean Adûnaic names, since the use of these was not then yet connected with rebellion against Eru. But as Legolas's mention of Nimrodel shows there was an ancient Elvish port near Dol Amroth, and a small settlement of Silvan Elves there from Lórien.[10] The legend of the prince's line was that one of their earliest fathers had wedded an Elf-maiden: in some legends it was indeed (evidently improbable) to have been Nimrodel herself; more probably in other tales it was one of Nimrodel's companions who was lost in the upper mountain glens.[11]

In any case I do not imagine Imrahil as bearded.

NOTES

1 Hobbits are stated to be beardless in the *Prologue* to *The Lord of the Rings* (LR:3).

2 Some years earlier, however, Tolkien had written (VT41:9) that: "Elves did not have beards until they entered their third cycle of life. Nerdanel's father [cf. XII:365–6 n.61] was exceptional, being only early in his second." And in any event, in *The Lord of the Rings* it is said of Círdan the Shipwright that: "Very tall he was, and his beard was long" (LR:1030).

3 On the longevity of the Númenóreans, cf. chap. XVII, "Elvish Ages & Númenórean", in part one of this book, as well as chaps. XI, "Lives of the Númenóreans", and XII, "The Ageing of Númenóreans", in part three.

---

he were a descendant of Elendil from Isildur not Anárion. But from Pelendur onwards the Ruling Stewards were determined not to receive any such claimant, but to remain supreme rulers of Gondor. It may anyway be observed that though Quenya names were not used, those used were probably *all* the names of renowned heroes in the royal lines of old as recorded in legend. Some may come from tales now lost; but Húrin, Túrin, Hador, Barahir, Dior, Denethor, Orodreth, Ecthelion, Egalmoth, Beren are from legends recorded.

4 Tar-Aldarion, whose only child, Ancalimë, was female, at some point before the end of reign in S.A. 1075, changed the Númenórean law of succession "so that the (eldest) daughter of a King should succeed, if he had no sons" (UT:219–20). This was long after the birth of Silmariën in S.A. 521 (UT:219, 225 n.4).

5 Cf. LR:759.

6 Tolkien here replaced "discovered" with "investigated".

7 I.e. LR:1039, 1052–3.

8 With "*in the name of the King* until he shall return" cf. LR:1052.

9 I.e. LR:872.

10 Cf. LR:339–41.

11 Christopher Tolkien quoted this passage (in slightly differently edited form) at UT:248.

VI

DESCRIPTIONS OF CHARACTERS

In 1970 Allen & Unwin published a poster-sized *Map of Middle-earth*, executed by the artist Pauline Baynes, and based upon that included in *The Lord of the Rings*. On the map itself are a series of vignettes portraying various locations significant to the story, such as the Barrow-Downs and Minas Tirith; and above and below the map proper, Baynes depicted the members of the Fellowship of the Ring, the Black Riders, Gollum, Shelob, and other enemies of the West. On seeing the finished art, Tolkien wrote a set of comments on these depictions of places and characters. Some of these comments are appreciative: e.g. Tolkien found four of the vignettes, sc. those depicting the Teeth of Mordor, the Argonath, Barad-dûr, and Minas Morgul, particularly well-executed, and described them as agreeing "remarkably with my own vision ... *Minas Morgul* is almost exact"; and he found the depiction of Aragorn good, those of Sam and Gimli "good enough", and that of Boromir to be "the best figure, and most closely related to the text". Other comments are less positive: e.g. of the vignettes he singled out those of Minas Tirith and Hobbiton for particular dislike; and of the depictions of characters he most disliked those of Gandalf, Legolas, Gollum, the Black Riders (though he found them "impressive as sinister cavaliers", he decried the addition of "*hats* and *plumes*" and the "relief" of "their hell-black with elvish *green*"), and Shelob (faulting in particular the positioning of her legs as "all apparently growing out of her head") – also that of Bill the Pony: "On the scale of the men and the hobbits Bill is no pony. Also he was represented as having become the special care and friend of Sam, who should be leading him". In the course of these comments he offers details of how some of these characters appeared in his own vision (some of which have been presented elsewhere),[1] as well as on the personality and roles of some, and these details are selected and arranged for presentation here.[2]

The map in question is reproduced on p. 385 of the catalogue of the recent Bodleian exhibition *Tolkien: Maker of Middle-earth* (Catherine McIlwaine, 2018), q.v.

Gandalf

In the story he was one of the Immortals, an emissary of the Valar. His visible form was therefore a guise in which he walked among the peoples of Middle-earth, a cloak for his power, wisdom, and compassion. But his body was not a phantom: it was corporeal and could suffer and be hurt, and though more slowly than mortal men he aged and was at the time of the story white-haired and bent with care and labour. (He had then been wandering – the Grey Pilgrim – mostly on foot through all the Westlands for some two thousand years). His looks, and his manners, had touches of the comic or grotesque (especially to hobbit-eyes), reflecting the sense of humour of a fundamentally humble spirit. Even the rare glimpses that he gave to those whom he specially loved of the founts of hope and mirth that lay beneath were touched with it; a figure strongly built with broad shoulders, though shorter than the average of men and now stooped with age, leaning on a thick rough-cut staff as he trudged along – at the side of Aragorn.* Gandalf's hat was wide-brimmed (a shady hat, H. p. 14) with a pointed conical crown, and it was *blue*; he wore a long *grey* cloak, but this would not reach much below his knees. It was of an elven silver-grey hue, though tarnished by wear – as is evident from the general use of grey in the book.

If I had known that Pauline Baynes was going to make a picture of Gandalf, I could have shown her a sketch I made long ago, showing him coming up the path to Bilbo's hole with his ("battered") blue hat more or less so.[3] Or better: the picture from which my personal vision of him was largely derived. This is a picture postcard acquired years ago – probably in Switzerland.[4] It is one of a series of six taken from the work of a German artist J. Madlener, called *Gestalten aus Märchen und Sage* ['Characters from Stories and Legends']. Alas! I only got one called *Der Berggeist* ['The Sorcerer', lit. 'The Mountain-spirit'].

---

* Incidentally: Aragorn is provided with a staff, much more suitable for Gandalf, though Aragorn is never described as using one.

On a rock under a pine-tree is seated a small but broad old man with a wide-brimmed round hat and a long cloak talking to a white fawn that is nuzzling his upturned hands. He has a humorous but also compassionate expression – his mouth is visible and smiling because he has a white beard but no hair on his upper lip. The scene is a woodland glade (pine, fir, and birch) beside a rivulet with a glimpse of rocky mountain-towers in the distance. An owl and four other smaller birds are looking on from the branches of the trees. The Berggeist has a green hat, and a scarlet cloak, blue stockings and light shoes. I altered the colours of hat and cloak to suit Gandalf, a wanderer in the wild, but I have no doubt that when at ease in a house he wore light blue stockings and shoes.

He was the friend and confidant of all living creatures of good will (I 375).[5] He differed from Radagast and Saruman in that he never turned aside from his appointed mission ("I was the Enemy of Sauron", III 294)[6] and was unsparing of himself. Radagast was fond of beasts and birds, and found them easier to deal with; he did not become proud and domineering, but neglectful and easygoing, and he had very little to do with Elves or Men although obviously resistance to Sauron had to be sought chiefly in their cooperation. But since he remained of good will (though he had not much courage), his work in fact helped Gandalf at crucial moments. Though it is clear that Gandalf (with greater insight and compassion) had in fact more knowledge of birds and beasts than Radagast, and was regarded by them with more respect and affection. (This contrast is already to be seen in *The Hobbit* 124-5. Beorn, a lover of animals, but also of gardens and flowers, thought Radagast a good enough fellow, but evidently not very effective.)

Legolas

The Legolas of the story was an Elvish prince of Sindarin race (III 363), clad in the *green and brown* of the Silvan Elves over whom his father ruled (I 253): tall as a young tree (II 28), lithe, immensely strong, able swiftly to draw a great war-bow and shoot down a Nazgul,* [7] endowed with the still tremendous vitality of elvish bodies, so hard and resistant to hurt that he went only in light shoes over rock or through snow (I 306), the most tireless of all the Fellowship.[8]

---

* He speaks slightingly of the archers of Rohan (II 137) in the battle of the Hornburg, in which he was the companion of Aragorn and Eomer in the hottest of the fighting. He was in the vanguard of the Army of the West.

Hobbits

Halflings was derived from the Númenórean name for them (in Sindarin *Periannath*). It was given first to the Harfoots, who became known to the rulers of Arnor in the eleventh century of the Third Age; later it was also applied to the Fallohides and Stoors. The name thus evidently referred to their height as compared with Númenórean men, and was approximately accurate when first given. The Númenóreans were a people of great stature. Their full-grown men were often seven feet tall.

The descriptions and assumptions of the text are not in fact haphazard, and are based on a standard: the average height of a male adult hobbit at the time of the story. For Harfoots this was taken as 3 ft. 6; Fallohides were slimmer and a little taller; and Stoors broader, stouter, and somewhat shorter. The remarks in the *Prologue* [concerning the height of hobbits] are unnecessarily vague and complicated, owing to the inclusion of references to supposed modern survivals of the race in later times; but as far as the LR is concerned they boil down to this: the hobbits of the Shire were in height between 3 and 4 feet, never less and seldom more. They did not of course call themselves *Halflings*.

Heights

The *Quendi* were in origin a tall people. The Eldar were those who accepted the invitation of the Valar to remove from Middle-earth and set forth on the Great March to the Western Shores of Middle-earth. They were in general the stronger and taller members of the Elvish folk at that time. In Eldarin tradition it was said that even their women were seldom less than 6 ft. in height; their full-grown elfmen no less than 6 ft. 6, while some of the great kings and leaders were taller.

The Númenóreans before the Downfall were a people of great stature and strength, the Kings of Men; their full-grown men were commonly 7 ft. tall, especially in the royal and noble houses. In the North where men of other kinds were fewer and their race remained purer this stature remained more frequent. Elendil the Tall, leader of the Faithful who survived the Downfall, was said to have surpassed 7 ft., though his sons were not quite so tall. Aragorn, his direct descendant, in spite of the many intervening generations, must still have been a very tall and strong man with a great stride; he was probably at least 6 ft. 6. Boromir, of high Númenórean lineage, would not be much shorter: say 6 ft. 4.

These figures [of the Fellowship] are thus all too short. Gandalf even bent must have been at least 5 ft. 6; Legolas at least 6 foot (probably more); Gimli is about the height that the hobbits should have been, but was probably somewhat taller; the hobbits should have been between 3 ft. 4 and 3 ft. 6. (I personally have always thought of Sam as the shortest, but the sturdiest in build, of the four).

Dwarves were about 4 ft. high at least. Hobbits were lighter in build, but not much shorter; their tallest men were 4 ft., but seldom taller. Though nowadays their survivors are seldom 3 ft. high, in the days of the story they were taller, which means that they usually exceeded 3 ft. and qualified for the name of *Halfling*. But the name "halfling" must have originated circa Third Age 1150, getting on for 2,000 years (1868) before the War of the Ring, during which the dwindling of the Númenóreans had shown itself in stature as well as in life-span; so that it referred to a height of full-grown males of an average of, say, 3 ft. 5.

The dwindling of the Dúnedain was not a normal tendency, shared by peoples whose proper home was Middle-earth; but due to the loss of their ancient land far in the West, nearest of all mortal lands to "The Undying Realm". In both Arnor and Gondor, apart from mixture of race, the Númenóreans showed a dwindling of height and longevity in Middle-earth that became more marked as the Third Age passed. The much later dwindling of hobbits must be due to a change in their state and way of life; they became a fugitive and secret people, driven as Men, the Big Folk, became more and more numerous, usurping the more fertile and habitable lands, to refuge in forest or wilderness: a wandering and poor folk, forgetful of their arts and living a precarious life absorbed in the search for food and fearful of being seen; for cruel men would shoot them for sport as if they were animals. In fact they relapsed into the state of "pygmies". The other stunted race, the Drúedain, never rose much above that state.

Gollum

Gollum was according to Gandalf one of a riverside hobbit people– and therefore in origin a member of a small variety of the human race, although he had become deformed during his long inhabiting of the dark lake. His long hands are therefore more or less right. Not his feet. They are exaggerated. They are described as *webby* (Hobbit 88), *like a swan's* (I 398), but had prehensile toes (II 219). But he was very thin – in the LR emaciated, not plump and rubbery; he had for his size a *large head* and a *long thin neck*, very large eyes (protuberant), and thin lank hair. He is often said to be dark or black. At his first mention (Hob. 83) he was "dark as darkness": that of course means no more than that he could not be seen with ordinary eyes in the black cavern – except for his own large luminous eyes; similarly "the dark shape" at night (I 399, 400). But that does not apply to the "black (crawling) shape" (II 219, 220), where he was in moonlight.[9]

Gollum was never *naked*. He had a pocket in which he kept the Ring (Hob. 92). He evidently had black garments (II 219), and in the "eagle" passage (II 253),[10] where it is said that from far above, as he lay on the ground, he would look like "the famished skeleton of some child of Men, its ragged garment still clinging to it, its long arms and legs almost bone-white and bone-thin". His skin was white, no doubt with a pallor increased by dwelling long in the dark, and later by hunger. He remained a human being, not an animal or a mere bogey, even if deformed in mind and body: an object of disgust, but also of pity – to the deep-sighted, such as Frodo had become. There is no need to wonder how he came by clothes or replaced them: any consideration of the tale will show that he had plenty of opportunities by theft, or charity (as of the Wood-elves), throughout his life.

Black Riders

They are clearly described as being themselves *invisible* and clad in long black cloaks with great *hoods* that hung down over their faces, so that people they met would not realize that they had no visible faces (I 84).[11] Neither could their hands be seen. In any case horsemen so accoutred would have worn gauntlets. Nor of course would their limbs have been so thin and emaciated if visible.

Shelob

Shelob is not described in precise spider terms; but she was "most like a spider" (II 334).[12] As such she was enormously magnified; and she had two horns and two great clusters of eyes. But she had the characteristic tight constriction of spiders between the front section (head and thorax) and the rear (belly) – this is called (II 334) her "neck", because the rear portion is swollen and bloated out of proportion. She was *black*, except for the underpart of her belly, which was "pale and luminous" with corruption. She would have eight legs, properly disposed, four a side, where they could function as organs of movement and seizure.

NOTES

1 Not always identified as such. See in particular UT:286–7 (beginning with "The remarks [on the stature of Hobbits]"); LRRC:4, 107, 229, 447, 493.

2 In extracting and arranging these elements from the MSS I have been highly selective and taken liberty in their ordering. As such I make no attempt to indicate excluded or elided passages, or where I have provided capitalization and punctuation to turn an extract into its own sentence.

3 This sketch, titled *One Morning Early in the Quiet of the World*, is reproduced as fig. 1 of *The Art of the Hobbit*, (Hammond and Scull, 2012) p. 20.

4 Just where and when Tolkien acquired the *Berggeist* postcard have been questioned; see TCG II:761–2 for the details.

5 I.e. LR:359.

6 I.e. LR:971

7 "(II 137)": i.e., LR:532.

8 The page-citations in this paragraph are to LR:1082, 240, 426, and 292, respectively.

9 The page citations to LR in this paragraph are to LR:382, 613, 382–4, 613–14, respectively

10 I.e., LR: 613 and 644, respectively.

11 I.e., LR:74.

12 I.e., LR:725.

VII

MIND-PICTURES

This text arose as a digression in the text presented in chap. XIV, "The Visible Forms of the Valar and Maiar", below. It was previously published in slightly different form in *Parma Eldalamberon* 17, (2007), p. 179.

For further discussion of communication between minds, see chap. IX, "*Ósanwe-kenta*", below.

The High Elves distinguished clearly between *fanar*, the "physical" raiment adopted by the Spirits in self-incarnation, as a mode of communication with the Incarnates,[*] and other modes of communication between minds, that might take "visual" forms.

They held that a superior "mind" by nature, or one exerting itself to its full in some extremity of need, could communicate a desired "vision" direct to another mind. The receiving mind would translate this impulse into the terms familiar to it from its use of the physical organs of sight (and hearing) and project it, seeing it as something external. It thus much resembled a *fana*, except that in most cases, especially those concerned with minds of less power (either as communicators or receivers) it would frequently be less vivid, clear or detailed, and might even be vague or dim or appear half-transparent. These "visions" were in Quenya called *indemmar* 'mind-pictures'.[†]

---

[*] In the L.R. a notable example is provided by the *Istari* who appeared among Elves and Men in the likeness of old Men.

[†] Cf. Q *indo* 'mind' and √*em* 'depict, portray'. A *quanta emma* or *quantemma* was a 'facsimile', a complete detailed visual reproduction (by any means) of a visible thing.

Men were receptive of them; according to the records of the time, mostly when presented to them by the Elves. To receive them from another human being required a special urgency of occasion, and a close connexion of kinship, anxiety or love between the two minds.

In any case *indemmar* were by Men mostly received in sleep (dream). If received when bodily awake they were usually vague and phantom-like (and often caused fear); but if they were clear and vivid, as the *indemmar* induced by Elves might be, they were apt to mislead Men into taking them as "real" things beheld by normal sight. Though this deceit was never intentional on the part of the Elves,* it was often by them [i.e., Men] believed to be.

---

* Of old. The matter of corrupted or malicious elvish beings is elsewhere considered. According to the Elves these were mainly disembodied Elves, who had met with some mortal damage, but rebelled against the summons to their spirits to go to their place of Awaiting. Those who so rebelled were mostly those who had been slain in the course of some wrong-doing. Thus they wandered as "houseless" elf-souls, invisible except in the form of *indemmar* that they could induce in others, and filled often with malice and envy of the "living", whether elvish or human.

VIII

KNOWLEDGE AND MEMORY

Among the "several pages of roughly written notes" at the end of the c. 1957 manuscript version (A) of *Laws and Customs among the Eldar* (see X:250) are two lengthy notes, written by contrast in a clear hand, but likewise in black nib-pen, concerning (broadly speaking) the nature of knowledge and of memory among the Eldar. The first of these arose as a long digression on the opening of the note concerning Elvish knowledge of the "Fate of Men" that Christopher Tolkien labels "(ii)" (X:251), sparked by the words "'supposed' or 'guessed'" there.

TEXT 1

The Eldar hold some things "for certain": they therefore *know* or *assert* things, when the evidence or authority is sufficient for certainty. They *judge* and have an *opinion*, when the evidence is sufficient to consider with reason (or the authority worthy of attention), but incomplete (or not compulsive). When the evidence is very incomplete (and there is no authority) they *suppose* or *surmise*. When the evidence is too incomplete for reasonable inference, or is not known they *guess*. This last process they do not usually distinguish from *feign* or *pretend* [save] only in this: that *guessing* implies a wish to know (and would use more evidence if that were available); it is intended to correspond as far as possible to fact, independent of the guessing mind; whereas *feigning* refers primarily to the mind itself, and is rather an exercise, or amusement, of the mind, independent of fact.[1]

They distinguish all these from *divining*, which is neither *guessing* nor *feigning*; for they hold that the *fëa* can arrive directly at knowledge, or close to it, without reasoning upon evidence or learning from living authority. Though *divining* is, they say, truly only a swift mode of learning from authority: since the *fëa* can only learn (apart from reasoning) by direct contact with other minds, or at the highest by "inspiration" from Eru. (This is truly called "divining".) This contact can at times take place between embodied minds of the same order without bodily contact or proximity. Minds of a higher Order, such as the Valar (including Melkor) can more easily influence those of a lower order (such as the Eldar) from afar. They cannot thus coerce or dictate, though they can inform and advise.* This too (except at great need) they do only when the mind is of its consent or desire opened to them: particularly, as when one of the Eldar calls one of the Valar by name in some need or doubt; generally as when one of the Eldar places himself under the protection and guidance of Manwë or Varda (or other Vala).[2]

The occupations of the embodied mind awake are an obstacle to such contacts, lower or higher. They occur therefore, the Eldar say, most often in "sleep" – not in "dreams". But "dreaming" and "sleeping" are to the Elves other than to Men. In sleep the *body* may, as in Men, cease from all activities (save those essential to life, such as breathing); or it may rest from this or that activity or function† as the *fëa* directs. While it is so, the mind may seek repose also, and be utterly quiet, but it may be absorbed in its own activity: "thinking" – that is, reasoning or remembering, or devising and designing; but these things are at will and of volition. The state that with the Elves nearest resembles human "dreaming" is when the mind is "feigning" or devising.‡ It is when the mind is quiet and inactive that it most readily receives and perceives contacts from without.[3]

---

* Melkor alone seeks to dominate or coerce minds, and for this uses fear: this is one of the greatest wrongs that he commits.

† Thus an Elf may stand "asleep" with eyes wakeful, and yet hardly breathe, and with his ears closed to all sound.

‡ Though it is more aware and controlled than in Men, and is usually fully remembered (if the *fëa* so desires).

TEXT 2

Note on Elvish Memory, especially of the *Reborn*, & its relation to Language[4]

It will be seen that by *rebirth* the memory of things and happenings in the past may be for the Eldar long and abundant and fresh. (Fresh since the "Waiting"[5] does not in their memory occupy time: to an Elf that had waited a thousand years the events of a thousand years before would seem by that space the nearer than to one who had not.) But this is not *complete*. Those who had passed through a Waiting often desired to forget some or all of their past, and they were relieved of their memory of such things. Others, remembering, would not communicate their recollection.[6]

There was one matter in which *rebirth* did not assist their "lore" – though this might be expected to be otherwise. This was the history and lore of *language* and the speech of bygone days. In such matters the Eldar were dependent mostly, as are we, upon visible records, or upon the "lore" consciously stored in the minds of those concerned with the branch of history. "Upon lore" not memory, that is – instinctive memory for the language of any Elf is that of the time in which he speaks; the languages of other *times* (as of other peoples and places) he must learn consciously, or deliberately store in mind as a thing separate from unpremeditated speech, the immediate and "natural" clothing of his thought. Not all the Eldar can do this, or do it readily and accurately; only "loremasters" specially concerned with "lore of tongues" commit such things (as for example the language of the period in which they are at that time) to visible record, or to the storehouse of mental lore.

Thus it will be seen that an Elf, remembering the past, must, if he will communicate it, clothe it in language. But to them "language" is essentially an art of the cohering *fëa* and *hrondo*,[7] and the chief product of their cooperation. The reborn Elf must learn language anew, and he will therefore re-clothe all his memory in the language of the later time (even as his *fëa* is reclothed in a body belonging to that time).

But it may be asked: "Will he not remember *sounds*? And will he not remember things that have been said to him and by him?" The answer is *yes* and *no*. In the disbodied Waiting he had *no* language (for that requires a body and is not required without one), only "thought". Through this interval all memory of his former life has passed; and it must, therefore, be re-clothed. He will, of course, remember *sounds*, and find words to describe those heard long ago, even as he might describe light, or colours, or emotions. But, say the Eldar, "language" is not *sounds*. Things said or heard in "language" are remembered as thoughts or meanings, and must be re-embodied in those modes of expression which at any given time a "speaking creature" uses without reflection.

Thus, those specially gifted to observe and recall variations of *sound* (as others may be gifted to observe and recall *colour*) might be able to recall and to repeat a sequence of spoken sounds heard long before. But this sequence would be dissociated from meaning, even as it would be, if an Elf found it written down in an ancient book; and it would have to be translated or deciphered by reference to the context of remembered scenes in which it occurred (aided by resemblances which it might still possess to other known tongues or periods of tongues). Thus it has come to pass that the Eldar possess much accurate lore concerning the speech-sounds used in days long past, but the linguistic memories of the Reborn are in other respects only like broken fragments of old books that must be reinterpreted and deciphered by lore and reasoning.

> The text ends here, near the bottom of a page; or rather, the text *in this mode of relation* ends here. For in the margins of the page the topic of memory and "reclothing" of speech is taken up again in a new mode, with a first-person narrator, sc. Ælfwine – the c. 900 A.D. Anglo-Saxon mariner who serves as an interlocutor with the Elves, and especially with the loremaster Pengoloð, in numerous texts of this period[8] – as indicated by the words: "Quoth Ælfwine" written faintly but ornately in pencil in the left margin.

To me the Eldar said: "You may understand this by considering the case of Men. Suppose now that a Man listened to a discourse in his own tongue and understood it in full as spoken. If then that by some chance, strange but not impossible, by change of life, by exile, or by some sickness, his mother-tongue were to be changed and utterly forgotten, how would he report the discourse? He would reclothe its meaning in the language that he now used as the natural expression of meanings. For the Eldar, contemporary languages (of common origin), which we should call kindred languages, or dialects according to the degree of divergence, and the same language lineally considered at widely sundered periods, present almost identical problems. In their earlier days their language (as other characteristics) changed hardly less quickly than those of Men."

NOTES

1 The sense Tolkien here gives to *feign* harkens back (according to the *OED*) to a previous, primary and material sense (now obsolete) 'to fashion, form, shape'. This sense derives from Middle English, Old French, and ultimately from Latin *fingere* 'to form, mould, feign', whence both *fiction* and *figment*.

2 Cf. the invocations of Varda (using her Sindarin name, Elbereth) by Frodo on Weathertop (LR:195) and Sam in Cirith Ungol (LR:729). For more on the nature of and constraints on contact between minds, see the next chapter.

3 Cf. LR:442: "Legolas already lay motionless, his fair hands folded upon his breast, his eyes unclosed, blending living night and deep dream, as is the way with Elves."

4 On the matter of Elvish "rebirth", following the death of their body, see chap. XV, "Elvish Reincarnation", below.

5 That is, of the disembodied *fëa* of an Elf in the Halls of Mandos.

6 At a later time, Tolkien set an "X" against, and bracketed, the passage beginning with "But it is not *complete*", in red ball-point pen, and wrote: "No! If they would take up *life* they *must* take up *memory* again".

7 At a later time, again in red ball-point pen, Tolkien altered "*hrondo*" here to "*hröa*". There is no independent evidence that the word *hröa* for 'body' was in use until after the typescript text B of *Laws and Customs among the Eldar* was made in c. 1958 (see X:141–3, 209, 304).

8 See, e.g., the numerous examples in *Morgoth's Ring*, and especially the probably closely contemporary text *Dangweth Pengoloð* (XII:396-402) which treats more briefly some of the same matters of speech and memory as here.

IX

ÓSANWE-KENTA

The far-ranging essay entitled by Tolkien in Quenya *Ósanwe-kenta*, 'Enquiry into the Communication of Thought', occupies eight typescript pages, numbered 1–8 by Tolkien. It is presented and (self-)described as a "résumé" (see below) or "abbreviation" (X:415) by an unnamed redactor[1] of another work of the same title that the Elvish Loremaster Pengolodh "set at the end of his *Lammas* or 'Account of Tongues'" (*ibid.*).[2] While thus a separate document, it nonetheless is closely associated and no doubt closely contemporary with the longer essay that Tolkien titled *Quendi and Eldar* (the bulk of which has been published in *The War of the Jewels*), with which it is located among Tolkien's papers.[3]

According to Christopher Tolkien, one of the copies of *Quendi and Eldar* is "preserved in a folded newspaper of March 1960", and notes written by his father on this paper and on the cover of the other copy include the *Ósanwe-kenta* among the Appendices to *Quendi and Eldar* (X:415). Christopher concludes that this complex of materials, including the *Ósanwe-kenta*, "was thus in being when the newspaper was used for this purpose, and although, as in other similar cases, this does not provide a perfectly certain *terminus ad quem*, there seems to be no reason to doubt that it belongs to 1959–60" (*ibid.*).

The eight typescript pages presented here appear to comprise the sole extant text of the *Ósanwe-kenta*; if it was preceded by any typescript or manuscript versions, they have apparently not been preserved. In the top margin of the first of these pages, Tolkien has written the three lines of its present title in ink. He has also numbered the first seven pages in the upper right-hand corner by hand,

and written the notation "*Ósanwe*" to the left of the numeral on each of these pages, also in ink; but the page number and notation are typed in the same positions on the eighth page. This suggests that Tolkien may have paused, or perhaps originally concluded the essay, somewhere on the seventh page, and written the short title and page number on those pages he had typed at that point, before the eighth page was begun. If so, he may have done so at the break on the seventh page indicated by a blank space before the paragraph beginning "If we speak last of the 'folly' of Manwë". The typescript has also been emended at points by Tolkien in ink, chiefly in correction of typographical errors, though on a few occasions supplying a change of wording. Save in a very few instances these changes have been incorporated silently in this edition.

For further discussion of the phenomenon of thought-communcation, see see chap. VII, "Mind-Pictures", above, and text 2, "Concerning Spirit", of chap. XIII, "Spirit", below.

This text was previously published, in a slightly different form, in *Vinyar Tengwar* 39 (1998).

Ósanwe-kenta

"Enquiry into the Communication of Thought"
(résumé of Pengolodh's discussion)

At the end of the *Lammas* Pengolodh discusses briefly direct thought-transmission (*sanwe-latya* 'thought-opening'), making several assertions about it, which are evidently dependent upon theories and observations of the Eldar elsewhere treated at length by Elvish loremasters. They are concerned primarily with the Eldar and the Valar (including the lesser Maiar of the same order). Men are not specially considered, except in so far as they are included in general statements about the Incarnates (*Mirröanwi*). Of them Pengolodh says only: "Men have the same faculty as the Quendi, but it is in itself weaker, and is weaker in operation owing to the strength of the *hröa*, over which most men have small control by the will".

Pengolodh includes this matter primarily owing to its connexion with *tengwesta* ['language']. But he is also concerned as an historian to examine the relations of Melkor and his agents with the Valar and the Eruhíni,[4] though this also has a connexion with "language", since, as he points out, this, the greatest of the talents of the *Mirröanwi*, has been turned by Melkor to his own greatest advantage.

Pengolodh says that all *minds* (*sáma*, pl. *sámar*) are equal in status, though they differ in capacity and strength. A mind by its nature perceives another mind directly. But it cannot perceive more than the existence of another mind (as something other than itself, though of the same order) except by the *will* of both parties.* The degree of *will*, however, need not be the same in both parties. If we call one mind G (for guest or comer) and the other H (for host or receiver), then G must have full intention to inspect H or to inform it. But knowledge may be gained or imparted by G, even when H is not seeking or intending[5] to impart or to learn: the act of G will be effective, if H is simply 'open' (*láta*; *látië* 'openness'). This distinction, he says, is of the greatest importance.

"Openness" is the natural or simple state (*indo*) of a mind that is not otherwise engaged.† In "Arda Unmarred" (that is, in ideal conditions free from evil)[6] openness would be the normal state. Nonetheless any mind may be *closed* (*pahta*). This requires an act of conscious will: *Unwill* (*avanir*). It may be made against G, against G and some others, or be a total retreat into privacy (*aquapahtië*).

Though in "Arda Unmarred" openness is the normal state, every mind has, from its first making as an individual, the right to close; and it has absolute power to make this effective by will. *Nothing can penetrate the barrier of Unwill.*‡

All these things, says Pengolodh, are true of all minds, from the Ainur in the presence of Eru, or the great Valar such as Manwë and Melkor, to the Maiar in Eä, and down to the least of the *Mirröanwi*. But different states bring in *limitations*, which are not fully controlled by the will.

The Valar entered into Eä and Time of free will, and they are now in Time, so long as it endures. They can perceive nothing outside Time, save by memory of their existence before it began: they can

---

* Here *níra* ('will' as a potential or faculty) since the minimum requirement is that this faculty shall not be exerted in denial; action or an act of will is *nirme*; as *sanwe* 'thought' or 'a thought' is the action or an act of *sáma*.

† It may be occupied with thinking and inattentive to other things; it may be "turned towards Eru"; it may be engaged in "thought-converse" with a third mind. Pengolodh says: "Only great minds can converse with more than one other at the same time; several many confer, but then at one time only one is imparting, while the others receive".

‡ No mind can, however, be closed against Eru, either against His inspection or against His message. The latter it may not heed, but it cannot say it did not receive it.

recall the Song and the Vision. They are, of course, open to Eru, but they cannot of their own will "see" any part of His mind. They can open themselves to Eru in entreaty, and He may then reveal His thought to them.*

The Incarnates have by the nature of *sáma* the same faculties; but their perception is dimmed by the *hröa*, for their *fëa* is united to their *hröa* and its normal procedure is through the *hröa*, which is in itself part of Eä, without thought. The dimming is indeed double; for thought has to pass one mantle of *hröa* and penetrate another. For this reason in Incarnates transmission of thought requires *strengthening* to be effective. Strengthening can be by *affinity*, by *urgency*, or by *authority*.

Affinity may be due to kinship; for this may increase the likeness of *hröa* to *hröa*, and so of the concerns and modes of thought of the indwelling *fëar*; kinship is also normally accompanied by love and sympathy. Affinity may come simply from love and friendship, which is likeness or affinity of *fëa* to *fëa*.

Urgency is imparted by great need of the "sender" (as in joy, grief, or fear); and if these things are in any degree shared by the "receiver" the thought is the clearer received. *Authority* may also lend force to the thought of one who has a duty towards another, or of any ruler who has a right to issue commands or to seek the truth for the good of others.

These causes may strengthen the thought to pass the veils and reach a recipient mind. But that mind must remain open, and at the least passive. If, being aware that it is addressed, it then closes, no urgency or affinity will enable the sender's thought to enter.

Lastly, *tengwesta* ['language'] has also become an impediment.[7] It is in Incarnates clearer and more precise than their direct reception of thought. By it also they can communicate easily with others, when no strength is added to their thought: as, for example, when strangers first meet. And, as we have seen, the use of "language" soon becomes habitual, so that the practice of *ósanwe* (interchange of thought) is neglected and becomes more difficult. Thus we see that the Incarnate tend more and more to use or to endeavour to use *ósanwe* only in great need and urgency, and especially when *lambë* ['speech'] is

---

* Pengolodh adds: "Some say that Manwë, by a special grace to the King, could still in a measure perceive Eru; others more probably, that he remained nearest to Eru, and Eru was most ready to hear and answer him".

unavailing; as when the voice cannot be heard, which comes most often because of distance. For distance in itself offers no impediment whatever to *ósanwe*. But those who by affinity might well use *ósanwe* will use *lambë* when in proximity, by habit or preference. Yet we may mark also how the "affine" may more quickly understand the *lambë* that they use between them, and indeed all that they would say is not put into words. With fewer words they come swifter to a better understanding. There can be no doubt that here *ósanwe* is also often taking place; for the will to converse in *lambë* is a will to communicate thought, and lays the minds open. It may be, of course, that the two that converse know already part of the matter and the thought of the other upon it, so that only allusions dark to the stranger need be made; but this is not always so. The affine will reach an understanding more swiftly than strangers upon matters that neither have before discussed, and they will more quickly perceive the import of words that, however numerous, well-chosen, and precise, must remain inadequate.

The *hröa* and *tengwesta* have inevitably some like effect upon the Valar, if they assume bodily raiment. The *hröa* will to some degree dim in force and precision the sending of the thought, and if the other be also embodied the reception of it. If they have acquired the habit of *tengwesta*, as some may who have acquired the custom of being arrayed, then this will reduce the practice of *ósanwe*. But these effects are far less than in the case of the Incarnate.

For the *hröa* of a Vala, even when it has become customary, is far more under the control of the will. The thought of the Valar is far stronger and more penetrant. And so far as concerns their dealings one with another, the affinity between the Valar is greater than the affinity between any other beings; so that the use of *tengwesta* or *lambë* has never become imperative, and only with some has it become a custom and preference. And as for their dealings with all other minds in Eä, their thought often has the highest authority, and the greatest urgency.

Here Pengolodh adds a long note on the use of *hröar* by the Valar. In brief he says that though in origin a "self-arraying", it may tend to approach the state of "incarnation", especially with the lesser members of that order (the Maiar). "It is said that the longer and the more the same *hröa* is used, the greater is the bond of habit, and the less do the 'self-arrayed' desire to leave it. As raiment may soon cease to be adornment, and becomes (as is said in the tongues of both Elves and Men) a 'habit', a customary garb. Or if among Elves and Men it be worn to mitigate heat or cold, it soon makes the clad body less able to endure these things when naked". Pengolodh also cites the opinion that if a "spirit" (that is, one of those not embodied by creation) uses a *hröa* for the furtherance of its personal purposes, or (still more) for the enjoyment of bodily faculties, it finds it increasingly difficult to operate without the *hröa*. The things that are most binding are those that in the Incarnate have to do with the life of the *hröa* itself, its sustenance and its propagation. Thus eating and drinking are binding, but not the delight in beauty of sound or form. Most binding is begetting or conceiving.[8]

"We do not know the *axani* (laws, rules, as primarily proceeding from Eru) that were laid down upon the Valar with particular reference to their state, but it seems clear that there was no *axan* against these things. Nonetheless it appears to be an *axan*, or maybe necessary consequence, that if they are done, then the spirit must dwell in the body that it used, and be under the same necessities as the Incarnate. The only case that is known in the histories of the Eldar is that of Melian who became the spouse of King Elu-thingol. This certainly was not evil or against the will of Eru, and though it led to sorrow, both Elves and Men were enriched.

"The great Valar do not do these things: they beget not, neither do they eat and drink, save at the high *asari* ['festivals'], in token of their lordship and indwelling of Arda, and for the blessing of the sustenance of the Children. Melkor alone of the Great became at last bound to a bodily form; but that was because of the use that he made of this in his purpose to become Lord of the Incarnate, and of the great evils that he did in the visible body. Also he had dissipated his native powers in the control of his agents and servants, so that he became in the end, in himself and without their support, a weakened thing, consumed by hate and unable to restore himself from the state into which he had fallen. Even his visible form he could no longer master, so that its hideousness could not any longer be masked, and it showed forth the evil of his mind. So it was also with even some of his greatest servants, as in these later days we see: they became wedded to the forms of their evil deeds, and if these bodies were taken from them or destroyed, they were nullified, until they had rebuilt a semblance of their former habitations, with which they could continue the evil courses in which they had become fixed".* [9]

---

* Pengolodh here evidently refers to Sauron in particular, from whose arising he fled at last from Middle-earth. But the first destruction of the bodily form of Sauron was recorded in the histories of the Elder Days, in the *Lay of Leithian*.

Pengolodh then proceeds to the abuses of *sanwe*. "For" he says, "some who have read so far, may already have questioned my lore, saying: 'This seems not to accord with the histories. If the *sáma* were inviolable by force, how could Melkor have deceived so many minds and enslaved so many? Or is it not rather true that the *sáma* may be protected by greater strength but captured also by greater strength? Wherefore Melkor, the greatest, and even to the last possessing the most fixed, determined and ruthless will, could penetrate the minds of the Valar, but withhold himself from them, so that even Manwë in dealing with him may seem to us at times feeble, unwary, and deceived. Is this not so?'

"I say that it is not so. Things may seem alike, but if they are in kind wholly different they must be distinguished. *Foresight* which is prevision,[10] and *forecasting*[11] which is opinion made by reasoning upon present evidence, may be identical in their prediction, but they are wholly different in mode, and they should be distinguished by loremasters, even if the daily language of both Elves and Men gives them the same name as departments of wisdom".*

In like manner, extortion of the secrets of a mind may seem to come from reading it by force in despite of its unwill, for the knowledge gained may at times appear to be as complete as any that could be obtained. Nonetheless it does not come from penetration of the barrier of unwill.

There is indeed no *axan* that the barrier should not be forced,

---

* Pengolodh here elaborates (though it is not necessary for his argument) this matter of "foresight". No mind, he asserts, knows what is not in it. All that it has experienced is in it, though in the case of the Incarnate, dependent upon the instruments of the *hröa*, some things may be "forgotten", not immediately available for recollection. But no part of the "future" is there, for the mind cannot see it or have seen it: that is, a mind placed in time. Such a mind can learn of the future only from another mind which has seen it. But that means only from Eru ultimately, or mediately from some mind that has seen in Eru some part of His purpose (such as the Ainur who are now the Valar in Eä). An Incarnate can thus only know anything of the future, by instruction derived from the Valar, or by a revelation coming direct from Eru. But any mind, whether of the Valar or of the Incarnate, may deduce by reason what will or may come to pass. This is not *foresight*, not though it may be clearer in terms and indeed even more accurate than glimpses of foresight. Not even if it is formed into visions seen in dream, which is a means whereby "foresight" also is frequently presented to the mind. Minds that have great knowledge of the past, the present, and the nature of Eä may predict with great accuracy, and the nearer the future the clearer (saving always the freedom of Eru). Much therefore of what is called "foresight" in careless speech is only the deduction of the wise; and if it be received, as warning or instruction, from the Valar, it may be only deduction of the wiser, though it may sometimes be "foresight" at second hand.

for it is *únat*, a thing impossible to be or to be done, and the greater the force exerted, the greater the resistance of the unwill.[12] But it is an *axan* universal that none shall directly by force or indirectly by fraud take from another what he has a right to hold and keep as his own.

Melkor repudiated all *axani*. He would also abolish (for himself) all *únati* if he could. Indeed in his beginning and the days of his great might the most ruinous of his violences came from his endeavour so to order Eä that there were no limits or obstacles to his will. But this he could not do. The *únati* remained, a perpetual reminder of the existence of Eru and His invincibility, a reminder also of the co-existence with himself of other beings (equal in descent if not in power) impregnable by force. From this proceeds his unceasing and unappeasable rage.

He found that the open approach of a *sáma* of power and great force of will was felt by a lesser *sáma* as an immense pressure, accompanied by fear. To dominate by weight of power and fear was his delight; but in this case he found them unavailing: fear closed the door faster. Therefore he tried deceit and stealth.

Here he was aided by the simplicity of those unaware of evil, or not yet accustomed to beware of it. And for that reason it was said above that the distinction of openness and active will to entertain was of great importance. For he would come by stealth to a mind open and unwary, hoping to learn some part of its thought before it closed, and still more to implant in it his own thought, to deceive it and win it to his friendship. His thought was ever the same, though varied to suit each case (so far as he understood it): he was above all benevolent; he was rich and could give any gift that they desired to his friends; he had a special love for the one that he addressed; but he must be trusted.

In this way he won entry into many minds, removing their unwill, and unlocking the door by the only key, though his key was counterfeit. Yet this was not what he most desired: the conquest of the recalcitrant, the enslavement of his enemies. Those who listened and did not close the door were too often already inclined to his friendship; some (according to their measure) had already entered on paths like his own, and listened because they hoped to learn and receive from him things that would further their own purposes. (So it was with those of the Maiar who first and earliest fell under his domination. They were already rebels, but lacking Melkor's power and ruthless will they admired him, and saw in his leadership hope of effective rebellion.) But those who were yet simple and uncorrupted in "heart"* were at once aware of his entry, and if they listened to the warning of their hearts, ceased to listen, ejected him, and closed the door. It was such as these that Melkor most desired to overcome: his enemies, for to him all were enemies who resisted him in the least thing or claimed anything whatsoever as their own and not his.[13]

Therefore he sought means to circumvent the *únat* and the unwill. And this weapon he found in "language". For we speak now of the Incarnate, the Eruhíni whom he most desired to subjugate in Eru's despite. Their bodies being of Eä are subject to force; and their spirits, being united to their bodies in love and solicitude, are subject to fear on their behalf. And their language, though it comes from the spirit or mind, operates through and with the body: it is not the *sáma* nor its *sanwe*, but it may express the *sanwe* in its mode and according to its capacity. Upon the body and upon the indweller, therefore, such pressure and such fear may be exerted that the incarnate person may be forced to speak.

So Melkor thought in the darkness of his forethought long ere we awoke. For in days of old, when the Valar instructed the Eldar newcome to Aman concerning the beginning of things and the enmity of Melkor, Manwë himself said to those who would listen: "Of the Children of Eru Melkor knew less than his peers, giving less heed to what he might have learned, as we did, in the Vision of their Coming. Yet, as we now fear since we know you in your true being, to everything that might aid his designs for mastery his mind was keen to attend, and his purpose leaped forward swifter than ours, being bound by no *axan*. From the first he was greatly interested in 'language', that talent that the Eruhíni would have by nature; but we did not at once perceive the malice in this interest, for many of us shared it, and Aulë above all. But in time we discovered that he had made a language for those who served him; and he has learned our tongue with ease. He has great skill in this matter. Beyond doubt he will master all tongues, even the fair speech of the Eldar. Therefore, if ever you should speak with him beware!"

"Alas!" says Pengolodh, "in Valinor Melkor used the Quenya with such mastery that all the Eldar were amazed, for his use could not be bettered, scarce equalled even, by the poets and the loremasters."

---

* *enda*. This we translate 'heart', though it has no physical reference to any organ of the *hröa*. It means "centre", and refers (though by inevitable physical allegory) to the *fëa* or *sáma* itself, distinct from the periphery (as it were) of its contacts with the *hröa*; self-aware; endowed with the primeval wisdom of its making which made it sensitive to anything inimical in the least degree.

Thus by deceit, by lies, by torment of the body and the spirit, by the threat of torment to others well loved, or by the sheer terror of his presence, Melkor ever sought to force the Incarnate that fell into his power, or came within his reach, to speak and to tell him all that he would know. But his own Lie begot an endless progeny of lies.

By this means he has destroyed many, he has caused treacheries untold, and he has gained knowledge of secrets to his great advantage and the undoing of his enemies. But this is not by entering the mind, or by reading it as it is, in its despite. Nay, for great though the knowledge that he gained, behind the words (even of those in fear and torment) dwells ever the *sáma* inviolable: the words are not in it, though they may proceed from it (as cries from behind a locked door); they must be judged and assessed for what truth may be in them. Therefore, the Liar says that all words are lies: all things that he hears are threaded through with deceit, with evasions, hidden meanings, and hate. In this vast network he himself enmeshed struggles and rages, gnawed by suspicion, doubt, and fear. Not so would it have been, if he could have broken the barrier, and seen the heart as it is in its truth unveiled.

If we speak last of the "folly" of Manwë and the weakness and unwariness of the Valar, let us beware how we judge. In the histories, indeed, we may be amazed and grieved to read how (seemingly) Melkor deceived and cozened others, and how even Manwë appears at times almost a simpleton compared with him: as if a kind but unwise father were treating a wayward child who would assuredly in time perceive the error of his ways. Whereas we, looking on and knowing the outcome, see now that Melkor knew well the error of his ways, but was fixed in them by hate and pride beyond return. He could read the mind of Manwë, for the door was open; but his own mind was false and even if the door seemed open, there were doors of iron within closed for ever.

How otherwise would you have it? Should Manwë and the Valar meet secrecy with subterfuge, treachery with falsehood, lies with more lies? If Melkor would usurp their rights, should they deny his? Can hate overcome hate? Nay, Manwë was wiser; or being ever open to Eru he did His will, which is more than wisdom. He was ever open because he had nothing to conceal, no thought that it was harmful for any to know, if they could comprehend it. Indeed Melkor knew his will without questioning it; and he knew that Manwë was bound by the commands and injunctions of Eru, and would do this or abstain from that in accordance with them, always, even knowing that Melkor would break them as it suited his purpose. Thus the merciless will ever count on mercy, and the liars make use of truth; for if mercy and truth are withheld from the cruel and the lying, they have ceased to be honoured.[14]

Manwë could not by duress attempt to compel Melkor to reveal his thought and purposes, or (if he used words) to speak the truth. If he spoke and said: *this is true*, he must be believed until proved false; if he said: *this I will do, as you bid*, he must be allowed the opportunity to fulfill his promise.*

The force and restraint that were used upon Melkor by the united power of all the Valar, were not used to extort confession (which was needless); nor to compel him to reveal his thought (which was unlawful, even if not vain). He was made captive as a punishment for his evil deeds, under the authority of the King. So we may say; but it were better said that he was deprived for a term, fixed by promise, of his power to act, so that he might halt and consider himself, and have thus the only chance that mercy could contrive of repentance and amendment. For the healing of Arda indeed, but for his own healing also. Melkor had the right to exist, and the right to act and use his powers. Manwë had the authority to rule and to order the world, so far as he could, for the well-being of the Eruhíni; but if Melkor would repent and return to the allegiance of Eru, he must be given his freedom again. He could not be enslaved, or denied his part. The office of the Elder King was to retain all his subjects in the allegiance of Eru, or to bring them back to it, and in that allegiance to leave them free.

Therefore not until the last, and not then except by the express command of Eru and by His power, was Melkor thrown utterly down and deprived for ever of all power to do or to undo.

Who among the Eldar hold that the captivity of Melkor in Mandos (which was achieved by force) was either unwise or unlawful? Yet the resolve to assault Melkor, not merely to withstand him, to meet violence with wrath to the peril of Arda, was taken by Manwë only with reluctance. And consider: what good in this case did even the lawful use of force accomplish? It removed him for a while and relieved Middle-earth from the pressure of his malice, but it did not uproot his evil, for it could not do so. Unless, maybe, Melkor had indeed

---

* For which reason Melkor often spoke the truth, and indeed he seldom lied without any admixture of truth. Unless it was in his lies against Eru; and it was, maybe, for uttering these that he was cut off from return.

repented.* But he did not repent, and in humiliation he became more obdurate: more subtle in his deceits, more cunning in his lies, crueller and more dastardly in his revenge. The weakest and most imprudent of all the actions of Manwë, as it seems to many, was the release of Melkor from captivity. From this came the greatest loss and harm: the death of the Trees, and the exile and the anguish of the Noldor. Yet through this suffering there came also, as maybe in no other way could it have come, the victory of the Elder Days: the downfall of Angband and the last overthrow of Melkor.

Who then can say with assurance that if Melkor had been held in bond less evil would have followed? Even in his diminishment the power of Melkor is beyond our calculation. Yet some ruinous outburst of his despair is not the worst that might have befallen. The release was according to the promise of Manwë. If Manwë had broken this promise for his own purposes, even though still intending "good", he would have taken a step upon the paths of Melkor. That is a perilous step. In that hour and act he would have ceased to be the vice-gerent of the One, becoming but a king who takes advantage over a rival whom he has conquered by force. Would we then have the sorrows that indeed befell; or would we have the Elder King lose his honour, and so pass, maybe, to a world rent between two proud lords striving for the throne? Of this we may be sure, we children of small strength: any one of the Valar might have taken the paths of Melkor and become like him: one was enough.

---

* Some hold that, though evil might then have been mitigated, it could not have been undone even by Melkor repentant; for power had gone forth from him and was no longer under the control of his will. Arda was marred in its very being. The seeds that the hand sows will grow and multiply though the hand be removed.

NOTES

1 It is of course tempting to identify this redactor, and that of *Quendi and Eldar*, as Ælfwine, the Anglo-Saxon mariner who was the translator/transmitter of and commentator upon other works of Pengolodh, such as the *Quenta Silmarillion* (V:201, 203–4, 275 fn.) and, notably, *Lhammas B* (cf. V:167).

2 While Pengolodh's *Lammas* 'Account of Tongues' here is, within the sub-creation, the same work as his *Lhammas* (the text published in *The Lost Road*), it appears that it refers to an unwritten (or, at any rate, no longer extant) version of that work that differs in certain respects. The published *Lhammas*, for instance, does not end with a discussion of "direct thought-transmission", as the present text states of the *Lammas*; and the *Note on the "Language of the Valar"* that concludes *Quendi and Eldar*, said to be "summarized" from Pengolodh's comments at the beginning of his *Lammas* (XI:397), is very much longer and more detailed than the very brief, general statement that begins the *Lhammas* (V:168). (At least one contemporary reference to the *Lammas* may, however, have been to the extant *Lhammas*: see XI:208–9 n. §6.)

3 A note on one of the title pages of *Quendi and Eldar* indicates that the *Ósanwe-kenta* was intended by Tolkien as an adjunct to the longer essay: "To which is added an abbreviation of the *Ósanwe-kenta* or 'Communication of Thought'" (X:415). Furthermore, Christopher Tolkien notes that his father used the title *Quendi and Eldar* not only for the longer essay, but also to include the *Ósanwe-kenta* and another brief essay on the origin of Orcs (the latter published in *Morgoth's Ring*, cf. pp. 415 ff.). All three essays are extant in typescript versions that are "identical in general appearance" (X:415).

   The association of the *Ósanwe-kenta* with *Quendi and Eldar* also extends to terminology and subject matter. For example, the *Ósanwe-kenta* employs certain linguistic terms defined and discussed in some detail in *Quendi and Eldar* (e.g. *tengwesta*, *lambë*) in a manner that assumes that the definitions and distinctions given there are already known. Further, the *Ósanwe-kenta* amplifies certain statements in the *Note on the 'Language of the Valar'* that concludes *Quendi and Eldar*: e.g. that "It was the special talent of the Incarnate, who lived by *necessary* union of *hröa* and *fëa*, to make language" (XI:405); and, more strikingly, that "the Valar and Maiar could transmit and receive thought directly (by the will of both parties) according to their right nature", although their "use of bodily form ... made this mode of communication less swift and precise" (XI:406). It likewise amplifies upon "the speed with which ... a *tengwesta* may be learned by a higher order", by the aid of direct "transmission and reception of thought" in conjunction with "warmth of heart" and "desire to understand others", as exemplified by the quickness with which Finrod learned the Bëorian language (*ibid.*)

   In its remarkable natural and moral philosophical range, the *Ósanwe-kenta* also has strong affinities with other, similarly philosophical, and closely contemporary writings published in *Morgoth's Ring*: e.g. *Laws and Customs among the Eldar*, the *Athrabeth Finrod ah Andreth*, and many of the briefer writings collected in Part V, "Myths Transformed". Of these, of particular note in connection with the present essay are texts II (X:375 ff.), VI *Melkor Morgoth* (X:390 ff.), and VII *Notes on motives in the Silmarillion* (X:394 ff.), all in some manner concerned with the motives and methods of Melkor and his dealings with Manwë and the other Valar and the Incarnates. The beginning of part (ii) of this last text (X:398 ff.) is especially noteworthy; though very much briefer and less detailed than the *Ósanwe-kenta*, it is also concerned with "thought-transference" and with many of the same philosophical issues surrounding it as are discussed in the present text.

4　In this and every subsequent instance, "Eruhíni" has been altered by Tolkien from typed "Eruhin" (cf. X:320).

5　Tolkien replaced "willing" with "intending" in the act of typing.

6　The concept of the Marring of Arda was much elaborated by Tolkien among the closely contemporary writings published in *Morgoth's Ring* (for the many references, see X:455). Cf. also XI:401.

7　Tolkien wrote "an impediment" above deleted "a barrier".

8　On the "binding" nature of the use by those not naturally incarnate of a body for bodily pleasures, see Body and Spirit in App. I.

9　This is perhaps a reference to the c. 1925–31 *Lay of Leithian* (cf. III:252–4, ll.2740–2822), where it is said that Sauron (then called Thû) escaped from Huan as "A vampire shape with pinions vast", though leaving behind "a wolvish corpse". In the published *Silmarillion* (S:175), however, it is plain that Sauron yields to Lúthien and is let loose by Huan *in order to avoid* his bodily destruction.

10　Cf. the discussion of *essi apacenyë* 'names of foresight', given by a mother to her child in the hour of its birth in indication of "some foresight of its special fate" (X:216).

11　Tolkien wrote "forecasting" in the margin as a replacement for deleted "predicting".

12　With this statement of the *impossibility* of forced penetration of the mind, compare the first paragraph of part (ii) of the *Notes on motives in the Silmarillion* (X:398–9), which appears to say that such an act is possible, though forbidden and, even if done for "good" purposes, criminal.

13　With this discussion of Melkor's deceitful methods of winning entry through the door of the *sáma*, it is interesting to compare the contemporary depiction of his failed attempt to cozen, flatter, and entice Fëanor into allowing him to enter through the (physical) door of Formenos, in the second-phase expansion of the *Quenta Silmarillion* chapter "Of the Silmarils and the Unrest of the Noldor" (X:280 §54, also S:71–2).

14　This sentence originally ended: "they have ceased to be [?– and] have become mere prudence".

X

NOTES ON *ÓRË*

Among the papers associated with the c. 1968 *Shibboleth of Fëanor* (published in part in *The Peoples of Middle-earth*), located now between the final typescript page of the essay proper and the first of the manuscript pages concerning the names of the sons of Fëanor and the legend of the death of his youngest son (cf. XII:352 ff.), is a single, apparently unrelated but closely contemporary typescript sheet. It is the beginning of what once may (or would) have been a substantial essay on the Common Eldarin root GOR and its descendants, which Tolkien has titled in ink with its Quenya derivative: "*óre*"; and numbered "1".

This text has been previously published, in a somewhat different form, in *Vinyar Tengwar* 41 (2000).

Órë

Common Eldarin GOR: Quenya *or*, Telerin *or*, Sindarin *gor*; associated with Common Eldarin √OR in Quenya and Telerin,[1] but probably not in Common Eldarin semantically connected. Nearest to the original sense is 'warn', but (a) it did not refer only to dangers, evils, or difficulties ahead; and (b) though it could be used of the influence of one person upon another by visible or audible means (words or signs) – in which case 'counsel' was nearer to its sense – this was not its chief use. This can best be explained by consideration of its principal derivative. This was in Common Eldarin *$g\bar{o}r\ddot{e}$: Quenya *órë*, Telerin *ōrë*, Sindarin *gûr*.

Quenya *órë* is glossed in *The Lord of the Rings* (III 401)[2] 'heart (inner mind)'. But although it is used frequently in the *LR* in the phrase "my heart tells me",[3] translating Quenya *órenya quete nin*, Telerin *ōre nia pete nin*, Sindarin *guren bêd enni*, 'heart' is not suitable, except in brevity, since *órë* does not correspond in sense to any of the English confused uses of "heart": memory, reflection; courage, good spirits; emotion, feelings, tender, kind or generous impulses (uncontrolled by, or opposed to the judgements of reason).

What the *órë* was for Elvish thought and speech, and the nature of its counsels – it says, and so advises, but is never represented as commanding – requires for its understanding a brief account of Eldarin thought on the matter. For this purpose the question whether this thought has any validity as judged by human philosophy or psychology, present or past, is of no importance; nor do we need to consider whether Elvish minds differed in their faculties and their relation with their bodies.

The Elves thought there was no fundamental difference in the given faculties; but that for reasons of the separate history of Elves and Men they were differently used. Above all the difference of their bodies, which were nonetheless of the same structure, had a marked effect: the human body was (or had become) more easily injured or destroyed, and was in any case doomed to decay by age and to die, with or without the will to do so, after a brief time. This imported into human thought and feeling "haste": all desires of the mind and the body were far more imperious in Men than in Elves: peace, patience, and even full enjoyment of present good were greatly lessened in Men. By an irony of their fate, though their personal expectation of it was brief, Men were always thinking of the future, more often with hope than dread, though their actual experience gave little reason for the hope. By a similar irony the Elves, whose expectation of the future was indefinite – though before them, however far off, loomed the shadow of an End – were ever more and more involved in the past, and in regret – though their memories were in fact laden with sorrows. Men, they said, certainly possessed (or had possessed) *óre*; but owing to the "haste" spoken of above they paid little attention to it. And there was another reason more dark (connected the Elves thought with human "death"): the *órë* of Men was open to evil counsel, and was not safe to trust.* [4]

---

* Cf. above "or had become". The Eldar surmised that some disaster had befallen Men before they became acquainted with them, sufficient to damage or alter the conditions under which they lived, especially with regard to their "death" and their attitude towards it. But of this Men, even the Atani with whom they became closely associated, would never speak clearly. "There is a shadow behind us", they would say, but would not explain what that meant.

The typescript ends at the bottom of the page. If any continuation of this typescript text ever existed, it is apparently no longer extant. There are, however, manuscript pages among Tolkien's linguistic papers containing what is apparently draft material not long preceding this typescript, that may give some indication of how that more finished text may have continued. This group of manuscript notes is written on both sides of three sheets of Allen & Unwin publication notices, variously dated 12th January or 9th February, 1968 (providing a *terminus a quo* for these notes). These were written very hastily, and the handwriting is in places exceedingly difficult of interpretation, even to Tolkien, who has, here and there, and more or less tentatively, glossed his own handwriting.

órë in nontechnical language, glossed 'heart, inner mind', nearest equivalent of 'heart' in our application to *feelings*, or *emotions* (courage, fear, hope, pity, etc.) including baneful ones. But it is also used more vaguely of things arising in the mind or entering the mind (*sanar*) which the Eldar regarded as sometimes the result of deep reflection (often proceeding in sleep) and sometimes of actual messages or influences on the mind – from other minds, including the greater minds of the Valar and so *indirectly* from Eru.[5] (So at this period it was supposed Eru even "spoke" directly to his Children.)[6] Hence the frequent expression *órenya quete nin* = "my heart tells me" used of some deep feelings (to be trusted) that some course of action etc. is to be [?approved] or [?] will happen [? ?]. This in Quenya was often associated with √*or-* 'up/-rise' as if it were 'arising' = things that arise and come up into the *sanar*, disturbing or colouring or warning it, and often actively determining its judgement, *nāmie* 'a single judgement or desire' (*sanwe* 'thought' > *nāma* 'a judgement or desire' > *indo* 'resolve' or 'will' > action), but it is probably another case of lost *h*.

'Mind' is *sanar* (for 'thinker'): of which *indo* 'will' was regarded either as a part or as a function of *sanar*.

Common Eldarin √HOR = 'urge, impel, move' but only of "mental" impulse; it differs from √NID in having no reference to physical action or force.[7]

(h)ore nin karitas = "I feel an urge/wish/desire to do it".

ore nin karitas nō (but) *namin alasaila* = 'I would like / feel moved to do so but judge it unwise'.

ōrenya quēta nin = "my heart is saying to me".

Mind, 'reflector, thinker' = Q. *sanar*; 'will' = *indo*; '(pre)monition' = *óre*.[8]

Emotions are divided into two "intertwined" things:

1) physical impulses provided by the *body*, for its preservation, pleasure, propagation, physical fear, desire, hunger, thirst, sexual desire, the physical side of love when the "wedding" of *hröa* and *fëa* was most close, etc.

2) impulses arising in the *fëa*, either from its own nature or as affected by horror, love/pity/[? ?], anger, hate; hate being a crucial case. It was in later Eldarin history a product of pride/self-love and emotion of rejection (or most corrupt, revenge) on those opposing one's will or desire; but there was a real "hate" far more impersonal, affecting the *fëa* only as one of animosity, of things that were evil, "against Eru", destructive of other things, especially living things.[9]

The Eldar thought[10] that some disaster, perhaps even amounting to a "change of the world" (sc. something that affected all its later history), had befallen Men which altered their nature, especially with regard to "death". But of this Men, not even the Atani with whom they became closely associated, could never speak more clearly than to refer to "the shadow behind us" or "the dark we have fled from". There exists however a curious document called the "Debate of Finrod and Andreth".[11] Finrod was one of the Noldorin Kings known as *Firindil* or *Atandil* 'friend of Men' most interested in them or sympathetic. Andreth was a woman, a 'wise-woman' of the Atani who it would appear had loved and been loved by his brother Eignor ('sharp flame') [Aegnor in the *Athrabeth*], but had (as Andreth thought) finally rejected her as of an inferior race. From this debate it would appear that Andreth believed that death (and especially the fear of it) had come upon Men as a punishment or result of some disaster – rebellion against Eru the Eldar guessed; and that there had not been any original intention that Men should be brief or fleeting. This document appears to have been actually of Mannish origin probably deriving from Andreth herself.

For (as far as we can now judge) [from] the legends (mainly of Elvish origin probably, though coming down to us through Men) it would seem clear that Men were not intended to have Elvish longevity, limited only by the life of the Earth or its endurance as a habitable place for incarnates. They were *privileged*, the Elves would have said, to have passed with free will out of the physical world and time (the circles of the world), but after a much greater life-span than now most actually possessed. The life of the Númenóreans before their fall (the 2nd fall of Man?) was thus not so much a special gift as a restoration of what should have been the common inheritance of Men, [to live] for 200–300 years. Aragorn claimed to be the last of the Númenóreans.[12] The "disaster" the Elves thus suspected was some rebellion against Eru taking [the] form of accepting Melkor as God.[13] One consequence of this was that the *fëa* was [?impaired] and Melkor had claim upon those who had rebelled against him and sought the protection of Eru, and access to [? ?] *óre* which [?amazed ? ?] but were [?useless] and only the wisest of Men could distinguish between [?his] evil promptings and the true *óre*.

> Despite the difficulty of the end of this passage, enough is legible that its meaning seems clear: through their acceptance of him as God, Melkor gained access to the *órë* of Men, so that only the wisest of Men could distinguish between the uncorrupted counsel of the *órë* and the evil promptings of Melkor. Cf. the statement in the typescript text that "the *órë* of Men was open to evil counsel, and was not safe to trust".

The Elves distinguished between the *fëa* (< **phayā*) as 'spirit/soul' and *hröa* (< **srawā*) 'body'. To the *fëa* [?primarily] they attributed *sanar* 'the mind' which functions in part with the will *indo* derived from judgements of the *sanar* based on evidence brought to it by the senses or experiences but also by the *órë*. This was held to be a power or function of the 'inner mind' ....[14]

> Another difficult manuscript note, located in the same bundle as (but not with) the preceding manuscript notes, and likewise written on an Allen & Unwin publication notice dated 9 Feb. 1968, reads:

hor- to be glossed 'warn' though this does not refer only to evils or dangers. It may be used of one person speaking to another but is mainly used impersonally as in *ora nin* 'it warns me' or in phrase *órenya quete nin* 'my heart tells me' and is regarded as "arising" from some inner source of wisdom or knowledge independent of the knowledge or experience gathered from the senses, which wisdom [?was sometimes due] to influence of greater, wiser minds, such as those of the Valar.

NOTES

1 *The Etymologies* gives the base ORO- 'up; rise; high; etc.', whence Q. *óre* 'rising' (V:379).

2 I.e., LR:1123.

3 Cf. LR:59, 266, 797, 802.

4 This footnote continues with an incomplete sentence: "But during the".

5 The word "indirectly" replaced original "mediately".

6 An exceedingly difficult marginal note against this paragraph reads, so far as I can determine: "[? heart] what one might call [? ? ? ?] feelings, a presentiment [? ? believe though this does not] arise from evidence [?gathered] by [?one's] conscious mind."

7 In apparently closely contemporary writings (i.e., c. Jan. 1968) elsewhere in Tolkien's papers, the verbal base √NID is glossed 'force, press(ure), thrust'. Among the Quenya derivatives given there are the noun *indo* 'the mind in its purposing faculty, the will', and the verb *nirin* 'I press, thrust, force (in a given direction)', which "though applicable to the pressure of a person on others, by mind and 'will' as well as by physical strength, could also be used of physical pressures exerted by inanimates".

8 In the top margin of the page, above these glosses, is an exceedingly difficult note, which so far as I am able to make out reads: "*hóre* also the conscience. The inner or inherent knowledge of what was good for the health of the [?mind & soul ? the good ? ?] beyond wisdom of experience [? ? pity ? ? ?].

9 Tolkien here wrote: "Q. *felme* | *feafelme* | *hroafelme*", presumably to be translated as 'impulse, emotion', 'spirit-impulse', and 'body-impulse', respectively.

10 The word "thought" here replaced earlier "believed" in the act of writing.

11 This is the c. 1959 text published as *Athrabeth Finrod ah Andreth* in *Morgoth's Ring* (X:303 ff.).

12 Cf. LR:1062. Aragorn also states there that he had been given "a span thrice that of Men of Middle-earth". Cf. chaps. XVIII, "Elvish Ages & Númenórean", in part one of this book, and XI, "Lives of the Númenóreans", and XII, "The Ageing of Númenóreans", in part three.

13 Cf. *The Tale of Adanel*, X:345–9; also X:351 and 354–6. As first written, the manuscript read "a god"; "god" was then altered to "God". The indefinite

article was not deleted, but presumably should have been, and so has been removed here editorially. With the fallen nature of Men, in Elvish and Mannish thought, see chaps. XII, "Concerning the Quendi in Their Mode of Life and Growth", in part one of this book. See also THE FALL OF MAN in App. I.

14 Tolkien's handwriting becomes extremely difficult at this point; so far as I can determine, the note continues: "because though not physical [?] were [?] it was [? ?] of the *fëa* [?when] it was [? heart] of the [?] by the [?impact] of the experience of its *hroa* / body [?] the *óre* [? ?]."

XI

FATE AND FREE WILL

Some time c. 1968 (much of the text presented here is written on the backs of printed Allen & Unwin reprint notices dated 12th Jan. 1968), Tolkien turned to considerations of two Quenya words encountered and glossed in *The Lord of the Rings*: *ambar* 'world' and *umbar* 'fate'; and of their precise meanings and etymological and semantic relationship. Amidst a linguistic discussion of certain points of Elvish phonology, Tolkien cited the Eldarin base MBAR underlying both these Quenya words, as well as the related Sindarin forms *amar* 'world' and *amarth* 'fate':

MBAR: basically 'settle, establish' but with a considerable semantic development, being especially applied to 'settlement', sc. the settling of a place, occupation (permanently) and ordering of a region as a "home" (of a family or people) > to erect (permanent) buildings, dwellings?[1]

Tolkien goes on to cite various derivatives of this base, including:

Quenya and Telerin *ambar*, Sindarin *amar* 'world', 'the great habitation'.

Beneath these glosses he added a note of clarification:

The full implications of this word cannot be understood without reference to Eldarin views and ideas concerning "fate" and "free will". (See note on these points.) The sense 'world' – applied usually to this Earth – is mainly derived from sense 'settlement': "the great habitation" (οἰκουμένη)[2] as "home of speaking creatures" esp. Elves and Men. (*ambar* 'world' differed from *Arda* in reference. *Arda* meant 'realm' & was this earth as the *realm* ruled by Manwë (the Elder King) vice-regent of Eru, for benefit of the Children of Eru.) But though *mbar-* was naturally mostly used of the activities and purposes of rational creatures, it was not limited to these. It thus could refer to the conditions and established (physical) processes of the Earth (as established at its Creation directly or mediately by Eru), which was part of Eä, the Universe; and so approached in some uses the sense 'Fate', according to Eldarin thought on the subject. Thus Q. *ambarmenië* 'the way of the world' ("world" by the way never meant "people"), the fixed, and by "creatures" unalterable, conditions in which they lived.

Then, a little further on in this discussion of derivatives of MBAR, Tolkien cites:

Sindarin *amarth* 'Fate'. This sense is an application of the basic sense, augmented by its formation, of *mbar*: 'permanent establishment/order'; 'Fate' especially (when applied to the future): sc. the order and conditions of the *physical* world (or of Eä in general) as far as established and pre-ordained at Creation, and that part of this ordained order which affected an individual with a *will*, as being immutable by his personal will.

The "note on these points" that Tolkien refers to here in connection with fate and free will arose in an earlier version of this same discussion of certain strictly linguistic points, beginning on a sheet which Tolkien subsequently titled "Fate" (after bracketing the discussion of MBAR and striking out the more strictly linguistic discussion that preceded it), and continuing on for four more pages, the first of which Tolkien titled "Fate and Free Will". The text begins in a clear hand in black nib-pen, with various notes and alterations made in blue ball-point pen, but this ends half-way down the second page, where Tolkien switched to pencil and began scrawling very hastily through the third page. Fortunately, on the fourth page Tolkien recapitulated, in blue ball-point pen and a much more careful hand, (nearly) all that he had written so hastily before. To this he added some footnotes in red ball-point pen. A final very difficult and faint paragraph was added in light pencil.

I give here the reading of the second version, which for the most part follows the first version very closely, but interpolate one significant paragraph (here set in square brackets) of the first version that is lacking in the second into the body of the text.

This text was previously published in a slightly different editorial form in *Tolkien Studies* vol. VI (2009). Ellipses indicate the omission of more strictly linguistic or otherwise technical passages.

MBAR 'settle, establish' (hence also, settle a place, settle in a place, establish one's home) also to erect (permanent buildings, dwellings, etc.); extended form *ṃbarat* with greater intensity. From this was derived S. *barad* 'tower' (not of a tall slender building, but in the sense of the Tower of London) great permanent building of defensive strength, as in *Barad-dûr*.* The Quenya form would have been *marto ... but this word was lost and generally replaced by *ostō > osto*, S. *ost* (as seen in *os(t)giliath*).† Common Eldarin *ṃbar'tă* 'permanent establishment' > *fate* of the world in general as, or as far as, established and pre-ordained from creation; and that part of this "fate" which affected an individual person, and not open to modification by his free will.‡

In Q. * *ṃbar'tă* > *umbart-* > *umbar* (genitive *umbarto*) 'Fate' ... in S. *amarth*. .... The word from the simple stem *mbar-* ... was *ambara* 'establishment', Q. *ambar* 'the world', T. *ambar*, S. *amar* (not found).

---

* But Minas Ithil and especially Minas Anor (Tirith) were 'towers' in the sense of *barad*, but derived their names from their high central tower, in days when the main dwelling-city of Gondor was at Osgiliath.

† Originally 'fortification', defence, not necessarily very large or permanent; a defensive camp with walls of earth and a ditch was an *osto*.

‡ E.g. one of the Eldar would have said that for all Elves and Men the shape, condition, and therefore the past and future physical development and destiny of this "earth" was determined and beyond their power to change, indeed beyond the power even of the Valar to alter in any large and permanent way. (They distinguished between "change" and redirection. Thus any "rational [?will-user]" could in a small way move, re-direct, stop, or destroy objects in the world; but he could not "change" [them] into *something else*. They did *not* confuse analysis with change, e.g. water/steam, oxygen, hydrogen.) The Downfall of Númenor was "a miracle" as we might say, or as they a *direct action of* Eru within time that altered the previous scheme for all remaining time. They would probably also have said that Bilbo was "fated" to find the Ring, but not necessarily to surrender it; and then if Bilbo surrendered it Frodo was fated to go on his mission, but not necessarily to destroy the Ring — which in fact he did not do. They would have added that *if* the downfall of Sauron and the destruction of the Ring was part of Fate (or Eru's Plan) then if Bilbo had retained the Ring and refused to surrender it, some other means would have arisen by which Sauron was frustrated: just as when Frodo's will proved in the end inadequate, a means for the Ring's destruction immediately appeared — being kept in reserve by Eru as it were.

This was to the Eldar more obviously related to *mbar'ta* than we might feel it to be, since "fate" so far as they recognized it was conceived as a much more physical obstacle to will.

They would not have denied that (say) a man was (may have been) "fated" to meet an enemy of his at a certain time and place, but they would have denied that he was "fated" then to speak to him in terms of hatred, or to slay him. "Will" at a certain grade must enter into many of the complex motions leading to a meeting of persons; but the Eldar held that only those efforts of "will" were "free" which were directed to a fully *aware purpose*. On a journey a man may turn aside, choosing this or that way – e.g. to avoid a marsh, or a steep hill – but this decision is mostly intuitive or half-conscious (as that of an irrational animal) and has only an immediate object of easing his journey. His setting-out may have been a free decision, to achieve some object,* but his actual course was largely under *physical* direction – and it *might have* led to/or missed a meeting of importance. It was this aspect of "chance" that was included in *umbar*. See L.R. III p. 360: "a chance-meeting as we say in Middle-earth".[3] That was said by Gandalf of his meeting with Thorin in Bree, which led to the visit to Bilbo. For this "chance", not purposed or even thought of by either Thorin or Gandalf, made contact with Gandalf's great "will", and his fixed purpose and designs for the protection of the NW frontiers against the power of Sauron. If Gandalf had been different in character, or if he had not seized the opportunity, the "chance" would, as it were, have failed to "go off" (misfired). Gandalf was not "fated" to act as he did then. (Indeed his actions were most odd, idiosyncratic, and unexpectable: Gandalf was a powerful "free will" let loose, as it were, among the physical "chances" of the world.)[4]

Umbar thus relates to the net-work of "chances" (largely physical) which is, or is not, used by rational persons with "free will". That aspect of things which *we* might include in Fate – the "determination" that we each carry about with us in our given created character (which later acts and experience may modify but not fundamentally change) was *not* included in *Umbar* by the Eldar; who said that if it was in any way similar it was on a different "plane". But the ultimate problem of Free Will in its relation to the *Foreknowledge* of a Designer

---

* Thus if a man set out on a journey with the *purpose* of finding his enemy, and the purpose then of doing this or that (pardoning him/asking his pardon/cursing him/seeking to slay him): That purpose governs the whole process. It may be frustrated by "chance" (– in fact he never met him –) or it may be helped by chance (– in fact against likelihood he did meet him), but in the latter case if he did evil he could not [?throw] the blame on "chance".

(both of the plane of *Umbar* and of the *Mind* and the blending of both in Incarnate Mind), Eru, "the Author of the Great Tale", was of course not resolved by the Eldar.

[But they would have said it is the continual clash of *umbar*, the "chances" of *ambar* as a fixed arrangement which continues to work out inevitably (except only for "miracle": a direct or mediate intervention of Eru, from *outside umbar* and *ambar*), and purposeful *will* that [?ramifies] a story or tale (as an excerpt from the total drama of which Eru is the Author or as that Drama itself). Until the appearance of *Will* all is mere preparation, interesting only on a quite different & lower plane: like mathematics or observing the physical events of the world or in a similar way the workings of a machine. *Will* first appeared with the Ainur/Valar, but *except for Melkor* and those he dominated their wills being in accord with Eru effected little change in *Ambar* or deflected *Umbar*.][5]

They said that, though this likeness is only a "likeness", not an equation, the nearest experience of the Incarnates to this problem is to be found in the author of a tale. The author is not in the tale in one sense, yet it all proceeds from him (and what was in him), so that he is present all the time.* Now while composing the *tale* he may have certain general designs (the plot for instance), and he may have a clear conception of the character (independent of the particular tale) of each feigned actor. But those are the limits of his "foreknowledge". Many authors have recorded the feeling that one of their actors "comes alive" as it were, and does things that were not foreseen at all at the outset and may modify in a small or even large way the process of the tale thereafter. All such unforeseen actions or events are, however, taken up to become integral parts of the tale when finally concluded. Now when that has been done, then the author's "foreknowledge" is complete, and nothing can happen, be said, or done, that he does not know of and will or allow to be. Even so, some of the Eldarin philosophers ventured to say, it was with Eru.

> The note originally ended here, about a third of the way down the page; but at a later point (judging by the change of writing implement), Tolkien added one more very rough and faint paragraph (readings marked here as uncertain are for the most part very uncertain indeed), apparently applying the simile of "the author of a tale" to his cosmogonic myth:[6]

---

* If one "character" in the tale is the author then he becomes as it were only a lesser and partial picture of the author in imagined circumstances.

Let the Music of Ainur [be an] ancient legend from Valinórean days. First stage: the music or "concert" of voices and instruments – Eru takes up alterations by their created wills ("good" or bad) and adds of His own. Second stage: the theme now transformed is made into a Tale and presented as visible drama to the Ainur, bounded but great. Eru had not [?complete] foreknowledge, but [?after it His] fore-knowledge was complete to the smallest detail – but He did not reveal it all. He veiled the latter part from the eyes of the Valar who were to be actors.

NOTES

1 The query mark is Tolkien's own. The symbol ">" is commonly used in lin-guistics to mean "yielded", either in form (by phonological development) or meaning (by semantic variation). Here the meaning is that from the basic sense 'settle, establish' arose the sense 'to erect permanent buildings or dwellings'.

2 Greek οἰκουμένη 'inhabited region; the inhabited world'.

3 I.e. LR:1080.

4 Cf. also Gandalf's statement, "I did no more than follow the lead of 'chance'" in *The Quest of Erebor* (UT:322).

5 This paragraph, interpolated from the first version of the note, continues with a partial sentence: "Ambar is complex enough, but only Eru who made and designed both Ambar (the processes of Eä)". Tolkien interrupted the sentence at this point to provide an etymological note on Eä, which reads: "*Eä* 'it is' only = the total of Ambar: the given material and its processes of change. Outside Eä is the world/sphere of aware purpose and will". This was followed at the bottom of the page by an etymological note on the Quenya word for 'will':

?DEL: Q. *lēle*, v[erb] *lelya* (*lelinye*): To *will* with conscious purpose, immediate or remote. To be willing, to assent, consent, agree – quite different, for it partakes of *will* but is an additional [?accident]. A man may say "I [?wish], I agree, I will" to some proposition of another without special purpose of his own (but he may also have reflected that it fits in with some design of his own and so agree to it as he might not otherwise have done).

6 The apparent ascription to Eru here of less than complete foreknowledge of the Music and the resulting Tale, in apparent contradiction of the absolute omniscience ascribed to God in both Catholic and classical theistic thought, may help explain the apparently hesitant nature of this roughly and faintly written addition. In any event, as Tolkien wrote before applying the simile of an author of a tale to Eru, it is "only a likeness ... the nearest experience of the Incarnates to this problem".

XII

THE KNOWLEDGE OF THE VALAR

This text arose as a long digression in "The Visible Forms of the Valar and Maiar", given here as chap. XIV below. Like that text, it was previously published in slightly different form in *Parma Eldamberon* 17 (2007), pp. 177–9.

The Knowledge of the Valar;
or Elvish ideas and theories concerned with them

[The Valar] remained in direct contact with Eru, though they, as far as the legends go, usually "addressed" Him through Manwë the Elder King. No doubt these legends are somatomorphic[1] (sc. almost as anthropomorphic as are our own legends or imagination), and most Elves, when speaking of Manwë appealing to Eru or having converse with Him, imagined him as a figure, even more majestic than one of their own ancient kings, standing in attitude of prayer or supplication to the Valar.* By *nature* one of the Valar, or of those of the prime order of created spirits to which they belonged, would *be* in the presence of Eru only by presenting themselves in thought. The Eldar, and still less the Elves of Middle-earth (and again still less Men, especially those who had no contact with Elves or shunned it), knew little of such things; but they believed that "direct" resort to Eru was not allowed to them, or at least not expected of them, except in gravest emergency. The Valar were themselves "on trial" – an

---

* At this time there was no way for the Incarnate *direct* to Eru, and though the Eldar knew well that the power of the Valar to counsel or assist them was only delegated, it was through them that they sought for enlightenment or aid from Eru.

aspect of the mystery of "free will" in created intelligences. They had a sufficient knowledge of the will of Eru and his "design" to undertake the responsibility of guiding its development by means of the great prowess given to them and according to their own reason and intelligence.

There was, however, one element in the Design of Eru that remained a mystery: the Children of Eru, Elves and Men, the Incarnate. These were said to have been an *addition* made by Eru Himself *after* the Revelation to the primal spirits of the Great Design. They were *not* subject to the subcreative activities of the Valar, and one of the purposes of this addition was to provide the Valar with objects of love, as being in no way their own subject, but having a direct relationship to Eru Himself, like their own but different from it. They were, or were to be, thus "other" than the Valar, independent creations of His love, and so objects for their reverence and true (entirely unselfregarding) love. Another purpose they had, which remained a mystery to the Valar, was to complete the Design by "healing" the hurts which it suffered, and so ultimately not to recover "Arda Unmarred" (that is the world as it would have been if Evil had never appeared), but the far greater thing "Arda Healed".*

With regard to Elves and Men Eru had made one absolute prohibition: the Valar were *not to attempt* to dominate the Children (even for what might seem to the Valar to be their good), neither by force nor fear nor pain, nor even by the awe and reverence that their wisdom and overwhelming majesty might inspire if fully revealed. The minds of the Children were not open to the Valar (except by the free will of the Children), and could not be invaded or violated by the Valar except with disastrous consequences: their breaking and enslaving, and the substitution in them of the dominating Vala as a God in place of Eru.[2]

It was for this reason that the Valar adopted the *fanar*;[3] but they did this also out of the love and reverence for the Children that they conceived when Eru first revealed to them His idea of them. From that time onwards they had ever looked and longed for the coming of Elves and Men into the world.

The Valar – all save one, Melkor – obeyed this prohibition by Eru,

---

* "Evil", in the arrogance and egotism of Melkor, had already appeared in the first attempts of the Spirits to express the Design of Eru communicated to them only in pure direct "thought". This was represented as taking the form of *music:* the Music of the Ainur (Holy Ones). In this Melkor, and those influenced by him, had introduced things of Melkor's own thought and design, causing great discords and confusion.

according to their wisdom.* But there was thus introduced an element of uncertainty into all their operations after the Coming of the Elves and Men. The wills and desires and the resultant deeds of the Elves remained forever in some measure unpredictable, and their minds not always open to admonition and instruction that was not (as was forbidden) issued as commands supported by latent power. This was even more evident in the case of Men, either by their nature, or by their early subjection to the lies of Melkor, or by both. It was also held by some that the Valar had even earlier failed in their "trials" when wearying of their destructive war with Melkor they removed into the West, which was first intended to be a fortress whence they might issue to renew the War, but became a Paradise of peace, while Middle-earth was corrupted and darkened by Melkor, long unopposed. The obduracy of Men and the great evils and injuries which they inflicted upon themselves, and also, as their power increased, upon other creatures and even upon the world itself, was thus in part attributable to the Valar. – not to their wilful revolt and pride, but to *mistakes* which were not by design intended to oppose the will of Eru, though they revealed a failure in understanding of His purposes and in confidence in Him.

NOTES

1 That is, imagining or projecting a bodily form onto (in this case) spiritual beings.

2 On the openness of minds, see chap. IX, "*Ósanwe-kenta*", above; on the substitution of a Vala as God in place of Eru, see chap. X, "Notes on *Órë*", above.

3 See chap. XIV, "The Visible Forms of the Valar and Maiar", below.

---

* This is said because the invitation given to the Eldar to remove to Valinor and live unendangered by Melkor was not in fact according to the design of Eru. It arose from anxiety, and it might be said from failure in trust of Eru, from anxiety and fear of Melkor, and the decision of the Eldar to accept the invitation was due to the overwhelming effect of their contact, while still in their inexperienced youth, with the bliss of Aman and the beauty and majesty of the Valar. It had disastrous consequences in diminishing the Elves of Middle-earth and so depriving Men of a large measure of the intended help and teaching of their "elder brethren", and exposing them more dangerously to the power and deceits of Melkor. Also since it was in fact alien to the nature of the Elves to live under protection in Aman, and not (as was intended) in Middle-earth, one consequence was the revolt of the Noldor.

XIII

SPIRIT

Text 1

This text is located in Tolkien's linguistic papers with a group of etymological notes that Tolkien has dated to Sep. 1957. Further supporting the date of this text to 1957 is the use of the word *hrondo* 'body', whereas this form was abandoned by 1959 for *hröa* (see X:141–3, 209, 304). It is written in an increasingly hasty hand in black nib-pen.

This text was first published in slightly different form in *Parma Eldalamberon* 17 (2007), pp. 124–5.

Eldar did not confound ordinary "breath" of the lungs with "spirit". The particular spirit indwelling in a body they called *fëa* [< *fáyā*]; spirit in general as a kind of being they called *fairë*. These terms were chiefly applied to the spirits or "souls" of Elves (and Men); since though these were held to be of a *similar* sort to those of the *máyar* (and Valar), they were not identical in nature: it was part of the nature of a *fëa* to desire to dwell in a body (*hrondo*), and by that mediary or instrument to operate upon the physical world; and the *fëa* did not and could not make its own body, according to its desire, or conception of itself, but could only modify its given or appointed *hrondo* by indwelling (as a living person may modify a house, filling it with a sense of his own personality, even if no visible physical alterations are made in its shape).

But the Eldar held that "spirits", the more as they had more native inherent power, could *emit* their influence to make contact with or act upon things exterior to themselves: primarily upon other spirits, or other incarnate persons (via their *fëar*), but also in the case of great spirits (such as the Valar or greater *máyar*) directly upon physical things without the mediacy of bodies normally necessary in the case of "*fairondi*" or incarnates. To describe this they used (but by deliberate symbolism – taken e.g. from such cases as their breathing upon a cold or frosted surface, which was then melted) the √*thū-* (or √*sū*). In addition Manwë, the most powerful spirit in Arda, in this respect was Lord of Air and Winds, and the winds were in primitive Eldarin thought to be especially his emission of power for himself. Hence *thūlē 'blowing forth' was used = 'spirit' in this special sense: the emission of power (of will or desire) from a spirit. [?Formulated] on *sū chiefly were Q *sūre* *(ĭ)*, S *sūl*. Cf. *Manwë Sūlimo* or *Thūrimo*, *thūle*, S *Thū*.

The Eldar still hold that *winds* may be [?such] and not all are naturally [?made] sc. that the air is [?easily] disturbed by direct will or [?alternatively] that [?the ?] of such power may seem to incarnates like a wind.

TEXT 2

> This text is written in a clear hand in black nib-pen on three sides of two sheets of Oxford examination paper. It was gathered by Tolkien with "Primal Impulse" (chap. II of part two of this book), but is presented here separately. There are two pieces of internal evidence that have bearing on its date. First is the use of the word *hrondo* 'body', whereas this form was abandoned by 1958 for *hröa* (see X:141–3, 209, 304). Second in the apparently inadvertent reference to the language "N." (that is, Noldorin) when citing the form *gwae*; this suggests that the change whereby Sindarin came to be the name of the Welsh-like Elvish language formerly and for long called Noldorin, was still relatively recent. I would therefore date this text to no later than 1957.

Concerning "Spirit"

The Eldar retained, even after their dwelling in Aman and their instruction by the Valar, many traces in their language of more primitive thought and theory.

At no time did they confuse, or identify, ordinary "breath" of the lungs, with "spirit". (They were indeed slow in arriving at the conception of a difference between "spirit" and "body" in their own case.) But they were much impressed by wind and all movements of air, especially as accompanying the passage of things going with speed, and (as they declared) the coming and going of other beings than themselves. The words for wind and motions of the air were therefore also used of, or modified and applied in use to, manifestations of "spirit", or incorporeal presences and operations.

The chief ancient stems concerned were: √*thū*/*thus*- 'blow, cause an air movement': √*sū*/*sur* 'blow, move with audible sound (of air)': the latter being seldom applied except to actual wind. The two stems owing to tendency in Quenya of *s*/*r* and *s*/*th* to coalesce became much confused. Q. *thussë*, *sussë* 'puff (of air)' (S. *thus*, *thos*); *súrë* (**sūri*) 'wind', &c. are only used of wind. But Q. *thúlë* usually equals '(movement of) spirit', whence S. *súl* = 'wind'; and *thû* = 'movement of spirit' (*thus*- ?).[1] In the title *Manwë Thúlimo*/*Súrimo*, later *Súlimo*, we see the blending.

Later the Eldar used the word Q. *fëa* (**phăyā*, from stem √*phay*) for the particular spirit indwelling in a given body or *hrondo*. In Sindarin we have *fân* (**phănā*) and *rhond*, *rhonn*. "Spirit" of this kind,[2] as a variety or mode of being was called in Q. *fairë* (**phai-rĭ*), in S. *faen* (**phainĭ*) = 'vapour'.

Also **wā*, **swā*, **wa-wa*, **swa-swa*, **swar*, etc. as "echoic" representations of sound of wind. Q. *hwá*; *hwarwa* 'violent wind'. N. *gwae* is apparently < **wā-yo* > *gwoe* > *gwae*. But *gwaew* < **wagmē*, Q. *vangwë* 'storm'.

These seem based on quite different analogies. √*pha*/*phay*/*phan* appear in origin to have referred to *exhalations*, as mists upon water or steams and the like. Cf. Q. *fanya* 'cloud' (S. *fein*, *fain* 'pallid, white', diaphanous), *fanwë* 'vapour, steam'.* [3]

In Quenya these terms: *fëa*, *fairë* were chiefly applied to the spirits or "souls" of Incarnates (Elves and Men); since though these were held to be of a similar mode of being to the Ainur, Valar, and Máyar,[4]

---

* Not that in Elvish thought "spirits" were conceived of as weak, thin, or only partly real: on the contrary *naked* and *obdurate* are the two adjectives most frequently applied to *fëar*. But the Eldar assert that "phantoms", reminding one of half-luminous exhalations, can be seen. They say that the *fëa* or spirit "remembers" its body (which it has inhabited in every part equally) and can present this mental picture to other *fëar* in a vapour or more or less wavering form, according to the clarity of vision and sensitivity of either party; this "phantom" is frequently seen (by those so gifted even among Men, but more readily by Elves) at or soon after the departure of a *fëa* from its body.

they were *not* identical in nature. They had no power, or very little power, of direct action upon other things or beings, and it was an important aspect of the nature of a *fëa* to desire to dwell in a body (*hrondo*), and by that mediacy or instrument to operate upon the *physical* world. Also, since the *fëa* was given a body at once, upon its entry into Eä, it had no experience or memory of separate existence. Death (that is separation from its body) was therefore for it an unnatural and unhappy condition.[5] Also, a *fëa* did not and could not make for itself any body, according either to its nature or its conception of itself, though it could and did modify and inspire its *hrondo* by indwelling – somewhat as a living person may modify and fill with a sense of its personality a house that it lives in long, even if it make no visible alteration in the shape of its dwelling. Whereas a Máya's normal experience was "disembodied"; its experience began before Eä, it had far more power over physical things, a far clearer and more accurate conception of itself – it could therefore "array" itself in forms of its own choosing. These might be only "phantoms", as were the appearances of disembodied *fëar*; but not necessarily so. By a "phantom" (Q. *nima* or *nimulë*; S. *nîf, nivol* = lit. a 'seeming') was meant an appearance having no existence in the *physical* world, existing only as a conception/memory/picture in one mind, and more or less accurately transferred direct to another. The Valar and greater Máyar were held to have made for themselves real bodies – ascertainable by Incarnates by all their senses, and occupying space; though since maintained by their true selves indestructible – in the sense that garments may be removed or repaired.

The Eldar believed that "spirits", and the more so as they had greater inherent native powers, could "emit" their influence to make contact with or act upon things exterior to themselves: primarily and most easily upon other spirits, or upon the *fëar* of Incarnates; but also in the case of the greater Máyar (of whom the Valar were the chief) directly upon physical things without the mediacy of corporeal instruments.* [6]

This direct action upon *things* was held to be quite different from direct calling of attention from other spirits. The latter was a *natural operation* within one mode of being, it being of the nature of spirits to

---

* The ordinary use of bodily instruments was usually necessary to an Incarnate (*mirondina*); though those in whom the *fëa* was dominant (a matter usually of *age*; for though some *fëar* were endowed from the beginning with greater power than others, all *fëar* were held to grow more dominant with respect to their *hrondo* as their life advanced) could do this in a small degree, and in a greater degree affect other *fëar* — by what we should call 'telepathy', Q. *palantimië* or *palanyantië*.

be aware of one another. The former was an exhalation of *dominance* of one mode over another; and according to the Eldar all exertions of dominance make demands upon those who exert the power – something of their "spirit" is expelled, and transferred to the thing in a lower mode. Hence all tyrants slowly consume themselves, or transfer their power to things, and can only control it so long as they can [?possess or control the thing with its ?] but power is dissipated. So Morgoth had become in fact *less* powerful than the other Valar, and much of his native power had passed into things [? ?diminished ?] Hence his malice could live on after his extrusion.

The words used to describe this action or emission of "power" were derived (apparently) by analogy from emission of breath, and such physical phenomena as breathing upon frost (which melts). In addition Manwë, who was held to be Lord of Air and Winds, was the most powerful of the Valar in this respect, and the most powerful spirit in Arda.

Following this text, Tolkien worked out two sentences in Quenya illustrating Manwë's "spirit in action" (Q. *thúlë/súlë*) from afar. The literal translations following each Quenya sentence are my own:

"And the spirit of Manwë went out* and the servants of Melkor were stayed"; or "and the hearts of the Eldar heard afar [?off] and were comforted / or obeyed."

Ar thúlë Manwëo etsurinye ar Eldaron indor turyaner.[7]
["And the spirit of Manwë blew forth and the hearts of the Eldar obeyed."]

Sustane Manwëo súle ten i indo Sindicollo ar he lastane ar carnes.[8]
["The spirit of Manwë blew unto the heart of Thingol and he listened and did it."]

Between these two Quenya sentences, Tolkien provided the following glosses and derivations:[9]

★thusya 'go forth' (as an emission) [>] Q. *thuzya* [>] *surya* 'blow' intr., [pa.t.] *surinyë*
★thusta, thúta 'send on' [>] Q. *susta* 'blow' tr., [pa.t.] *sustanë; súta,* [pa.t.] *sútanë.*

---

* Here *thúlë/súlë* 'spirit ([?in action])'.

NOTES

1 The question mark here is Tolkien's own, expressing that S. *thû* is perhaps derived from earlier *thus*.

2 That is, "spirit" as a "manifestation" or "incorporeal presence" (see the end of the second paragraph.

3 With "mental picture" in this footnote, see "Mind-Pictures" above.

4 For "Máyar" as a seldom-used form of the name "Maiar" see chap. VII, "The March of the Quendi", n. 11, above

5 On the natural unity of body and spirit in Incarnates, see BODY AND SPIRIT in App. I.

6 Q. *palanyantië* was altered from "*palannexe*" in the act of writing. For more on telepathy between spirits, see chaps. VII, "Mind-Pictures", and XI, "*Ósanwe-kenta*", above.

7 As first written, this sentence read: "*Ar thúle Manwëo etturinye etsurinye ar[?a] Melkoro*", before "*Melkoro*" (gen. 'of Melkor') was struck out; the whole being apparently an aborted translation of "And the spirit of Manwë went out and the servants of Melkor were stayed". While *etturinye* was not likewise struck out, I take it as intended to be replaced by following *etsurinye* in light of *surinye* in the subsequent jottings (q.v.). Similarly, "*Eldaron indor*" replaced the deleted false starts: "*in indor Eld in Eldar*" in the act of writing. Both in this and in the following Quenya sentence, the three occurrences of the conjunction "*ar*" was revised from, apparently, original "*ara*".

8 As first written, this sentence began with the false start: "*Sustane i sul*". The genitive form "*Sindicollo*" 'of Thingol' was altered from original "*Sindicolluo*" in the act of writing.

9 I have provided the mark "*" (indicating a primitive form) editorially, regularized Q *sūta(ne)* to *súta(në)*, and rearranged some items to indicate the "historical" and phonological developments implied by these forms.

XIV

THE VISIBLE FORMS OF
THE VALAR AND MAIAR

This text occupies five sides of six sheets of unlined paper, lettered (a)–(e) by Tolkien. It is written in a clear hand in black nib-pen. It is located in a bundle of sheets among Tolkien's linguistic papers that date from c. 1967, and is both near to and associated with the text presented in chap. VI, "Dwellings in Middle-earth", in part three of this book.

This text was previously published in slightly different form in *Parma Eldalamberon* 17, (2007), pp. 174–7.

√*phan-*. The basic sense of this was 'cover, screen, veil', but it had a special development in the Eldarin tongues. This was largely due to what appears to have been its very ancient application to *clouds*, especially to separate floating clouds as (partial) veils over the blue sky, or over the sun, moon, or stars. This application of the most primitive derivative ⋆*phanā* (Q *fana*, S *fân*) was so ancient that when ⋆*phanā* (or other derivatives) was applied to lesser, handmade, things this was felt to be a transference from the sense 'cloud', and words of this group were mainly applied to things of soft textures, veils, mantles, curtains and the like, of white or pale colours.

In Sindarin *fân* remained the usual word for 'cloud', floating clouds, or those for a while resting upon or wreathing hills and mountain-top. The derivative (properly adjectival in form) ⋆*phanyā* became *fain*, used as an adjective meaning 'dim, dimmed' (applied to dimmed or fading lights or to things seen in them) or 'filmy, fine-woven etc.' (applied to things that only partially screened light, such as a canopy of young still half-transparent leaves, or textures that veiled but only half-concealed a form). As a noun it was used of vague shapes or fleeting glimpses, especially of "apparitions" or figures seen in dreams.

In Quenya, owing to close relations of the Eldar in Valinor with the Valar and other lesser spirits of their order, *fana* developed a special sense. It was applied to the visible bodily forms adopted by these spirits, when they took up their abode on Earth, as the normal "raiment" of their otherwise invisible being. In these *fanar* they were seen and known by the Eldar, to whom glimpses of other and more awe-inspiring manifestations were seldom given. But the Elves of Valinor asserted that unclad and unveiled the Valar were perceived by some among them as lights (of different hues) which their eyes could not tolerate; whereas the Maiar were usually invisible unclad, but their presence was revealed by their fragrance.* [1]

The old word *fana* thus became used in Quenya only in this special and exalted sense: the visible form or "raiment" (which included both the assumed bodily shape and its vesture) in which a Vala or one of the lesser angelic spirits, not by nature incarnate, presented itself to bodily eyes. Since these *fanar* usually appeared "radiant" (in some degree), as if lit by a light within, the word *fana* acquired in Quenya an additional sense as 'shining shape', and this addition of radiance affected other derivatives of the same "base".

Valar ar Maiar fantaner nassentar fanainen ve quenderinwe koar al larmar. (*Nasser ar Kenime Kantar Valaron ar Maiaron*: a preserved fragment of Quenya lore): "The Valar and Maiar veiled their true-being in *fanar*, like to Elvish bodies and raiment" from "The Natures and Visible Shapes of the V. and M."

Thus the word for 'cloud' was in Quenya supplied by the derivative *fanya* (cf. I 394),[2] which was no longer used as an adjective. But this was used only of white clouds, sunlit or moonlit, or of clouds reflecting sunlight as in the sunset or sunrise, or gilded and silvered at the edges by moon or sun behind them. The hands of Varda were

---

* This applied only to those uncorrupted. Melkor, they said, was invisible, and his presence was revealed only by great dread and by a darkness that dimmed or blotted out the light and hues of all things near him. The Maiar corrupted by him stank. For this reason neither he nor any of the evil Maiar ever approached one of the Eldar that they wished to persuade or deceive except clad in their *fanar*. These they could still make to appear beautiful to Elvish eyes, if they wished — until after the great treachery of Melkor and the destruction of the Trees. After that Melkor (Morgoth) and his servants were perceived as forms of evil and enemies undisguised.

(like all her *fana*) of shining white. After the Darkening of Valinor she lifted them up, palms eastward, in a gesture of rejection,[3] as she summoned up in obedience to the decree of Manwë, her spouse, the "Elder King", the vast mists and shadows that made it impossible for any living thing to find again the way westward to the shores of Valinor. Her hands are thus compared poetically in "Galadriel's Lament" to clouds – white and shining still above the rising darkness that swiftly engulfed the shores and the mountains, and at last her own majestic figure* upon the summit of Oiolossë.[4]

This Quenya meaning of *fana* after the coming of the Exiles to Middle-earth was also assumed by Sindarin *fân*, at first in the Sindarin as used by the exiled Noldor, and eventually also by the Sindar themselves, especially those in close contact with the Noldor or actually mingled with them. No doubt this use aroused in the minds of the Sindar who had not seen the Valar in their own sacred land of Aman a mental picture of a majestic figure robed as if in shining cloud seen far away.[5] *Fanuilos* was thus a title of, or second name for Elbereth, made after the coming of the Exiles, and conveyed in full some such meaning as "bright angelic figure, far away upon *Uilos* (= Oiolossë)," or "– angelic figure ever-snow-white (shining afar)".[6]

Though the Sindar had failed to reach Valinor (and some were embittered by what they considered their desertion on the Western Shores of Middle-earth) their hearts were still "westward" and they treasured what they knew or could learn about the Valar. In the far off days of their "Awaking" they had been visited and protected by Oromë in his *fana* as a great horseman mounted upon Nahar and bearing his mighty horn, the *Valaróma*. Their king Elwë, later known as *Elwë Sindikollo* or in Sindarin form *(Elu) Thingol*, had been one of the three emissaries borne by Oromë to Valinor to the council of the Valar at which it was resolved to invite all the Elves who were willing to remove and dwell in the Far West under the protection of the Valar and out of the reach of Morgoth. He had thus seen and had converse with the Valar in their most majestic *fanar*. His wife Melian was one of the lesser spirits of the same order, a Maia of great beauty and wisdom, so that, at least among the "wise" of Doriath, much was known about the Valar. Varda whom none of the Sindar had seen

---

* The *fanar* of the great Valar were said by the Eldar who had dwelt in Valinor usually to have had a stature far greater than that of the tallest Elves, and when performing some great deed or rite, or issuing commands, to have assumed an awe-inspiring height.

(save Elwë), was there called *El-bereth* (a name of the same meaning as Quenya *Elentári*) ['Star-queen']....

The *fanar* of the *Valar* were not "phantoms", but "physical": that is, they were not "visions" arising to the mind, or implanted there by the will of a superior mind or spirit, and then projected,* [7] but received through the bodily eyes.†

The Valar had a command, great individually, *almost* complete as a united council, over the physical material of Eä (the material universe). Their *fanar* which were originally devised out of love for the "Children of Eru", the Incarnate, whom they were to guard and counsel, had the properties of the material of which the *köar* (or bodies) of the Elves (and also of Men) were formed: sc. they were not transparent, they cast shadows (if their inner luminosity was dimmed); they could move material objects, and were resisted by these, and resisted them. These *fanar* were, however, also personal expressions (in terms suitable to the apprehension of the Incarnate) of their individual "natures" and functions, and were usually also clad in vestures of similar purpose.

But it is often mentioned in the legends that certain of the Valar, and occasionally of the Maiar, "passed over the Sea", and appeared in Middle-earth. (Notably Oromë, Ulmo, and Yavanna.) The Valar and Maiar were essentially "spirits", according to Elvish tradition given being before the making of Eä. They could go where they willed, that is could be present at once at any point in Eä where they desired to be.‡

A briefer but related and apparently contemporary note elsewhere in Tolkien's linguistic papers provides these additional details:

[Q. *fana*] was used of the "raiment" or "veils" in which the Valar presented themselves. These were the *bodily forms* (like those of Elves and Men), as well as any further vestures, in which the Valar were

---

* These were called in Quenya *indemmar* 'mind-pictures'.

† Or mainly so: the power of the presence of one of these spirits no doubt affected the reception and was responsible, for instance, for the impressions of "radiance" with which the "vision" was endowed.

‡ Subject only to special limitations voluntarily taken upon themselves or decreed by Eru. Thus after the final establishment of Arda, when the Valar, the spirits destined to be most concerned with this chosen stage for combat with Melkor, took up their abode on Middle-earth, they no longer passed beyond its confines. That is, according to Elvish tradition they remained, usually clad in their *fanar*, in physical residence on earth as its guardians.

self-incarnated. These *fanar* they assumed when after their demiurgic activities they came and dwelt in *Arda* ('the Realm'), that is the Earth; and they did so because of their love and yearning for the "Children of Eru", for whom they were to prepare the world, and for a time to govern it. The future forms of the bodies of Elves and Men they knew, though they had no part in their making. In these forms they presented themselves to the Elves (though they could assume other and wholly alien shapes), appearing usually as persons of majestic (but not gigantic) stature.

NOTES

1 In the footnote, the words "as forms of evil and enemies undisguised" replaced original "as enemies of dreadful shape". But with this cf. the statement at UT:254 n.7 that when in the Second Age in Eregion, long after Melkor's destruction of the Two Trees, Sauron "came among the Noldor he adopted a specious fair form". With the fragrance of uncorrupted spirits see ODOUR OF SANCTITY in App. I.

2 I.e. LR:377.

3 With this gesture of rejection, cf. chap. III, "Eldarin Hands, Fingers, and Numerals" above.

4 Cf. LR:377–8.

5 A deleted footnote at this point read:

The *fanar* were physical or had the properties of material substances, i.e. were not transparent, could move other objects, cast shadows (if not themselves shining) and were resisted by or offered resistance to other physical things. But the Vala (or Maia) could move or pass over Sea. For their bodies were self-made. They houseless as spirits could go where they would (either slowly or immediately), and could then reclothe themselves. In Middle-earth they usually occluded their radiance.

6 Cf. *The Road Goes Ever On* (1968), p. 66.

7 With *indemmar* cf. chap. VII, "Mind-Pictures", above.

XV

ELVISH REINCARNATION

The complex of texts presented here spans from about 1959 to 1972. The first part of text 1A was published at X:361–2, but I give it here again for ease of comparison with the commentary and the partial, revised version (1B) that follows it. For Christopher Tolkien's own discussion and citation from these texts, cf. X:265–8, 362–6, XII:382, 390–1 n.17.

These texts were published (with the assistance of Christopher Tolkien and myself) in somewhat different form by Michaël Devaux in *La Feuille de la Compagnie*, vol.3, *J.R.R. Tolkien, l'effigie des Elfes* (2014).

TEXT 1A

This typescript text of nine sides, lettered by Tolkien A–I (with two additional, supplanted sides, lettered Cx and Dx) is described and partially presented by Christopher Tolkien at X:361–2, who dates it to c. 1959.

The Converse of Manwë with Eru
concerning the death of the Elves and how it might
be redressed; with the comments of the Eldar added

Manwë spoke to Eru, saying: "Behold! an evil appears in Arda that we did not look for: Thy First-born Children, whom Thou madest immortal, suffer now severance of spirit and body. Many of the *fëar* of the Elves in Middle-earth are now houseless; and even in Aman there is one. The houseless we summon to Aman, to keep them from the Darkness, and all who hear our voice abide here in waiting.

"What further is to be done? Is there no means by which their lives may be renewed, to follow the courses which Thou hast designed? And what of the bereaved who mourn those that have gone?"

Eru answered: "Let the houseless be re-housed!"

Manwë asked: "How shall this be done?"

Eru answered: "Let the body that was destroyed be re-made. Or let the naked *fëa* be re-born as a child."

Manwë said: "Is it Thy will that we should attempt these things? For we fear to meddle with Thy Children."

Eru answered: "Have I not given to the Valar the rule of Arda, and power over all the substance thereof, to shape it at their will under My will? Ye have not been backward in these things. As for My First-born, have ye not removed great numbers of them to Aman from the Middle-earth in which I set them?"

Manwë answered: "This we have done, for fear of Melcor,[1] and with good intent, though not without misgiving. But to use our power upon the flesh that Thou hast designed, to house the spirits of Thy Children, this seems a matter beyond our authority, even were it not beyond our skill."

Eru said: "I give you authority. The skill ye have already, if ye will take heed. Look and ye will find that each spirit of My Children retaineth in itself the full imprint and memory of its former house; and in its nakedness it is open to you, so that ye may clearly perceive all that is in it. After this imprint ye may make for it again such a house in all particulars as it had ere evil befell it. Thus ye may send it back to the lands of the Living."

Then Manwë asked further: "O Ilúvatar, hast Thou not spoken also of re-birth? Is that too within our power and authority?"

Eru answered: "It shall be within your authority, but it is not in your power. Those whom ye judge fit to be re-born, if they desire it and understand clearly what they incur, ye shall surrender to Me; and I will consider them."[2]

Comments

1. The Valar were troubled, not only because of the case of Finwë and Míriel but because of the Avari, and of the Sindar; for Middle-earth was perilous to bodies, and many had died, even before the Eldar came to Aman. And they discovered that, though those *fëar* that obeyed their summons were safe from the Darkness, to be naked was

against their nature.[3] Therefore the Dead were unhappy, not only because they were bereaved of friends, but because they could do no deed nor achieve any new design without the body.[4] Many therefore turned inwards, brooding upon their injuries, and they were hard to heal.

2. The Valar feared to meddle with the Children, since they were not in the design of Eä in which they had assisted. Also Eru had forbidden them to coerce their wills, daunting their minds by dread of the power of the Valar, or even amazing them with wonder of their beauty and majesty. But they deemed that since the rule of Arda was committed them, it was within their authority to hinder any creature from deeds of evil, or to restrain it from what might prove hurtful to itself or to others. By "coercing the will" they understood the domination or enslaving of the mind of a lesser creature, so that it might say "I will", assenting to this or that against its true nature and inclination, until it lost, maybe, the power of choice. But they held it within their authority, which must otherwise become void in all dealings with those that had minds and wills, to deny to it, if they could, the means to achieve its purposes and desires, if these were evil or hurtful. For by the gift of will, Eru had not guaranteed to any less than Himself that this will should always be effected, be it good or evil.[5] And even the lesser creatures had the power to hinder the deeds of others, and the right to do so, if they judged the deeds to be wrong, albeit their judgement of what was evil or hurtful was far less secure than the judgement of the Valar, who knew clearly (according to their capacity) the will of Eru. Nonetheless, the removal of the Eldar from Middle-earth went to the limits of their authority, as they well understood; and not all of the Valar had believed this to be wise.

3. It is clear that the Valar had power and skill, among them, to form from the substance of Arda any thing, however intricate in design, of which they knew and fully perceived the pattern. But as was seen in the case of Aulë and the Dwarves they had no power to give free mind and will to anything that they made. With regard to the Dead, however, the living mind of the *fëa* already existed, and the Valar had only to make for it a house in all things the same as the one that it had lost. This they could now do with the authority of Eru.

4. Some then asked whether the *fëa* re-housed was the same person as before the death of the body. It was agreed that it was the same person, for these reasons. "What means this word *same*?" the loremasters said. 'It means two things: *in all respects equivalent*; but also *identical in history*.'

"With regard to spirits: No *fëa* can be repeated; each proceeds separately and uniquely from Eru, and so remains for ever separate and unique. It may indeed resemble some other *fëa* so closely that observers may be deceived; but it can then only be said to be *like* the other. If it is said to be the *same* as the other (though this is not said by the wise), this can only mean that it resembles the other in all features of its character so closely that the two, unless present together, cannot be distinguished, save by intimate knowledge of both. We say *by intimate knowledge*, not meaning knowledge only of the different histories of these two, but because we hold, and all observation confirms us, that no two *fëar* are in truth exactly alike or equivalent.

"With regard to things without life, and to things with life corporeal only, it may seem that all these also are unique in history, that is in the Unfolding of Eä and the Tale of Arda. But here two things require thought. First: 'In what degree things without even life corporeal can be distinguished as the *same* (or identical) on the one hand, and as *equivalent* on the other.' Second: 'How does it concern a thing with life corporeal (still more a person with a life spiritual also), if the material in which it is embodied is changed, the pattern of the embodiment being maintained or restored?'

"To speak of things without life. In history, maybe, one quantity of iron (for example) is not the *same* as any other equal quantity of iron; for both co-exist in time, occupying different places, and they will do so while Eä lasts, even though each quantity or aggregation of iron may be dispersed into smaller quantities. But this difference concerns IRON only, that is the total of this *nassë* (or material) that exists in Arda (or in Eä, maybe). For later-made and higher forms, whether having life (from Eru and his vice-gerents), or the shaping of art (from minds incarnate), this difference has no importance or meaning, and all fractions of IRON (or other *nassë*) are in value or virtue the *same*."* [6]

---

* Or nearly so. They may indeed be "virtually", that is in all operations or effects in the service of higher forms, identical. But the loremasters tell us that they may be in themselves not wholly and exactly equivalent. Some of the loremasters hold that the substance of Arda (or indeed of all Eä) was in the beginning one thing, the *erma*; but not since the beginning has it remained one and the same, alike and equivalent, in all times and places. In the first shapings this primary substance or *erma* became varied and divided into many secondary materials or *nassi*, which have within themselves various patterns, whereby they differ one from another inwardly, and outwardly have different virtues and effects. In so far, therefore, as the separate *nassi* maintain their characteristic patterns within, all fractions of the same *nassë* are equivalent and indistinguishable, and with regard to higher forms may be said to be "the same". But the Valar, through or by whom these variations were effected as the first step in the production of the riches of

Thus for all the purposes of constituting a form that uses (say) IRON in its embodiment, the substitution of one fraction of IRON for another equal fraction will have no effect upon life or identity. It is commonly said, for instance, that two rings (differently shaped by art) are made "of the same stuff", if they are both made (say) of GOLD. And "same" is rightly used, when the higher thing that uses lower materials for its embodiment is considered.

Still more truly is the word "same" used, if we consider things with life corporeal. For life corporeal consists in a pattern, existing in itself (from the mind of Eru, directly or mediately), and neither derived from the *nassi* used in its embodiment, nor imposed by other living things (as by the art of the Incarnate). Though it may indeed be part of the nature of the living thing to use certain materials and not to use others in the development of its pattern.

This is because the living patterns, though conceived as it were outside Eä, were destined to be realized within Eä (having respect to the qualities of the *erma* and *nassi* of Eä), and therefore "select" – not by will or awareness of their own good, but by the nature of the unfolding pattern, which is to seek realization as near to its primal and unconditioned form as possible – those materials by which they may be "best" realized. "Best", but not perfectly: that is, not in any case exactly according to the conceived and unrealized pattern. But such "imperfection" is not an evil, necessarily.[7] For it does not seem that Eru designed Eä so that living things should each in their kind exactly exhibit the primal life-pattern of that kind,[8] and that all members of one kind (as, say, beeches) should be exactly alike. Rather His design is more akin to the Art of the Incarnate, in which the pattern conceived may be endlessly varied in individual examples, and according to the chances of materials and conditions in Arda. To perceive the patterns, and their kinship, through living variation is a chief delight of those who survey the wealth of the living things of Arda. Neither is there a

---

Eä, and who therefore have full knowledge of the *nassi* and their combinations, report that there are minute variations of pattern within one *nassë*. These are very rare (and their origins or purposes the Valar have not disclosed); yet it can thus happen that in comparing a quantity of one *nassë* with another equal quantity of the same *nassë* the subtle in skill may find that the one quantity contains *únehtar* (the smallest quantities possible in which the interior pattern that distinguishes it from other *nassi* is exhibited) varying somewhat from the norm. Or both quantities may contain the variant *únehtar*, but in different numbers. In such cases the two quantities will not be precisely equivalent; though it may be held that the difference between them is so incalculably small that their virtues as materials for the making of embodiments of living patterns are indistinguishable.

fast distinction between "kinds" and the variations of individuals. For some kinds are more akin to others in pattern, and may seem to be only variations of some older and common pattern. This the Valar say is how the variety of Arda was indeed achieved: beginning with a few patterns, and varying these or blending pattern with pattern.[9]

Thus it may occur that for a living thing its "proper", that is, its best, materials are scarce, so that it may be obliged to use these in different proportions from those which are "proper", or even to use other materials. If these changes do not actually impair its development so that it perishes, still its form may be modified; and the modifications may be thought to be "due" to the *nassi*. But rightly viewed they are not so. The *nassi* are passive, the living pattern is active; and though the realization of the pattern may be otherwise than it would have been with "better" materials, the modified form is due to the operation of the living upon the unliving.

Another thing which distinguishes the living from the unliving is that the living employ Time in their realization. In other words it is part of their nature to "grow", using such material as is needed or is available to them for their embodiment. So that a living pattern does not exist fully at any one moment of time (as do unliving patterns); but is complete only with the completion of its life. It cannot therefore rightly be seen instantly, and is only imperfectly envisaged even with the help of memory. Only those who conceived its pattern and whose sight is not limited to the succession of time can, for instance, see the true shape of a tree.

We say that unliving things or patterns do "exist fully at any one instant of time", meaning, for instance, that IRON is always IRON, just so and nothing more nor less, whenever observed or considered. So long, that is, as its characteristic inner pattern is maintained. If this is or could be changed, it would not be IRON, or a portion of IRON, "growing" and working out the full pattern of IRON according to iron-nature. It would rather be that iron was changed into something else, and became another *nassë*, whether by force external applied to it, or by its own instability. Though in the case of certain *nassi* that appear "by nature" to be thus "unstable", breaking up or changing their inner patterns normally under like conditions, it may be thought that we have an adumbration in a lower order of the normal nature of a higher order.[10] For such adumbrations are to be seen in all orders. Nonetheless they are only "adumbrations" and not the same processes. Just as the apparent growth of crystals foreshadows but does not forestall the growth of plants.

Some may say: "But are not many unliving things subject to change without loss of identity?" We answer: "No. These things are things in name only: that is, they are distinguished from their surroundings by minds, and not by their own interior nature. Or they have shapes and individuality derived also from minds, and imposed upon the unliving material by art."

Thus the Incarnate may distinguish, say, a mountain from the land about it, giving it a name, such as *Dolmed* [one of the Blue Mountains]. But what are the bounds of Dolmed? Some may say "here it begins" or "here it ends"; but others may say otherwise; and if the bounds are agreed, it will be by custom or convention of people, not by the nature of the land. Neither would its bounds in Time be clear, so that one of the Incarnate living many ages might say "now Dolmed has begun to be" or "now it has ceased". For this aggregation of materials upon the surface of Arda has no inner individuality distinguishing it from the adjacent material. The distinction is applied by minds receiving the impression of a shape that can be held in memory; and it is by their memory alone that it is name-worthy.

A face perceived by eyes in the markings on a wall, or in the weatherings of a rock, or in the discolorations of the Moon, is not a face in itself, but only for a beholder (and maybe not for all beholders). Such perceptions are related to Art, and not to the forms which living things exhibit by their own nature apart from any beholder.

As for works of art or craftsmanship, these things resemble corporeal living things in having a shape that does not belong to the material used in their embodiment. But this shape lives (so to speak) only in the mind of the maker. It is not part of Arda (or Eä) apart from that mind; and it may indeed only be recognized as a "shape" by that mind, or by others of like kind. Those who had never had need or thought of a staff, if they saw one, might not distinguish it from any chance piece of wood. For the most part the Incarnate do, or think that they do (for they may be deceived by the chances of Arda), recognize the purposeful touches of shaping hands in things of art or craft, even when the purpose is not known. But this is because they are like minds, and have experience in themselves of this mode of shaping. Moreover shapes of this mode are only name-worthy when complete, either completely finished, or so far made that their ultimate form may be foreseen or nearly guessed.

In this way, therefore, living forms (not imposed) may be distinguished from those given by craftsmen. The living forms grow; but they have at all stages a true form that is name-worthy. Being part of a total shape, extending over Time, each instant of their existence partakes in that reality (or realization). We may speak of a "young" tree (or "sapling"), and of a "young" man (or "child"), judging the form to be tree or man, but because of memory and experience deeming (not always rightly) that this tree or man is in an early stage of its development. But beholding a craftsman making a chair we should not call its first stage a "young" chair. We should say at different moments that he was making something of (say) wood; that he was making a piece of furniture; and that he was going to make a chair (when the shape was so far advanced that we could guess this). But we should not call his work "a chair" until it was finished.

Thus when we speak of things named, we must distinguish three kinds. Some have a shape and being of their own, which we did not give, and which would exist so, even if we did not exist: these are living things, which though we may use them, have as primary purpose to be themselves. Some have their individuality only in the names given to them by name-givers, and have only such bounds as the name-givers ascribe to them. This name-giving is related to the arts of the Incarnate. For either the mind of the name-giver, though no work of his hands is involved, selects from Arda a memorable shape that he might have made or might make if he had the skill and power; or he attributes that which he sees, as a mountain or lake, to the work of a mind that had purpose (such as one of the Valar). Some, the third kind, have shapes given to them by Incarnate minds with purposes belonging to the minds and not to the materials. But since all things in Arda are akin, the form of Art respects the nature of the material, and should do so.

All that has been said concerning things of life corporeal applies fully to the Incarnate also. For they use a body of life corporeal. But with regard to the Incarnate this must be added: their bodies are governed indeed, as are bodies without *fëar*, by living and growing patterns; but over that again is now the indwelling spirit, which exerts power over the life corporeal, and so over the material also. When the *fëa* is strong, and when it is not weakened by the Shadow so as to be turned away from its good, it sustains the life corporeal (as a master may support and succour a servant), so that it too is strong, to complete itself and to resist affronts from without, or to heal and restore any injuries to its embodiment.

Much more, then, than in even a healthy living thing without *fëa*, its being must be sought in its life-pattern rather than in the material of its body; so that change in that material, or the substitution of equivalent materials, as long as these are adequate for the continuation of the life and coherence of the housing body, will not affect its identity and individuality.

For the individuality of a person resides in the *fëa*. A *fëa* alone may be a person. In the case of the Incarnate, though they are by nature embodied, their identity resides no longer, as it does in things of corporeal life only, in that embodiment, but in the identity of the *fëa* and its memory. A *fëa* of this kind requires a "house" by which it may inhabit Arda and operate in it. But a house exactly equivalent is sufficient for it – for it will *exactly* correspond to its memory of its former house, and that memory being in the mind only and incorporeal will not be concerned with the history of the material used in the realization (so long as it is fitted for this purpose) but with the form only. Therefore, returning, the *fëa* will inhabit the rebuilt house gladly.

Even so, one might go on a journey, and while he was away lightning might come and destroy his house. But if he had friends of subtle skill, who while he was away re-built his house and all its appurtenances that had been ruined in exactly the same shapes, he would come back to this house, and call it his own, and continue his life there as before. And even if his friends reported to him what they had done, would he not still be content, giving to the house re-built the same name as the old house had, and deeming that the evil chance had been healed?

He would be content, or at least he would accept with gratitude the work of his friends and find in it a sufficient means for the carrying on of his life in the same mode as was his wont. Alas! it might well chance that the house, or something within it, had for him a value not residing in itself or its fashion, but attributed to it by him, the owner: as being, for instance, the gift of one whom he loved. With the counterfeit (that is, the exact copy) he might then not be wholly content, saying "this is not the same thing as the one that is lost". But this would be because he loved the *history of the thing*, rather than any other quality it had possessed, and because that history was connected with a loved person he attributed to it part of that love. This is part of the mystery of love, and of the singling out by love of one thing alone in its oneness and history unique, which is of the nature of the Incarnate. Such losses not even the re-housing of the Dead, under the authority of the One, can avoid, for it deals with the future, not the past. Death is death; and it may be healed or amended, but it cannot be made not to have been.

Nonetheless one of the Dead re-housed, with whatsoever regret death may bring, will remain the same person; and will inhabit and continue the life of the housing body, as if no evil had befallen it. To doubt this is as if one were to doubt that a craftsman remained the same person, when, after a work upon which he laboured was destroyed, he laboured again with fresh material to make that work again, or to finish it.

It is then, we see, the relation of the *fëa* to its housing that makes possible the re-building of this house without change of identity in the whole person. If we return to consideration of living things without *fëar* this will become clear. Of these it is true to say that they all are unique in history and according to the Tale of Arda. To speak of trees, for example. Each tree is unique; for no other tree can occupy the same situation (comprising both the time and the room of its growth). If it ends or is destroyed, then it cannot appear again in the Tale of Arda.

Some may say, nonetheless: "Yet its being resided mainly in its pattern, as a single exemplar of the pattern of its kind. What then, if after that embodiment of the pattern was destroyed, the pattern was reconstituted from the *same materials* (that is, identical) wherewith it was before embodied? Will then the 'new' tree be other than the 'old' tree, even in history? All those who knew the tree and mourned its loss will rejoice; and Arda will suffer no loss or change, for both the pattern and the materials will be as they were before the damage and in the same relations. Would it not be truer to say then, even in history: 'This tree at this date suffered the marring (or destruction) of its body; but soon after *it* (*sc.* the tree) was made again and so continued its life'? And what if the re-making was accomplished not with identical materials but with equivalents? The difference between 'equivalents' of the order of *nassi* has, as we have seen, no importance for forms of a higher order."

To this it may be answered: "This is a proposition of thought only. In any case we have here to consider not the materials (whether identical or equivalent), but the nature of corporeal pattern. This is not 'of Eä', but its embodiment belongs to a particular date or period within Arda. When this embodiment is destroyed, the co-operation of pattern and material and Time (which is the being of the tree) is ended. It cannot be begun again (even if identical materials are used); it can only be counterfeited. For the pattern is a 'design' extending through a period of time, which therefore at any moment before its completion envisages the future and has an energy, as it were, impelling the growth to continue the development to its end. At the moment of the dissolution of its work, from whatever cause, that impulse ceases.

We may say, if we limit ourselves to the particular thing considered, not involving ourselves with wider or deeper matters, that it was the 'fate' in Arda of this tree to fail of full achievement. This may become clearer, if we reflect not on premature death but on the natural death of living things of short duration. If the tree dies, having fulfilled its span, who can remake it? It was both its 'fate' and its nature by design to live so long and no longer; its pattern is complete and ended; it is all 'past' and has no more 'future'."

For this reason the Valar themselves do not claim ever to *re-make the same tree*, whether its loss be mourned or not, but only (if they will) to restore to the wealth of Arda a thing equivalent. They do not undo history. This cannot indeed be done without the undoing of Eä. Therefore, it is only the Elves that the Valar can, under the authority of Eru, "re-house". For it is their nature *not* to end within Arda. Those whose nature it is to end within Arda, that is to die naturally, they cannot and do not re-house, as is seen in the case of Men. Even so, the restored body of one of the Elves, is only an "equivalent", and it is the *fëa* which provides continuity, since this still has a "future" in Arda.

In all this we have not considered the Great Pattern, or the Major Patterns: to which we refer when we speak of *kinds*, or *families*, or *descent*. Men often liken these things to Trees with branches; the Eldar liken them rather to Rivers, proceeding from a spring to their outflow into the Sea.

Now some hold that as the matters of Eä proceed from a single *erma* (if this indeed be true), so the life of living things comes from one beginning or *Ermenië*

The text ends here, about ¾ down the page. For the continuation of this last line of thought, see chap. II, "The Primal Impulse" in part three of this book.

TEXT 1B

This typescript text of two sides is briefly referred to by Christopher Tolkien at X:361 as an abandoned "second, more ample version of the 'Converse'". It doubtless is closely contemporary with text 1A.

Beginning of a revised & expanded version of
"The Converse"

Manwë spoke to Eru, saying: "Behold an evil appears in Arda that
we did not look for: thy first-born children, whom thou madest
immortal, suffer now severance of spirit and body, and many of the
fëar of the Elves are houseless. These we summon to Aman, to keep
them from the Darkness, and here they abide in waiting, all who
obey our voice. What further is to be done? Is there no means by
which their life may be renewed and follow the courses that thou
hast designed? For the *fëa* that is naked is maimed and can accomplish no new thing according to the desire of its nature. And what of
the bereaved that live still but mourn those that have gone?"

Eru answered: "Let the houseless be re-housed!"

And Manwë asked: "Is it thy will that we should attempt this? For
we fear to meddle with thy children".

And Eru said: "Verily ye shall not coerce their wills, nor daunt their
minds with wonder or with dread. But ye may instruct them in truth
according to your knowledge; and in Arda Marred ye may hinder
them from evil, and restrain them from what is hurtful to their kind.

"And have I not given to the Valar the rule of Arda, and power
over all the substance thereof, to shape it at their will under my will?

"This then ye may do. The Dead that hear your summons and
come to you ye shall judge. The innocent shall be given the choice to
return into the lands of the Living. If they choose this freely, ye shall
send them back. In two ways this may be done. The former body, as
it was before the injury that caused death, may be restored. Or the *fëa*
may be re-born according to kind.

"Have ye not seen that each *fëa* retaineth in itself the imprint and
memory of its former house (even if it be not itself fully aware of
this)? Behold! the *fëa* in its nakedness may be wholly perceived by
you. Therefore after this imprint ye shall make again for it such a
house in all particulars as it had ere evil befell it. Thus ye may send it
back to the lands of the Living.

"Let this be done soon, for the innocent that desire it; soonest for
those who suffer death as children; for they will have need of their
parents, and their parents of them. Yet of times the choice is committed to the Valar, according to the needs of each case and the chances
of Arda. Great evils and sorrows will come to pass there; and it may
not always be expedient to send those who have been slain, by wounds
or by grief, too swiftly back into the perils that overcame them.

"As for the wrong-doers, who will increase in Middle-earth, ye shall be their judges, be their ill deeds great or small. Surely your judgement of the naked *fëa* shall not go astray. Those who submit to you ye shall correct and instruct, if they will hear your words; and when ye deem that they have been healed and brought back to good will, they too may return in like manner, if they wish. But the obdurate ye shall retain until the End. The time and place of each return ye shall choose.

"As for re-birth according to kind: those who choose this must know fully what this meaneth; and the time of return shall be in my will, which they must await. For understand that, as hath been said, each *fëa* retaineth the imprint of its former body and of all that it hath experienced therethrough. That imprint cannot be erased, but it may be veiled, though not for ever. Even as each *fëa* must of nature remember Me (from whom it came), yet that memory is veiled, being overlaid by the impress of things new and strange that it perceives through the body. So it shall be that for a *fëa* re-born all its past, both in life and in waiting, will be veiled and overlaid by the strangeness of the new house in which it will awake again. For the re-born shall be true children, awaking anew to the wonder of Arda.

"In this the Dead who are re-born shall find recompense for their injuries. But let those who desire re-birth be assured of this: memory of the past will return. Slowly, maybe, and fitfully, as by strange hints and monitions or by knowing things unlearned, the re-born will become aware of their state, until even as they become full-grown and the *fëa* cometh to its mastery they will recall their former life.

"This may bring them sorrow, for they will not be able to take up their former life, but must continue in the state and under the name that they now bear. Yet this sorrow will be redressed, by greater wisdom (for the *fëa* of the re-born will be twice nourished by parents); and it will be strong to endure, and patient and prudent.

"Nonetheless, because of this danger in returning memory, I counsel you that not to all the houseless shall ye offer this choice of re-birth. In the first place those who are to be re-born ye should judge to be wise. Also it were best that they should be the young in death, who have not had long life nor formed binding ties of love or duty with others. In no case shall they be those who were wedded.

"For the re-born could not return to their former spouse; neither could they take another. Marriage is both of the body and of the spirit. Therefore those who have a different body cannot resume a union made in another body. But since they are the same person as before, who was wedded, they cannot take a new spouse: for identity of person resideth in the *fëa*, and in its memory. This unnatural state shall not be permitted.

"If there are any who having heard these things still desire re-birth, say to them: 'It lieth with Ilúvatar. We will present your prayers to Him. If He denies you, ye shall speedily know, and ye must be content with other choice. If He assents, He will call you in due time, but until then you must abide in patience'."

Is it lawful for one of the Dead to summon another from the Living (such as a beloved spouse) to Mandos? Unlawful, were it possible. For the Dead, if innocent, may return to those whom they love. If guilty, they may not meddle again with the Living, not at least until they are cleansed. But they cannot summon any of the Living unless through the Valar; and this the Valar must refuse to do.

Is it lawful for two wedded persons (or others that are bound by love) both (or all of them) to remain in Mandos together, if death shall have brought them thither together? It is lawful. They may not be compelled to return. But if they have duties to the Living (as parents to children, maybe), then ye may dissuade them from abiding with just argument.

Text 2

This text, which Christopher Tolkien paraphrased and excerpted at X:363–4 and dates there by implication to c. 1959 (cf. X:304) is written in increasingly hasty black nib-pen on five sides of six torn half-sheets, and on three of the four half-sides of a folded (but not torn) sheet, and on one side of an additional torn half-sheet. Complicating the dating of this text is the note on the additional half-sheet, which bears the date: "June 1966" (given here as an extensive footnote on the sentence: "Could possibly the 'houseless' *fëa*, in proper case, be allowed to/instructed how to rebuild its own 'house' from memory?") However, as a commentary on the primary text, it may well have been written at some remove from the primary text.

Reincarnation of Elves

Dilemma: It seems an *essential* element in the tales. But:

How accomplished? 1) *Rebirth*? 2) Or re-making of a *counterfeit equivalent body* (when original one destroyed)? Or *both*?

1) Most difficult in result; much easiest to arrange.

The most *fatal* objection is that it contradicts the fundamental notion that *fëa* and *hröa* were each *fitted* to the other. Since *hröar* have a physical descent, the body of rebirth, having different parents, must be different, and *should* cause acute discomfort or pain to the reborn *fëa*.

There are *many other* objections: as

(a) unfairness to second parents to foist a child on them whose *fëa* already had experience and a character – unless they were consulted. How could they be?

(b) Problem of *memory*. Unless identity of *personality*, and conscious continuity of experience were preserved, re-birth would offer *no* consolation for death and bereavement. If memory were preserved and (eventually) regained by the re-born, this would produce difficulties. Not so much psychological as practical. (The idea in previous considerations of double joy, and memory of two youths or springs as a recompense for "death" is good enough psychologically.)

(c) But if memory and continuity of personality is preserved (as it must be) then we must suppose (as has been supposed in previous treatments) that the reborn *fëa* would assimilate its new body to its memory of the former, and would when "full grown" become visibly as interiorly the same person again.

What then of its relations to former kin and friends, and especially to a *former spouse*? It could only re-marry the former spouse: in fact it must do so – but then there would be a discrepancy of age, and rebirth must be at least swift. No time for Mandos to consider how long he should keep them "houseless"!

(d) How could re-marriage be arranged for, or opportunity of re-meeting?

2) Difficulties are here "mechanical". How could the Valar re-make an exactly equivalent body – which of them would do this (or all)? It could only be done in *Aman* (certainly under such conditions as prevailed during Exile of Ñoldor). How would the rehoused *fëa* then be sent back? *The only solution* seems to be this:

There was no provision for re-incarnation in the Music known to the Valar. Elves were not supposed to die. The Valar soon found many houseless spirits gathered in Mandos. E.g. some "deaths" probable even on Great March. (There need only be few.)[11]

They did nothing until the case of Míriel* made the matter immediate. Because they did not "understand" the Children, and were not
competent or permitted to meddle. Manwë then directly appealed to
Eru for counsel.

Eru accepts and ratifies the position – though clearly he thinks the
Valar should have contested Melkor's domination of Middle-earth
earlier, and made it "safe for the Elves" – they had not enough *estel*
['trust'] that in a *legitimate war* Eru would not have allowed Melkor to
so damage Arda that the Children could not come, or live in it. The
fëar of the Dead all go to Mandos in Aman: or rather they are now
summoned thither by the authority given by Eru. A place is made for
them. (They may refuse the summons, because they must remain
free wills.)

The Valar have power in Aman to re-build bodies *for the Elves*. The
naked *fëa* is open to their inspection – or at least *if it desires reincarnation it will co-operate* and reveal its memory. The memory is so
detailed that a houseless *fëa* can induce in another *fëa* a picture of it
(if it tries: hence notion of "phantoms" – which are indeed mental
appearances).[12] The new body will be made of identical materials to
a precise pattern. Here there will come discussion of nature of "iden-
tity-equivalence" in material constructions.

The rehoused *fëa* will *normally* remain in Aman. Only in very
exceptional cases as Beren and Lúthien will they be transported
back to Middle-earth. (*How* perhaps need not be made any clearer
than the mode by which the Valar in physical form could go from
Aman to Middle-earth.) Hence *death* in Middle-earth had much of
same sort of sorrow and sunderance for Elves and Men. But as
Andreth saw the *certainty* of living again and *doing* things in incarnate form – if desired – made a vast difference in death as a personal
terror. After removal of/? destruction of Aman as physical part of
Arda – there could be no return. Only way of reunion of bereaved
was by death of both parties – though after end of Beleriand and
Battle which destroyed Morgoth the bereaved could *voyage* to Aman.
They usually did! After destruction of Númenor, *only* the Elves
could normally do this.

---

* Míriel is thus first case – *there were no* dead in Aman before that. Hence accom-
modation in House of Vairë.

Could possibly the "houseless" *fëa*, in proper case, be allowed to/ instructed how to rebuild its own "house" from memory?* [13]

This solution seems to fit the tales well enough. In fact very well. But of course the exact nature of existence in Aman or Eressëa after its "removal" must be dubious and unexplained. Also how "mortals" could go there at all!

The latter not very difficult. Eru committed the Dead of mortals also to Mandos. (That had been done long before: Manwë knew they would be mortal.) They waited then a while in recollection before going to Eru. The sojourn of say Frodo in Eressëa – then on to Mandos? – was only an extended form of this. Frodo would *eventually* leave the world (desiring to do so). So that the sailing on ship was equivalent to death.

Memory by a *fëa* of experience is evidently powerful, vivid, and complete. So the underlying suggestion is that "matter" will be taken up into "spirit", by becoming part of its knowledge – and so rendered timeless and under the spirit's command. As the Elves remaining in Middle-earth slowly "consumed" their bodies – or made them into raiments of memory? The resurrection of the body therefore (at least as far as Elves were concerned) was in a sense *incorporeal*. But while it could pass physical barriers *at will*, it could *at will* oppose a barrier to matter. If you touched a resurrected body you *felt* it. Or *if it willed* it could simply elude you – disappear. Its *position in space* was *at will*.

---

* The houseless *fëa itself rebuilt* its *hröa* to fit. This is far and away the best solution. This power might be limited, e.g. by requiring permission; by only being possible in Aman, etc. Transport of the re-housed *fëa* back to its "home" (or place of death) could be more frequent, but always according to the judgement of Mandos. This permission would principally depend on cause of death and/ or the worth of an elf concerned. An elf whom Mandos judged should be long retained "naked" would not usually be allowed to return to Middle-earth — things and relationships would have changed there. An elf allowed quickly to re-house itself might "return" very soon after death.

This power of the *fëa* to rebuild its "house" is much the best, because only the *fëa* can *inherently and by experience* know its own house. Its memory is so strong that it can in another *fëa* (incarnate) induce a picture of it, so that it seems a phantom form. A "phantom" is the reverse of vision = seeing. Vision reaching the mind/*fëa* via the bodily senses is transformed into a "picture" (which *may* be then preserved in memory). But if a mind receives a pictorial impression *direct* it *may* (if itself sufficiently interested or impressed) translate this into "sight", and the physical organs being stimulated will see — a phantom, which not being produced by a physical [?presentation] cannot be touched, but can be walked through. Since "eyes" will project a vision forwards and this will *retreat* (keeping same apparent distance away) or will vanish as soon as the "seer" reaches the point at which it was externalized.

Text 3

This text, located among the small collection of very late writings that Christopher Tolkien calls "Last Writings" (XII:377) and thus dating from 1972–3, is written in a clear hand in black nib-pen on two sides of a single sheet. Christopher Tolkien refers to this text at XII:382 and 390 n.17.

On 'rebirth', reincarnation by restoration, among Elves. With a note on the Dwarves.[14]

Restoration of Elvish bodies. The whole matter of Elvish beliefs and theories concerning their "bodies" and the relations of these to their "spirits" – which for the purposes of this mythology are treated as "true" and derived by the Elvish lore-masters from the Valar – is set out in various places elsewhere. But it may here be noted that the Eldar held that an Elf's spirit (*fëa*) had a complete knowledge of every detail of its body in general and in particulars peculiar to it as a unique thing. This knowledge it retained when spirit and body were divorced: in fact it then became clearer, for Elves in health seldom *consciously* thought about their bodies, unless they had a special interest in such "lore"; whereas a disembodied spirit yearned for its body as its natural and unique housing, and in the Halls of Waiting dwelt much in memory of its lost companion. Now the Valar, sub-creators under Eru, could make use of this memory; without any interrogation, since the mind of a disembodied spirit was open to them completely, and with far keener insight and knowledge than any possessed by the spirit itself. From this "inspection", having among them as a whole a complete power over the physical substances of Middle-earth, they could reconstitute a body totally suitable to the deprived spirit.* [15]

The notion, which appears in some places in the *Silmarillion*, as yet unrevised, that Elvish reincarnation was achieved, or was sometimes achieved, by rebirth as a child among their own kindred, must be abandoned – or at least noted as a false notion.† For the Elves

---

* And therefore "identical", though there is no space here to discuss the precise meaning of this.

† E.g. possibly of "Mannish" origin, since nearly all the matter of the *Silmarillion* is contained in myths and legends that have passed through men's hands and minds, and are (in many points) plainly influenced by contact and confusion with the myths, and theories, and legends of Men.

believed and asserted that they had learned this from the Valar, that Eru alone could create "spirits" with *independent*, though secondary, being; and that each of these spirits was individual and unique. Yet He had made the "spirits" of His Children (Elves and Men) of such a nature that they needed physical bodies and loved them, and would love and need the beauties and wonders of the physical world about them. But he delegated the procreation of bodies to the Children: that is, to be accomplished according to their wills, and choice of partners and of times and places, though otherwise the process was beyond their powers and skill. He, said the Elves, thus designed to produce that strange and marvellous combination of unique being with a "housing" that had descent and kinship within the physical order, which was the peculiar character of His Children. Therefore since the creative power of Eru was infinite (both outside and within the confines of His great Design in which we have part) it would be absurd, indeed unthinkable, to imagine him showing, as it were, a niggardliness in using again an unfortunate houseless spirit to inhabit a new body. For even if this was produced by parents of close kinship, it would *not* be its own, nor fully acceptable to it. Moreover to do this would be wrong; since a spirit that had already been born preserved a full memory of its former incarnate life, and if this was in some way veiled so that it was not immediately accessible to its consciousness, it could not be obliterated, and this would contribute to its unease: it would be "maladjusted",* a defective creature. Whereas if it consciously preserved its memory, as certainly those *fëar* did that the Valar restored, it would not be a true child, and would have a false relation to its second parents (whom it would know to be such), to their grief and to their deprivation of the great joy that Elves had in the early years of their children.

The matter of the Dwarves, whose traditions (so far as they became known to Elves or men) contained beliefs that appeared to allow for re-birth, may have contributed to the false notions above dealt with. But this is another matter which already has been noted in the *Silmarillion*. Here it may be said, however, that the reappearance, at long intervals, of the person of one of the Dwarf-fathers, in the lines of their Kings – e.g. especially Durin – is not when examined probably one of re-birth, but of the preservation of the *body* of a former

---

* Not as we now say with reference to a human person that is ill at ease with its environment (social or physical), but in the very centre of its being from the moment of its "re-birth".

King Durin (say) to which at intervals his spirit would return. But the relations of the Dwarves to the Valar, and especially to the Vala Aulë, are (as it seems) quite different from those of Elves and Men.

NOTES

1 For the implications of the form *Melcor* for dating this and other texts, see my editorial introduction to chap. XVII, "Death", below.

2 As first typed, this paragraph read:

Eru answered: "It shall be within your authority, but it is not within your power. Those [for whom ye judge that re-birth >>] whom ye judge fit to be reborn, if they desire it ye shall [?name] to Me, and they must then await My will. I shall consider them and understand clearly what they incur.

Tolkien then typed an alternative to this paragraph, subsequently struck through:

Eru answered: "It is in your power; but ye shall have authority to choose from among those who desire it the *fëar* for whom re-birth is fitting, but ye find any that desire re-birth, ye shall instruct them, and if when they learn all that is entailed they still desire it, they shall be reserved to Me, to await my will.

3 On the natural unity of *hröa* ('body') and *fëa* ('spirit') in Incarnates, see BODY AND SPIRIT in App. I.

4 As first typed, this sentence ended:

they could not do anything nor achieve any new design, since by nature they were made to work through the body.

5 For the "gift of will" and its limits, see chap. XI. "Fate and Free Will", above.

6 With the concept of the *erma* as a single, undifferentiated first thing or matter, see PRIME MATTER in App. I. With the concept of a "pattern" that defines the kind and identity of a material and its "virtues and effects", cf. "The Primal Impulse" (below), and cf. HYLOMORPHISM in App. I. Noting that *únehtar* are, it appears, quite literally "atoms" (i.e., 'indivisible things'), the discussion of minute and rare variations of the *únehtar* of a *nassë* (material) is highly reminiscent of the phenomenon of isotopes of elements, as for example deuterium (^{2}H) of hydrogen. The form "*únehtar*" replaces earlier "*únexi*" (of the same apparently literal meaning, but with nominal rather than deverbal derivation).

7 For evil as a lack in the conceived and unrealized pattern, see EVIL (AS LACK OF PERFECTION) in App. I.

8 For more on the "primal life-pattern", see chap. II, "The Primal Impulse", in part three of this book.

9 For the blending and varying of the patterns of living things, again see "The Primal Impulse"; and cf. EVOLUTION (THEISTIC) in App. I.

10 Tolkien would have been aware of the "unstable" nature of certain elements that decay and become other elements over time, as for example when uranium (^{238}Ur) through a chain of mutations becomes various other elements before stabilizing as lead (^{206}Pb).

11 Tolkien later drew a vertical line and the word "no" in red ball-point pen against the last three sentences of this paragraph. At apparently the same time he added the footnote naming Míriel the "first case", also in red ball-point pen. For the ramifications of Míriel's death being the first in Aman, see X:269–71.

12 Cf. chap. VII, "Mind-Pictures", above.

13 This footnote entered as a long comment, dated "June 1966" by Tolkien, on the final page of this small bundle of papers. Regarding the apparent finality here of the decision that the houseless fëa "itself rebuilt its hröa to fit … is far and away the best solution", see text 3 in this chapter, and XII:391 n.17.

14 As first written, this text was titled: "Some notes on 'Glorfindel'".

15 The matter of "identity" of materials and bodies is discussed extensively in text 1A, "The Converse of Manwë with Eru", in this chapter.

XVI

FROM *THE STATUTE OF FINWË AND MÍRIEL*

Christopher Tolkien notes (X:253 n.15) that there is a shift in the text of *The Statute of Finwë and Míriel*, in which a break – at "'So be it!' said Manwë" (X:247), not at the end of a page – precedes a continuation at the top of a subsequent page – with: "Therefore the Statute was proclaimed..." – in a rougher script than what preceded (usually a mark of Tolkien taking up and resuming a work at a later date). It happens, though, that an apparently supplanted text, and the *original recto* of the continuation page, intervenes. Though not struck through, much of it was marked with square brackets, which often indicates Tolkien considering its deletion, or perhaps removal to another place. I give this unused/supplanted text here in full.

It was asked, also: What if the bereaved spouse afterwards, by some ill chance, be also slain or die; or if the second spouse also die. Who then shall be the spouse of whom?

It was answered: If the bereaved spouse die, while remaining unhoused clearly he (or she) is the spouse "in will" of the one left among the Living. For the former union was dissolved and is no more; and moreover the second one to die may still be reborn and return to the one left, whereas the first to die is doomed to remain in Mandos. Not otherwise is it if all three die. Still the union of the first and second is no more, whereas the second and third may return and take up their marriage again. But since marriage is of the body, being unachieved or of the will only in the unhoused, the first and the second and the third may meet in Mandos (if they will) in friendship.

Nonetheless this is one of the ways in which the Statute may breed grief and not healing. For the meeting in Mandos of those that have been willing to dissolve their union, or of the one that came first in love and the other that succeeded that, cannot be like to the meeting of those between whom no shadow of inconstancy has fallen.

All the preceding text was bracketed, but not actually struck out. Beneath this, and in the left margin of the page, is written:

It was asked: What those in the Waiting do, and whether they have care for those that live, or knowledge of the events in Arda. It was answered: They *do* nothing; for *doing*, in a creature of dual nature, requires the body, which is the instrument of the *fëa* in all its actions. If they desire to *do*, they desire to return. They think, using their minds (so to speak, for they are their minds) as they are capable, upon their contents. These are the memories of their life;[1] but they may also learn in Mandos, if they *seek* knowledge. As for those whom they have left in life, or the events of Arda, again they may learn much, if they desire to do so. It is said that they can see some things from afar through the eyes of others to whom they were dear, but in no way so as to disturb or influence the minds of the living, for good or ill. Were they to attempt this, their sight would be veiled. But in Mandos all the events of the Tale of Arda (such as knowable to others than Eru; for the secrets of minds are not readable even by the Valar)[2] are recorded, and to this knowledge and history they have access according to their [?measure] and will.

NOTES

1 What I give here as "life" actually looks most like "live", but might also be "love".

2 For the impregnability of minds even for the Valar, see chap. IX, "*Ósanwe-kenta*", above.

things would have died that were limited to a period of time (that is, those whose total shape was small); and that many things were by nature of this shorter duration. But the end would not have been abhorrent to look on.[1] (It would no doubt to the Incarnate have still held the pain of loss and farewell. But that is in part due to the mystery of love within Time;[2] and in part due to the fact that the Incarnate only entered in to the design of Eä after the rebellion of Melcor; so that their whole being is bound up with the Marring. This, some hold, it is the will of Eru that they should redress or atone, by the suffering of love.) The end of things of short duration would not, the Eldar hold, have been abhorrent; for living out their lives completely and unmarred, they would have completely used up and discarded the material of their embodiments,[3] waning slowly (as they had begun to wax slowly) through changes recessive and yet no less beautiful than the changes progressive at the other end of their lives, until they disappeared. But herein the Eldar maybe are importing into their thought of Arda Unmarred the thoughts of hearts destined to live only in Arda Marred and within Time. Is it not the loss of the thing that was, and the love of its former shape, now dissolving, that makes the process of this dissolution painful, or sometimes horrible? (Not all the things that *seem* evil or unnatural to the Incarnate are the fruit of the works of Melcor.) If the process of dissolution be the right or natural way of the return of the material to the common use of Arda, it would not be painful or horrible to those not bound by Time, who would still see the living thing in all its duration, as a pattern complete.[4] The moment that pattern was complete (which is the precise moment of death) the remaining material would have no concern for those who loved the living thing. If it became slime, this would not be felt worse than the slime in which its growth began. It would be no part of living things loved.[5]

But to this the Eldar answer: True: regret and sorrow come to the Incarnate from love that is (for the duration of Arda) bound within Time. But decay and dissolution is not abhorrent solely because of this. To speak of *olvar* (that is, plants): The soil in which it springs has no part in it (until it is taken up as food by the life of the growing thing, and appears transformed into living and admirable form). The seed and the soil are clearly different. But at death it is not the surrounding earth nor the ground upon which the dead thing falls that seems horrible; it is the material of the thing itself that disintegrating seems horrible. And in Arda Marred this process may be long. Indeed death may be slow, and even before all life has departed the living thing may become sickly, or deformed. We do not think that this sickening and after it decay and putrescence can seem beautiful (as surely all things in Arda Unmarred should be) or at least not regrettable, to any minds whatsoever that love Arda, whether free from Time or bound therein.

Therefore we hold that death and decay in the kinds that we now see cannot be part of Arda Unmarred, in which we consider only "natural" death and the end of completed life, and not the deaths of violence. Also it may be thought that even those things that have by nature a short duration would in the health of Arda Unmarred have lived longer and more completely.

To speak of *kelvar* (that is, 'animals' or living things of all other kinds than the plants).[6] They do not grow in soil; but their bodies decay into slimes and loathsome forms before they are dispersed. Their end cannot therefore be likened to their beginning.

It would seem a wise conclusion that death, or the ending of living things of short duration, is now otherwise in Arda Marred than it might have been; and it has been marred in special by Melkor. For he desires ever new things and loves nothing that has been or already is; and at first he recked not how things were removed to make room for others, but came at last in his hatred and despite of all things (even those which he himself devised) to rejoice in their defilement.[7] On the other hand the Incarnate cannot rightly conceive of Arda Unmarred, in this matter of death, for they in their begetting by Eru belong to Arda Marred.[8] And this is most clearly seen herein: they are as it were the heirs and participators in death by violence. They cannot live without causing the death or ending untimely of living things that have corporeal life. Some of the Eldar (and some Men) eschew the slaying of *kelvar* to use their bodies as meat, feeling that these bodies, resembling in different degrees their own, are in some way too near akin. (Yet none of the Eldar hold that the eating of flesh, not being the flesh of the Incarnate and hallowed by the indwelling of the *fëa*, is sinful or against the will of Eru.) But even so they must kill and eat *olvar* or die; for it is their nature to be fed, as to their *hröar*, by living things corporeal, and things have a right to live according to their nature. Yet violence is done to the *olvar* (which have a kinship with the bodies of the Incarnate, be it remote), and these are denied the fulfilment of their own lives and final shapes. Therefore we must hold that the Incarnate belong by nature to Arda Marred and to a world in which death, and death by the violence of others, is accepted.[9] Neither Elves nor Men eat willingly things that have not died by violence.

II. Death of Incarnate Bodies

Incarnate bodies die also, when their corporeal coherence is destroyed. But not, by necessity, when or because the *fëa* departs. Usually the *fëa* departs only because the body is injured beyond recovery, so that its coherence is already broken. But what if the *fëa* deserts a body which is not greatly injured, or which is whole? It then, it might be thought, remains a living corporeal body, but without mind or reason; it becomes an animal (or *kelva*), seeking nothing more than food by which its corporeal life may be continued, and seeking it only after the manner of beasts, as it may find it by limbs and senses. This is a horrible thought. Maybe such things have indeed come to pass in Arda, where it seems that no evil or perversion of things and their nature is impossible. But it can have happened only seldom.

For the function of the body of one of the Incarnate is to house a *fëa*, the absence of which is unnatural to it; so that such a body is not ever in precisely the like case with a body that has never possessed a *fëa*: it has suffered loss. Moreover while the *fëa* was with it, the *fëa* inhabited it in every part or portion, less or greater, higher or lower.[10] The departure of the *fëa* is therefore a shock to the body; and except maybe in rare cases this shock will be sufficient to unloose its coherence, so that it will fall into decay. Nor in any case would the deserted body easily turn to feeding itself after the manner of beasts; for the matter of food (as all matters of governance) had long been directed by the *fëa*, and carried on by means beyond the reach of the body in itself; so that the mere beast senses were dulled, and the body undirected would be less skilful than an ordinary beast. Unless by chance much food of the kind required by it were ready to hand, it would therefore most likely soon perish by starvation, even if it survived the shock of the sunderance.

(The rare cases are those where sunderance has happened in Aman where there is no decay. Also others more horrible. For it is recorded in the histories that Morgoth, and Sauron after him, would drive out the *fëa* by terror, and then feed the body and make it a beast. Or worse: he would daunt the *fëa* within the body and reduce it to impotence;[11] and then nourish the body foully, so that it became bestial, to the horror and torment of the *fëa*.)

To speak of elf-bodies. An elf-body is by nature and function made to be the house of a permanent inhabitant, a *fëa* that cannot leave Time, nor go whence its return to the body is impossible. Such a body, therefore, will *wait* much longer, maintaining coherence and resisting decay, but then it will usually seem to sleep, lying passive and essaying nothing, not even the search for food, without the command of its master. (It cannot be fed without waking it, and thus killing it with shock, or rendering it beastlike.) But man-bodies deserted by the *fëa* perish swiftly. They are made to be the houses of *fëar* that, once they are severed from the body, *never return.* The body then has no function (and the shock of the separation is greater); and for the most part it soon decays and passes away into Arda.* [12] It is known to the Eldar that the *fëar* of Men (many or all, they do not know) go also to Halls of Waiting in the keeping of Námo Mandos; but what is there their fate, and whither they go when Námo releases them, the Eldar have no sure knowledge, and Men knowing little say many different things, some of which are fantasies of their own devising and are darkened by the Shadow. The wisest of Men, and those least under the Shadow, believe that they are surrendered to Eru and pass out of Eä. For which reason many of the Elves in later days under the burden of their years envied the Death of Men, and called it the Gift of Ilúvatar.

---

* Not always. Men report that the bodies of some of their Dead long maintain their coherence, and even sometimes endure in fair form as if they slept only. That this is true the Elves know by proof; but the purpose or reason is not to them clear. Men say that it is the bodies of the holy that sometimes remain long incorrupt: meaning those of whom the *fëar* were strong and yet were turned ever towards Eru in love and hope. This endurance of the body they believe, therefore, to be a sign from Eru for the increase of hope. For Men, even more than the Elves, abhor the sight of decay.

NOTES

1 Here and in the other two occurrences below, the word "abhorrent" is a penciled replacement for deleted "disgusting".

2 With the "mystery of love within Time", cf. the "Comments" section of text 1A, "The Converse of Manwë with Eru", of chap. XV, "Elvish Reincarnation", above.

3 The word "discarded" here is a typed replacement for original "absorbed".

4 Cf. the same concept of the complete pattern of living things through time in the text of chap. XV, "Elvish Reincarnation", just cited.

5 This last sentence is an addition to the typescript in pencil.

6 Here and at all subsequent occurrences, *kelvar* is written above and (apparently) was intended to replace original *cuivar*. A faint note at the end of the essay explains the change: "*kelvar = cuivar. cuy* = 'awake' not 'live'".

7 As first typed, the parenthetical statement in this sentence read: "(but most of those which he did not himself devise)". With the statement here that Melkor "desires ever new things and loves nothing that has been or already is", cf. the apparently closely contemporary chap. III, "Powers of the Valar" in part three of this book.

8 The words "by Eru" were a later insertion on the typescript.

9 As first typed, this sentence ended: "and to a world of which death, and death by the violence of others, is an accepted part".

10 On the unity of body and spirit in incarnates, see BODY AND SPIRIT in App. I.

11 As originally typed this clause read: "and reduce it to a stupor of horror so that it was impotent".

12 Cf. INCORRUPTIBILITY OF SAINTS in App. I.

PART THREE

THE WORLD, ITS LANDS,
AND ITS INHABITANTS

INTRODUCTION

By 1957 (see the introduction to part one of this book) Tolkien had decided that for astronomical verisimilitude the Sun and the Moon, instead of being formed from the last flowers of the Two Trees, long after the creation of Arda and the arrival of the Eldar in Valinor, must in fact have been (at least) coëval with Arda, and that the Elves must have known this astronomical fact. Tolkien was however thereby left with a dilemma that he never fully resolved: namely, how to incorporate this scientific truth into his mythology without eviscerating its distinctives. (I have long thought that if Tolkien had further decided that, when the world was made round at the Downfall of Númenor and the Undying Lands removed, Ilúvatar had further "demythologized" Arda and Eä – by making the Moon be simply a rocky orb, and the Sun and stars gaseous orbs, and making it appear that they had always been so, and the world always round – he could have preserved both his mythology and a conformance to modern scientific knowledge, and saved himself much time and thought and doubt.)

Even before this decision, from the mid-1940s on, Tolkien was greatly concerned to achieve astronomical and chronological verisimilitude in *The Lord of the Rings*. He expended great effort, for example, to make the movements of the various members of the separated Fellowship realistic, in terms of distance covered on foot or mounted each day (matters of which, as a former British Army officer with equestrian training, he had much experience); and further, to be accurate and precise in the matter of the phases and positions of the Moon (see L:74, 80; also VII:179–80, 367–9).

Unsurprisingly, when Tolkien resumed work on his *legendarium* after the completion of *The Lord of the Rings*, he brought this same concern for verisimilitude to bear. As seen in part one of this book,

"Time and Ageing", Tolkien expended considerable effort (both of thought and mathematics) to bring natural realism to the matters of Elvish population and migration. This third and final part comprises much wider-ranging texts, showing Tolkien's late consideration, in light of this concern, of broader aspects of his created world, its lands, and its inhabitants.

I

DARK AND LIGHT

This text, written in an at places exceedingly difficult scrawl in black ball-point pen, is found among a bundle of late papers, (nearly) all Allen & Unwin scrap paper dating from the late 1960s, containing writings in reconsideration of various matters of Elvish vocabulary and nomenclature.[1] One of the matters taken up in this bundle concerns certain Eldarin bases and concepts related to light and darkness. The first text from this bundle, which exists in three successive versions (labelled here A–C), shows Tolkien's development of what he describes as the Elves' "mytho-astronomical" picture of the world and the phenomena of dark and light.

Text 1A

√PHUY: Noldorin Q. *fuinë*, Vanyarin Q. *huinë*, S. *fuin*.[2] In Sindarin *fuin* was the ordinary word for 'night' without (originally) any sinister tone. It appears far back in Quendian history to have been imagined by the Elves as a "breath" that came out of the East as the Sun went down in the West, which brought a cool shadow that grew ever darker, beginning with *dōmē* 'twilight' until middle-night, *mori*; the process from *mori* > *dōmē* being reversed when the "breath of light" from the East drove the dark westward, where it was absorbed by Aman.[3] *phuinē* was this 'vapour-like darkness' (but S. *môr* was † [i.e. poetic], *fuin* became 'night')[4]

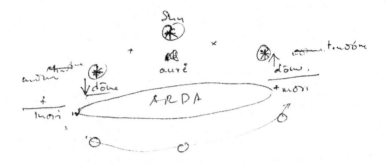

Tindómë followed darkness and began by being starlit still, until it grew to daylight; *undómë* followed light and became dark, and was the "sad twilight", an image or sign of the passing of beautiful things.

The text ends at the very bottom of the page. On the next sheet, Tolkien began a new and somewhat different and at points more "scientific" account of the Elvish conception of light and darkness:

Text 1B

The words for NIGHT, TWILIGHT, DAY were originally governed by the primitive Quendian imagination of the passage of the Sun; and also by their imagination of *light*. This they thought of as a "substance", ever the most tenuous and ethereal of all things, an emanation from *self-luminous*, light-giving things (such as fire on earth, and the Sun in heaven in particular) that continued, or could continue, in existence after issuing from its source, unless quenched, "swallowed", or extinguished by DARK. (*Dark* was also a substance, only less tenuous than Light, but was incalculably more abundant and prevalent than Light.) "Light-substance" was called *★linkwē* (Q. *linque*), "Dark-substance" was called *★phuine*.[5]

In light-giving things all the stars and all heavenly lights were included, except the Moon. The Quendi however seem to have guessed (and later been confirmed in it) that *Anar* the Sun and chief light-giver (*Kalantar*) of Arda was especially concerned with Arda and was far greater than any others because it was far *nearer*, though still very far away. Also they appear to have known or guessed that the Moon (*Ithil*) was not a light-giver, but a reflector. KAL = light from a light-giver (in Arda primarily from the Sun): ÑAL = reflected light. Certain stars (no doubt those we call planets) and among them especially Venus, which they called *Elmō* (and later mythologically *Eärendil*), they early observed were "wayward" and altered their places with regard to the "far-stars" (fixed stars). These they called companions of the Sun and thought them quite small heavenly bodies – derived from the Sun.

In their primitive mythology they thought that early in the time of Arda (long before it had been made habitable) the Valar during their strife with Melkor for the government of Arda, discovering the danger of darkness, which favoured the secret machinations and works of Melkor, had made the Moon (some thought out of a part of "Nether Arda", some thought bringing it from outside the realm of Anar) to reflect the light of Anar and reduce the darkness of NIGHT.

> This recapitulation and expansion likewise ends at the bottom of
> the page; and again Tolkien starts anew, on the following sheet, with
> another and still more "scientific" explanation:

Text 1A

The words for NIGHT, TWILIGHT, DAY, or their forms and applications in Elvish languages, require for their understanding the primitive Quendian imagination of the "shape" of *Arda* (our Earth) and the passage of the Sun (*Anar*); and also for their changes in the divergent Eldarin tongues a knowledge of the Elvish language.

The Quendian imagination of the shape of Arda and of the visible Heaven (Menel) above it, was due to the acute minds of a people endowed with sight far keener than the human norm. It was partly astronomical and "scientific", but crossed with a mythological or poetic talent. Even before their first acquaintance with the Valar they had evidently constructed a picture mytho-astronomical of the world, which was in some respects far nearer to our recent knowledge and theory than might be expected. This "picture" endured in their minds and coloured their myths even after the learned and most scientific among the High-elves who dwelt with the Valar had, or so it may perhaps be presumed, learnt far more the scientific truth (or what we now regard as the truth).

Their "imagination" was thus not properly a flat-earth cosmology; and it was *geocentric* only as regards the Sun, Moon, and certain stars ("companions of the Sun" or wayward stars = our planets). The "Solar System" – Sun, Moon, and wayward stars – was properly called *Arda* 'the Realm',[6] but *Arda* was commonly used of the Earth as the habitation of Elves and Men, to which the Sun etc. were tributary. The Earth or 'Middle-land' (Q. *en(en)dor*) was apparently conceived as *spheroid* (major axis 3, minor 2) with the major axis lying West > East. There was no childish pictorial myth of its supports: it was set there by the Maker (or his agents, and there remained by their will). It was not possible for terrestrial animals, nor Elves and Men, without wings, to reach the West and East Poles or the uttermost North or South, because it was cut by a deep circular chan[nel]

> Tolkien interrupts the text here, mid-word, above the following representation of the elliptical spheroid just described, its West and East Poles, a dot indicating its center-point, and perhaps a rough indication of the "deep circular channel" at its edges:

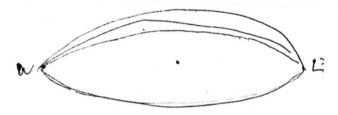

> Tolkien was however still not quite finished with his elaborations, writing "PTO" after the interrupted word, and starting one more reconsideration on the verso:

was conceived as an elliptical surface longer (3) than broad (2), its longer axis lying W–E. It was not flat, but rose up to its central point gradually. It seems to have been imagined as having an underportion of the same shape (nether Arda) which could not be inhabited since, not knowing of gravitation, the lower surface was supposed to be bare, solid and [?trackless,] and all unattached things (save only mist) would fall off. Later it was represented as an elliptical spheroid of [?some nature]. But

> Here Tolkien's attempts at presenting a "mytho-astronomical" account of the early Elvish conception of Arda was interrupted, at the start of a sentence, for (it seems) the last time, save for a final accompanying figure:

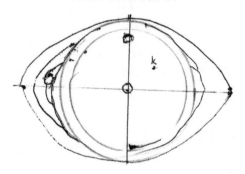

This again shows an elliptical Earth with a major East-West axis, and indicates its central high-point. There is no indication in these papers what the western and northern circles indicate, or the dot labelled "k"; but it can be conjectured that the circle to the extreme west indicates the abode of the Valar in Aman, and that perhaps "k" stands for *Kuiviénen*, the 'Water of Awakening', which in the *Annals of Aman* is said to lie "far off in Middle-earth, eastward of Endon (which is the midmost point) and northward" (X:72). If so, the northern circle may indicate Melkor's early northern abode, Utumno.

TEXT 2

Like the preceding text, this discussion is associated with an adjacent etymological note on an Eldarin base, which itself is reminiscent in its terminology to texts 1A and 1B above:

√LIK: 'glide, slide, slip, drip', applied to dew, water, [?watery] liquid or half-liquid substance (as sap, etc.). From this was derived the word *linkwe (Q. *linque*) 'light' as conceived as an ethereal substance independent (when once emitted) of the light-giver from which it emanates. This was preserved also in T. *limpi*, but not in Sindarin, where it was used only for 'dew'. *phuinē, its opposite (material substance), Q. *fuine*, became the ordinary Sindarin word, *fuin*, for night, between the twilights but including the darker parts of these. In Sindarin (which still conceived "light" and "dark" in the same way) the words used were: 'dark' *dû* or *dú(wath)*; 'light' *glae/glaegal* (√S. *glay-*).

Limlight, modernized from Rohanese *Limliht* (as in Story of Eärnil), which had no connexion with R. *lim* 'limb', but was a "translation name".[7] The original Sindarin name was *Limhir*; and evidently *lim-* was translated by R. *līht* and combined as a gloss with older *lim-*, leading to R. *Limliht(ēa)*.[8] But in what sense (*līht* 'not heavy' or *līht* 'bright') is not now clear; nor is the original meaning of the Sindarin certain.

Some older spellings, e.g. *Limphîr*, suggest that the first element was originally S. *limp* (n.) < **limpi* < C.E. **liŋkwi* (n.), Q. *linque* (n., adj.) '(bright/clear/gleaming) liquid'. This was applied (in Quenya) to dew (or to fine rain in sunshine); in Sindarin to pools or rills of clear clean water. It was probably in origin a "mythological" word – referring to the primitive Elvish conception of "light" as an actual substance (emitted by light-givers, but then independent), though ethereally fine and delicate. (Its opposite was **fuinē*, C.E. **phuiṇē* = the thin shadowy cloud of twilight and darkness that quenched **linkwi*.) The Rohirrim enquiring the meaning of *Limhir* might well [have been] told it meant 'clear, bright'; but that there was some uncertainty was suggested by the unusual, in Rohan, preservation of the old name + a gloss.

Another possibility is that the name really contains C.E. **slimbi*, S. *lhim*, Q. *hlimbë* 'sliding, gliding, slippery, sleek' – used often implying sleekness, a shiny or gleaming surface, or quick movement of swiftly moving or flowing things.[9]

NOTES

1 The exception is a typed, undated letter from one Andrew Cruickshank, advertising and raising funds for the Wordsworth Ryland Mount Trust, Ltd. This charity, registered in the U.K. on 6 Feb. 1970 (now dissolved), had as its aim: "To promote, encourage, maintain, improve and advance public education and in particular the education of the public in the life and work of William Wordsworth and to establish and maintain a museum to house and preserve all such articles and effects of literary and other nature having connection with William Wordsworth or his family."

2 In the margin against this Tolkien wrote the word "fwyn", which may be intended as representing the pronunciation of the Sindarin word *fuin* according to the conventions of Welsh orthography (though if so the spelling ought rather to be "ffwyn"). As first written, √PHUY had the start of a gloss: "prob. 'fog, mists', produced", struck through in the act of writing.

3 An apparent candidate replacement for the conception of night as a "breath" follows Tolkien's diagram in a very hasty hand:

as a wind that followed the Sun out of the East and drove its light away West (which [?alike] they conceived as a substance like ethereal liquid that otherwise [?would flow down] like a tenuous rain on the surface of Arda and in pools, as they imagined it to do in Aman) where the Sun carries it back again leaving Earth [? ? ? ?] of the Sun [?flowed] or spread her light over Arda until it again [?drives it off] Arda.

4 In the margin, against the accompanying figure, Tolkien later wrote, in pencil: "*linque* = liquid light".

5 A note written in the top margin of this page adds: "'darkness' conceived as a very thin misty substance had the ancient name of *★phuinē* (√PHUY 'breathe out'); 'light' conceived also as a very ethereal but shining substance had the ancient name of *★linkwē* (√LIK 'glide, slip')".

6 For the late (c. 1959) but obviously long-lived extension of the term *Arda* to encompass the entire solar system (not just the Earth, as earlier), cf. X:337, 349, 358 n.11, and esp. 375.

7 Tolkien "translated" the language of the Rohirrim into Old English, so here "Rohanese" (R) in fact stands for Old English (O.E.). The "Story of Eärnil" is apparently a reference to Eärnil II, the 32nd King of Gondor, and what is said of him in various parts of App. A of *LR*, though in fact the name *Limlight* does not there occur in connection with these passages. It may be that "Eärnil" here is a slip for *Eorl*, in which case see LR:1064.

8 O.E. *ēa* 'river' is a common element in English river-names, frequently as an ending becoming -*ey*. As first written, the original Sindarin name was "*Lim(p)-hir*".

9 A marginal note against this reads: "In that case it is possible (though unlikely?) that *līht* in R. had sense *levis*" (i.e., as Latin *levis* adj. 'light (not heavy)'). At the end of the text, Tolkien further notes that "[?Older] Rohanese had a voiceless initial *lh*, but in both Sindarin and R. this may have been voiced, or dissimilative for *mh*".

An earlier version of this possible derivation reads: "S. *limb* > *lim(m)* was from C.E. *limbi* 'smooth, sleek, sliding, gliding (slippery)', applied among other things to fish, snakes, light boats [?but] [of] shallow draught, waters or liquids flowing (down) or slipping along [? or ?]. But this would not have been interpreted by R. *līht* 'light' (lucent), and is not close to R. *līht* '*levis*'. It seems probable that the old name was actually < S. *limp*".

II

THE PRIMAL IMPULSE

The title is taken from Tolkien's cover page to a bundle of two texts (with draft materials), which reads:

Primal Impulse

"Spirit"

Fragments, incomplete, concerning "The Primal Impulse" and conceptions of "Spirit" and origins of terms for it in Elvish languages.

The first text, concerning "The Primal Impulse", is presented in this chapter; the second, concerning "Spirit", is presented as text 2 in chap. XIII, "Spirit", in part two of this book.

The first five pages after the cover sheet are torn half-sheets of candidates' examination script pages from University College Cork, Ireland, where Tolkien was an external examiner at various times throughout the 1950s (see TCG II:578). The sixth sheet is a single sheet of unlined paper. The text written on these sheets is all in black nib-pen, in a hand at points calligraphic and at others very hasty. Comparison of the text, particularly in points of terminology such as "pattern" and Q. *erma* 'prime substance' and *nassi* 'materials', with "The Converse of Manwë with Eru", presented as text 1 of chap. XV, "Elvish Reincarnation", in part two of this book, indicate that they are closely related and that this text likewise dates from c. 1959.

The text exists in two versions, called here A (the earlier) and B (the later). Preceding A is a single page of increasingly rough draft workings. B is a fair manuscript that follows A as emended closely, but ends before A does. I thus give here first text B, with citation in the notes of all significant differences with A as first written and as emended, and with the draft. I then give the preceding text A in full from the point where the later text B stops, again with citation in the notes of all significant differences with the draft.

TEXT B

The "prime impulse", of which the total unfolding is the Great Pattern (*Erkantië*),[1] having continuous life. This life will not be co-extensive with the Tale of Arda;[2] for as Arda began with the *Erma* ['prime substance'] and then the *nassi* ['materials'],[3] before the entry of the living things,[4] so doubtless the Great Pattern will end sooner, leaving the *nassi*, and they will be reduced to the *Erma*, until the Tale ends as it began.[5] Yet while it continues the *Erkantië* is unbroken and unceasing. Many points of its growth may cease and proceed no further: this is when a living thing perishes before it has produced any offspring or successor.[6] But the whole will not cease until such time as all living things then surviving shall no longer produce living offspring.[7]

This might happen by catastrophe, in which all living things perished;[8] or by the cessation of the impulse to generate as the Great Pattern worked at last towards its completion. But, since the pattern of any one living thing is not held to have ended until the embodiment is destroyed or dissolved, the Great Pattern could not strictly be said to have ended while still any living thing lived and endured, even if it did not generate. On the other hand the Elves are said to be "immortal within Arda", which should mean, as it is understood, that they will endure to the utter end of Arda. Thus it may be that Men and all other races of living things will perish and fail to generate, whereas (as seems likely since the process may be seen in operation) the Elves will long before the End have ceased to generate, and their *bodies* will have been consumed by their *fëar*.

But others hold – and their view seems to observe more clearly what is known by lore and experience of history – that this is not a true account of the beginning or ending of life in Arda. They maintain that *Ermenië* does not belong to Eä (and therefore not to Arda). It must be referred to the uttermost beginning: the "Theme of Eru", as He first propounded it, before the *Ainulindalë* in which the Spirits whom He had made and instructed cooperated in the elaboration and working out of the Theme. Thus the *Ermenië* (which is a 'Device of Eru')[9] being before the *Ainulindalë* is also before *Eä* (the Realization).[10]

For it is clear in such lore as we have received from the Valar that they set in motion the unfolding of different living patterns at many different points in the *Ainulindalë*, and therefore this was repeated in Eä. Within Eä we have then not one single *Ermenië* or Great Pattern, but a number of early or Major Patterns (*Arkantiër*).

The text ends here, about a third of the way down an otherwise empty page. Text A however continues:

TEXT A

For it seems clear in such lore as we have received from the Valar, that they started the unfolding of living patterns at many different points in the Music, and so also in Eä – only so can we understand the power which the Valar certainly have and certainly exercised in days of old, of *making things* with life corporeal[11] – as if one should set many springs flowing in different places.[12] These would not be related in history nor proceed from one fount; they would be akin or alike only through the nature of *water*, and because each stream would perforce obey the laws of the coherence of Eä, that are alike for all things, though directing them variously according to the situation of each. (As for instance all streams would flow downwards unless hindered, and wind swifter or slower according to the figure of the land.)

Thus we may observe the great complexity of corporeal life in Arda. Derived ultimately from the *Ermenië* of Eru, we have the "devices (or designs) of the Valar", separate each in time of conception and first effecting, whether coming successively from one of the Valar, or coming from more than one. These are the "major patterns" that we have spoken of.

Their number none but the Valar can know. These are not rightly called "akin" (unless by later mingling), for they are related only as proceeding from the same mind (as of one Vala) or from like minds (as of more than one of these), and their differences are given not developed within and by the operation of Arda. But these "major patterns" (*arkantiër*) developing in Arda will diverge whether by the design of their beginners, or by the varieties caused by the stuff of Arda which they must use, into different but similar groups of descendants. These are truly *akin* and members of races or tribes or families or houses. At last and in our time it is beyond the skill of any but the Valar to distinguish the likenesses due to the likeness of the minds of the Valar from those due to descent in Arda.[13]

And beyond this we have ever over All, Eru. That he introduced new things into the Music (not in the Theme) we are told; for thus began the conception of Elves and Men. (The Dwarves are a case rather of the separate beginnings by the Valar, though [? unless] Eru tolerated and blessed it.)

That he has never done so in other cases (of corporeal life or of incarnate) or that he never will do so again, none can say. The Valar report no such [?intrusive] things in the Music other than the coming of the Children. But since Eru was not bound by the Theme, nor by the *Ainulindalë* (as made by the Ainur), it would be rash to assert that He is or will be bound by Eä realized; since He is outside Eä but holds the whole of Eä in thought (by which it coheres).[14] Some of those things that appear suddenly in History and [?continue] then in obedience to Eä (or soon cease to be [?seen]) may indeed be due directly to Eru. (These things are called the signs of the Finger of Eru.)[15]

Now in most living things (not all) succession is by [?breeding], and by the mating or union of two. So those that mate, or [?bear] must be akin. It is possible therefore that those that may mate and produce offspring are *akin by descent*. Those that may not or do not do so are not akin however they may resemble others because of the kinship of their beginners. Yet even among the "kin" mating seems to require no very great sunderance of branches. So [?what seems but ? ? ? be akin] by descent [?though] remotely. Little is known of this. But we do know some things which are nonetheless not easy to understand. For instance we know that the First Born and the Second Born may mate, though this has rarely been done, and as for the High Elves, the Eldar, only twice. In Middle-earth unless tales be now [?] thrice: Beren/Lúthien, Idril/Tuor, Ancestors of Imrahil. We must say that it was the will of the Beginner of these two streams of life (Elves and Men), that is Eru, that it should be part of the corporeal nature to be capable of marriage and begetting – for certain purposes of the Tale, and no doubt only in the greater of the Eldar.[16]

Therefore (though Eru's power is inestimably greater and his will free)[17] it may well be that other beginners made interbreeding part of the capabilities of their respective streams or descents. Study will show maybe that by interweaving its pattern with an earlier, the earlier might be refreshed, and new variety come to being.[18]

But Eru even in intruding the Children took as their shape a form

[?that] though altered and refined, resembles in less or even in great degree the forms of beasts. The Children are not "akin" by descent with the beasts therefore but are related closely in the thought of Eru to them, and with the beasts the Children have ever felt kinship, even akin.

The *fëar* of the Elves and Men (and Dwarves via Aulë, Ents via Yavanna) were *intrusions* into Eä from outside. As the Valar were sent into Eä.[19]

NOTES

1 Text A originally gives this Quenya name of the "Great Pattern" as *Arkantië*, subsequently emended to *Erkantië*. In B it was first written as *erkantië* and then capitalized. It was written as *Erkantië* at its second occurrence.

2 The draft as first written has to this point: "the total unfolding of which is the Great Pattern. The whole life of this may not indeed be coextensive with the life of Arda". This was emended to replace "may" with "will", and "life of Arda" with "Tale of Arda".

3 For the meanings and distinction of *erma* 'prime substance' and *nassi* 'materials', see PRIME MATTER in App. I and the entries for these terms in App. II.

4 Text A has here "before the entry into the Tale of the living things"; this is not found in the "draft" at all.

5 The draft here continues with a parenthetical: "(As a great monument upon which History has been written in Life by hands from outside.)" No such corresponding statement is found in either subsequent version.

6 Text A reads here: "which is when a living creature perishes before it has begotten or born any seed, or offspring, or heir".

7 Text A reads here: "But the whole will not cease, until such time as no single living thing produces living offspring". Also in text A the passage corresponding to that here from "Yet while it continues" to this point originally followed the passage corresponding to what is the third paragraph in text B, beginning "But others hold". In A this passage entered as an interpolation, with an arrow indicating that it was to be inserted before the passage corresponding to the third paragraph in text B.

The corresponding passage in the draft, which as in text A follows the passage corresponding to what is the third paragraph in text B, is brief and different enough (chiefly in metaphor) to give here in full:

This [the *Ermenië*] continues through the ages in continuity. For though some branches occasionally may wither and end as some rivulets run into sand and clay and come not to the Sea. And that is when living creatures perish before they have begotten or born or produced seed or offspring or heir.

8 The corresponding passage in text A is a parenthetical statement, reading: "(This may come about in turmoils made by Melcor in his last attempt to achieve mastery or revenge of destruction)". For the significance of the spelling "Melcor", see my editorial introduction to the text given as chap. XVII, "Death", in part two of this book.

9 As suggested by the Eldarin base √MEN- 'have as object, (in)tend, proceed, make for, go towards' PE17:93) and its derivative *mēnie 'determination' (PE17:94), Tolkien apparently uses "device" here not only in the modern sense given it in the *OED* as "6 Something devised or contrived for bringing about some end or result"; but also in one or both senses (now considered obsolete) given it in the *OED* as: "†2 Purpose, intention" and "3 †b. Will or desire as expressed or conveyed to another; command, order, direction, appointment".

10 As first written, this sentence ended: "*before* and *not part* of Eä (the Realization)". Both text A and the draft (so far as it goes) correspond here quite closely with B.

11 But cf. the opening of the next text.

12 The aside beginning "only so can we understand" entered as an (apparently) contemporary note in the top margin of the page, with marks indicating that it should be inserted here.

13 For the blending and varying of the patterns of living things, again see "The Converse of Manwë and Eru", text 1 of chap. XV of part two of this book, as well as EVOLUTION (THEISTIC) in App. I.

14 Cf. EXISTENCE, CONTINGENCY OF in App. I.

15 See X:244: "'new things', manifesting the finger of Ilúvatar, as we say". Cf. Exodus 8:19, referring to the miraculous plague of gnats: "Then the magicians said unto Pharaoh, This is the finger of God."

16 Tolkien here replaced "wedded unio[n]" with "marriage" in the act of writing. Before starting the next paragraph, Tolkien made here a rough figure, concerning the union of Half-elves and some of their offspring: "*Half Elven*: Arwen Aragorn. | Dior - || | Earendil. Elrond/Celebrian".

17 Tolkien began here, and then deleted in the act of writing, a clause reading: "yet it will work a".

18 Tolkien here replaced "another" with "earlier" (at the first occurrence), and "things" with "variety", in the act of writing.

19 The fourth (and final) paragraph of the brief draft text has here:

The *fëar* of Elves and Men and still later things (Ents? Dwarves) were intrusions by Eru, like the Valar – *Aule* and the Dwarves. *Yavanna* and the Ents. *Maiar* could take forms of Eagles etc. – [?these] were *sent* into Eä. They are not *of* Eä, but Eru's agent *in* Eä.

III

POWERS OF THE VALAR

This typescript text occupies both sides of a single sheet of the same University College Cork, Ireland, examination script pages as used for "The Primal Impulse", with which it is closely related, and it also likely dates from c. 1959.

Powers of the Valar[1]

The Valar had power to endue things that they designed with corporeal life; but they could not make things with independent minds or spirits: sc. they could not make things of equal order, but only ones of lower order. In ultimate truth they did not in fact "make" even corporeal life, which proceeded from Eru. But they had assisted in the general design of Eä, and severally, in different degrees and modes, in the production from the *erma* (or prime substance) of things of many kinds.[2] The idea of life and growth came from Eru, but the Valar, under Him, devised the shapes and forms of living things. When Eru gave being to this design, in general and particular, and it became Eä, unfolding in Time, He set in motion life and growth, or those processes which would in time lead to this. But when he permitted the Valar to descend into Time, to carry out in Eä (or reality) the things that they had designed in thought, then viewed in Time they appeared to make things which were alive. Indeed it is held that being themselves in Time they experienced the making as a new thing, differing in this experience little, save in degree of power and art, from the makers or artists among the Incarnate. Neither they nor the Incarnate could make things utterly new; they could not "create" after the manner of Eru, but could only make things out of what already existed, the *erma*, or its later variations and combinations.

The Valar, however, had of course far greater power over their material. Not only had they enormously greater force of will, scope of mind, and subtlety of skill, but they had complete understanding of the *erma* and of the structure of its variations, since they had themselves (under Eru) designed and brought about these variations, and their combinations. Or rather, among them all such knowledge was to be found; for individually they had possessed from their own creation, and had shown in their assistance in the designing of Eä, different talents, and each of them possessed some skill or knowledge of his or her own.

The Children, the Incarnate, were introduced into the design of Eä by Eru, and the Ainur had no part in devising even their corporeal forms. They had, of course, a vision of them in thought, received from the mind of Eru; but they were not "in" the thought of any one of the Valar (as were the forms of things the making of which had been deputed to them). They were not realized fully until they appeared in history. It was for this reason that the Valar feared to meddle even in the matter of the bodies of the Children, until Eru gave them special authority. For they revered the Children, as beings to them holy (in that they came from Eru directly and not mediately). Indeed the vision of the Children to be had great effect upon the minds of the Valar; as was seen in the case of Aulë and the making of the Dwarves, or above all in the delight that the Valar had to make for themselves forms like to those of Men and Elves (according to their foresight, or to their actual sight later). These forms were to them, as it were, their most favoured raiment, in which they most often (but not always) were clothed.[3]

It is said that of the Valar Manwë had the greatest knowledge, so that no lore or arts of any of the others were to him a mystery; but that he had less desire to make things of his own, great or small; and under the cares of the Kingship of Arda the desire ceased, for his mind and heart were given rather to healing and restoration. The harms and evils of Melcor[4] were to him the greatest grief, and he ever sought to redress them or turn them to good.

Melcor on the other hand desired even with passion to make things of his own, being restless and unsatisfied with all that he did, were it lawful or unlawful. Within Eä he had small love for anything that had been, desiring always new things and strange. He would ever be altering what he had made, and would meddle with the works of the other Valar, changing them, if he could, or destroying them in wrath if he could not. Though his mind was swift and piercing, so that, if he would, he might have surpassed all his brethren in knowledge and understanding of Eä and all that is therein, he was impatient and overweening (believing his powers of mind greater than they were).[5] Too quickly he assumed that he had grasped all the nature of a thing, or all the causes of an event; and his plans and works often went amiss for that reason. But he learned no wisdom from this, and charged his failures ever upon the malice of the Valar, or the jealousy of Eru.

Since he had no love even for the things that he had himself made, he came at length to reck not at all how things had come into being, considering neither their natures nor their purposes. Thus he desired only to possess things, to dominate them, denying to all minds any freedom outside his own will, and to other creatures any value save as they served his own plans. Thus it was seen in Arda that the things made or designed by Melcor were never "new" (though at first he strove to make them so) but were imitations or mockeries of works of others.

NOTES

1　Tolkien supplied this title in pencil in the top margin.

2　With *erma* 'prime substance' cf. PRIME MATTER in App. I.

3　Cf. chap. XIV, "The Visible Forms of the Valar and Maiar", in part two of this book.

4　For the implications of the form *Melcor* for dating this and other texts, see my editorial introduction to chap. XVII, "Death" in part two of this book.

5　As originally typed, this sentence began: "Though his mind was swift, swiftest maybe of all the Valar, and piercing...".

IV

THE MAKING OF *LEMBAS*

These two brief texts are located close to each other in a bundle of pages among Tolkien's linguistic papers. Both are written on the versos of printed Allen & Unwin reprint notices dated 12th Jan. 1968. Text 1 is extracted from a larger typescript text, while text 2 is a hastily written note in black ink. For more on the constitution and nature of *lembas* see XII:403–5; and cf. the next chapter here.

TEXT 1

In Elvish legend the secret of the making [of] "waybread" – an essential preparation for the Great Journey to the Western Shore – was taught them by Oromë. He brought as a gift from Manwë and Varda the seed of wheat, and instructed the Quendi in the manner of growing, harvesting, and storing it; but the grinding of flour, its kneading, and baking into (unleavened) "bread" was committed to the "bread-women".* [1]

---

* In Common Eldarin *khābā, originally applied to most vegetable foods, but after the coming of corn was restricted to those made from grain. The Quenya words were háva (collective) and havar (< *khabar) 'a loaf, or cake of bread'. "Bread-women" were called hávanissi.

Text 2

"Waybread": art taught by Oromë to the Three Elderwomen of the Elves.[2] It was made from meal [?ground] wheat-corn (specially brought to them by Oromë). This "Western Corn", it is said, slowly diminished in virtue on the Great Journey, owing to the dim sunlight,[3] and there was no more Western Corn seed left when they arrived in Beleriand. But when the Noldor came back they brought with them new corn – and [it] by a special grace of pity by Manwë and Varda did not fail and was still in vigour till the end of the First Age. Galadriel was one of the chief inheritors of it and of the art. But at the time of L.R. only in Lórien did the Western Corn survive, and the art was known only to herself and her daughter Celebrían (wife of Elrond) and her daughter Arwen. With Galadriel's departure and the death of Arwen, the Western Corn and Waybread were lost forever in Middle-earth.

NOTES

1 An unfinished and then deleted passage at this point reads:

At first the grain was used entirely for making the special "waybread" needed on long journeys in the wild, as was the original purpose of the gift of the Valar. But after the Great Journey was ended

Regarding the "bread-women", see X:214.

2 "Three Elderwomen" – that is, apparently, the three women among the first six Elves to awake, in the *Cuivienyarna* named as Iminyë, Tatië, and Enelyë (XI:421; and cf. chap. VIII, "Eldarin Traditions Concerning the 'Awakening'", in part one of this book).

3 The word "dim" here replaced original "lack of"; i.e., "owing to the lack of sunlight". For the implication that the Sun existed from the Awakening onward, but that its light was dimmed, see text II of the section "Myths Transformed" of *Morgoth's Ring* (and particularly X:377–8).

V

NOTE ON ELVISH ECONOMY

This text, located among Tolkien's linguistic papers, is written on the verso of a printed Allen & Unwin notice dated 9th Feb. 1968. The text was first written hastily in red ball-point pen, and subsequently overwritten and expanded in black nib-pen. So far as can now be determined, the black nib layer closely follows the red ball-point original, except for the final paragraph, which is original to the black nib layer.

Note on Elvish Economy

Arable. The Sindar did not practice agriculture until long after the departure of the other Eldar.[1] Of the "economics" of Valinor we know nothing except that [?initially] food was provided for the Eldar – *not* without all labour, in which they delighted and made it the occasion of song and festivals.[2] But the grain (of some kind not native to Middle-earth)* was *self-sown* and only needed *gathering* and the *scattering* of 1/10 (the tithe of Yavanna) of the seed on the field.

The Dwarves had an agriculture – which in early times they practiced when isolated and unable to buy grain etc. by barter. They had invented a "plough" of some sort – which they *dragged* as well as steered themselves: they were tough and strong – but they did not delight in such labour of necessity.[3]

The Kingdom of Doriath was a woodland realm, and had only a little open ground, except on its east borders where they kept some small kine and sheep. Beyond the Girdle of Melian (eastward) there

---

* From it was descended the grain for *lembas.*

was much open land (prairie) of wide extent. The Sindar (E. Sindar) not under the rule of Thingol dwelt and practiced not only cattle-rearing and sheep-farming, but also grain-growing and other food crops; on which they prospered because both Doriath west and the Dwarves east were ready to buy what they could. *Flax* was grown in Doriath; and the Sindar there were adepts in spinning and weaving it. They knew some metallurgy and had good weapons on the Great Journey owing to the teaching of Oromë. For long on the Great Journey they had depended on the arms and swords, spears, bows, etc. made in their first home; or during their sojourns – if they could then find metals. In Beleriand they were eventually aided by the Dwarves, who assisted (very willingly!) in search for metals. Iron was found in the Gorgoroth![4] And later also in western parts of Ered Wethrin. There was silver there also. But of *gold* they had very little, except what was washed out by Sirion near Doriath's borders or at its Delta. But the Exiles were heavily ornamented with gold, of which the total that they brought must have amounted to a great weight. Before his death Fëanor had explored (as much as possible) the ground looking for metals. It was the discovery of *silver, copper, and tin* about Mithrim that contributed greatly to his rashness in trying too soon to conquer and own, entirely, this North region. But it was known that the best and most abundant *iron ore* was in Thangorodrim.

The Eldar were not in the Common Eldarin period ignorant of either horticulture or agriculture. These things they had begun to develop by their own skill and inventiveness at a date long before the Great Journey; but by the teaching of Oromë their practice was greatly improved. The Eldar hoarded a great deal of food before they set out; but they took with them not only weapons (hunting and defense) but light cultural tools.[5] Their sojourns during this age-long journey were often prolonged – so prolonged that at each stage some remained content and stayed behind.

NOTES

1 As first written, this sentence began: "The Eldar had no arable culture".

2 The word here read tentatively as "initially" entered as an interlinear insertion above "food".

3 I have set this passage concerning the Dwarves in a separate paragraph editorially (in the original, it begins at the top of a page side, and there is no break in the text between it and what is presented here as the subsequent paragraph), in order to clarify that (as I interpret the text) it is the Dwarves, "tough and strong", that had invented a plough that they both dragged and steered themselves.

4 That is, in the Ered Gorgoroth, north of Doriath and south of Taur-na-Fuin.

5 The word "cultural" was altered from "agricultural" by strikethrough of the initial letters.

VI

DWELLINGS IN MIDDLE-EARTH

This text, which is written for the most part in a clear hand in black nib-pen, arose in conjunction with a detailed linguistic consideration of Q. *ambar* 'world' and *umbar* 'fate', and their close relation in origin. It is located in a bundle of sheets among Tolkien's linguistic papers that date from c. 1967, and is both near to and associated with the texts presented in chaps. XI, "Fate and Free Will" (q.v.), and XIV, "The Visible Forms of the Valar and Maiar", in part two of this book.

This text was published in somewhat different form in *Parma Eldalamberon* 17 (2007), pp. 104–9. I have omitted here without indication many passages of primarily linguistic and etymological matters.

Eldarin **ambar(a)* 'the Settlement',* Q. *ambar*, S. *amar* had the sense of settlement, appointed place, as applied to the major Settlement of all: the Earth as the appointed dwelling place or home of Elves (and Men). The decision and choice was in this case attributed to Eru.

It was no doubt the coalescence in form in Sindarin of *m̥bar* and

---

* English *settle* in its various branches of meaning closely resembles the development of the meanings of √*mbar*: thus *settlement* can mean the act of colonizing or taking up an abode, or the area or place so occupied (by a family or community); or (the terms of) an agreement fixed after debate. The development was not, however, the same: the senses of *settle* proceed from a sense 'place in or take up' a firm position, especially in a place that seems suitable; from which the sense of settling affairs that were in confusion or doubt arose. √*mbar* meant basically to make a decision, and the meanings relating to dwelling or occupying land proceeded from that.

ambar that caused the assimilation of **amar* in sense of 'fate' to the verb *amartha-* which had no reference to habitation. In Sindarin *amar* 'settlement' continued to be used in the sense of 'this world, the Earth', though with the increase of knowledge it often excluded *Aman* even before its removal from the "circles of the world" after the Downfall. In Quenya *ambar*, though often apparently used as an equivalent of 'the Kingdom of Arda' (*Ardaranyë*), in fact meant 'this Earth', the planet, as a whole, including *Aman* until its removal, but excluding other parts of "the Kingdom of Arda" under the guardianship and headship of Manwë (Sun, moon, etc.). *Tenna Ambar-metta* 'Until World's-end' thus meant "until the end of the finite time during which the Earth is appointed (by its *umbar*: see below) to endure, at least as a region inhabited by the Children (Elves and Men)".

In Quenya the other derivative of √*mar*: *umbar* meant a decision, issuing in an ordinance or decree by some authority; hence also it might mean the fixed arrangements, conditions, and circumstances proceeding from such a decree. It was a word of lofty associations, mainly used of the dispositions and will of *Eru*, with regard to Creation as a whole (in full, *Eämbar*), to "this World" in particular, or to persons of great importance in events.*

The simplest form of this base **mbără* became a much-used word or element in primitive Eldarin: which may be rendered 'dwelling'. This application was probably a development during the period of the Great Journey to the Western Shores, during which many halls of varying duration were made by the Eldar at the choice of their leaders, as a whole, or for separate groups. This element survived in various forms in Quenya and Sindarin with sense-changes due to the divergent history of the Eldar that passed over Sea and of those remaining in Beleriand.

The principal forms were the primitive simple form P.E. **mbăr(a)* > uninflected *mbār*, inflected *mbăr*; and the derivative form **mbardā*. The former survived in Quenya in the archaic word *már*, which was used with a defining genitive or more often in genitival compound: as *Ingwemar*, *Valimar*, *Eldamar* (among the Eldar normally living and dwelling in it). This signified, when added to a personal name the 'residence' of the (named) head of a family, and included the adjacent lands attached to the permanent buildings or dwelling-houses

---

* *Umbar* could thus correspond to History, the known or at least the already unfolded part, together with the *Future*, progressively realized. To the latter it most often referred, and is rendered *Fate* or *Doom*. But this is inaccurate, so far as genuine Elvish, especially High-elvish, is concerned, since it was not in that use applied only to evil events.

developed by the Eldar in Aman. When added to the name of a "kin-dred" it referred to the whole area occupied or owned by them, in which they were settled and were "at home" as long as they remained a united people. (*Eldamar* is thus translated *Elvenhome*.) It thus became in many cases synonymous with Q *nórë* (in composition often reduced to -*nor*), though this was only applied to large regions or countries, and was not added to the names of single persons.

The derivative form **mbardā* became in Quenya *marda* 'a dwell-ing'. This normally referred to the actual dwelling place, but was not limited to buildings, and could equally well be applied to dwellings of natural origin (such as caves or groves). It was nonetheless the near-est equivalent to "house" in most of its senses.* The words for buildings were derived from the base √*tam* 'construct' and √*kaw* 'shelter'. The former is seen in the very primitive and simple form **tamō*, translated 'smith', but meaning a craftsman in wood, stone, or metal: carpenter (carver), mason (sculptor), or smith. The oldest, derived product word was **taman-* (Q *taman*, S *tavn*) 'a thing made by handicraft'. 'Dwelling-house' is thus most closely represented in Quenya by *martan* (*martam-*) or the longer *martaman* (pl. *martamni*).

From √*kaw* was made the simple primitive form **kawā* > Q *köa*, applied to any 'shelter' (contrived and not natural), temporary or, in Aman, more often permanent, and applied to what we might call "outhouses", huts, sheds, booths. The later and more precise form, using the old instrumental suffix -*mā*, *kauma* remained in use for any protection or shelter natural or otherwise, sc. against sun, or rain, or wind – or against darts. It was often used = shield.

In Sindarin, owing to the quite different circumstances and history of the Eldar left behind in Beleriand, the development was different. Before the coming of the Exiles from Eldamar a large part of the Sindar lived in primitive conditions, mostly in groves or forest-land; permanent built dwellings were rare, especially those of smaller kind corresponding more or less to our "a house". The natural talents of the Quendi had already begun to develop many crafts before the beginning of the westward journey of the Eldar. But though the jour-ney had an object, in this period the Eldar became accustomed to a nomadic mobile life, and after reaching Beleriand they long

---

* Not to the use of "house" as the name of a (small) separate building with a function such as *bake-house*, *wood-house*; nor to the use of "house" as a family especially of power or authority. The former in Quenya was usually *köa* (see below). The latter was represented by words for "kindred".

continued with it, even after those among the Sindar who still desired to cross the Sea had abandoned hope. Thus the earliest essays of the Sindar in masonry were on the West Coasts in the realm of Círdan the Shipbuilder: harbour-works, quays, and towers. After the return of Morgoth to Thangorodrim their building remained undomestic, being mainly devoted to defensive works. Their skill developed rapidly during their association with the Dwarves of the Ered Luin, and later was still more enhanced by the great arts of the exiled Noldor. These latter had great effect in those regions where the Exiles and the Sindar were intermingled; but the Exiles' arts and habits had little or no influence in Doriath, the realm of Thingol, owing to his hatred of the Sons of Fëanor. In Doriath the only great permanent dwelling was Menegroth, which had been constructed with the aid and advice of the Dwarves: excavated not "built", and underground in the manner of the Dwarves: grim, strong, secret, though made beautiful within by the Valian arts of Melian. Outside the buildings of this period, the Siege of Angband, were mainly of defensive or warlike character: walls and battlements and forts. Even the great "house" of Finrod, *Minas Tirith*, as its name 'Tower of Watch' signifies, on an island in Sirion, was primarily a fort intended to command the accesses into Beleriand from the North. Only in Gondolin, a secret city, was the art of the Exiles fully employed in building fair houses as dwellings. But the Noldor generally built family houses in their territories, and often established communities within encircling walls in the manner of "towns". The Men who later entered Beleriand and became their allies adopted the same customs.

VII

THE FOUNDING OF NARGOTHROND

This text is extracted from a typescript text among Tolkien's linguistic papers that he titled "REVISION of Q[uenya] and S[indarin]" and dated 1969. I have omitted here without indication many passages of primarily linguistic and etymological matters.

[The Sindarin stem] *philig-* is mostly confined to specific places in the old tales of Beleriand. Its chief interest comes from its use in the "title" or by-name of King Finrod *Felagund* (said traditionally to have meant 'den-dweller', or specifically 'brock, badger').* This puzzled the earlier loremasters since the ending *-gund* could not be interpreted from Eldarin. The Sindarin word *fela* could be derived from a stem *phelga* or *philga*. It was used of minor excavations made by wild animals as dens or lairs, and also as temporary dwellings by wandering folk, Dwarvish or Elvish; it was usually distinguished from the larger caves of geological formation used and extended by stone-workers. It was thus naturally used of the "setts" of badgers (which seem to have existed in great numbers in parts of Beleriand). There were a number of such *fili* (pl. of *fela*, < **felʒi* < **phelgai*) on the west bank of the lower Narog river where it flowed along the feet of the great hills, "the hunters' Wold". But they were made or at least long occupied by Dwarves, of the strange and sinister kind known as

---

* This nick-name was probably actually given to Finrod not by Dwarves but by the Sons of Fëanor at least partly in derision. There was no great love between the Sons of Fëanor and the children of Finarphin, though they hid their enmity at need. (As when Curufin and Caranthir dwelt in the shelter of Nargothrond after the defeat of the Elves by Morgoth in the North). Moreover the Sons of Fëanor had much communication with the Dwarves of Nogrod and Belegost.

the Petty Dwarves: in origin, as was later known, descended from Dwarves banished for evil deeds from the great mansions of their kind.

During the Siege of Angband, while Morgoth was (or seemed to be) contained in his fortress by the Elvish armies and most of Beleriand had peace, Finrod was visited by dark forebodings – he was the wisest and most farseeing of the chieftains of the Noldor – that Morgoth was only biding his time, and would break and overwhelm the ring of the besiegers. He therefore made great journeys, exploring the lands, especially in southern and western Beleriand. It is told that when he came upon the Narog rushing down its steep course under the hills' shadow, he resolved to make there a secret fortress and store-houses against evil days, if he could; but the river could not be crossed at that place, and in the far banks he saw the opening of many caves. The tale of his dealings with the Petty Dwarves who still lingered there, remnant of a once more numerous folk, is told elsewhere. But during the years of peace that still remained Finrod carried out his design, and established the great mansions that were later called Nargothrond (< *Narog* + *ost-rond*), the cavernous halls beside the Narog. In this labour he had at first help from the Petty Dwarves and their feigned friendship; for which he rewarded them generously until Mîm their chieftain made an attempt to murder him in his sleep and was driven out into the wild.

VIII

MANWË'S BAN

This text is located among the "Last Writings" which Christopher Tolkien dated to the last year of his father's life (see XII:377). It is written in a clear hand in black nib-pen on the versos of two sheets of a printed Allen & Unwin "Publication Note" that is dated Feb. 1970. It arose in connection with, and was originally a part of, the text *Glorfindel II* that was published at XII:378–82. I supply the beginning of the first paragraph of this text from that printed at XII:380.

Elves were destined to be "immortal", that is not to die within the unknown limits decreed by the One, which at the most could be until the end of the life of the Earth as a habitable realm. Their death – by any injury to their bodies so severe that it could not be healed – and the disembodiment of their spirits was an "unnatural" and grievous matter. It was therefore the duty of the Valar, by command of the One, to restore them to life, if they desired it. But this restoration could be withheld or delayed by Manwë, for some grave reason: such as very evil deeds, or any works of malice of which a disembodied spirit remained unrepentant.[1] Now Glorfindel of Gondolin was one of the exiled Ñoldor, rebels against the authority of Manwë, and they were under a ban imposed by him: they could not return in bodily form to the Blessed Realm in any manner.* Not while the Ban was in force.

---

* By physical means, as by a ship, it was made impossible, after the rape of the Telerian ships at Alqualondë, nor could any living creature of Middle-earth, such as birds, however strong, cross the Great Sea. And all the Valar and Maiar were forbidden by Manwë to set foot on the land where the Ñoldor dwelt. Some say on any soil of Middle-earth at all.

This ban was as is told in the "Silmarillion" never fully revoked. Though after the defeat and downfall of Melkor[2] and his creatures from Middle-earth a general pardon was granted to all the Exiles who would accept it, those who then left Middle-earth did not dwell actually in Valinor, but in a special region of the great Isle of Eressëa that was set aside for them. There they could visit Valinor from time to time, but could not abide there long.

It must be supposed that Manwë intended to maintain the Ban – unless commanded by The One to lift it in any particular case, or in general – until some change unforeseen by him in the unfolding of the history of Middle-earth occurred.

Some of the Lore-masters later,* considering the events which led to the lifting of the Ban (as far as Elves were concerned) debated this matter. The One, all-seeing, knew of the imposition of the Ban, and permitted it; he also permitted its maintenance for long years, in the terms devised by Manwë, though these might seem too severe even on the Ñoldor, and were a great loss to the other Elves, and also to other folk and creatures. In particular, making any communication between the Ñoldor and the Valar impossible prevented the Ñoldor, in particular or as a people, from expressed repentance, or pleading for pardon and help. Some, therefore, of these loremasters concluded that Manwë, and the Council of the Valar, erred: because of their anger; and also because, though they possessed foreknowledge of history (since the making of the Music, and the vision that Eru thereafter presented to them of the unfolding history that it had generated), certain important matters had become dark to them. They had had no part in the creation of the Children of Eru, Elves and Men, and could not ever with complete assurance foresee the actions working of their independent wills.

But the wiser ones among them rebuked them, saying: Ye cannot say that the Valar *erred*, in so grave a matter, seeing that Eru knew and permitted the actions and commands of Manwë, for this is to attribute error to Him.[3] Moreover, ye misrepresent and exaggerate the workings of the Ban and so call in question its justice. As far as concerns the Ñoldor, they obtained precisely what they demanded: freedom from the sovereignty of Manwë, and therefore also from any protection or assistance by the Valar, or indeed any meddling with their affairs. They had been advised and solemnly taught by Manwë

---

* That is, in Númenor. And herein may be seen (though this debate was begun early in the history of that land) the first beginnings of that arrogance which ultimately destroyed that realm.

to what straits and griefs they would come, relying only on their own wisdom and power. They rejected him; and even before they had finally left the West Lands and reached Middle-earth, they did hideous deeds of robbery and bloodshed and treachery.[4] Then a large number of the Ñoldor, who had taken no part in this, went back to Valinor, and sought pardon and were granted it. Those that did not do so, even if not personally slayers, must share the blood guilt, if they accepted the freedom gained by it. That none of the Ñoldor should be allowed again to dwell in bodily form was an inevitable consequence. That none of the Valar or Maiar should appear in their lands to aid them was also inevitable. But it is not said that Manwë abandoned them, peoples over whom he had been appointed by Eru to be a vice-regent.[5] His messengers could come from Valinor and did so, and though in disguised form and issuing no commands, they intervened in certain desperate events.* [6]

Moreover the Valar had great knowledge of the war of the Ñoldor and Sindar against Melkor in Thangorodrim; for great hosts of Elves were slain in that war, and some came in spirit to Mandos† where all their deeds in Middle-earth were laid bare. And yet again: great and grievous as was the revolt of the Ñoldor, it was only a part of the griefs and anxieties of Manwë, only one aspect of his heavy kingship: the war against Melkor himself, which had now broken out again into new malignance. It was indeed Melkor who was the prime malefactor, the author and deviser of the revolt of the Ñoldor, though that was only again a small part of his assault upon the Valar and their land, which he had darkened and robbed of its primeval joy and beauty. From this he had escaped.

---

* The most notable were those Maiar who took the form of the mighty speaking eagles that we hear of in the legends of the war of the Ñoldor against Melkor, and who remained in the West of Middle-earth until the fall of Sauron and the Dominion of Men, after which they are not heard of again. Their intervention in the story of Maelor, in the duel of Fingolfin and Melkor, in the rescue of Beren and Lúthien is well known. (Beyond their knowledge were the deeds of the Eagles in the war against Sauron: in the rescue of the Ring Finder and his companions, in the Battle of Five Armies, and in the rescue of the Ringbearer from the fires of Mount Doom.)

† Men also, and doubtless from them also much was learned. But no question of their "restoration" arose. For this was not in the power of the Valar. It is said that they too dwelt in the Halls of Waiting assigned to their kind, but they were not judged, and abode there only until summoned by Eru, and departed whither neither the Valar nor the Elves knew.

NOTES

1 Cf. chap. XV, "Elvish Reincarnation", in part two of this book.

2 Tolkien struck through the words "and extrusion" between "downfall" and "of Melkor".

3 Tolkien labored on this admonition, first writing: "in so grave a matter, in making [?common]" (perhaps the start of "command"?), then striking out these last three words and replacing them with: "by doing things which Eru permitted, without attributing error to Him". He then struck out all from "a matter" to "Him", before continuing the effort on the next page with "a matter …". Further, in the left margin against this lengthy paragraph he very roughly wrote: "Debate concerning Manwë's Ban; was it just? not for the good of Elves and Men."

   The words "knew and permitted" in the continuation replaced "was in direct commun[ion]" in the act of writing.

4 As first written, the deeds of the Ñoldor are called "wicked" (rather than "hideous").

5 Tolkien first wrote "vice-ger" (i.e., for "vice-gerent") before changing this to "vice-regent" in the act of writing. Tolkien describes Manwë as a "vice-gerent" in chap. IX, "*Ósanwe-kenta*", in part two of this book.

6 For *Maelor* as a post-*LR* variant name of Maglor, see: III:353 and fn.; X:182 §41; and XII:318 n.7.

IX

ELVISH JOURNEYS ON HORSEBACK

This text is found in a bundle of manuscript material associated with the late typescript text B of *Of Maeglin*, which Christopher Tolkien describes at XI:316, 330 and dates to 1970. Portions of this text are drafting for texts already given at XI:332–3, 335–6 (q.v.). I give here some details among this material not previously published or cited.

Elvish journeys on horseback

We are not dealing with the movements of human cavalry with its slow pace (except in action): e.g., "walk" 3½ mph; "trot-walk" 5; "trot" 7, etc.![1] Elves (and their horses) were swifter in movement, hardier, and of greater endurance. At need an Eldarin rider could remain in the saddle for long hours with brief halts and light provision, while his horse maintained a high speed, and they could cover great distances in a day, with only a brief few hours' rest or sleep before going on again. But we are in the case of Eöl's journey to *Nogrod* and back not dealing yet with his desperate pursuit of the fugitives [Aredhel and Maeglin]. Eöl was "on a holiday", riding in the wild lands he loved, at ease, and he had allowed ample time in which to reach *Nogrod* before the Feast.

Riding at ease he would journey about 9 hours, and at what was for him and his horse the gentle speed of some 9 miles in the hour. Of this 9 hours he would spend about 1½ hours (more or less) in halts. He would thus only go about 70 miles or less in a day.

Eöl was by choice a night-rider, being night-sighted, and training his riding horses to suit him. (But he had, of course, no fear of being abroad by day, or at need of riding in sunlight.) At Midsummer* when sunset was about 8 pm and sunrise about 4 am, he would start about 7:30 in late evening and go on about 4:30 in early morning (9 hours).

But he could, without wearying himself or his horse, journey for longer hours, and at greater speed. For example, he could journey for 10 hours at an average of 10 mph, spending no more than 1½ hours in halts, and so cover easily 85 miles in a day.† Speed, however, naturally depended much upon the ground. From Elmoth to Gelion‡ the land was, north of the Andram, and the Falls below the last Ford§ over Gelion (just above the inflow of the River Ascar from the Mountains), mostly rolling plain, with large regions of big trees without thickets. There were several beaten tracks made originally by Dwarves from Belegost and Nogrod, the best (most used and widest) being from the Little Ford past the north of Elmoth and to the Ford of Aros, it crossed the Bridge of Esgalduin but went no further for, if the Dwarves wished to visit Menegroth and Thingol [?wished to see them they were][2]

Here the text, which has come to be written in very hasty and now rubbed pencil, becomes mostly illegible. Following the wholly illegible end of the last sentence above, some bits can be interpreted, including the names *Thargelion*, *Asgar*, and perhaps *Belegost*.

---

* Assuming a latitude of about 50° N, and an astronomical situation not greatly different from ours.

† At need he could, for at least 2 days together, cover 100 miles a day — and of course in desperate flight or pursuit go faster still, though this would be wearisome, and exhausting to his horse, even if watering was available.

‡ Now read *Gevolon* < Dwarf-name *Gabilān* ('great river').

§ In Map [cf. XI:331] *Sarn Athrad*, but this must be changed to *Harathrad* 'Southern Ford' (or *Athrad Daer*) in contrast to the much-used northern Ford where the River was not yet very swift or deep, nearly due east of Eöl's house (72 miles distant).

X

RIDER TO "THE WHITE RIDER"

Though not in fact among Tolkien's late writings, this seems an opportune place to bring to wider attention a text bearing on the history of the writing of *The Lord of the Rings*, as well as a charming if rejected scene involving Legolas and horses. This text is written on a torn half-sheet, and was originally intended as an insertion in the drafting of what became the chapter "The White Rider" (ch. 5 of Book III of *The Lord of the Rings*). At the top of the sheet a note Tolkien wrote: "If new ending of Chap. XXIII is used, this will not be required." To the right of this Tolkien wrote the number "XXVI", and at the far right are the words "3 rider". (As Christopher Tolkien notes, the chapter "The White Rider" "was numbered 'XXVI' from an early stage"; VII:425). The entire page was ultimately crossed out (the reason for its rejection is discussed in the commentary following the text). In the foreword to the 2nd edition of *LR* Tolkien says (xx–xxi), "I went on and so came to Lothlórien and the Great River late in 1941. In the next year I wrote the first drafts of the matter that now stands as Book III, and the beginnings of Chapters 1 and 3 of Book V." This strongly suggests that Tolkien drafted this rider early in 1942.

This text and the accompanying commentary by Patrick Wynne and Christopher Gilson were previously published in *Vinyar Tengwar* 27 (1993).

"What of our horses?" said Legolas.

"I was forgetting them," said Aragorn. "We cannot lead them into the Forest; there will be no food for them in there. They must be set free, so that they can return as they will to their own master. We do not know how long our search will take or whither it will lead us."

"But we do not yet know that it will take us into the Forest," said Gimli. "At least let us take the horses to the edge of the wood! It is a long walk from here to Theoden's halls, and you promised to ride back there with our borrowed mounts."

"When our quest was over or proved vain," said Aragorn.

"Let the horses judge!" said Legolas. "I will speak to them." Running lightly over the grass he returned to the tree under which they had camped, and going to the horses he untethered them, fondling their heads and whispering in their ears. "Go free now, Hasofel and Arod!" he said aloud. "Wait for us a while, but no longer than seems good to you!"

The horses looked solemnly at him for a moment, and then walked together behind the Elf towards the river-bank. There they stood quietly like folk on a doorstep when friends are taking their leave. As the companions went away up the slope they lifted their heads and whinnied, and then bending to the grass, afar they strayed together, browsing peacefully as if they were in their home-pasture.

The text apparently describes Aragorn, Gimli, and Legolas *on the morning after* their encounter with the old man by the campfire (cf. "[Legolas] returned to the tree under which *they had camped*"), when they are on the verge of entering Fangorn Forest proper. In *The Lord of the Rings* as published this occurs in "The White Rider", not "The Riders of Rohan"; the latter chapter ends on the previous night, with the three companions still camping by the eaves of the Forest. In Tolkien's numeration at the time of composition, "The Riders of Rohan" was numbered 'XXIII', and the significance of the note "If new ending of Chap. XXIII is used, this will not be required" seems to be this:

In "The Riders of Rohan" as published, at the end of the chapter the horses run away after the apparition of the mysterious old man: "The horses were gone. They had dragged their pickets and disappeared." (LR:443) But that chapter as originally written ended differently; in the original version, the horses were alarmed but did not flee: "The horses were restive, straining at their tether-ropes, showing the whites of their eyes. It was a little while before Legolas could quiet them." (VII:403) The insertion must have been written to accord with this earlier version of the story. Since the horses did not run away in chap. XXIII, it was necessary to account for what was done with them later in chap. XXVI when Aragorn, Legolas, and Gimli finally entered Fangorn. However, Christopher Tolkien states that by the time of the completion of the fair copy manuscript of "The White Rider", his father had changed the ending of "The Riders of Rohan" to its published form (VII:432). This, of course, is the "new ending of chap. XXIII" referred to in Tolkien's note at the top of the manuscript, and with this change the insertion to chap. XXVI became unnecessary.

XI

LIVES OF THE NÚMENÓREANS

This typescript text exists in three versions: Tolkien's typescript (A), its carbon copy (B) with no textual value save one brief marginal note concerning Aldarion's later change of succession law; and (C) an amanuensis fair copy, likewise with no textual value. The text given here is therefore A, which occupies four-and-a-half sides. Christopher Tolkien assembled selections from this text, and from that given in chap. XIII below, into the chapter *A Description of the Island of Númenor* in UT:165–72. He dated both of these texts to c. 1965 (UT:7).

In the typescript the text proper is followed by a series of (at times quite lengthy) author's notes. For the reader's convenience I have placed all but the longest of these as footnotes; the remaining two follow the text and are cited in the text with "[*Author's Note*]". The discussion of Númenórean life-spans that opens this text was referenced and paraphrased by Christopher Tolkien at UT:224–5 n.1. This discussion further echoes closely the matters and schemes Tolkien developed at length for the Elves in part one of this book, "Time and Ageing" (and cf. esp. chap. XVIII, "Elvish Ages & Númenórean", which likewise dates from 1965, in part one of this book).

Lives of the Númenóreans

Long life and Peace were the two things that the Edain asked for when the Valar offered them reward at the fall of Thangorodrim. Peace was readily granted; long life not so readily, and only after Manwë had consulted Eru.

Elros was treated specially. He and his brother Elrond were not actually differently endowed, so far as the purely physical potentiality of life was concerned; but since Elros elected to remain among the kindred of Men, he retained the chief human characteristic as compared with the Quendi: the "seeking elsewhither", as the Eldar called it, the "weariness" or desire to depart from the World. He died, or resigned life, when he was about 500 years old.

The remainder of the people were granted a life-span about five times as long as that of ordinary Men: that is, they would die, whether by free resignation or not, somewhere within the limits of 350 to 420 years.[1] Within these limits individuals, and also families, [*Author's Note 1*] differed in natural life-span, as they did before the Grace was given. The royal family or "Line of Elros" was in general longeval, and often lived for 400 years or a little more. In other families 400 years was less often achieved; though in families who had become allied with the Line of Elros by marriage (in the earlier generations) longeval individuals often appeared.

By this is meant that the "weariness" was not felt by the longeval until about the 400th year; how long they might have lived on into decrepitude, if they had "clung to life", is not known, because in the early generations they did not do so. "Clinging to life", and so in the end dying perforce and involuntarily, was one of the changes brought about by the Shadow and the rebellion of the Númenóreans. It was also accompanied by a shrinking of their natural life-span. These things first appeared in the 14th generation, that is, after the death of Tar-Atanamir in S.A. 2251.[2]

The increase of the Númenórean life-span was brought about by assimilating their life-mode to that of the Eldar, up to a limited point. They were however expressly warned that they had not become Eldar, but remained "mortal Men", and had been granted only an extension of the period of their vigour of mind and body. Thus (as the Eldar) they "grew" at much the same rate as ordinary Men:[3] gestation, infancy, childhood, and adolescence up to puberty and "full-growth" proceeded more or less as before; but when they had achieved full-growth they then aged or "wore out" very much slower, so that for them five years had about the same effect as one year for ordinary mortals.

The first approach of "world-weariness" was indeed for them a sign that their period of vigour was nearing its end. When it came to an end, if they persisted in living, then decay would, as growth had done, soon proceed at more or less the same rate as for other Men. Thus, if a Númenórean reached the end of vigour at about 400 years, he would then pass quickly, in about ten years, from health and vigour of mind to decrepitude and senility.

If one wishes, therefore, to find what "age" a Númenórean was in ordinary human terms of vigour and aptitude, this may be done so: (1) Deduct 20: since at 20 years a Númenórean would be at about the same stage of development as an ordinary person. (2) Add to this 20 the remainder divided by 5. Thus a Númenórean man or woman of years:

25 50 75 100   125 150 175 200 225 250 275 300 325 350 375 400 425

would be approximately of the "age":

21 26 31   36   41   46   51   56   61   66   71   76   81   86   91   96 101

But this numerical calculation omits certain factors. Númenórean mental development was also assimilated to some degree to the Eldarin mode. Their mental capacity was greater and developed quicker than that of ordinary Men; and it was dominant. After about seven years they grew up mentally with rapidity, and at 20 years knew and understood far more than a normal human of that age. A consequence of this, reinforced by their expectation of long-lasting vigour which left them with little sense of urgency in the first half of their lives, was that they very often became engrossed in lore, and crafts, and various intellectual or artistic pursuits, to a far greater degree than normal. This was particularly the case with men.

Desire for marriage, the begetting, bearing, and rearing of children, thus occupied a smaller place in the lives of Númenóreans, even of the women, than among ordinary Men. Marriage was regarded as natural for all, and once entered into was permanent; * [4] but like the Eldar they tended to make the period of parenthood (or as the Eldar called it, the "Days of the Children")[5] a single connected and limited period of their lives. This limitation was regarded as

---

* The Númenóreans were monogamous, as is later said. No one, of whatever rank, could divorce a husband or wife, nor take another spouse in the lifetime of the first. Marriage was not entered into by all. There was (it appears from occasional statements in the few surviving tales or annals) a slightly less number of women than men, at any rate in the earlier centuries. But apart from this numerical limitation, there was always a small minority that refused marriage, either because they were engrossed in lore or other pursuits, or because they had failed to obtain the spouse whom they desired and would seek for no other.

natural. The connexion, the treating of the period of child-bearing as an ordered and unbroken series, was considered proper and desirable, if it could be achieved. That the married pair should dwell together, with as few and short times of separation as possible, between say, the conception of their first child to at least the seventh birthday of the latest, was held to be the ideal arrangement. It was particularly desired by the women, who were naturally (as a rule) less engrossed in lore or crafts; and who had far less desire for moving about. [*Author's Note 2*]

Thus the Númenóreans, who seldom had more than four children in each marriage, would frequently produce these within a period of about 50 to 75 years (between the first conception and the last birth). The intervals between the children were long as a rule, in ordinary terms: often ten years, sometimes 15 or even as much as 20 years; never less than about five years.* But it has to be remembered in this regard that in proportion to their total life-span this period was only equivalent to one of about 10 to 15 years of normal human life. The intervals, if reckoned also according to their degree of approach towards the end of vigour and fertility, were thus equivalent to a

---

* Since in matters of growth, which included the conception and bearing of children, the Númenórean development differed little in speed from that of ordinary Men, these intervals seem long. But as has been said their mental interests were dominant; and also they gave great and concentrated attention to any matter that they took up. The matter of children, therefore, being of highest importance, was one that occupied most of the attention of the mother during bearing and infancy, and except in great households cast a great deal of the daily labour upon the father. Both were glad for a while to return to other neglected pursuits. But also (it was said by the Númenóreans themselves) they were in this matter more like the Eldar than other kinds of Men: in the begetting and still more in the bearing of a child far more of their vigour both of body and mind was expended (for the longevity of the later generations was, though a grace or gift, transmitted mediately by the parents). A rest both of body and will was, therefore, needed, especially by the women. After the conception of a child indeed desire for union became dormant for a while, in both men and women, though longer among the mothers.

This dominance was seen in other matters. If the Númenóreans were not lustful, they did not think the love of men and women less important or of less delight than did other Men. On the contrary they were steadfast lovers; and any breaches in the bonds and affection between parents, or between them and their children were thought great evils and sorrows. So with the delights of eating and drinking. Until the Shadow came there were in Númenor few gluttons or drunkards. No one ate or drank to excess, or indeed much at any one time. They esteemed good food, which was plentiful, and expended care and art in its cooking and serving. But the distinction between a "Feast" and an ordinary meal consisted rather in this: in the adornments of the table, in the music, and in the merriment of many eating together, than in the food; though naturally at such feasts food and wines of more rare and choice sorts would sometimes appear.

(rare) minimum of one year, with a more frequent allowance of two, three, or sometimes four years.

"Vigour", that is primarily bodily health and activity, and the period of fertility and child-bearing in women, were of course not co-extensive. The child-bearing period of women was similar to that of ordinary women, though reckoned in Númenórean terms. That is, it ranged from puberty (reached by Númenórean women not long before full-growth) to an "age" equivalent to a normal human 45 (with occasional extension towards 50). In years this means from about 18 to about 125 or a little more. But first children were seldom if ever conceived at the end of this time.

Thus a Númenórean woman might marry when 20 (marriage before full-growth was not permitted); but most usually she married at about 40 to 45 years ("age" 24 to 25). Marriage was considered unduly delayed in her case if postponed much beyond her 95th year ("age" about 35).* [6]

Men seldom married before their year 45 (age 25). Their time from the year 15 to 45 was usually engrossed in learning, in apprenticeship to one or more crafts, and (more and more as time went on) in seafaring. Postponement of marriage to about the 95th year (age 35) was very common; and, especially in the case of men of rank, high duty, or great talents, it was not seldom entered into as late as the 120th year (age 40). In the Line of Elros (especially among the children of actual kings), which was somewhat more longeval than the average and also provided many duties and opportunities (both

---

* Thus to mention the case of Erendis, wife of Tar-Aldarion, concerning whom there were several tales made (one has survived), since the events were held important: both as a rare case of dissension between the married, and because they caused an alteration in the laws of succession. She was not of the Line of Elros, but came of a Bëorian family of the West, who though descended from a kinswoman of Beren, were among the relatively short-lived. Her marriage with Aldarion (then Heir to the Sceptre) was delayed by his voyages until S.A. 870. Since she was born in 771, she was then of 99 years: that is, nearly 36, or indeed with regard to the shorter life-span of her people 38. After the birth of their child, Ankalimë, Aldarion went again oversea; and on his return late in 882 she was of years 111; that is, just over 38 (or in her family nearly 41), her expectation of children, and her desire for them, thus fast waning. In her anger (for she thought his departures wilful and selfish, though this was not in the main true), she rejected Aldarion, and they did not again dwell together nor have any more children. It was for this reason, and to obtain control of their daughter Ankalimë, to whom Erendis clung, that Tar-Aldarion, soon after he became king, altered the Law of Succession, so that a king's daughter, if he had no male heir (and later, if she were his eldest child and all her brothers younger) might, if she were willing, succeed to the Sceptre.

for men and women), marriage was often later than normal: for women 95 (age 35) was frequent; and for men might be as late as the 150th year (age 46) or even later. This had one advantage: that the "Heir to the Sceptre", even if the king's eldest child, would be able to succeed while still in full vigour, though he would probably have passed through the "Days of the Children" and be more free to devote himself to public concerns.*

Númenóreans were strictly monogamous: by law, and by their "tradition": that is by the tradition of the original Edain concerning conduct, afterwards re-inforced by Eldarin example and teaching. There were in the early centuries few cases of the breach of the law, or even of desire to break it. The Númenóreans, or Dúnedain, were still in our terms "fallen Men";[7] but they were descendants of ancestors who were in general wholly repentant, detesting all the corruptions of the "Shadow"; and they were specially graced. In general they had little inclination to, and a conscious detestation of lust, greed, hate and cruelty, and tyranny. Not all of course were so noble. There were such things as wickedness among them, at first very rarely to be seen. For they were not selected by any test save that of belonging to the Three Houses of the Edain. Among them were no doubt a few of the wild men and renegades of old days, and possibly (though this cannot be asserted) actual conscious servants of the Enemy.

A second marriage was permitted, by traditional law, if one of the partners died young, leaving the other in vigour and still with a need or desire of children; but the cases were naturally very rare. Death untimely, whether by sickness or mischance, seldom occurred in the early centuries. This the Númenóreans recognized as due to the "grace of the Valar" (which might be withheld in general or in particular cases, if it ceased to be merited): the land was blessed, and all things, including the Sea, were friendly to them. In addition the

---

* Ankalimë, daughter of Tar-Aldarion, who became the first Ruling Queen of Númenor, was exceptional in many ways. She was extremely long-lived (413 years); she had the longest reign (205 years) of any Ruler of Númenor after Elros; and she married very late: in her 127th year (age about 41) producing a son, Anárion, in her 130th year. With regard to more normal successions, it may be noted that Tar-Meneldur, born in S.A. 543, succeeded in 740 in his 197th year. He would in the usual course have probably resigned about 925 (when 382 years old, and after a reign of 185 years); his heir Aldarion would then have been 225 years old. Actually for domestic and political reasons he resigned in 883, and lived on in retirement (engaged in his favourite pursuit of astronomy) until 942. Thus Aldarion succeeded when 183 years old (age about 52) and had a long reign of 192 years, resigning in 1075, and dying in 1098.

people, tall and strong, were agile, and extremely "aware": that is they were in control of their bodily actions, and of any tool or material they handled, and seldom made absent-minded or blundering movements; and they were very difficult to take "off their guard". Accidents were thus unlikely to occur to them. If any did, they had a power of recovery and self-healing, which if inferior to that of the Eldar, was much greater than that of Men in Middle-earth.* Also among the matters of lore that they specially studied was *hröangolmë* or the lore of the body and the arts of healing.[8] Pride was no doubt their chief weakness, increased later by contact with Men of lesser kinds – though not at first: their first sentiments and motives were of pity and benevolence. They were also proud of their ancestry, in general and in particular, as a people and as individuals; and all men of all ranks kept scrolls of their descent. Descent "from Eärendil" or "from Beren and Lúthien" were their chief titles to nobility.

The later law, or rather custom, by which those of the royal house (especially the Heir) wedded only members of the Line of Elros, was not in the early generations possible. But in the days of Tar-Aldarion, or about the year 1000, there were numerous descendants of Elros sufficiently divergent in kinship. (Marriage with kin nearer than second cousin was at all times prohibited, until the latter days of the Shadow, even in the royal house.) This rule of royal marriage was never a matter of law, but it became a custom of pride: a symptom of the growth of the Shadow, since it only became rigid when in fact the

---

* Sicknesses or other bodily disorders were very rare in Númenor until the latter years. This was due both to the special grace of health and strength given to the race as a whole, but especially due to the blessing of the land itself; and also in some measure no doubt to its situation far out in the Great Sea: animals were also mostly free from disease. But the few cases of sickness provided a practical function, so far as one was needed, for the continued study of *hröangolmë* (or physiology and medicine) in which the practisers of simple leechcraft among the Edain had received much instruction from the Eldar, and in which they were able still to learn from the Eressëans, so long as they would. In the first days of the coming of Númenórean ships to the shores of Middle-earth it was indeed their skill in healing, and their willingness to give instruction to all who would receive it, that made the Númenóreans most welcomed and esteemed.

Since some of the Númenórean crews that went on the first long voyages of exploration (far south and east of Lindon) fell sick or contracted diseases prevalent in the lands that they visited, it was feared by many in Númenor that the Venturers or explorers might bring back disease to the land. It was this fear in especial that made Tar-Meneldur opposed to his son Tar-Aldarion's longer voyages, and caused a coolness between father and son for a long time. But it was found that those of the sick who were brought back living (few in fact died abroad before the actual settlements of Númenóreans in Middle-earth) soon recovered fully in their own land, and their diseases were not propagated.

distinction between the Line of Elros and other families, in life-span, vigour, or ability, had diminished or altogether disappeared.

Author's Notes

[*Note 1*] The Númenóreans were not of uniform racial descent. Their main division was between the descendants of the "House of Hador" and the "House of Bëor". These two groups originally had distinct languages; and in general showed different physical characteristics. Each House had, moreover, numerous followers of mixed origin. The people of Bëor were on the whole dark-haired (though fair-skinned), less tall and of less stalwart build; they were also less long-lived. Their Númenórean descendants tended to have a smaller life-span: about 350 years or less. The people of Hador were strong, tall, and for the most part fair-haired. But the chieftains of both Houses had already in Beleriand intermarried. The Line of Elros was regarded as belonging to the House of Hador through Eärendil (son of Tuor, the great-great-grandson of Hador); but it was also descended on the distaff side from the House of Bëor through Elwing wife of Eärendil, daughter of Dior, son of Beren (last chieftain of the House of Bëor, and seventh in direct descent from Bëor).

The Númenórean language was in the main derived from the speech of the people of Hador (much enlarged by additions from the Elven-tongues at different periods). The people of Bëor had in a few generations abandoned their own speech (except in the retention of many personal names of native origin) and adopted the Elven-tongue of Beleriand, the Sindarin. This distinction was still observable in Númenor. Nearly all Númenóreans were bilingual. But where the main mass of settlers came from the people of Bëor, as was the case especially in the North-west, Sindarin was the daily tongue of all classes and Númenórean (or *Adûnayân*) a second language. In most parts of the country Adûnayân was the native language of the people, though Sindarin was known in some degree by all except the stay-at-home and untravelled of the farming folk. In the Royal House, however, and in most of the house of the noble or learned, Sindarin was usually the native tongue, until after the days of Tar-Atanamir.

Sindarin used for a long period by mortal Men naturally tended to become divergent and dialectal; but this process was largely checked, at any rate so far as the nobles and learned were concerned, by the constant contact that was maintained with the Eldar in Eressëa, and later with those who remained in Lindon in Middle-earth. The Eldar came mostly to the West regions of the country. Quenya was not a spoken tongue. It was known only to the learned, and to the families of high descent (to whom it was taught in their early youth). It was used in official documents intended for preservation, such as the Laws, and the Scroll and Annals of the Kings, and often in more recondite works of lore. It was also largely used in nomenclature. The official names of all places, regions, and geographical features in the land were of Quenya form (though they usually also had local names, generally of the same meaning, in either Sindarin or Adûnayân). The personal names and especially the official and public names of all members of the Royal House, and of the Line of Elros in general, were given in Quenya form. The same was true of some other families, such as the House of the Lords of Andúnië.

[*Note 2*][9] Númenor was a land of peace; within it there was no war or strife, until the last years. But the people were descended from ancestors of a hardy and warlike kind. The energy of the men was chiefly transferred to the practice of crafts; but they were also much occupied in games and physical sports. Boys and young men loved especially to live, when they could, freely in the open and to journey on foot in the wilder parts of the land. Many exercised themselves in climbing. There were no great mountains in Númenor. The sacred Mountain of the Menel-tarma was near the centre of the land; but it was only about 3,000 feet high, and was climbed by a spiral road from its southern base (near where was the Valley of the Tombs, in which the kings were buried) up to its summit. But there were rocky and mountainous regions in the promontories of the North and North-west and South-west, in which some heights were about 2,000 feet. The cliffs, however, were the chief places of climbing for the daring. The cliffs of Númenor were in places of great height, especially along the west-facing coasts, the haunts of innumerable birds.

In the Sea the strong men took their greatest delight: in swimming or in diving; or in small craft for contests of speed in rowing and sailing. The hardiest of the people were engaged in fishing: fish were abundant, and at all times one of the chief sources of food for Númenor. The cities or towns where many people congregated were all by the coast. From the fisher-folk were mostly drawn the special class of mariners, who steadily increased in importance and esteem. At first the Númenórean craft, still largely dependent on Eldarin models, were engaged only in fishing, or in coastwise journeys from port to port. But it was not long before the Númenóreans by their own study and devices improved their art of ship-building, until they could venture far out into the Great Sea. It was in S.A. 600 that Vëantur, Captain of the King's Ships under Tar-Elendil, first achieved a voyage to Middle-earth and back. He brought his ship *Entulessë* ('Return') to Mithlond on the Spring winds (which often blew strongly and steadily from the West) and returned in Autumn of the following year. After that sea-faring became the chief outlet for daring and hardihood among the men of Númenor. It was Aldarion son of Tar-Meneldur who formed the Guild of Venturers to which all the tried mariners belonged, and many young men even from the inland regions sought admission.

The women took little part in these things, though they were generally nearer to men than is the case with most races in stature and strength, and were agile and fleet of foot in youth. Their great delight was in dancing (in which many men also took part) at feasts or in leisure time. Many women achieved great fame as dancers, and people would go on long journeys to see displays of their art. They did not, however, greatly love the Sea. They would journey in need in the coastwise craft from port to port; but they did not like to be long aboard or to pass even one night in a ship. Even among the fisher-folk the women seldom took part in the sailings. But nearly all women could ride horses, treating them honourably, and housing them more nobly than any other of their domestic animals. The stables of a great man were often as large and as fair to look upon as his own house. Both men and women rode horses for pleasure. Riding was also the chief means of quick travel from place to place; and in ceremony of state both men and women of rank, even queens, would ride, on horseback amid their escorts or retinues.

The inland roads of Númenor were for the most part "horse-roads", unpaved, and made and tended for the purpose of riding. Coaches and carriages for journeying were in the earlier centuries little used; for the heavier transport went largely by sea. The chief and most ancient road, suitable for wheels, ran from the greatest port, Rómenna, in the East, north-west to the royal city of Armenelos (about 40 miles), and thence to the Valley of Tombs and the Menel-tarma. But this road was early extended to Ondosto within the border of the Forostar (or Norlands), and thence straight west to Andúnië in the Andustar (or Westlands); it was however little used for wheeled vehicles of travel, being mainly made and used for the transport by wains of timber, in which the Westlands were rich, or of stone of the Norlands, which was most esteemed for building.

Though the Númenóreans used horses for journeys and for the

delight of riding they had little interest in racing them as a test of speed. In country sports displays of agility, both of horse and rider, were to be seen; but more esteemed were exhibitions of understanding between master and beast. The Númenóreans trained their horses to hear and understand calls (by voice or whistling) from great distances; and also, where there was great love between men or women and their favorite steeds, they could (or so it is said in ancient tales) summon them at need by their thought alone.[10]

So it was also with their dogs. For the Númenóreans kept dogs, especially in the country, partly by ancestral tradition, since they had few useful purposes any longer. The Númenóreans did not hunt for sport or food; and they had only in a few places upon the borders of wild lands any great need of watch-dogs. In the sheep-rearing regions, such as that of Emerië, they had dogs specially trained to help the shepherds. In the earlier centuries country-men also had dogs trained to assist in warding off or tracking down predatory beasts and birds (which to the Númenóreans was only an occasional necessary labour and not an amusement). Dogs were seldom seen in the towns. In the farms they were never chained or tethered; but neither did they dwell in the houses of men; though they were often welcomed to the central *solma* or hall, where the chief fire burned: especially the old faithful dogs of long service, or at times the puppies. It was men rather than women who had a liking to keep dogs as "friends". Women loved more the wild (or "unowned") birds and beasts, and they were especially fond of squirrels, of which there were great numbers in the wooded country.

Of these matters more is said elsewhere, concerning the tame (or "owned") animals of Númenor, the native beasts and birds, and the imported.

This last topic is taken up in chap. XIII , "Of the Land and Beasts of Númenor", below.

NOTES

1 Cf. Christopher Tolkien's reference to and commentary on this statement at UT:224 n.1.

2 Tolkien here follows *The Tale of Years* at LR:1083. In *The Line of Elros* Tar-Atanamir is instead said to have died in 2221 (UT:221, and cf. 226 n.10).

3 Regarding the comparability of the growth-rate of the Eldar, from gestation to maturity, to that of Men, see Tolkien's considerable hesitation and elaborations on this point throughout part one of this book, "Time and Ageing".

4 A deleted and much briefer note here reads:

That is, no other union was possible while both partners were alive. Not for any reason or need, e.g. not to provide a king with an heir.

On the permanence of marriage, see the discussion of ~MARRIAGE in App. I.

5 See the repeated discussion of the "Days of the Children" among the Eldar in part one of this book.

6 Cf. *Aldarion and Erendis* in UT:173–217.

7 With "fallen Men" see the *Athrabeth Finrod ah Andreth* in *Morgoth's Ring*, and chaps. XII, "Concerning the Quendi in Their Mode of Life and Growth", in part one of this book, and X, "Notes on *Órë*", in part two of this book. See also THE FALL OF MAN in App. I.

8 As first written, the Quenya term for "lore of the body" was given as *hröanissë*.

9 Portions of this long digression were taken up, in slightly different form, by Christopher Tolkien into *A Description of Númenor*: cf. UT169, 171.

10 "By their thought alone": cf. chap. IX, "*Ósanwe-kenta*", in part two of this book.

XII

THE AGEING OF NÚMENÓREANS

Apparently in conjunction with writing the preceding text, and so probably likewise c. 1965, Tolkien wrote two brief texts, both written in black nib-pen, giving more precise tabulations of the differences in the age of maturity and subsequent rates of ageing between the Line of Elros and other Númenóreans. I give them in what appears to be their chronological order.

Text 1[1]

	Númenóreans	Line of Elros
Manhood	20	20
Full-growth	25	25 – 30
Youth	25 – 125 (or later)	25 – 200 (or later)
Vigour	25 – 175 (or later)	25 – 300 (or later)
Coming of weariness	200 – 225 (or later)	350 – 400 (or a little later)

The best time for marriage was held to be in "youth", though it could be delayed during the years of vigour. For the Line of Elros it was seldom entered into in the first years of youth; and seldom after the last years.

Marriage could by nature take place thus between manhood and the end of the years of vigour; but it was seldom entered into in the first years of youth or delayed until (or beyond) their end. For the Line of Elros about the year 100 was held to be the high or best time for wedding; for others, about the year 50. But many women were married earlier than this; for them (in the Royal line) 50 was the high time, and 30 for others, and they have children seldom after 150.

TEXT 2

	Númenóreans	Line of Elros
Manhood	20	25[2]
Full-growth	25	25 – 30
Maturity[3]	c. 50	c. 100 – 150
Youth	25 to 125 (or later)	25 to 200 (or later)
Vigour	25 to 175 (or later)	25 to 300 (or later)
Coming of weariness	200 (or later: seldom later than 250)	c. 400 (or a little later)

The time of "maturity" (which implied full-growth of mind as well as body) was held to be the best time for marriage; normally about the age 50, or for the Line of Elros 100. But marriage was often delayed by men of keen mind, eager in various pursuits, and especially by those who turned towards the Sea. It could be delayed until near the end of the years of "vigour"; but this was seldom done.

Women came to womanhood and full-growth in the same time as men, but their "youth" (beyond which they seldom bore children) lasted less long. They were married younger (as a rule), and thus for the most part took husbands older than themselves. Yet their lives were often longer than those of men, for they were more tenacious of the world and their pursuits therein, wearying less soon, and less willing to depart.

Marriage years:

	Normal	Royal
Men	50–100	100–150
Women	30–75	50–100

Extremes:

	Normal	Royal
Men	20–175	25–250
Women	20–125	25–200

I give here a note from the same bundle of papers, separate from the above, but consonant with it:

The long life of the Númenóreans was in answer to the actual prayers of the Edain (and Elros). Manwë warned them of its perils. They asked to have more or less the "life-span of old", because they wanted to learn more.

As Erendis said later, they became a kind of imitation Elves; and their Men had so much in their heads and desire of doing that they ever felt the pressure of time, and so seldom rested or rejoiced in the present. Fortunately their wives were cool and busy – but Númenor was no place for great love.

NOTES

1 Both texts have in their top margins the similar final part of a preceding text, reading (in text 1):

... to be great loss, if either father or mother were long absent during the childhood-years of their daughters and sons.

2 As first written, the age of manhood in the Line of Elros was 20; this was changed in red ball-point pen to 25.

3 This row for maturity was inserted sometime after the rows for full-growth and youth were written.

XIII

OF THE LAND AND BEASTS
OF NÚMENOR

This typescript text follows directly on from the text given in chap. XI, "Lives of the Númenóreans", above, and occupies most of ten sides; it is extant in precisely the same three versions, A–C, and again the text given here is that of A. Significant portions of this text were incorporated, with some modifications, into *A Description of the Island of Númenor* (UT:165–72), hereinafter DN. There are however considerable portions that have not previously been published. Christopher Tolkien dated this text as well to c. 1965 (UT:7).

Of the land and beasts of Númenor

The opening paragraph of the text is echoed in that of *DN* (UT:165) but it is there much compressed:

Accurate charts of Númenor were made at various periods before its downfall; but none of these survived the disaster. They were deposited in the Guildhouse of the Venturers, and this was confiscated by the kings, and removed to the western haven of Andúnie; all its records perished. Maps of Númenor were long preserved in the archives of the Kings of Gondor, in Middle-earth; but these appear to have been derived in part from old drawings made from memory by early settlers; and (the better ones) from a single chart, with little detail beyond sea-soundings along the coast, and descriptions of the ports and their approaches, that was originally in the ship of Elendil, leader of those who escaped the downfall. Descriptions of the land, and of its flora and fauna, were also preserved in Gondor; but they were not accurate or detailed, nor did they distinguish clearly between the state of the land at different periods, being vague about its condition at the time of the first settlements. Since all such matters were the study of men of lore in Númenor, and many accurate natural histories and geographies must have been composed, it would appear that, like nearly all else of the arts and sciences of Númenor at its high tide, they disappeared in the downfall.

DN then follows the present text closely, though the description of the general shape of Númenor provides a few additional details:

The promontories, though these were not all of precisely the same shape or size, were roughly 100 miles across and rather more than 200 miles long. A line drawn from the northernmost point of the Forostar to the southernmost of the Hyarnustar lay more or less directly north and south (at the period of the maps); this line was somewhat more than 700 miles long, and each line drawn from the end of one promontory to the end of another and passing through the land (along the borders of the Mittalmar) was more or less of the same length.

The Mittalmar was above the general level of the promontories, not reckoning the height of any mountain or hills in these; and at the settlement appears to have had few trees and to have consisted mainly of grasslands and low downs. Nearly at its centre, though somewhat nearer the eastern edge, stood the tall mountain, called the Menel-tarma, Pillar of the Heavens. It was about 3,000 feet high above the plain.*

The text again continues as in DN with few significant differences save for the details that: the position of the Meneltarma in Mittalmar was "nearly at its centre, though somewhat nearer the eastern edge", that it "was about 3,000 feet high above the plain", and that it was "in places" unscalable in the "last 500 feet" before the summit; "Towards the great North Cape the land rose to rocky heights of some 2,000 feet, the highest of which (Sorontil) rose straight from the sea in tremendous cliffs"; that Tar-Meneldur's

---

* The lower slopes of the Menel-tarma were gentle and partly grass-covered, but the mountain grew ever steeper, and the last 500 feet were in places unscalable, save by the climbing road.

tower was "the first and greatest of the observatories of the Númenóreans"; that the "great curved indentation" of the Bay of Eldanna was "warm, almost as warm as the southernmost lands"; that Eldalondë was "almost at [the Bay's] centre, not far from the borders of the Hyarnustar"; that the *yavanna-mírë* had "rose-like flowers and globed and scarlet fruits"; that in Númenor the *mallorn* reached "at its tallest height almost 600 feet", that its fruit "was a small nut-like fruit, with a silver shale, pointed at the end", and some were "given as a gift by Tar-Aldarion to King Finellach Gil-galad of Lindon [*deleted*: and there the *malinorni* grew during the Second Age of Middle-earth]"; that the river Siril "became in the last 50 miles of its course a slow and winding stream; for the land here was almost flat, and not high above sea level"; that the village Nindamos lay "upon the east side of the Siril close to the sea" and that "Great seas and high winds hardly ever troubled this region. In later times much of this land was reclaimed, and formed into a region of great fish-haunted pools with outlets to the sea, about which were rich and fertile lands".

Where *DN*, however, comes to describe the Hyarrostar and the Orrostar (UT:168–9), the present text shows significant differences, including a long discussion of the fauna and flora of Númenor not found in the later text, as well as considerable detail of distances and populations in the island. I therefore give this middle section here in full.

The south-facing and south-western parts of the Hyarrostar closely resembled the corresponding parts of the Hyarnustar; but the remainder, though high above the sea, was flatter and more fertile. Here grew a great variety of timber; and after the days of Tar-Aldarion, who began the regular care of forestry, some of the chief plantations were in this region: devoted largely to the production of materials for ship-yards.

The Orrostar was cooler, but was protected from the north-east (whence came the colder winds) by highlands that rose to a height of 2,100 feet near the north-eastern end of the promontory. In the inner parts, especially in those adjacent to the Kingsland, much grain was grown.

The chief feature of Númenor were the cliffs, already often mentioned. The whole land was so posed as if it had been thrust upward out of the Sea, but at the same time slightly tilted southward. Except at the southern point, already described, in nearly all places the land fell steeply towards the sea in cliffs, for the most part steep, or sheer. These were at the greatest height in the north and north-west, where they often reached 2,000 feet, at the lowest in the east and south-east. But these cliffs, except in certain regions such as the North Cape, seldom stood up directly out of the water. At their feet were found shorelands of flat or shelving land, often habitable, that ranged in width (from the water) from about a quarter of a mile to several miles. The fringes of the widest stretches were usually under shallow water even at low tides; but at their seaward edges all these strands plunged down again sheerly into profound water. The great strands and tidal flats of the south also ended in a sheer fall to oceanic depths along a line roughly joining the southernmost ends of the south-west and south-east promontories.

It would appear that neither Elves nor Men had dwelt in this island before the coming of the Edain. Beasts and birds had no fear of Men; and the relations of Men and animals remained more friendly in Númenor than anywhere else in the world. It is said that even those that the Númenóreans classed as "predatory" (by which they meant those that would at need raid their crops and tame cattle) remained on "honourable terms" with the newcomers, seeking their food so far as they could in the wild, and showing no hostility to Men, save at times of declared war, when after due warning the husbandmen would, as a necessity, hunt the predatory birds and beasts to reduce their numbers within limits.

As has been said, it is not easy to discover what were the beasts and birds and fishes that already inhabited the island before the coming of the Edain, and what were brought in by them. The same is also true of the plants. Neither are the names which the Númenóreans gave to animals and plants always easy to equate with or relate to the names of those found in Middle-earth. Many, though given in apparently Quenya or Sindarin forms, are not found in the Elvish or Human tongues of Middle-earth. This is partly due, no doubt, to the fact that the animals and plants of Númenor, though similar and related to those of the mainlands, were different in variety and seemed to require new names.

As for the major animals, it is clear that there were none of the canine or related kinds. There were certainly no hounds or dogs (all of which were imported). There were no wolves. There were wild cats, the most hostile and untameable of the animals; but no large felines. There were a great number, however, of foxes, or related animals. Their chief food seems to have been animals which the

Númenóreans called *lopoldi*. These existed in large numbers and multiplied swiftly, and were voracious herbivores; so that the foxes were esteemed as the best and most natural way of keeping them in order, and foxes were seldom hunted or molested. In return, or because their food-supply was otherwise abundant, the foxes seem never to have acquired the habit of preying upon the domestic fowl of the Númenóreans. The *lopoldi* would appear to have been rabbits, animals which had been quite unknown before in the north-western regions of Middle-earth.[1] The Númenóreans did not esteem them as food and were content to leave them to the foxes.

There were bears in considerable numbers, in the mountainous or rocky parts; both of a black and brown variety. The great black bears were found mostly in the Forostar. The relations of the bears and Men were strange. From the first the bears exhibited friendship and curiosity towards the newcomers; and these feelings were returned. At no time was there any hostility between Men and bears; though at mating times, and during the first youth of their cubs they could be angry and dangerous if disturbed. The Númenóreans did not disturb them except by mischance. Very few Númenóreans were ever killed by bears; and these mishaps were not regarded as reasons for war upon the whole race. Many of the bears were quite tame. They never dwelt in or near the homes of Men, but they would often visit them, in the casual manner of one householder calling upon another. At such times they were often offered honey, to their delight. Only an occasional "bad bear" ever raided the tame hives. Most strange of all were the bear-dances. The bears, the black bears especially, had curious dances of their own; but these seem to have become improved and elaborated by the instruction of Men. At times the bears would perform dances for the entertainment of their human friends. The most famous was the Great Bear-dance (*ruxöalë*)[2] of Tompollë in the Forostar, to which every year in the autumn many would come from all parts of the island, since it occurred not long after the Eruhantalë, at which a great concourse was assembled. To those not accustomed to the bears the slow (but dignified) motions of the bears, sometimes as many as 50 or more together, appeared astonishing and comic. But it was understood by all admitted to the spectacle that there should be no open laughter. The laughter of Men was a sound that the bears could not understand: it alarmed and angered them.[3]

The woods of Númenor abounded in squirrels, mostly red, but some dark brown or black. These were all unafraid, and readily tamed. The women of Númenor were specially fond of them. Often they would live in trees near a homestead, and would come when invited into the house. In the short rivers and streams there were otters. Badgers were numerous. There were wild black swine in the woods; and in the west of the Mittalmar at the coming of the Edain were herds of wild kine, some white, some black. Deer were abundant on the grasslands and in and about the forest-eaves, red and fallow; and in the hills were roe-deer. But all seem to have been somewhat smaller of stature than their kin in Middle-earth. In the southern region there were beavers. About the coasts seals were abundant, especially in the north and west. And there were also many smaller animals, not often mentioned: such as mice and voles, or small preying beasts such as weasels. Hares are named; and other animals of uncertain kind: some that were not squirrels, but lived in trees, and were shy, not of men only; others that ran on the ground and burrowed, small and fat, but were neither rats nor rabbits. In the south there were some land-tortoises, of no great size; and also some small freshwater creatures of turtle-kind. The animals named *ekelli* seem to have been urchins or hedgehogs of large size, with long black quills. They were numerous in some parts, and treated with friendship, for they lived mostly upon worms and insects.

There seem to have been wild goats in the island, but whether the small horned sheep (which were one of the varieties of sheep-kind that the Númenóreans kept) were native or imported is not known. A small kind of horse, smaller than a donkey, black or dark brown, with flowing mane and tail, and sturdy rather than swift, is said to have been found in the Mittalmar by the settlers. They were soon tamed, but throve and were well-tended and loved. They were much used in the farms; and children used them for riding.

Many other beasts there were no doubt that are seldom named since they did not generally concern Men. All must have been named and described in the books of lore that perished.

Sea-fish were abundant all about the coasts of the island, and those that were good to eat were much used. Other beasts of the sea there were also off the shores: whales and narwhal, dolphins and porpoises, which the Númenóreans did not confuse with fish (*lingwi*), but classed with fish as *nendili* all those that lived wholly in the water and bred in the sea. Sharks the Númenóreans saw only upon their voyages, for whether by the "grace of the Valar" as the Númenóreans said, or for other cause they did not ever come near the shores of the island. Of inland fish we hear little. Of those that live in the sea partly, but enter the rivers at times, there were salmon in the Siril, and also in the Nunduinë, the river that flowed into the sea at Eldalondë, and on its way made the small lake of Nísinen (one of the few in

Númenor) about three miles inland: it was so called because of the abundance of sweet-smelling shrubs and flowers that grew on its banks. Eels were abundant in the meres and marshes about the lower course of the Siril.

The birds of Númenor were beyond count, from the great eagles down to the tiny *kirinki* that were no bigger than wrens, but all scarlet, with high piping voices the sounds of which were on the edge of human hearing. The eagles were of several kinds; but all were held sacred to Manwë, and were never molested nor shot, not until the days of evil and the hatred of the Valar began. Not until then did they on their part molest men or prey on their beasts. From the days of Elros until the time of Tar-Ankalimon, son of Tar-Atanamir, some two thousand years, there was an eyrie of golden eagles in the summit of the tower of the king's palace in Armenelos. There one pair ever dwelt and lived on the bounty of the king.

The birds that dwell near the sea, and swim or dive in it, and live upon fish, abode in Númenor in multitudes beyond reckoning. They were never killed or molested by intent by the Númenóreans, and were wholly friendly to them. Mariners said that were they blind they would know that their ship was drawing near home because of the great clamour of the shore-birds. When any ship approached the land seabirds in great flocks would arise and fly above it for no purpose but welcome and gladness. Some would accompany the ships on their voyages, even those that went to Middle-earth.

Inland the birds were not so numerous, but were nonetheless abundant. Some beside the eagles were birds of prey, such as the hawks and falcons of many kinds. There were ravens, especially in the north, and about the land other birds of their kin that live in flocks, daws and crows and about the sea-cliffs many choughs. Smaller song-birds with fair voices abounded in the fields, in the reedy meres, and in the woods. Many were little different from those of the lands from which the Edain came; but the birds of finch-kind were more varied and numerous and sweeter-voiced. There were some of small size all white, some all grey; and others all golden, that sang with great joy in long thrilling cadences through the spring and early summer. They had little fear of the Edain, who loved them. The caging of song-birds was thought an unkind deed. Nor was it necessary, for those that were "tame", that is: who attached themselves of free will to a homestead, would for generations dwell near the same house, singing upon its roof or on the sills, or even in the *solmar* or chambers of those that welcomed them. The birds that dwelt in cages were for the most part reared from young whose parents died by mischance or were slain by birds of prey; but even they were mostly free to go and come if they would. Nightingales were found, though nowhere very abundant, in most parts of Númenor save the north. In the northern parts there were large white owls, but no other birds of this race.

Of the native trees and plants little is recorded. Though some trees were brought in seed or scion from Middle-earth, and others (as has been said) came from Eressëa, there seems to have been an abundance of timber when the Edain landed. Of trees already known to them it is said that they missed the hornbeam, the small maple, and the flowering chestnut; but found others that were new to them: the wych-elm, the holm-oak, tall maples, and the sweet chestnut. In the Hyarrostar they found also walnuts; and the *laurinquë* in which they delighted for its flowers, for it had no other use. This name they gave it ('golden rain') because of its long-hanging clusters of yellow flowers; and some who had heard from the Eldar of Laurelin, the Golden Tree of Valinor, believed that it came from that great Tree, being brought in seed thither by the Eldar; but it was not so. Wild apple, cherry, and pear also grew in Númenor; but those that they grew in their orchards came from Middle-earth, gifts from the Eldar. In the Hyarnustar the vine grew wild; but the grape-vines of the Númenóreans seem also to have come from the Eldar. Of the many plants and flowers of field and wood little is now recorded or remembered; but old songs speak often of the lilies, the many kinds of which, some small, some tall and fair, some single-bloomed, some hung with many bells and trumpets, and all fragrant, were the delight of the Edain.

To the land the Edain brought many things from Middle-earth: sheep, and kine, and horses, and dogs; fruiting trees; and grain. Water-fowl such as birds of duck-kind or geese they found before them; but others they brought also and blended with the native races. Geese and ducks were domestic fowls on their farms; and there also they kept multitudes of doves or pigeons in great houses or dovecotes, mainly for their eggs. Hen-fowl they had not known and found none in the island; though soon after the great voyages began mariners brought back cocks and hens from the southern and eastern lands,[4] and they throve in Númenor, where many of them escaped and lived in the wild, though harried by the foxes.

The legends of the foundation of Númenor often speak as if all the Edain that accepted the Gift set sail at one time and in one fleet. But this is only due to the brevity of the narrative. In more detailed histories it is related (as might be deduced from the events and the numbers concerned) that after the first expedition, led by Elros, many other ships, alone or in small fleets, came west bearing others of the Edain, either those who were at first reluctant to dare the Great Sea but could not endure to be parted from those who had gone, or some who were far scattered and could not be assembled to go with the first sailing.

Since the boats that were used were of Elvish model, fleet, but small, and each steered and captained by one of the Eldar deputed by Círdan,* it would have taken a great navy to transport all the people and goods that were eventually brought from Middle-earth to Númenor. The legends make no guess at the numbers, and the histories say little. The fleet of Elros is said to have contained many ships (according to some 150 vessels, to others two or three hundred) and to have brought "thousands" of the men, women, and children of the Edain: probably between 5,000 or at the most 10,000. But the whole process of migration appears in fact to have occupied at least 50 years, possibly longer, and finally ended only when Círdan (no doubt instructed by the Valar) would provide no more ships or guides. In that time the number of the Edain that crossed the Sea must have been very great, though small in proportion to the extent of the island (probably some 180,000 square miles). Guesses vary between 200,000 and 350,000 people.[5] After a thousand years the population seems not to have much exceeded 2 million. This was greatly increased later; but outlet was found in the Númenórean settlements in Middle-earth. Before the Downfall the population of Númenor itself may have been as many as 15 million.†

The Edain brought with them much lore, and the knowledge of many crafts, and numerous craftsmen who had learned from the Eldar, directly or through their fathers, besides preserving lore and traditions of their own.

---

* It seems to have been long before the Númenóreans themselves ventured far to sea in ship, after the Elvish steersmen had returned, taking with them most of the original vessels of the migration. But they had shipwrights who had been instructed by the Eldar; and from these beginnings they soon devised vessels more suitable to their own uses. The first ships of heavier draught were made for the coastwise traffic between ports.

† The increase was slow, in spite of the absence of disease and the rarity of death by misadventure, because of the long lives of the Númenóreans in which they produced few children: the average in each "generation" being somewhat more than three times half the total number of the generation, less than four to each possible marriageable pair. At least one third of the original immigrants produced no children in Númenor.

As mentioned in chap. XII, "Lives of the Númenóreans", above, the last paragraph at UT:169 was taken up from a long, digressive author's note to that text; it is not present in the current text, which instead continues, with no significant variation, with that found at UT:170 ("But they could bring with them few materials..."), save for additional details regarding metals found in Númenor:

Lead they also had. Iron and steel they needed most for the tools of the craftsmen and for the axes of the woodsmen.

Also, regarding weapons in Númenor, this text has:

But no man wore a sword in Númenor, not even in the days of the wars in Middle-earth, unless he was actually armed for battle. Thus for long there were practically no weapons of warlike intent made in Númenor. Many things made could of course be so used: axes, and spears, and bows. The bowyers were a great craft. They made bows of many kinds: long bows, and smaller bows, especially those used for shooting from horse-back; and they also devised cross-bows, at first used mainly against predatory birds. Shooting with bows was one of the great sports and pastimes of men; and one in which young women also took part. The Númenórean men, being tall and power-ful, could shoot with speed and accuracy upon foot from great long bows, whose shafts would carry to great distance (some 600 yards or more), and at lesser range were of great penetration. In later days, in the wars upon Middle-earth, it was the bows of the Númenóreans that were most greatly feared.

Finally, the long concluding paragraph of DN concerning the pur-suits of men (UT:171), which Christopher Tolkien also took up from "Lives of the Númenóreans", is absent here; instead, the text concludes with:

These things are said for the most part of the days of the bliss of Númenor, which lasted well nigh two thousand years; though the first hints of the later shadows appeared before that. Indeed it was their very arming to take part in the defence of the Eldar and Men of the West of Middle-earth against the wielder of the Shadow (at length revealed as Sauron the Great) that brought about the end of their peace and content. Victory was the herald of their Downfall.

NOTES

1 The European rabbit (as distinct from hares) was in fact a relative latecomer to northwestern Europe.

2 As first typed, the Quenya term for (apparently) 'bear-dance' was *ruxopandalë*.

3 As first typed, the laughter of Men was said to be "a sound that the bears resented".

4 According to current accounts, the ancestor of the modern chicken originated in Asia, and did not reach Europe until about 3000 BC.

5 As first typed, the estimate was between "300,000 and 500,000".

XIV

NOTE ON THE CONSUMPTION
OF MUSHROOMS

This typescript text is a short passage rejected by Tolkien from the
essay published as *The Drúedain* in UT:377–87; I start the passage
at the point (UT:378) that immediately precedes this note.

[The Drúedain's] knowledge of all growing things was almost equal
to that of the Elves (although untaught by them), discerning those
that were poisonous, or useful as medicaments, or good as food. To
the astonishment of Elves and other Men they ate funguses with
pleasure, many of which looked to others (Men and Hobbits) dangerous; some kinds which they specially liked they caused to grow
near their dwellings. The Eldar did not eat these things. The Folk of
Haleth, taught by the Drúedain, made some use of them at need;
and if they were guests they ate what was provided in courtesy, and
without fear. The other Atani eschewed them, save in great hunger
when astray in the wild, for few among them had the knowledge to
distinguish the wholesome from the bad, and the less wise called
them ork-plants and supposed them to have been cursed and
blighted by Morgoth.

A rough pencil note in the margin reads: "Delete all this about
funguses, too like Hobbits".

XV

THE NÚMENÓREAN CATASTROPHE
& END OF "PHYSICAL" AMAN

This text, written in a somewhat hasty hand in black nib-pen, occupies three half-sides of the recto and verso of a folded sheet. It
follows on immediately from the text presented as text 2 in chap.
XV, "Elvish Reincarnation", in part two of this book, and appears to
be contemporary with that text, thus likewise dating from c. 1959.

The Númenórean Catastrophe & End
of "Physical" Aman[1]

Is Aman "removed" or destroyed at the Catastrophe?

It *was* physical. Therefore it could not be removed, without
remaining visible as part of Arda or as a new satellite! It must either
remain as a landmass bereft of its former inhabitants or be destroyed.

I think now that it is best that it should *remain* a physical *landmass*
(America!). But as Manwë had already said to the Númenóreans: "It
is not the *land* that is hallowed (and free of death), but it is hallowed
by the dwellers there" – the Valar.

It would just become *an ordinary land*, an addition to Middle-
earth, the European-African-Asiatic contiguous landmass. The *flora
and fauna* (even if different in some [?items] from those of Middle-
earth) would become ordinary beasts and plants with usual conditions of mortality.

Aman and Eressëa would be the memory of the *Valar and Elves* of
the former land.

The Catastrophe would no doubt do great damage and change to the configuration of Aman. Partly, especially on West [*sic*; read "East"?] side, sunk into Sea.

But how then would the corporeal union of *fëar* and *hröar* be maintained in an Aman of memory only?

The answer, I think, is this.

The *Catastrophe* represents a definite *intervention* of *Eru* and therefore in a sense a change of the primal plan. *It is a foretaste of the End of Arda.* The situation is much later than "conversation of Finrod and Andreth"[2] and could not then be foreseen by anyone, *not even Manwë.* In a sense Eru moved forward the *End of Arda* as far as it concerned the Elves. They had fulfilled their function – and we approach the "Dominion of Men". Hence the vast importance of the *marriages* of Beren and Tuor – *providing continuity of the Elvish element!* The tales of the *Silmarillion* and especially of *Númenor* and *the Rings* are in a *twilight.* We do not *see* as it were a catastrophic end, but viewed against the enormous stretch of ages the *twilight period* of $2^{nd}/3^{rd}$ Ages is surely quite short and abrupt!

The Elves are *dying.* They whether in Aman or outside will become *fëar* housed only in *memory* until the true End of Arda. They must await the issue of the War [?and] only then; and of their *redemption* foreglimpsed by Finrod:[3] for their true returning (corporeal or in Eru's equivalent!) in Arda Remade.

NB Melkor (*inside* Eä) only really becomes evil after the achievement of Eä in which he played a great and powerful part (and in its early stages in accord with the fundamental Design of Eru). It was jealousy of Manwë and desire to dominate the Eruhíni that drove him mad. It was the matter of Arda (as a whole but particularly of *Imbar*)[4] that he had corrupted. The Stars were not (or most of them were not) affected.

He became more and more incapable (like Ungoliantë!) of extricating himself and finding scape in the vastness of Eä, and became more and more physically involved in it.

It is evident from the haste of his writing and the fluidity of his conceptions that Tolkien is here thinking on paper (as he often did). Not only does some of this thinking apparently contradict long-standing "facts" of the then-unpublished mythology: e.g., the discord, envy, and desire for dominance of Melkor – in short, rebellion against Eru and His design – *during* the Music and *prior to* entering Eä; but also events depicted in the already-published *Lord of the Rings*: e.g., Frodo's bodily journey to a seemingly very physical Tol Eressëa.

NOTES

1 This title was provided by Tolkien in red ball-point pen.

2 That is, the *Athrabeth Finrod ah Andreth* given in X:303–60.

3 Cf. X:319.

4 Cf. X:337: "It is certainly the case with the Elvish traditions that the principal part of Arda was the Earth (*Imbar* 'the Habitation') ...."

XVI

GALADRIEL AND CELEBORN

The two texts presented here are located in a bundle of papers comprising 1) manuscript drafting and writing in black nib-pen on Oxford college documents dated 1955, to which Tolkien subsequently gave the title "Concerning Galadriel & Celeborn", and 2) a late typescript on printed sheets containing the 1968 radio script of *The Hobbit* (see TCG I:760). Parts of this typescript were quoted (pp. 256–7, 267) or paraphrased (e.g. pp. 253, 266–7) in *Unfinished Tales*. See there also for the complex nature of the various and at times contradictory accounts of the history of Galadriel and Celeborn, of which the present texts are but a part.

Text 1

Concerning Galadriel & Celeborn

Galadriel: daughter of Finarphin and sister of Finrod (Felagund). Quenya name *Alatáriel* 'blessed queen', Sindarized as *Galadriel* (*galad* = 'bliss'). She wedded Celeborn (grandson of Elmo, brother of Thingol)[1] at about the end of the First Age. For love of Celeborn (who did not wish to leave Middle-earth), at the downfall of Angband and the ruin of Beleriand she crossed the Eryd Lindon into Eriador. Celebrían was born c. S.A. 300; Amroth c. 350.[2]

Eventually Galadriel and Celeborn, with a following mainly of Noldor (but of course also Sindar and perhaps? some Nandor) established (c. S.A. 750) the realm of Eregion west of the Misty Mountains, and maintained friendship with the Dwarves of Moria.

They had access to the great Nandorin realm on the other side of the Mountains (where afterwards Lórien was: as a remnant of much greater woods joining up with Mirkwood on both sides of Anduin). This realm was then called *Lōrinand* because of its golden trees: 'Golden Vale' (N[andorin] *lōri* 'gold' = Q. *laurë*); and also *Norlindon* – because its people still called themselves *Lindë* (*Lindar*) – 'land of the Lindar'.[3] The chief craftsman of Eregion was Celebrimbor.

Galadriel and Celeborn are regarded as High Lord and Lady of all the Eldar of the West.

Sauron visited the Elves; but was rejected by Gil-galad in S.A. 1200. He visits Eregion and is rejected by Galadriel and Celeborn. He sees that he has met his match (or at least a very serious adversary) in Galadriel; he dissembles his wrath, and gets round Celeborn. The Noldorin Smiths under Celebrimbor admit him and begin to learn from him (so in a sense the story of Fëanor is repeated). Galadriel and Celeborn leave Eregion c. S.A. 1300 and retreat (through Moria) to Lórinand (with many of their *non*-Noldorin following): they are well received, and teach to the Lindar many things, warning them especially against Sauron.

1697: At fall of Eregion many fleeing Elves come through (via Moria) and swell the ranks of Sindarin speakers. The Lindar become more and more Sindarized.

The text ends here, at the bottom of a page;[4] but on the next page Tolkien begins an expanded account of Celebrimbor's dealings with Sauron:

But Sauron was more successful with the Ñoldor of Eregion, especially with Celebrimbor (secretly anxious to rival the skill and fame of Fëanor). When Sauron visited Eregion he sees quickly that he has met his match in Galadriel – or at least that in her he would have a chief obstacle. So he concentrated on Celebrimbor; and soon had all the Smiths of Eregion under his influence. Eventually he gets them to revolt against Celeborn and Galadriel. These pass through Moria and take refuge in Lórinand (c. S.A. 1350).

When Celebrimbor discovers the designs of Sauron and repents – and hides the Three Rings – Sauron invades Eriador from the south, and besieges Eregion. Celeborn and Amroth with Nandor and Dwarves come through Moria to the west. Gilgalad sends help under Elrond from Lindon. But he is not in time to assist much. Sauron breaks into Eregion and lays it waste. Celebrimbor is slain personally by Sauron, but Sauron does not get the Three Rings. His wrath now blazes. Elrond with all (the few) refugees from Eregion he can gather fight a vanguard action and draw away N.W. He founds a stronghold in Imladris.

When Celeborn heard of onset of Sauron (fearing to keep the Three Rings himself) he sent one to Galadriel in Lórinand by Amroth. Celeborn makes a sortie and breaks out and joins Elrond but cannot get back.

In the top margin of this page Tolkien made various calculations based on the dates cited in this text, and corresponding time-spans in *yéni* (the "long years" of the Elves, equating to 144 solar years). These accompanied the following statement:

Amroth was already prince in S.A. 850, only 32 *yên* [when he] passed in T.A. 1981.[5]

In the accompanying calculations it can be discerned that Tolkien assigned his birth to S.A. 750, and that Amroth was thus 32 *yéni* plus 64 solar years = 4,672 solar years old when he passed. A different chronology, in which Amroth is made somewhat older at his passing, is worked out in the left-hand margin:

Amroth born S.A. 300. 2 in S.A. 588. In S.A. 1350 he was 29. In S.A. 1697 he was 31. In S.A. 3441 nearly 44 (43/117). In T.A. 1693 [he was] 11/109 older = 55/82.

These ages, however (with the exception of the first, being precisely 2 *yéni* after S.A. 300), cannot be reconciled with a *yên* of 144 solar years. The accounting of Amroth's ages through the end of the Second Age in 3441 must refer rather to an apparent age, in terms of human maturation, not actual age in *yéni* (e.g., in S.A. 1350 Amroth would have been just over 7 *yéni* old, not 29; and in S.A. 3441 he would have been just under 22 *yéni* old, not 44).[6] As is shown in part one of this book, the intertwined issues of the age and maturation rate of the Elves, and implications for the chronology, occupied Tolkien greatly in his later years.

In the top margin of the (apparently much later) cover page, above the prominent title, Tolkien very roughly wrote (and then struck through) the following:

Galadriel is made *sister* of Finrod. In youth she was fond of wandering afar. She often visited the Teleri of Alqualondë (her mother was sister of Olwë and Elwë). There she was often a companion of Teleporno ('silver-tall'). Celeborn's kinship from a younger brother of Olwë and Elwë: Nelwë.

Account of Galadriel's quarrel with the sons of Fëanor at sack of Alqualondë. How she fought with Celeborn. She nonetheless went into Exile because though she did not love the sons of Fëanor she was personally proud and rebellious and wished for freedom.

TEXT 2

The Names *Galadriel, Celeborn & Lórien*[7]

The name *Alatáriel* is Telerin in form; its original meaning was 'maid of the glittering coronal'. It was a compound of three elements, in Common Eldarin (C.E.) form (1) **ñalatā* 'a glitter' (of reflected light); (2) the base RIƷ 'to wreathe'; (3) the feminine suffix **-el, -elle*. From **rīʒā* and the suffix was made the word **rīʒelle* 'a woman bearing a garland', specially applied to maidens wearing garlands at festivals. In Telerin initial *ñ* was lost; and with loss of medial ʒ and shortening of the word at the end of long names *-riel* was produced; the whole name thus became Alatáriel.[8]

The name *Telepornë* is also Telerin in form. It meant 'silver tree'. It was a compound of C.E. **kyelep-* 'silver' and **ornē* 'tree' (originally and usually applied to the taller, straighter, and more slender trees, such as birches),* a noun form related to the adj. **ornā* 'uprising, tall' (and straight). C.E. **kyelep-* became in T. *telep-*. In Sindarin its form was *celeb*. Its true Quenya form was *tyelpë, tyelep-* (as in the surname of Írildë, S. *Idril: tyeleptalëa* 'silver-footed'). This was still the form in Old Quenya, and survived in many old names; but later the form *telpë* became usual. This was due to the influence of Telerin. The Teleri prized silver above gold; and their skill as silversmiths was esteemed even by the Noldor. For a similar reason *Telperion* was more generally used than *Tyelperion* as the name of the White Tree of Valinor. This

---

* The stouter and more spreading trees, such as oaks and beeches, were called in C.E. *galadā* 'great growth'; though this distinction was not always observed in Quenya, and disappeared in Sindarin. In S. *orn* < **ornē* fell out of common use and was used only in verse and songs, though it survived in many names, of trees and persons. All trees were called *galað* < **galadā*.

was held in great honour by the Teleri (who it is said devised its name), though the Vanyar and Noldor gave greater love to Laurelin the Golden.

The base *ñal- fell out of use in Quenya, surviving only in the derivatives ñalda 'bright, polished', and angal 'a mirror' from *aññala (cf. Angal-limpe 'Mirrormere').[9] There was no Quenya form of C.E. *ñalatā (it would have been *ñalta).

These names were later given a Sindarin form in Middle-earth. This presented no difficulty, and the names became naturally Galadriel and Celeborn. But when later Celeborn and Galadriel became the rulers of the Elves of Lórien (who were mainly in origin Silvan Elves and called themselves the Galaðrim) the name of Galadriel became associated with trees, an association that was aided by the name of her husband, Celeborn, which also appeared to contain a tree-word (his name was however in fact derived from *ornā 'upraised, high, tall', of stature),[10] so that outside Lórien among those whose memories of the ancient days and Galadriel's history had grown dim her name was often altered to Galaðriel. Not in Lórien itself.[11]

> There follow the passages excerpted at UT:256–7; one of these was
> paraphrased by Christopher Tolkien, and it reads:

and after the first arising of Barad-dûr and in the long wars against Sauron in the Second Age they became much diminished and hid themselves in fastnesses of Greenwood the Great (as it was still called): small and scattered peoples, hardly to be distinguished from Avari.

> Following this excerpt, the text continues with passages likewise
> paraphrased by Christopher at UT:253 n.5, 267. I give them here
> in full.

Lórien is probably an alteration of an older name now lost. It is actually the Quenya name of a region in Valinor, often also used as the name of the Vala to whom it belonged: it was a place of rest and shadowy trees and fountains, a retreat from cares and griefs. The resemblance cannot be accidental. The alteration of the older name may well have been due to Galadriel herself. As may be seen generally, and especially in her song (I 389),[12] she had endeavoured to make Lórien a refuge and an island of peace and beauty, a memorial of ancient days, but was now filled with regret and misgiving, knowing that the golden dream was hastening to a grey awakening. It may be noted that Treebeard (II 70)[13] interprets *Loth-lórien* as 'Dreamflower'.

A Gondorian commentator states that the older name was *Lawarind*. He names no authority; but it seems likely. It probably contains the C.E. stem *(g)lawar-* 'golden light', and is a derivative that in Quenya form would be **lawarē-nde* > *laurende* (with the suffix frequent in place-names): cf. Q. *laure*, S. *glawar*, T. *glavare*. The reference was to the mallorn-trees. Treebeard also says that the earlier name given by the Elves was *Laurelindórenan*. This is very likely a composition in Treebeard's manner of *Laurelinde-nan(do)*, and *Laure-ndóre*, both Quenya names and probably also due to Galadriel. The second contains *-ndor* 'land'; the first is assimilated to *Laure-linde* (meaning more or less 'singing gold'), the name of the Golden Tree of Valinor. Both are easily taken as based on **lawarind* and alterations of it to resemble the names of Valinor, for which Galadriel's yearning had increased as the years passed to an overwhelming regret. *Lórien* was the name most used since in form it could be Sindarin.[14]

The element *-nan* 'valley' was derived from C.E. base NAD 'hollow' of structures or natural features more or less concave with rising sides.* In Sindarin this gave *nand* which as other words ending in *nd* remained in stressed monosyllables but > *nann* > *nan* in compounds.[15]

Galadhon, only in *Caras Galadhon*, which evidently meant 'Fortress of the Trees'; but the word *caras* is not found in Sindarin: it may derive from the same Silvan dialect as the reported name *Lawarind*, and be related to Q. *caraxë*, applied to a defensive earth wall surmounted by sharp stakes or standing stones; though in Caras Galadhon the palisade had disappeared and only the deep moat remained outside the great wall reinforced by stone. The adjectival/genitival *-on* is not Sindarin,[16] and was probably taken over from the older Silvan name of what was no doubt originally a much more

---

* Derivatives were **nadmā* > Q. *nanwa* 'a (large) bowl' or similar artefact; **nandā* 'hollow' (not used of things empty inside but those open above); **nandē* 'a valley, bottom', originally used only of not very large areas the sides of which were part of their own configuration. Vales or valleys of great extent, plains at the feet of mountains, etc. had other names. As also had the very steep-sided valleys in the mountains such as Rivendell. Those such as the valley of Gondolin which were more or less circular, but deeply concave, and had high mountains at the rim were called **tumbu*. The vale of Gondolin was actually called *i Tumbo* (in full *i Tumbo Tarmacorto* 'the vale of the high-mountain circle', in Sindarin *Tum Orchorod*) and usually in S. *Tumladen* 'Wide valley'.

primitive structure, though the first element was Sindarized – the tree word was probably still recognizable as a descendant of C.E. *galada (Q. *alda*, T. *galada*, S. *galaδ*).

NOTES

1 See UT:233–4.

2 The birth-years of Celebrían and Amroth – and even whether Amroth was a child of Galadriel and Celeborn – were points on which Tolkien vacillated considerably. See the various references to both in part one of this book, and in *Unfinished Tales*.

3 "Norlindon" replaces struck-through "Lindoriand", and "land of the Lindar" was first written as "land of the Lendar".

4 A barely legible note in the bottom margin here begins: "Galadriel has desire for Sea [?] and dwell in [?] or in Dol Amroth".

5 Tolkien corrected original "750" to "850". The actual text here appears to read: "If Amroth was already prince in S.A. [750 >>] 850 [*deleted*: ?be] only 32 *yên* [?and have] passed in T.A. 1981" (the word "If" appears to have been added later); but this is obviously a fluid and somewhat garbled thought, so I have extracted and presented the bare facts of it editorially.

6 This may explain why Tolkien has marked the ages 2, 29, and 31 with a "+"; but no such mark is made against the subsequent ages. But, T.A. 1693 is indeed 11 *yéni* + 109 sun-years later than S.A. 3441; so something in this accounting is awry, or at least inconsistent.

7 This title was added by Tolkien in the top margin, in ball-point pen.

8 On an adjacent sheet – bearing the same title and likewise in typescript – occurs a different version of this opening paragraph and etymological discussion:

The name *Galadriel* is in this form Sindarin. Its original meaning was 'lady of the glittering coronal', referring to the brilliant sheen of her golden hair, which in her youth she wore in three long braids, the middle one being wound about her head. *Celeborn* is also in this form Sindarin, but originally meant 'silver-tall'. Both names were, however, originally Telerin: *Alatáriel* and *Teleporno*. This may seem strange, since Galadriel was of the Noldor, the sister of Finrod son of Finarphin son of Finwë, and one of the greatest of that House; but it may be understood by reference to the *Tale of Celeborn and Galadriel*.

Galadriel was formed from the base ÑAL 'shine, glitter', applied to light reflected from water, metal, glass, gems, etc. From this was derived a triconsonantal form *ñalata* '(reflected) radiance'. The base RI3 meant 'wind about, wreathe'; derivatives were *ri3 'a wreath, garland' (Q. *ría* also *ríma* 'fillet, snood'). The suffix -*el*, -*elle* (developed in C.E.) was a feminine ending, parallel to the masculine -*on*, *ondo*; a *ri3el(le) was a woman bearing a garland on her head, usually applied to maidens wearing garlands of flowers at festivals. *ñalata-ri3elle would this mean 'maiden crowned with a garland of radiance'. The name was given to her by Teleporno, and accepted by her.

Galadriel was a daughter of Finarphin son of Finwë first king of the Noldor. She was called *Nerwen* 'man-maiden' because of her strength and stature, and her courage. She loved to wander far from the home of her kin.

Following this are some roughly handwritten etymological notes in ink:

Q *ñal* obsolete except in *ñalda* 'bright, polished' (of metal). *angal* ([?] *aŋŋala*) 'a mirror' or *angalailin* 'mirrormere'. *ŋalatā-ri3el(le) = *Alatáriel*. Quenyarized *Altáriel*? RGEO *Altariello* gen.

The reference to "RGEO" is to the 1968 song-book *The Road Goes Ever On*, in which the poem *Namárië* is described by Tolkien in Quenya as "*Altariello nainië Lóriendessë*", i.e. 'Galadriel's lament in Lórien".

Finally, some related draft notes read:

Galadriel was a Sindarin name given to (and accepted by) her after her coming to Beleriand, meaning 'lady of the golden crown' or 'coronal', referring to the braids of her golden hair (braided high).

9 Tolkien corrected original *Angal-mille* to *Angal-limpe* in ink. In connection with the Eldarin words for 'mirror', this is a convenient place to cite a passage in separate but contemporary writings among Tolkien's linguistic papers concerning an object of Elvish technology:

[Q.] *ñaltalma*, the name of an Eldarin device for signalling from afar (like a heliograph, though it is said to have been also usable in a clear moon). Its form and the manner of manipulating it are not recorded, but it must have contained a bright surface. It was however evidently small, able to be slipped into a slender pouch or pocket, and the flash that it gave would not have been visible by human eyes, at any rate not at a distance. In what way the flashes, received by a watcher when suitably directed, conveyed a message is also now unknown. The *ñaltalma* was, as most such things, in later days attributed to Fëanor; but was probably far older. (Similar devices were used by the Sindar, and there is no mention of their being among the many things learned by the Sindar from the Exiles). The Sindarin name was *glathralvas* 'flashing glass/crystal'.

The heliograph, a mirrored signalling device (usually employing Morse code), was a standard device in the British Army from the 19th century through 1960. Tolkien, who trained in military signalling in 1914–15 and became Battalion Signalling Officer in 1916 (TCG I:62, 92), would have been well familiar with the device. The manual he was issued during his training, *Signalling: Morse, Semaphore, Station Work, Despatch Riding, Telephone Cables, Map Reading* (ed. E.J. Solano, 1915; see TCG I:79) says of the heliograph (p. 6) that: "In the case of flag or lamp signals the distance is usually less in broken or hilly ground and misty atmosphere, and greater on level ground and in clear atmosphere. In India, Africa, and Egypt, for instance, upon hilly ground, stations for signalling by heliograph may be separated by seventy miles or more. On the other hand, in Britain and other European countries it may not be possible to use the heliograph at all, owing to want of sunlight, and its range is usually limited to twenty-five miles in sunshine, owing to the prevalence of mist and haze in the atmosphere."

10 As typed, this sentence ended: "… Celeborn, which actually contained a tree-word"; it was altered to the given reading via a marginal note in ball-point pen.

11 As first typed the text here continued: "No doubt the same association was made by its people, but *galad* was the form they gave to the S. word *galað* 'tree'. They spoke Sindarin, and some among them were actually Sindar; but their daily language was modified by their former tongue. This had not preserved the sounds ð and þ and these were turned into *d* and *s*." This passage was subsequently struck through in ink.

12 I.e. LR:372–3.

13 I.e. LR:467.

14 The continuation "and alterations of it …" after "based on *lawarind*" arose in very rough writing on the page, in ink and in-line with the text and interposing the resumption of the typescript. This first version reads:

and alterations of it to resemble names of Valinor for which, as is plain, Galadriel's longing increased year by year to at last an overwhelming regret. Lórien was the name most used in the Third Age, since formally it could also be a Sindarin name [*deleted*: though in Sindarin it would more properly be spelt *Lorien* since in Sindarin the [?quantity augmented ? only] an]

The point of the deleted passage seems to be that the *o* of the Sindarin reflex of *★lawarind* would not be marked as long, since (in accordance with usual Sindarin development) it arose from earlier *★aw(a)* by (in this position) monophthongization and shortening.

15 The footnote on *tumbu here was subject to much emendation and reconsideration. As first typed, the form appears to have been *tumbā, and Q. *iTumbo* (and *i Tumbo*) was emended in ink from original *iTumba* (and *i Tumba*); and *Tum Orchorod* is a replacement for original *Tum Orodgerth*. A rough note in ink above this note, apparently referring to Rivendell (S. *Imladris*) reads: "Cf. *imbē* a variation of *imbi* 'between', now used of a cleft of great length in mountains between very high walls of stone; Q. *imbilat* = S. *imlad*)". A rough note in ink below this note reads: "No. t*umbŭ* = deep of vale, v[ale?] referred to the great volcanic mare in midst of the crater-valley." (It is possible for "mare" to be read as "mere", but the former's use for dark, flat pseudo-oceans of ancient, hardened volcanic flow seems more apposite.) This consideration of the Vale of Gondolin in turn gave rise to still another rough note in ink, filling the bottom half of the page, on the name, history, and nature of Gondolin:

Gondolin. Q. Ondolinde 'Singing Stone' [? ?]

That the site had been occupied by Dwarves meant [?first] who had done much of the work – bringing the stones and leveling the land and building the walls of the central fortress – [?which by ? ? only rea? by ?]. It was the Noldor who [? ? ?] built a [?steel] bridge from the outer shore of the lake across the [? ?] of the lake to the [? ?]. [? ? ? ? ?] of the return of Morgoth to Thangorodrim and Turgon had found the Tumbo deserted. The name *Gondolin* in Sindarin [?] Gondolin(d) is probably [? ? ?] Quenya [? ? ? ? ?] before [?] foundation. Though somewhere supposed [? ?] to have been Eldarized from some older Dwarvish [?name but ? ? ?] contact!

16 A later, rough marginal note in ink here reads: "A genitival a of relationship, pl. -*on*, occurred in O.S., but only preserved in names of the [? or ?]. *Dagnir Laurunga*." With this latter name, cf. the epitaph *Dagnir Glaurunga* *'Slayer of Glaurung' on Túrin's grave marker (S:226, UT:145). An etymological figure in ink on the following page shows the development of this genitival ending in Old Sindarin, accounting for the preservation of word-final -*a* where the normal loss of all final syllables makes final vowels uncommon in Sindarin:

*-*āga*, [pl.] *āgam* > $\tilde{a}$, $\tilde{a}m$/ $\tilde{a}n$. Final $\bar{a}$ > *a* (not *o*!), but $\tilde{a}n$ > *on*.

XVII

SILVAN ELVES AND SILVAN ELVISH

The two texts presented here are both late typescripts, occupying sides (six and six, respectively) of printed Allen & Unwin notices dated 1968. The first of these is evidently closely associated with texts published in *Unfinished Tales* as *The Disaster of the Gladden Fields*, *Cirion and Eorl*, and *The History of Galadriel and Celeborn*; as well as the texts presented just above as chap. XVI, "Galadriel and Celeborn". The first text itself makes explicit reference to the first and second of those *UT* texts, and Christopher Tolkien quotes portions of it in the latter of these (UT:257–9). The second text arose in conjunction with that given as *The Problem of Ros* in *The Peoples of Middle-earth*, and is excerpted from a longer discussion of Silvan Elvish, with particular focus on the etymology of the name *Amroth*; its discussion of S. *rath* 'climb' and its connection with *Amroth* was referenced in UT:255 n.16.

TEXT 1

Nomenclature

Silvan Elvish (SE), and names recorded as being derived
from (dialects of) that language.

This language was evidently related to Sindarin; but its characteristics have not been defined. For (as may be supposed) little information is available, beyond a few personal names and place names. The Wood-elves played a valiant part in the War of the Ring, but appear to have given no assistance in the ancient War of the Three Jewels.[1]

In the fragmentary survivals of the legends of the Great Journey there are mentions of several secessions from the march, either by accident (some small parties lost their way) or by deliberate abandonment of the journey through weariness and loss of hope. For the most part these secessions were made by groups of the Lindar, the most numerous of the Eldar, who had been the most reluctant to leave their ancient home, and marched more slowly westward, always in the rear.* [2] The Eldar of Ossiriand, the Green Elves, though wood-dwellers, were of quite different origin, which does not here concern us; they were probably in origin of Noldorin kinship.[3] The Wood-elves of the time of the War of the Ring appear to have been those Teleri and their descendants who were dismayed by the Hithaeglir or Misty Mountains† and abandoning the march settled in the then greater and denser forests between the Anduin and the mountains, in the region in later days bounded north and south by the rivers Gladden and Limlight.[4] How the Eldar had crossed the Anduin is not told,[5] but the legends appear to describe that river as very different from its later shape in that region: wider and slower and forming great lakes at intervals in what were afterward the grassy lands of the Vales of Anduin. Such land would be attractive to the Lindar, who from their earliest days had a greater love of water than the other kindreds, and had already devised small boats to row or sail on the lakes of their own land before the days of the Great Journey. It was no doubt by their craft that eventually all three hosts reached the feet of the mountains and were faced by the labour and perils of finding ways through them. The legends speak of a sojourn of many years and long debates before the Vanyar and Noldor after long exploration began the crossing "by the pass under the Red Mountain".‡ They were followed by some two-thirds of the Teleri. A third, mainly belonging to the folk of Olwë, had become during the delay well contented, and

---

* Hence they were called by the Vanyar and Noldor the *Teleri*, the backward; but those who eventually reached Valinor retained their own name (Lindar, or in their tongue *Lindai*). Lindarin (L) is thus used for the language of the Teleri of Valinor, in many ways the most archaic and least changed of the Eldarin languages.

† These at that remote time appear to have been continuous with the White Mountains.

‡ Probably that mountain afterwards known as *Caraðras*; though unless its awe-inspiring peak was magnified in legend, it was then loftier than in later ages. "Under" plainly means "under the shadow of"; for there were as yet no Dwarves in those mountains, and the mines of Moria had not been begun. Neither, fortunately for the Eldar, had the Orks of Morgoth yet reached those regions.

remained behind. There was no contact between these Silvan Elves and the Grey Elves, the Sindar, who in the event also remained in Middle-earth and never crossed the Great Sea, until the Second Age and the ruin of Beleriand. In Mannish terms that was a time as long maybe as all the years that now lie between us and the War of the Ring.[6] Any tongues of Men, however close akin, would in such a time have diverged beyond recognition. It was not so with the Elvish languages. They changed indeed, in Middle-earth at any rate, in much the same ways as do our languages, but much more slowly. For as Elvish sight and hearing were limited in range as ours are, and yet were keener and of greater range, so were their memories of things seen and heard. In the First Age after the end of the Great Journey, in a thousand years the unheeded change in the speech of the Elves that remained "on the hither shores", that is in Middle-earth, was no more than in two generations of Men.* Thus, although the dialects of the Silvan Elves, when they again met their long separated kindred, had so far diverged from Sindarin as to be hardly intelligible, little study was needed to reveal their kinship as Eldarin tongues.† Though the comparison of the Silvan dialects with their own speech greatly interested the loremasters, especially those of Noldorin origin, little is now known of the Silvan Elvish. The Silvan Elves had invented no forms of writing, and those who learned this art from the Sindar wrote in Sindarin as well as they could. By the end of the Third Age the Silvan tongues had probably ceased to be spoken in the two regions that had importance at the time of the War of the Ring: Lórien and the realm of Thranduil in northern Mirkwood. All that survived of them in the records was a few words and several names of persons and places.[7]

Those names that are Elvish (at least in form) in the North East may naturally be supposed to have been originally devised in the Silvan tongue of Thranduil's realm, which had extended into the woods surrounding the Lonely Mountain, before the coming of the Dwarves in exile from Moria, and the invasions of the Dragons

---

* In Valinor the conditions were different. Change though it was imperceptibly slow proceeded even in the Blessed Realm; but unheeded change in speech was controlled by memory and design, and the chief changes, which were considerable, were due to changes in "taste" and to inventiveness both in vocabulary and the devices of language.

† Their divergence might be compared with that of the Scandinavian dialects from the English at the time of the Norse settlements in England, though it was in some respects somewhat greater, and in some regions (notably Lórien) mixed language developed, in which Sindarin was dominant but was infected by many words and names of Silvan origin.

of the far North. The Elvish folk of this realm had migrated from the south, being the kin and neighbours of the Elves of Lórien, but they had dwelt east of Anduin. Their movement had at first been slow, and they had for a long time remained in contact with their kin west of the river. Their unrest did not begin until the Third Age. They had been little concerned in the wars of the Second Age; but in that age they had grown to a numerous people, and their king Oropher* led a great host to join Gilgalad in the Last Alliance; but he was slain and many of his following in the first assault upon Mordor.[8] Afterwards they lived in peace, until a thousand years of the Third Age had passed. Then as they said a Shadow fell upon Greenwood the Great and they retreated before it as it spread ever northward, until at last Thranduil established his realm in the North-east of the forest and delved there a fortress and great halls underground.†[9] Maybe now more than 500 years had passed between the loss of all communication between

---

* He was the father of Thranduil, father of Legolas.

† Oropher was of Sindarin origin (cf. LR III 363) and no doubt his son was following the example of King Thingol, long before in Doriath; though his halls were not to be compared with Menegroth. He had not the arts nor the wealth nor the aid of the Dwarves; and compared with the Elves of Doriath his Silvan folk were rude and rustic. He had come among them with only a handful of Sindar, and they were soon merged with the Silvan Elves, adopting their language and taking names of Silvan form and style. This they did deliberately; for they (and other similar adventurers forgotten in the legends or only briefly named) came from Doriath after its ruin, and had no desire to leave Middle-earth, nor to be merged with the other Sindar of Beleriand, dominated by the Noldorin Exiles for whom the folk of Doriath had no great love. They wished indeed to become Silvan folk and to return, as they said, to the simple life natural to the Elves before the invitation of the Valar had disturbed it. Thus already in the Second Age Oropher had withdrawn northward beyond the confluence of the Gladden and Anduin: to be free from the power and encroachments of the Dwarves of Moria, and still more, after the fall of Eregion, from the "domination" of Celeborn and Galadriel. They had passed through Moria with a considerable following of Noldorin Exiles and dwelt for many years in Lórien. Thither they returned twice before the Last Alliance and the end of the Second Age; and in the Third Age, when the Shadow of Sauron's recovery arose, they dwelt there again for a long time. In her wisdom Galadriel foresaw that Lórien would be a stronghold and point of power to prevent the Shadow from crossing the Anduin in the war that must inevitably come before it was again defeated (if that were possible); but that it needed a rule of greater wisdom and strength than the Silvan folk possessed. Nonetheless, it was not until the disaster in Moria, when by means beyond the foresight of Galadriel Sauron's power actually crossed the Anduin and Lórien was in great peril, its king lost, its people fleeing and likely to leave it deserted to be occupied by Orks, that Celeborn and Galadriel took up their permanent abode in Lórien, and its government. But they took no title of King or Queen, and were the guardians that in the event brought it unviolated through the War of the Ring.

Thranduil's folk and their southern kindred before disaster befell Lórien and their last king, Amroth, was lost. In that time their Silvan tongue would have suffered no perceptible changes.

> The text ends, or at any rate is interrupted, here, near the top of the page and above a large empty space.[10] However, starting at the top of the next page, which Tolkien numbered continuously with this one, is typescript text that, if not exactly continuous with the foregoing – it is disjoint with the preceding passage and partially repetitive of the text, as for example in the stated motive of Oropher's withdrawal northwards – is clearly contemporary with it, and may represent a partial reconsideration and redirecting of its course.[11] Long extracts from its beginning are quoted in *Unfinished Tales* (pp. 258–9), as indicated.

In the records of the Third Age all that remains of the Silvan language is a few local words and several names of persons and places. These are mostly derived from Lórien; but the names that are Elvish in form found in the Northeast must have originally been devised in the Silvan tongue of King Thranduil's realm, which had extended into the woods surrounding the Lonely Mountain and growing along the west shores of the Long Lake, before the coming of the Dwarves exiled from Moria and the invasion of the dragon.

> The latter half of this sentence and several subsequent paragraphs are published at UT:258–9. Following this lengthy excerpt, the text continues:

[Thranduil] had not long returned when the disaster of the Gladden Fields occurred. When he retreated from the War in the first year of the Third Age he heard ill news: the Orks of the north regions of the Misty Mountains had also multiplied and spread southwards and many had crossed the Anduin and were infesting the eaves of Greenwood.

The history of the Orks is naturally obscure and whence these Orks had come is not known. In the final destruction of Thangorodrim and the casting out of Morgoth, their begetter, those in his immediate service had been destroyed, though no doubt some escaped and fled east into hiding. But in the Second Age Sauron, when he turned back to evil, had gathered to his service all the Orks that were scattered far and wide in the Northern world, cowed and masterless, furtive lurkers in dark places. He rekindled the lusts of their black hearts; and to some he showed favour and fed them lavishly, breeding and training them into tribes of strong and cruel warriors.

In the Second Age the presence of the lesser and more furtive Orks in the mountains between Carn Dûm and the Ettenmoors had long been known to the Elves and the Dúnedain; but they were not yet much troubled by them.[12] These Orks feared the Elves and fled from them; and they did not dare to approach the dwellings of Men or to assail them on their journeys, unless a lone man or a few rash adventurers strayed near their hiding places. But things had changed. While the greater part of the strength of Elves and Men had been drawn away south to the war with Mordor, they had become more bold and their scattered tribes had become leagued together and had dug a deep stronghold beneath Mount Gundabad. Slowly they were creeping southward.

But these Orks could not have caused the disaster of the Gladden Fields; they would not have dared even to show themselves to Isildur. For though he was marching north with only a small company, maybe no more than two hundreds,* [13] they were his picked body-guard, tall knights of the Dúnedain, war-hardened, grim and fully armed.[14] There can be no doubt that Sauron, well informed of the Alliance and the gathering of great forces to assail him, had sent out such troops of Orks as

Here the text breaks off, midsentence and at the bottom of a page. At this break, in the bottom margin, Tolkien later wrote: "Continued in Disaster of the G[ladden] F[ields]".[15]

---

* While Isildur stayed for a year or more in Gondor re-establishing its order and its bounds (as is told in the Tale of Cirion and Eorl, that drew on ancient chronicles now lost), the main forces of the realm of Elendil in Arnor had returned to Eriador by the Númenórean road from the Fords of Isen to Lake Evendim. When Isildur at last felt free to return to his own realm, he was in haste, and he wished to come first to Imladris where he had left his youngest son and his wife. The western road would take him far out of his way; for he could not strike north from the road because of the treacherous marshes of the Gwathló; he would have been obliged to follow the road to Evendim until it crossed the great East-West Road of Arnor, only some 40 miles east of the Baranduin. That led straight to Imladris, but it was more than 300 miles from the road-crossing to Imladris, as great a distance as from the inflow of the Celebrant to the high pass in the Mountains leading to Imladris, if one went north along the Anduin. (By that pass a great part of Gilgalad's army had come on the way to Mordor.) He therefore determined to march north up the vales of Anduin.

TEXT 2

In L.R. I 355[16] Legolas speaks of this custom [dwelling in trees] as if it was universal among the Galadhrim of Lórien, and was used "even before the Shadow came",* but it was not in fact a habit of the Silvan Elves in general. It was developed in Lórien by the nature and situation of the land: a flat land with no good stone, except what might be quarried in the mountains westward and brought with difficulty down the Celebrant.† Its chief wealth was in its trees, a remnant of the great forests of the Elder Days, of which the chief were the great *mellyrn* ('golden-trees') of vast girth and immense height. East and west the land was bounded by the Anduin and by the mountains, but it had no clearly defined borders northward and southward.

The text continues with the excerpt given at UT:260–1, resuming with:

But in the later days of which we speak Lórien had been a land of uneasy vigilance. The dwelling in trees was not universal. The *telain* or 'flets' were in origin either refuges in trees to be used in cases of

---

* By which he does not (probably) refer far back to the end of the first millennium of the Third Age, when a shadow fell on Greenwood the Great and it began to be called Mirkwood: see Tale of Years, L.R. III 366 [i.e. LR:1085]; though it was no doubt this "Shadow" spreading from Dol Guldur that caused the Galadhrim who lived in the southern parts of Greenwood to retreat further and further north, and eventually made communication with those that remained west of Anduin rare and difficult. He is principally thinking of the end of the second millennium, when the power of Sauron, now revived, was felt in all the lands east of Anduin and was a growing threat to the narrow lands between it and the Misty Mountains. It is not recorded how long Amroth had been king of Lórien, but either as hereditary chieftain, associated with Galadriel and Celeborn as "advisers and guardians", or alone in times of their absence, he must have dwelt ever since Third Age 1000 in growing disquiet, until the disaster (no doubt ultimately due to Sauron) of T.A. 1980 when a Balrog arose in Moria and it was abandoned by the Dwarves and became filled with the servants of Sauron. Nimrodel and many others of the Silvan folk fled south, and Amroth seeking for Nimrodel never returned. Lórien would no doubt have been deserted and left open to Sauron if Celeborn and Galadriel had not returned and taken over the rule, supported by the Elves of Noldorin and Sindarin origin, who were already a large part of the people of Lórien.

† In this task at one time the Elves had the assistance of the Dwarves of Moria. For these had had alliances and friendship with the Elves of Eregion, and they were well-disposed to Lórien, where many of the survivors of Eregion had taken refuge.

attack or invasion, or most often (especially those high up in great trees) outlook posts from which the land and its borders could be surveyed by Elvish eyes. Such an outlook post, used by the wardens of the north marches, was the flet in which Frodo spent the night. The abode of Celeborn in Caras Galadon was also of the same origin: its highest flet, which the Fellowship of the Ring did not see, was the highest point in the land. Earlier the great flet of Amroth at the top of the great mound or hill of Cerin Amroth (piled by the labour of many hands) had been the highest, and was principally designed to watch Dol Guldur across the Anduin. The conversion of these telain into permanent dwellings was a later development, and only in Caras Galadon were such dwellings numerous. But Caras Galadon was itself a fortress, and only a small part of the Galadhrim dwelt within its walls. Living in such lofty houses was no doubt at first thought remarkable, and Amroth was probably the first to do so.* It is thus from his living in a high *talan* that his name – the only one that was later remembered in legend – was most probably derived.

If so it is connected with a stem RATH meaning 'climb' – with hands and feet, as in a tree or up a rocky slope. This is recorded in Quenya only in *raþillo* (*rasillo*) 'squirrel' and *rantala* 'ladder' (< **ran-þlā*).[17] In Lindarin *rath-* was still the stem of a normal "strong" verb 'to climb'; a (professional or habitual) climber was *rathumo*, but in compounds the agental form was *-rathō*, as in *orotrātho* 'mountain-climber'. In Sindarin, clearly connected derivatives are not found.[18]

Both Quenya and Lindarin also possessed a word *ratta*, which might be a derivative (by lengthening the medial consonant, a frequent device in Primitive Eldarin) from either **rattha* or **ratta* from the stem RAT,†[19] and in senses seems to be a blend of both. It meant 'a track'; though often applied to ways known to mountaineers, to

---

* Unless it was Nimrodel. Her motives were different. She loved the waters and the falls of Nimrodel from which she would not long be parted; but as times darkened the stream was too near the north borders and in a part where few of the Galadhrim now dwelt. Maybe it was from her that Amroth took the idea of living in a high flet.

† The stem RAT (of which RATH was probably an emphatic variation in Primitive Eldarin) meant 'to find a way', applied to persons journeying in the wild; to travel in roadless land; and also to streams and rivers and their courses. A derivative was P.E. **rantā*, applied to the tracks and trails of travellers or explorers that had become habitual and could be followed by others. It was also, especially in Sindarin, applied to the courses of rivers, as in *Celebrant* ('Silverlode'). Cf. also the *Gondrant*, the stone-trail of the great wains of the quarriers in the Stonewain Valley, *Tum Gondregain*, north of Minas Tirith.

passes in the mountains and the climbing ways to them, it was not confined to ascents. It could be used of tracks across a marshland, or trails (blazed or sometimes marked by guide-stones) in forests. This is evidently the origin also of S. *rath*, the short vowel of which shows that it had a double consonant medially and was not derived from a simple form of RAT such as **rathā*. It had the same senses as Q., L. *ratta*, though in mountainous country it was most used of climbing ways. In Minas Tirith, in the Númenórean Sindarin that was used in Gondor for the nomenclature of places, *rath* had become virtually equivalent to 'street', being applied to nearly all the paved ways within the city. Most of these were on an incline, often steep.

The naming had probably come down from the early days of Gondor when the rocky hill of Amon Anor was yet uninhabited, except by a small fort on its summit reached by winding paths and rough-hewn steps. It was in those days of less importance than Minas Ithil, the centre of the Watch that was kept on the deserted land of Mordor. The chief purpose of the fort (Minas Anor) was then to guard the place of the Tombs of the Kings which were built on a long pier of rock which joined the outlier, Amon Anor, to the main mass of the great Mindolluin behind it. Thus one of the oldest of the *raths* of Minas Tirith must have been the steep winding way that led down to the Tombs and then along the rocky way between them: the Rath Dínen, the Silent Street, as it was called; though in the time of the L.R. this name was applied only to the great way between the numerous tombs. The ancient *rath* had been replaced by a broad winding way, cut in the rock of the hill, that wound down without steps, and fenced on the outward edge with a low wall and carved balusters: *Dúnad in Gyrth*, the Descent of the Dead.

NOTES

1 As first typed, this sentence began: "The Wood-elves played only a small part in the War of the Ring".

2 The gloss "backward" should not be understood in a culturally pejorative sense, but rather literally: "those at the back", i.e., as opposed to "forward"; cf. XI:382.

3 The remark here that the Green-elves (Q. *Laiquendi*, S. *Laegrim*) "were probably in origin of Noldorin kinship" seemingly represents a late reversion to an earlier ascription of kinship that had otherwise been firmly displaced by 1951 (but see X:158) in favor of Telerin kinship (see X:83, 89 §62, 93; X:163–4, 169–71 §§28–9; XI:13).

4 That is, in the same river-bounded region in which Lórien lay in the Third Age. Tolkien's note that the Misty Mountains (Hithaeglir) "at that remote time appear to have been continuous with the White Mountains" (Ered Nimrais) would seem to imply that the Gap of Rohan, which by the Third Age separates the two mountain ranges, was not yet in existence during the Great March in the First Age.

5 But cf. chap. VIII, "The March of the Quendi", in part one of this book, at the entry for VY 1130/91.

6 As first typed, this sentence began: "In Mannish terms that was a time maybe longer than all the years". In a letter from Oct. 1958, Tolkien states that he "imagine[s] the gap [between the Fall of Barad-dûr and the present] to be about 6000 years" (L:283 fn).

7 The end of this lengthy paragraph, beginning at "although the dialects of the Silvan Elves" (without the interposed notes) is given at UT:257.

8 Here and at the first two occurrences of the name "Oropher" in Tolkien's following, lengthy note, as first typed, the name of Thranduil's father is given as "Rogner". Tolkien altered the latter of these occurrences to "Oropher", and "Oropher" appears *ab initio* in the subsequent text; so it is here supplied editorially at the first two occurrences as well. The beginning of the lengthy note, through the words "before the invitation of the Valar had disturbed it", editorially clarified and combined with the sentence on which it comments, is quoted at UT:259. I have also adopted here Christopher's editorial substitution of "Menegroth" for the typescript's "Menegrond", which (so far as I can determine) appears nowhere else. It must be noted though that Tolkien himself let the name stand, despite other corrections; and further that in the linguistic situation of the c. 1936 *Etymologies* the element *roth* of *Menegroth* is specifically Doriathrin element corresponding to Noldorin (later Sindarin) *r(h)ond* (cf. V:384 s.v. ROD; also XI:414–15, and VT46:12 s.vv. ROD, ROT-); so that "Menegrond" in the present context may in fact be a specifically Sindarin form of the otherwise always-employed Doriathrin "Menegroth".

9 The opening of this footnote was previously published at UT:259. "LR III 363" = LR:1082. "Thither they returned twice before the Last Alliance": in the contemporary *History of Galadriel and Celeborn*, upon the revolt in Eregion of the Mírdain at the instigation of Sauron, Galadriel alone passed through Khazad-dûm to Lórinand (UT:237), took up rule, and remained there until she departed to seek Celeborn at Imladris, prior to the Council there (UT:240). At some point after the Council, Galadriel and Celeborn departed to dwell in what later came to be Dol Amroth until, upon the disaster in Khazad-dûm in T.A. 1981, Galadriel took up rule in Lórinand again, and Celeborn joined her (ibid.).

10 There is strong evidence that Tolkien did not originally intend to end or interrupt the text here. First, it is plain that Tolkien began the continuation of the long note on Oropher and Thranduil at the bottom of the same page so as to allow ample space above for continuation of the main text. Moreover, on the verso of the page – i.e., the original recto of the Allen & Unwin publication notice on which this text was typed – Tolkien took such pains to make so full use of blank areas that he not only continued the note on Oropher and

Thranduil in the top margin of the notice (upside-down with respect to the printing on the notice), but also interspersed the note's final lines in the gaps between the paragraphs of the notice. Finally, the last letters of the last word, "changes", of the main text, before the long gap, are dim, as though the typewriter ribbon had suddenly run out, which might have occasioned an unplanned pause in composition, that, in the event, was not resumed.

11 In the top margin of the page Tolkien at some later point wrote: "Continuation of Discussion of Silvan Elvish, diverging (when discussing Thranduil & his removal northward) into a brief account of Isildur's fall".

12 I take this opportunity, though it is not strictly speaking late writing, to record an (ultimately cancelled) manuscript rider by Tolkien to a typescript version of what became "The Tale of Aragorn and Arwen" in *LR* App. A. The source and context of this rider is cited at XII:268: "Arador was the grandfather of the King". The rider, titled "Rider A", reads:

Trolls had lived in the north of the Misty Mountains since days before memory, especially near the Ettenmoors; but they increased in numbers and wickedness while the realm of Angmar lasted. They then retreated east of the mountains, but about 300 years before the War of the Ring they returned and began to trouble Eriador, in spite of the vigilance of the Rangers, making dens in the hills even as far from the mountains as the North Downs. In the time of Arador a band threatened the house of the Chieftain, which was then in woods near the Hoarwell north of the Trollshaws, though many of the Dúnedain lived in the woods between Hoarwell and Loudwater.

13 Re: "as is told in the Tale of Cirion and Eorl": In published texts at least, this tradition is not related in the texts presented in *Cirion and Eorl* in *Unfinished Tales*, but is rather reflected in the opening paragraphs of *The Disaster of the Gladden Fields*: cf. UT:271.

14 In Tolkien's lengthy, digressive note on Isildur, as first typed, the motive for Isildur's northerly rather than western route is that "there were as yet no other roads in Eneðwaith or Minhiriath, and after Tharbad he would have had to strike north through pathless and in part marshy land to gain the great East-West Road of Arnor near Amon Sûl, or go further". With this note cf. UT:278 n.6.

15 This is no doubt a reference to at least a draft of the text presented as *The Disaster of the Gladden Fields* in *Unfinished Tales*; see especially p. 273 and pp. 282–3 n.20. In fact, a bit of such drafting, apparently early, is found on the same verso page as the final lines of the lengthy note on Oropher and Thranduil mentioned above (and plainly predates the present text, because it is written in what was originally the top margin of the publication notice, which had that space been available to Tolkien when finishing the long note, he would surely have utilized). Though very rapidly written and indeed illegible in parts, it appears to read:

along the paths made by the Silvan Elves near the eaves of the forest. There had been heavy rains for some days past, and Anduin [? far ?] its deep channel was swollen with swift water. On a drear day of Autumn, when the Sun was sinking in the reddened cloud beyond the distant peaks of the Mountains, they drew level with the south reaches of the Gladden Fields [? they heard]. In the fading light

With this cf. UT:272.

16 I.e. LR:341.

17 While it may be (but probably isn't) a mere coincidence, it is worth noting the name *Ratatoskr* in Norse mythology of the squirrel that runs up and down the world-tree Yggdrasil bearing messages. While this is now generally etymologized as meaning "drill-tooth" or "bore-tooth", it had long been suggested that the initial element *rata-* meant 'traveller' or 'climber'.

18 The text here originally continued with an attempted but rejected explanation of the Sindarin word *rath* 'street' as related to RATH:

In this case Sindarin shared with Quenya a stem RAP [*sic*] 'climb'; and the only derivative of RATH is *râth*. (The word *rath* in Sindarin especially as applied to the steep stairway from the citadel of Minas Tirith to the place of the Tombs appears to be related, and may be. But its short vowel indicates descent from CE *ratt-*.) This in the Númenórean Sindarin of Gondor that was used in the nomenclature of places (and generally in that of persons) was applied to all the longer roadways and streets of Minas Tirith. Nearly all of these were on an incline, often steep; but the connection of *rath* with 'climb' is seen clearly in the Rath Dínen, the Silent Street, which was a steep stairway leading down from the Citadel of Minas Tirith to the Tombs. The vowel of *rath* was however short in the pronunciation; for 'climb' the word used was amrad- 'find a way up', derived from stem RAT, no doubt originally related to RATH (an emphatic variation).

A stem RAP 'climb' is attested in somewhat earlier linguistic writing: cf. PE22:127. At the end of this typescript, Tolkien writes:

The relation of *-roth* to this stem RATH is probably this: it was a form of the agental agent seen in L. *-rātho*, sc. *amroth* was < *ambarātho* meaning 'up-climber, high climber'. In that case Silvan Elvish had shifted the P.E. $*\bar{a} > o$, though independently of Sindarin, and probably without the complications seen in Sindarin, in which P.E. $*au$ and $*\bar{a}$ had both become δ (open as in English pronunciation of *au*), and then $> au$, which however only remained in stressed monosyllables, and otherwise again reverted to *o*. This evidence of the existence of a stem *rath* 'climb' in Silvan Elvish connects it with Lindarin rather than Sindarin ultimately. This accords with history, since the strayers from the Great Journey evidently belonged mainly to the rear host of the Lindar of whom Olwë was the chieftain.

19 "*Celebrant*" 'Silverlode': "lode" here has the same meaning that it does in "lodestone", i.e., 'way, course'; it is derived from Old English *lād* of the same meaning. In late Middle English it came to mean a 'watercourse', i.e. the course of a brook or stream.

XVIII

NOTE ON THE DELAY OF GIL-GALAD
AND THE NÚMENÓREANS

This text is written in a fairly clear hand in black nib-pen on a single page of a printed Allen & Unwin publication notice dated 19th Jan. 1970.

Note on the delay of Gil-galad and the Númenóreans
in attacking Sauron, *before* he could gather his forces.

It is now vain, and indeed unjust, to judge them foolish not to do, as in the end they were obliged to do, to have quickly gathered their forces and assailed Sauron. (See the *Debate of the Loremasters upon the Ban of Manwë* and his conduct as the Lord of Arda.)[1] They could not have any certain knowledge of Sauron's intentions, or his power, and it was one of the successes of his cunning and deceits that they were unaware of his actual weakness, and his need for a long time in which to gather armies sufficient to assail an alliance of the Elves and Western Men. His occupation of Mordor he no doubt would have kept secret if he could, and it would appear from later events that he had secured the allegiance of Men that dwelt in lands adjacent, even those west of Anduin, in those regions where afterwards was Gondor in the Ered Nimrais and Calenardhon. But the Númenóreans occupying the Mouths of Anduin and the shorelands of Lebennin had discovered his devices, and revealed them to Gil-galad. But until [S.A.] 1600 he was still using the disguise of beneficent friend, and often journeyed at will in Eriador with few attendants, and so could not risk any rumour that he was gathering armies. At this time he perforce neglected the East (where Morgoth's ancient power had been) and though his emissaries were busy among the multiplying tribes of eastern Men, he dared not permit any of them to come within sight of the Númenóreans, or of Western Men.*

The Orcs of various kind (creatures of Morgoth) were to prove the most numerous and terrible of his soldiers and servants; but great hosts of them had been destroyed in the war against Morgoth, and in the destruction of Beleriand. Some remnant had escaped to hidings in the northern parts of the Misty Mountains and the Grey Mountains, and were now multiplying again. But further East there were more and stronger kinds, descendants of Morgoth's kingship, but long masterless during his occupation of Thangorodrim, they were yet wild and ungovernable, preying upon one another and upon Men (whether good or evil). But not until Mordor and the Barad-dûr were ready could he allow them to come out of hiding, while the Eastern Orcs, who had not experienced the power and terror of the Eldar, or the valour of the Edain, were not subservient to Sauron – while he was obliged for the cozening of Western Men and Elves to wear as fair a form and countenance as he could, they despised him and laughed at him. Thus it was that though, as soon as his disguise was pierced and he was recognized as an enemy, he exerted all his time and strength to gathering and training armies, it took some ninety years before he felt ready to open war. And he misjudged this, as we see in his final defeat, when the great host of Minastir from Númenor landed in Middle-earth. His gathering of armies had not been unopposed, and his success had been much less than his hope. But this is a matter spoken of in notes on "The Five Wizards".[2] He had powerful enemies behind his back, the East, and in the Southern lands to which he had not yet given sufficient thought.

NOTES

1 That is, the text in chap. VIII, "Manwë's Ban", above.

2 Given at XII:384–5.

---

* That is, of the numerous tribes of Men, whom the Elves called Men of Good Will, who lived in Eriador and Calenardhon and the Vales of Anduin and in the Great Wood and the plains between that and Mordor and the Sea of Rhûn. In Eriador there were actually some of the remnants of the Three Houses of Men that had fought with the Elves against Morgoth. Others were of their kin, who (like the Silvan Elves) had never passed the Ered Luin, and others of remoter kin. But nearly all were descendants of ancient rebels against Morgoth. (Some evil men there were also.)

XIX

NOTE ON DWARVISH VOICES

This note is found on two sides of a narrow strip of paper located
with papers dating from c. 1969. It is written in a very hasty hand in
black fountain and ball-point pen.

It is false to make Dwarves [?uncreative] or poor linguists. They had
great interest in languages – which was more or less dormant until
they began to associate with other peoples – but they could not conceal
their *voices*. Phonetically they were acute and could pronounce learned
languages well, but their voices were very deep in tone with laryngeal
coloration, and they among themselves spoke in a laryngeal whisper.

They started with a [?purely] spoken language [?but ? ? ? ?]

But it is said in L.R. App[1] that the *Cirth* were first devised in
Beleriand by the Sindar – in a simple form they spread to the
Dwarves; the [?elaborating] of the Cirth under the influence of the
Tengwar is attributed to Daeron.

NB: the *invention* ascribed to Dwarves by Elrond[2] was of the invisible runes in moonletters only. All the same do not exaggerate
Dwarvish linguistic ability. Though devised by the Sindar (owing to
their enmity with the Dwarves of Nogrod and Belegost) it is probable
(and was held true by the Noldor) that the idea of runes cut in stone
etc. was derived ultimately from the Dwarves who had friendship
with the sons of Fëanor.

NOTES

1 Cf. LR:1117.

2 Cf. *The Hobbit* chap. III.

XX

NOTE ON THE DWARF ROAD

This typescript text, located in Tolkien's linguistic papers, is associated with but now separated from the late text, *The Disaster of the Gladden Fields* (UT:271–87).[1] It is typed on the verso of a sheet of a printed Allen & Unwin publication notice dated 1968. An apparently later version was paraphrased and partially quoted at UT:280–1 n.14, but this draft gives additional details on the history of the Dwarf Road. In the *UT* text there is no indication that the Dwarf Road extended south to Moria, but instead it descends from the Pass of Imladris.

The Dwarf Road, *Menn-i-Naugrim* had been made with great labour by the Longbeard Dwarves of Moria and their kin in the Iron Hills (Emyn Engrin) in the North-east.[2] The Dwarves of Moria had made a road from their gates north along the east skirts of the Misty Mountains, over the upper course of the Gladden, and so to the lowest point at which the Anduin could be bridged, somewhat above the beginning of its sudden descent. There they built a stone-bridge from which the Dwarf Road ran, straight and due east, across the vale and through the Forest to a bridge across the Celduin (River Running) made by the Dwarves of the Iron Hills, whence it ran on over open land, north-east to their iron mines.[3]

The making of the bridges and the first miles of the road through the forest was work of the First Age; the road was completed early in the Second Age when the population of Moria (and to a less extent also of the Iron Mines) was much increased by emigrants from the mansions in the Ered Luin. There was great traffic on the road in those days, until the forging of the Great Ring and the war between

Sauron and the Elves and their Númenórean allies, in which the Dwarves of Moria became involved because of their close friendship with the Noldor of Eregion. Sauron's power was however not full grown, and was far to the south and east. He invaded Eriador from the south and did not greatly trouble the north-lands.

NOTES

1 The paragraph preceding this passage corresponds to the opening paragraph of what became n.14 of the *Disaster* (UT:280). Here however it is numbered as note 10.

2 As first typed, the name (and translation) of the Dwarf Road was *Menn-i-Nyrn* (lit. 'Road of the Dwarves').

3 This paragraph was at some point struck through twice, lightly.

XXI

FROM *THE HUNT FOR THE RING*

This text, written in a clear hand in brown nib-pen, is associated with the mass of writings that Christopher Tolkien published as *The Hunt for the Ring* in *Unfinished Tales*, and describes as being "written after the publication of the first volume [of *The Lord of the Rings*] but before that of the third" (UT:11). Cf. LR:1091. The two Nazgûl involved are distinguished here as "E" (elsewhere identified as Khamûl, UT:348) and "F".

Sat. Sept. 24 [3018]. (Gandalf speeds across Enedwaith.) E picks up the Stock Road and overtakes Frodo at approaches to Woody End – probably by accident; he becomes uneasily aware of the Ring, but is hesitant and uncertain because of the bright sun. He turns into the woods and waits for night. After dark, becoming acutely aware of the Ring, he goes in pursuit; but is daunted by the sudden appearance of the Elves and the song of Elbereth.[1] While Frodo is surrounded by the Elves he cannot perceive the Ring clearly.

Sun. 25th. As soon as the Elves depart he renewed his hunt, and reaching the ridge above Woodhall is aware that the Ring has been there. Failing to find the Bearer and feeling that he is drawing away, E summons F by cries. E is aware of the general direction that the Ring has taken, but not knowing of Frodo's rest in the wood, and believing him to have made straight eastwards, he and F ride over the fields. They visit Maggot while Frodo is still under the trees. E then makes a mistake (probably because he imagines the Ringbearer as some mighty man, strong and swift): he does not lurk near the farm, but sends F *down* the Causeway towards Overbourn, while he goes north along it towards the Bridge. They tryst to return and meet one another at night; but do so just too late. F joins him soon after.

E is now well aware that the Ring has crossed the river; but the river is a barrier to his sense of movement. Also E and F (and all the Nazgûl) hate water; and they will not touch the Baranduin: its waters were to them "elvish", for it rose in Nenuial, which the Elves still controlled. (Frodo spends night at Crickhollow; Gandalf is drawing near to Tharbad.)

NOTES

1 Cf. LR:79ff.

XXII

THE RIVERS AND BEACON-HILLS OF GONDOR

This text has been previously published in *Vinyar Tengwar* 42 (2001). I describe and present it here much as I did in *VT*, though I have reduced considerably the more strictly linguistic and etymological content and (my own) commentary, without indication, and updated the editorial cross-references to *The Lord of the Rings* to match the current standard edition (which has continuous page-numbering).

This historical and etymological essay, titled only "*Nomenclature*" by its author, belongs with other, similar writings that Christopher Tolkien has dated to c. 1967–9 (XII:293–4) – including *Of Dwarves and Men*, *The Shibboleth of Fëanor*, and *The History of Galadriel and Celeborn* – and that were published, in whole or in part, in *Unfinished Tales* and *The Peoples of Middle-earth*. Indeed, Christopher Tolkien gave numerous excerpts from this essay as well in *Unfinished Tales*. He prepared a fuller presentation of the text for *The Peoples of Middle-earth*, but it was omitted from that volume on consideration of length. Christopher kindly provided me with both the full text of the essay and of his own edited version intended for *The Peoples of Middle-earth*. I have retained, with his gracious consent, as much of Christopher's own commentary as practicable, clearly identified as such throughout, while providing some additional commentary and notes of my own.

The essay consists of thirteen typescript pages, numbered 1 to 13 by Tolkien. A torn, unnumbered half-sheet bearing a manuscript note headed "*Far too complicated*" (amidst and referring to a lengthy, discursive discussion of the Eldarin number system, in particular the explanation of the numeral 5) was placed between pages 8 and 9 of the typescript. Another unnumbered sheet follows the last page of the typescript, bearing a manuscript note on the name *Belfalas* (which is paraphrased at UT:247). All of these sheets are various forms of printed Allen & Unwin notices, with Tolkien's writing confined to the blank sides, except in the case of the last sheet. Here, the printed side was used for manuscript drafting of Cirion's Oath in Quenya (already very near to the published version; cf. UT:305), which was continued on the top (relative to the printing) of the blank side. The note on *Belfalas* is written upside-down beginning at the bottom of the sheet (with respect to this drafting and the printing).

Concerning the origin and date of this essay, Christopher Tolkien writes: "On 30 June 1969 my father wrote a letter to Mr Paul Bibire, who had written to him a week before, telling him that he had passed the Bachelor of Philosophy examination in Old English at Oxford: he referred a little disparagingly to his success, achieved despite neglect of certain parts of the course which he found less appealing, and notably the works of the Old English poet Cynewulf (see *Sauron Defeated*, p. 285 note 36). At the end of his letter Mr Bibire said: 'Incidentally, there's something that I've been wondering about since I saw the relevant addition to the second edition [of *The Lord of the Rings*]: whether the River Glanduin is the same as the Swan-fleet' (for the reference see *Sauron Defeated*, p. 70 and note 15)." Christopher Tolkien has provided the relevant portions of his father's reply (which was not included in the collection of letters edited with Humphrey Carpenter):

It was kind of you to write to me again. I was very interested in your news of yourself, and very sympathetic. I found and find dear Cynewulf a lamentable bore – lamentable, because it is a matter for tears that a man (or men) with talent in word-spinning, who must have heard (or read) so much now lost, should spend their time composing such uninspired stuff.[1] Also at more than one point in my life I have endangered my prospects by neglecting things that I did not at that time find amusing! ...

I am grateful to you for pointing out the use of *Glanduin* in the Appendix A, III, p. 319.[2] I have no index of the Appendices and must get one made. The Glanduin is the same river as the Swanfleet, but the names are not related. I find on the map with corrections that are to be made for the new edition to appear at the end of this year that this river is marked by me as both Glanduin and various compounds with *alph* 'swan'.[3] The name *Glanduin* was meant to be 'border-river', a name given as far back as the Second Age when it was the southern border of Eregion, beyond which were the unfriendly people of Dunland. In the earlier centuries of the Two Kingdoms *Enedwaith* (Middle-folk) was a region between the realm of Gondor and the slowly receding realm of Arnor (it originally included Minhiriath (Mesopotamia)). Both kingdoms shared an interest in the region, but were mainly concerned with the upkeep of the great road that was their main way of communication except by sea, and the bridge at Tharbad. People of Númenórean origin did not live there, except at Tharbad, where a large garrison of soldiers and river-wardens was once maintained. In those days there were drainage works, and the banks of the Hoarwell and Greyflood were strengthened. But in the days of *The Lord of the Rings* the region had long become ruinous and lapsed into its primitive state: a slow wide river running through a network of swamps, pools and eyots: the haunt of hosts of swans and other water-birds.

If the name Glanduin was still remembered it would apply only to the upper course where the river ran down swiftly, but was soon lost in the plains and disappeared into the fens. I think I may keep Glanduin on the map for the upper part, and mark the lower part as fenlands with the name *Nîn-in-Eilph* (water-lands of the Swans), which will adequately explain Swanfleet river, III.263.[4]

alph 'swan' occurs as far as I remember only on III, p. 392.[5] It could not be Quenya, as *ph* is not used in my transcription of Quenya, and Quenya does not tolerate final consonants other than the dentals, *t*, *n*, *l*, *r* after a vowel.[6] Quenya for 'swan' was *alqua (alkwā)*. The "Celtic" branch of Eldarin (Telerin and Sindarin) turned *kw* > *p*, but did not, as Celtic did, alter original *p*. The much changed Sindarin of Middle-earth turned the stops to spirants after *l*, *r*, as did Welsh: so *⋆alkwā* > *alpa* (Telerin) > S. *alf* (spelt alph in my transcription).[7]

At the end of the letter Tolkien added a postscript:

I am myself much recovered – though it has taken a year, which I could ill afford.[8] I can walk about fairly normally now, up to two miles or so (occasionally), and have some energy. But not enough to cope with both continued composition and the endless "escalation" of my business.

At the head of the present essay, Tolkien wrote "*Nomenclature*", followed by: "Swanfleet river (L.R. rev. edition, III 263) and *Glanduin*, III App. A. 319"; and then by: "Queried by P. Bibire (letter June 23, 1969; ans. June 30). As more briefly stated in my reply: *Glanduin* means 'border-river'." The essay is thus seen to have arisen as an expansion and elaboration of the remarks in his reply.

The names of the Rivers

The essay begins with the lengthy excerpt and author's note given at UT:264–5 (and so not reproduced here). A few variances between the published text and the typescript are noteworthy: where the published text has *Enedwaith* the typescript reads *Enedhwaith* (this was an editorial change made in all excerpts from this essay containing the name in *Unfinished Tales*; cf. XII:328–9 n.66); and where the published text has *Ethraid Engrin*, the typescript has *Ethraid Engren*. In addition, a sentence referring to the ancient port called Lond Daer Enedh was omitted before the last sentence of the author's note on UT:264; it reads: "It was the main entry for the Númenóreans in the War against Sauron (Second Age 1693–1701)" (cf. LR:1083; and UT:239, 261–5). Also, against the discussion of the approach to Tharbad that closes the first paragraph on UT:264, Tolkien provided the cross-reference "I 287, 390".[9]

Tolkien then comments: "The names of the Rivers give some trouble; they were made up in a hurry without sufficient consideration", before embarking upon a consideration of each name in turn. Significant portions of this section of the essay have been given in *Unfinished Tales*. Extended passages are not repeated here, but their places in the essay are indicated.

Adorn

This is not on the map, but is given as the name of the short river flowing into the Isen[10] from the west of Ered Nimrais in App. A, III 346.[11] It is, as would be expected in any name in the region not of Rohanese origin, of a form suitable to Sindarin; but it is not interpretable in Sindarin. It must be supposed to be of Pre-Númenórean origin adapted to Sindarin.[12]

Of this entry, Christopher Tolkien notes: "On the absence of the name on the map – referring of course to my original map to *The*

Lord of the Rings, which was replaced long after by the redrawing made to accompany *Unfinished Tales* – see UT:261–2, footnote."

Gwathló

Of the next entry, headed "*Gwathlo (ló)*", Christopher Tolkien writes: "The long discussion arising from this name is found in UT:261–3, with the passage concerning the Púkel-men removed and cited in the section on the Drúedain, UT:383–4. In the latter passage the sentence 'Maybe even in the days of the War of the Ring some of the Drú-folk lingered in the mountains of Andrast, the western outlier of the White Mountains' contains an editorial change: the original text has 'the mountains of Angast (Long Cape)', and the form *Angast* occurs again more than once in the essay. This change was based on the form *Andrast* communicated by my father to Pauline Baynes for inclusion, with other new names, on her decorated map of Middle-earth; see UT:261, footnote."[13] A further editorial change may be noted: where the published text has *Lefnui* (UT:263, repeated in the extracted note on Púkel-men, UT:383) the typescript reads *Levnui*; cf. the entry for *Levnui* below.

An unused note against "the great promontory ... that formed the north arm of the Bay of Belfalas" (*ibid.*) reads: "Afterwards called still *Drúwaith (Iaur)* '(Old) Púkel-land', and its dark woods were little visited, nor considered as part of the realm of Gondor." Also, a sentence struck through by Tolkien, following "huge trees ... under which the boats of the adventurers crept silently up into the unknown land", (UT:263), reads: "It is said that some even on this first expedition came as far as the great fenlands before they returned, fearing to become bewildered in their mazes."

The discussion originally continued with the following etymological note, struck through at the same time as the deleted sentence:

The element -*ló* was also of Common Eldarin origin, derived from a base *(s)log*: in Common Eldarin *sloga* had been a word used for streams of a kind that were variable and liable to overflow their banks at seasons and cause floods when swollen by rains or melting snow; especially such as the Glanduin (described above) that had their sources in mountains and fell at first swiftly, but were halted in the lower lands and flats.

The deleted passage was replaced with that given at UT:263 starting at "So the first name they gave to it was 'River of Shadow', *Gwath-hîr, Gwathir*". It may be noted that the word *lô* in this passage was corrected on the typescript from *lhô*. A note on the name *Ringló*, omitted from the passage in *Unfinished Tales*, occurs after the words "*Gwathló*, the shadowy river from the fens". For this note, and its development, see the entry for *Ringló* below. After this note, an etymological statement intervenes before the last full paragraph of the excerpt published in *Unfinished Tales*:

Gwath was a common Sindarin word for 'shadow' or dim light – not for the shadows of actual objects or persons cast by sun or moon or other lights: these were called *morchaint* 'dark-shapes'.

Erui

Though this was the first of the Rivers of Gondor it cannot be used for 'first'. In Eldarin *er* was not used in counting in series: it meant 'one, single, alone'. *erui* is not the usual Sindarin for 'single, alone': that was *ereb* (< *erikwa*; cf. Q. *erinqua*); but it has the very common adjectival ending *–ui* of Sindarin. The name must have been given because of the Rivers of Gondor it was the shortest and swiftest and was the only one without a tributary.

Serni

Christopher Tolkien writes: "The statement about this name is given in the Index to *Unfinished Tales*, but with a misprint that has never been corrected: the Sindarin word meaning 'pebble' is *sarn*, not *sern*." The opening sentence reads: "An adjectival formation from S. *sarn* 'small stone, pebble' (as described above), or a collective, the equivalent of Q. *sarnie* (*sarniye*) 'shingle, pebble-bank'." An unused sentence, occurring before "Its mouth was blocked with shingles", reads: "It was the only one of the five to fall into the delta of the Anduin."

Sirith

This means simply 'a flowing': cf. *tirith* 'watching, guarding' from the stem *tir-* 'to watch'.

Celos

> Christopher Tolkien writes: "The statement about this name is given in the Index to *Unfinished Tales*. On the erroneous marking of Celos on my redrawn map of *The Lord of the Rings*, see VII:322 n. 9."

Gilrain

> A significant portion of the remarks on this river name was given in UT:242–5; but the discussion begins with a passage omitted from *Unfinished Tales:*

This resembles the name of Aragorn's mother, *Gilraen*; but unless it is misspelt must have had a different meaning. (Originally the difference between correct Sindarin *ae* and *ai* was neglected, *ai* more usual in English being used for both in the general narrative. So *Dairon*, now corrected, for *Daeron* a derivative of S. *daer* 'large, great': C.E. *daira* < base DAY; not found in Quenya. So *Hithaiglir* on map for *Hithaeglir* and *Aiglos* [for *Aeglos*].)[14] The element *gil-* in both is no doubt S. *gil* 'spark, twinkle of light, star', often used of the stars of heaven in place of the older and more elevated *el-, elen-* stem. (Similarly *tinwë* 'spark' was also used in Quenya). The meaning of *Gilraen* as a woman's name is not in doubt. It meant 'one adorned with a tressure set with small gems in its network', such as the tressure of Arwen described in L.R. I 239.[15] It may have been a second name given to her after she had come to womanhood, which as often happened in legends had replaced her true name, no longer recorded. More likely, it was her true name, since it had become a name given to women of her people, the remnants of the Númenóreans of the North Kingdom of unmingled blood. The women of the Eldar were accustomed to wear such tressures; but among other peoples they were used only by women of high rank among the "Rangers", descendants of Elros, as they claimed. Names such as *Gilraen*, and others of similar meaning, would thus be likely to become first names given to maid-children of the kindred of the "Lords of the Dúnedain". The element *raen* was the Sindarin form of Q. *raina* 'netted, enlaced'.

> In an accompanying etymological note Tolkien provides this detail regarding S. *raen*, Q. *raina*:

C.E. base RAY 'net, knit, contrive network or lace'; also [*deleted*: 'catch',] 'involve in a network, enlace'.... The word was only applied to work with a single thread; weaving with cross-threads or withes was represented by the distinct base WIG.

Of this note Christopher Tolkien writes: "*Tressure*, a net for confining the hair, is a word of medieval English which my father had used in his translation of *Sir Gawain and the Green Knight* (stanza 69): 'the clear jewels / that were twined in her tressure by twenties in clusters', where the original has the form *tressour*."

The entry then continues:

In *Gilrain* the element -*rain* though similar was distinct in origin. Probably it was derived from base RAN 'wander, stray, go on uncertain course', the equivalent of Q. *ranya*. This would not seem suitable to any of the rivers of Gondor....

The portion given in *Unfinished Tales* begins here (p. 242). The final sentence of the first extract from the discussion of *Gilrain* in UT:243 omits the ending; the whole sentence reads: "This legend [of Nimrodel] was well-known in the Dor-en-Ernil (Land of the Prince) and no doubt the name [*Gilrain*] was given in memory of it, or rendered in Elvish form from an older name of the same meaning." Also omitted was the paragraph following this sentence, which reads: "The flight of Nimrodel was dated by the chronologists at Third Age 1981. An error in Appendix B appears at this point. The correct entry read (still in 1963): 'The Dwarves flee from Moria. Many of the Silvan Elves of Lórien flee south. Amroth and Nimrodel are lost.' In subsequent editions or reprints 'flee from Moria....' to 'Silvan Elves' has been for reasons unknown omitted." The correct reading of this entry has been restored in later editions (LR:1087). In addition, the first sentence of the following paragraph, introducing the passage with which the extract given in *Unfinished Tales* resumes (p. 243), reads: "At that time Amroth was, in the legend, named as King of Lórien. How this fits with the rule of Galadriel and Celeborn will be made clear in a precis of the history of Galadriel and Celeborn." Finally, the last sentence of the last paragraph given on UT:244 was omitted; it reads: "Communication was maintained constantly with Lórien."

A typescript note appended after the first sentence on UT:245, against the phrase "the sorrows of Lórien, which was now left without a ruler", and subsequently struck through by Tolkien, reads:

Amroth had never taken a wife. For long years he had loved Nimrodel, but had sought her love in vain. She was of Silvan race and did
not love the Incomers, who (she said) brought wars and destroyed
the peace of old. She would speak only the Silvan Tongue, even after
it had fallen into disuse among most of the people. But when the
terror came out of Moria she fled away distraught, and Amroth followed her. He found her near the eaves of Fangorn (which in those
days drew much nearer to Lórien). She dared not enter that wood,
for the trees (she said) menaced her, and some moved to bar her
way. There they had long converse; and in the end they plighted their
troth, for Amroth vowed that for her sake he would leave his people
even in their time of need and with her seek for a refuge of peace.
'But there is no such"

> The deleted note ends here, in mid-sentence. As Christopher
> Tolkien notes (UT:242), this passage is the germ of the version of
> the legend of Amroth and Nimrodel given in UT:240–2.
>   The discussion of *Gilrain* concludes (following the first para-
> graph given on UT:245) with this note:

The river *Gilrain* if related to the legend of Nimrodel must contain
an element derived from C.E. RAN 'wander, stray, meander'. Cf. Q.
ranya 'erratic wandering', S. *rein, rain*. Cf. S. *randir* 'wanderer' in
Mithrandir, Q. *Rána* name of the spirit (Máya) that was said to abide
in the Moon as its guardian.

Ciril, Kiril

Uncertain, but probably from KIR 'cut'. It rose in Lamedon and
flowed westward for some way in a deep rocky channel.

Ringló

For the element *-ló* see discussion of *Gwathló* above. But there is no
record of any swamps or marsh in its course. It was a swift (and cold)
river, as the element *ring-* ['cold'] implies. It drew its first waters from
a high snowfield that fed an icy tarn in the mountains. If this at
seasons of snowmelting spread into a shallow lake, it would account
for the name, another of the many that refer to a river's source.

> Cf. the entry *Ringló* in the index to *Unfinished Tales*. This explana-
> tion of the name *Ringló* only arose in the course of the writing of

this essay; for in the discussion of *Gwathló* that Tolkien struck out he had originally added this note:

It the element *ló*] appears also in the name *Ringló*, the fourth of the Rivers of Gondor. It may be translated *Chillflood*. Coming down cold from the snows of the White Mountains in swift course, after its meeting with the Ciril and later with the Morthond it formed considerable marshes before it reached the sea, though these were very small compared with the fens of the Swanfleet (Nîn-in-Eilph) about Tharbad.

In the revised discussion of *Gwathló* (UT:263) this note was replaced by the following:

A similar name is found in *Ringló*, the fourth of the rivers of Gondor. Named as several other rivers, such as Mitheithel and Morthond (black-root), after its source *Ringnen* 'chill-water', it was later called *Ringló*, since it formed a fenland about its confluence with the Morthond, though this was very small compared with the Great Fen (*Lô Dhaer*) of the Gwathló.

Tolkien then struck out the latter part of this note (from "since it formed a fenland" through the end), replacing it with a direction to see the final explanation of *Ringló* given above, in which the element *lô* is not derived from fenlands near the coast ("there is no record of any swamps or marsh in its course") but from the lake that formed at the river's source "at seasons of snowmelting" in the mountains.

Morthond

Similarly the *Morthond* 'Black-root', which rose in a dark valley in the mountains due south of Edoras, called *Mornan* ['dark valley'], not only because of the shadow of the two high mountains between which it lay, but because through it passed the road from the Gate of the Dead Men, and living men did not go there.

Levnui

There were no other rivers in this region, "further Gondor," until one came to the *Levnui*, the longest and widest of the Five. This was held to be the boundary of Gondor in this direction; for beyond it lay the promontory of Angast and the wilderness of 'Old Púkel-land'

(Drúwaith Iaur) which the Númenóreans had never attempted to occupy with permanent settlements, though they maintained a Coast-guard force and beacons at the end of Cape Angast.

Levnui is said to mean 'fifth' (after Erui, Sirith, Serni, Morthond), but its form offers difficulties. (It is spelt *Lefnui* on the Map; and that is preferable. For though in the Appendices *f* is said to have the sound of English *f* except when standing at the end of a word,[16] voiceless *f* does not in fact occur medially before consonants (in uncompounded words or names) in Sindarin; while *v* is avoided before consonants in English).[17] The difficulty is only apparent.

Tolkien then immediately embarks on a long, elaborate, and complex discussion of the Eldarin numerals. Following this discussion, Tolkien (continuing westward on the map from Levnui) reintroduced the name *Adorn*, and repeated the substance of his earlier remarks: "This river, flowing from the West of Ered Nimrais into the River Isen, is fitted in style to Sindarin, but has no meaning in that language, and probably is derived from one of the languages spoken in this region before the occupation of Gondor by Númenóreans, which began long before the Downfall." He then continued:

Several other names in Gondor are apparently of similar origin. The element *Bel-* in *Belfalas* has no suitable meaning in Sindarin. *Falas* (Q. *falasse*) meant 'shore' – especially one exposed to great waves and breakers (cf. Q. *falma* 'a wave-crest, wave'). It is possible that *Bel* had a similar sense in an alien tongue, and *Bel-falas* is an example of the type of place-name, not uncommon when a region is occupied by a new people, in which two elements of much the same topographical meaning are joined: the first being in the older and the second in the incoming language.[18] Probably because the first was taken by the Incomers as a particular name. However, in Gondor the shore-land from the mouth of Anduin to Dol Amroth was called *Belfalas*, but actually usually referred to as *i·Falas* 'the surf-beach' (or sometimes as *Then-falas* 'short beach', in contrast to *An-falas* 'long beach', between the mouths of Morthond and Levnui). But the great bay between Umbar and Angast (the Long Cape, beyond Levnui) was called the Bay of Belfalas (*Côf Belfalas*) or simply of Bel (*Côf gwaeren Bêl* 'the windy Bay of Bêl'). So that it is more probable that Bêl was the name or part of the name of the region afterward usually called *Dor-en-Ernil* 'land of the Prince': it was perhaps the most important part of Gondor before the Númenórean settlement.

Christopher Tolkien writes: "With 'the windy Bay of Bêl' cf. the
poem *The Man in the Moon came down too soon* in *The Adventures of
Tom Bombadil* (1962), where the Man in the Moon fell 'to a foaming
bath in the windy Bay of Bel', identified as Belfalas in the preface to
the book. – This passage was struck through, presumably at once,
since the next paragraph begins again 'Several other names in
Gondor are apparently of similar origin'. A page of rapid manuscript found with the typescript essay shows my father sketching an
entirely different origin for the element *Bel*. I have referred to this
text and cited it in part in *Unfinished Tales* (p. 247), observing that it
represents an altogether different conception of the establishment of
the Elvish haven (*Edhellond*) north of Dol Amroth from that given
in *Of Dwarves and Men* (XII:313 and 329 n.67), where it is said that
it owed its existence to 'seafaring Sindar from the west havens of
Beleriand who fled in three small ships when the power of Morgoth
overwhelmed the Eldar and the Atani'. The manuscript page obviously belongs to the same very late period as the essay, as is seen
both from the paper on which it is written and from the fact that the
same page carries drafting for the Oath of Cirion in Quenya
(UT:305)." This manuscript page is given here in full:

Belfalas. This is a special case. *Bel-* is certainly an element derived
from a pre-Númenórean name; but its source is known, and was in
fact Sindarin. The regions of Gondor had a complex history in the
remote past, so far as their population was concerned, and the
Númenóreans evidently found many layers of mixed peoples, and
numerous islands of isolated folk either clinging to old dwellings, or
in mountain-refuges from invaders.* But there was one small (but
important) element in Gondor of quite exceptional kind: an Eldarin
settlement.[19] Little is known of its history until shortly before it disappeared; for the Eldarin Elves, whether Exiled Noldor or
long-rooted Sindar, remained in Beleriand until its desolation in the
Great War against Morgoth; and then if they did not take sail over
Sea wandered westward [*sic*; read "eastward"] in Eriador. There,
especially near the Hithaeglir (on either side), they found scattered
settlements of the *Nandor*, Telerin Elves who had in the First Age
never completed the journey to the shores of the Sea; but both sides
recognized their kinship as Eldar. There appears, however, in the
beginning of the Second Age, to have been a group of Sindar who

---

* Though none of the regions of the Two Kingdoms were before (or after!) the
Númenórean settlements densely populated as we should reckon it.

went south. They were a remnant, it seems, of the people of Doriath, who harboured still their grudge against the Noldor and left the Grey Havens because these and all the ships there were commanded by Círdan (a Noldo). Having learned the craft of shipbuilding* they went in the course of years seeking a place for havens of their own. At last they settled at the mouth of the Morthond. There was already a primitive harbour there of fisher-folk; but these in fear of the Eldar fled into the mountains. The land between Morthond and Serni (the shoreward parts of Dor-en-Ernil)

> The manuscript page ends mid-sentence, and without reaching an explanation of the element *Bel-*. Christopher Tolkien writes: "It was perhaps a purely experimental extension of the history, at once abandoned; but the assertion that Círdan was a Noldo is very strange. This runs clean counter to the entire tradition concerning him – yet it is essential to the idea sketched in this passage. Possibly it was his realization of this that led my father to abandon it in mid-sentence."

> The typescript resumes with a replacement of the rejected passage on *Belfalas* (and now avoiding discussion of that problematic name):

Several other names in Gondor are apparently of similar origin. *Lamedon* has no meaning in Sindarin (if it was Sindarin it would be referred to **lambeton-*, **lambetân-*, but C.E. *lambe-* 'language' can hardly be concerned). *Arnach* is not Sindarin. It may be connected with Arnen on the east side of Anduin. Arnach was applied to the valleys in the south of the mountains and their foothills between Celos and Erui. There were many rocky outcrops there, but hardly more than in the higher valleys of Gondor generally. Arnen was a rock outlier of the Ephel Dúath, round which the Anduin, south of Minas Tirith, made a wide bend.

Suggestions of the historians of Gondor that *arn-* is an element in some pre-Númenórean language meaning 'rock' is merely a guess.[20] More probable is the view of the author (unknown) of the fragmentarily preserved *Ondonórë Nómesseron Minapurië* ('Enquiry into the Place-names of Gondor'). On internal evidence he lived as far back as the reign of Meneldil, son of Anárion – no events later

---

* All Elves were naturally skilled in making boats, but the craft that were to make a long voyage over Sea, perilous even to Elven-craft until Middle-earth was far behind, required more skill and knowledge.

than that reign are mentioned – when memories and records of the early days of the settlements now lost were still available, and the process of naming was still going on. He points out that Sindarin was not well-known to many of the settlers who gave the names, mariners, soldiers, and emigrants, though all aspired to have some knowledge of it. Gondor was certainly occupied from its beginning by the Faithful, men of the Elf-friend party and their followers; and these in revolt against the "Adunaic" Kings who forbade the use of the Elvish tongues gave all new names in the new realm in Sindarin, or adapted older names to the manner of Sindarin. They also renewed and encouraged the study of Quenya, in which important documents, titles, and formulas were composed. But mistakes were likely to be made.[21] Once a name had become current it was accepted by the rulers and organizers. He thinks therefore that *Arnen* originally was intended to mean 'beside the water', sc. Anduin; but *ar-* in this sense is Quenya, not Sindarin. Though since in the full name *Emyn Arnen* the *Emyn* is Sindarin plural of *Amon* 'hill', *Arnen* cannot be a Sindarin adjective, since an adjective of such shape would have a Sindarin plural *ernain*, or *ernin*. The name must therefore have meant 'the hills of Arnen'. It is now forgotten, but it can be seen from old records that *Arnen* was the older name of the greater part of the region later called *Ithilien*. This was given to the narrow land between the Anduin and the Ephel Dúath, primarily to the part between Cair Andros and the southern end of the bend of Anduin, but vaguely extended north to the Nindalf and south towards the Poros. For when Elendil took as his dwelling the North Kingdom, owing to his friendship with the Eldar, and committed the South Kingdom to his sons, they divided it so, as is said in ancient annals: "Isildur took as his own land all the region of Arnen; but Anárion took the land from Erui to Mount Mindolluin and thence westward to the North Wood" (later in Rohan called the Firien Wood), "but Gondor south of Ered Nimrais they held in common."

Arnach, if the above explanation is accepted, is not then related to *Arnen*. Its origin and source are in that case now lost. It was generally called in Gondor *Lossarnach*. *Loss* is Sindarin for 'snow', especially fallen and long-lying snow. For what reason this was prefixed to Arnach is unclear. Its upper valleys were renowned for their flowers, and below them there were great orchards, from which at the time of the War of the Ring much of the fruit needed in Minas Tirith still came. Though no mention of this is found in any chronicles – as is often the case with matters of common knowledge – it seems probable that the reference was in fact to the fruit blossom. Expeditions to Lossarnach to see the flowers and trees were frequently made by the people of Minas Tirith. (See index Lossarnach, Imloth Melui 'sweet flower-valley', a place in Arnach.) This use of 'snow' would be specially likely in Sindarin, in which the words for fallen snow and flower were much alike, though different in origin: *loss* and *loth*, [the latter] meaning 'inflorescence, a head of small flowers'. *Loth* is actually most often used collectively in Sindarin, equivalent to *goloth*; and a single flower denoted by *elloth* (*er-loth*) or *lotheg*.

The names of the Beacon hills

The full beacon system, that was still operating in the War of the Ring, can have been no older than the settlement of the Rohirrim in Calenardhon about 500 years before; for its principal function was to warn the Rohirrim that Gondor was in danger or (more rarely) the reverse. How old the names then used were cannot be said. The beacons were set on hills or on the high ends of ridges running out from the mountains, but some were not very notable objects.

> The first part of this statement was cited in the section *Cirion and Eorl* in UT:315 n.35.

Amon Dîn

> This entry is given in full in UT:319 n.51 (last paragraph).

Eilenach and Eilenaer

> This entry is given in the same note in *Unfinished Tales*, but in this case slightly reduced. In the original the passage begins:

Eilenach (better spelt *Eilienach*). Probably an alien name; not Sindarin, Númenórean, or Common Speech. In true Sindarin *eilen* could only be derived from **elyen*, **alyen*, and would normally be written *eilien*. This and *Eilenaer* (older name of Halifirien: see that below) are the only names of this group that are certainly pre-Númenórean. They are evidently related. Both were notable features.

> The name and parenthetical note on *Eilenaer* entered here, as alterations to the typescript. Christopher Tolkien writes: "The name *Eilenaer* does not in fact occur in the account of Halifirien in this

essay: my father intended to introduce it, but before he did so he rejected that account in its entirety, as will be seen." At the end of the description of Eilenach and Nardol as given in *Unfinished Tales*, where it is said that the fire on Nardol could be seen from Halifirien, Tolkien added a note:

The line of beacons from Nardol to Halifirien lay in a shallow curve bending a little southward, so that the three intervening beacons did not cut off the view.

There follow statements concerning Erelas and Calenhad, elements of which were used in the index to *Unfinished Tales*.

Erelas

Erelas was a small beacon, as also was *Calenhad*. These were not always lit; their lighting as in *The Lord of the Rings* was a signal of great urgency. *Erelas* is Sindarin in style, but has no suitable meaning in that language. It was a green hill without trees, so that neither *er* 'single' nor *las(s)* 'leaf' seem applicable.

Calenhad

Calenhad was similar but rather larger and higher. *Calen* was the usual word in Sindarin for 'green' (its older sense was 'bright', Q. *kalina*). *-had* appears to be for *sad* (with usual mutation in combinations); if not misspelt this is from SAT 'space, place, sc. a limited area naturally or artificially defined' (also applied to recognized periods or divisions of time), 'divide, mark off', seen in S. *sad* 'a limited area naturally or artificially defined, a place, spot', etc. (also *sant* 'a garden, field, yard, or other place in private ownership, whether enclosed or not'). *Calenhad* would thus mean simply 'green space', applied to the flat turf-covered crown of the hill. But *had* may stand for S. *-hadh* (the maps do not use *dh*, but this is the only case where *dh* might be involved, except *Caradhras* which is omitted, and *Enedhwaith* which is misspelt *ened*).[22] *-hadh* would then be for *sadh* (in isolated use *sâdh*) 'sward, turf' – base SAD 'strip, flay, peel off', etc.[23]

Halifirien

> The essay ends (unfinished) with a long and notable discussion of the Halifirien; Tolkien's interspersed notes are collected together at the end of this discussion. With this account cf. UT:300–1, 303–5.

Halifirien is a name in the language of Rohan. It was a mountain with easy approach to its summit. Down its northern slopes grew the great wood called in Rohan the Firien Wood. This became dense in lower ground, westward along the Mering Stream and northwards out into the moist plain through which the Stream flowed into the Entwash. The great West Road passed through a long ride or clearing through the wood, to avoid the wet land beyond its eaves. The name Halifirien (modernized in spelling for *Háligfirgen*) meant Holy Mountain. The older name in Sindarin had been *Fornarthan* 'North Beacon'; the wood had been called *Eryn Fuir* 'North Wood'. The reason for the Rohan name is not now known for certain. The mountain was regarded with reverence by the Rohirrim; but according to their traditions at the time of the War of the Ring that was because it was on its summit that Eorl the Young met Cirion, Steward of Gondor; and there when they had looked forth over the land they fixed the bounds of the realm of Eorl, and Eorl swore to Cirion the Oath of Eorl – "the unbroken oath" – of perpetual friendship and alliance with Gondor. Since in oaths of the greatest solemnity the names of the Valar were invoked* [24] – and though the oath was called "the Oath of Eorl" in Rohan it was also called "the Oath of Cirion" (for Gondor was equally pledged to aid Rohan) and he would use solemn terms in his own tongue – this might be sufficient to hallow the spot.

But the account in annals contains two remarkable details: that there was at the place where Cirion and Eorl stood what appeared to be an ancient monument of rough stones nearly man-high with a flat top; and that on this occasion Cirion to the wonder of many invoked the One (that is God). His exact words are not recorded, [25] but they probably took the form of allusive terms such as Faramir used in explaining to Frodo the content of the unspoken "grace" (before communal meals)[26] that was a Númenórean ritual, e.g. "These words shall stand by the faith of the heirs of the Downfallen in the keeping of the Thrones of the West and of that which is above all Thrones for ever."

---

* Cf. the Coronation of Aragorn.

This would in effect hallow the spot for as long as the Númenórean realms endured, and was no doubt intended to do so, being not in any way an attempt to *restore* the worship of the One on the Meneltarma ('pillar of heaven'), the central mountain of Númenor,[*] but a reminder of it, and of the claim made by "the heirs of Elendil" that since they had never wavered in their allegiance they[†] were still permitted to address the One in thought and prayer direct.

The "ancient monument" – by which was evidently meant a structure made before the coming of the Númenóreans – is a curious feature, but is no support to the view that the mountain was already in some sense "hallowed" before its use in the oath-taking. Had it been regarded as of "religious" significance it would in fact have made this use impossible, unless it had at least been completely destroyed first.[‡] [27] For a religious structure that was "ancient" could only have been erected by the Men of Darkness, corrupted by Morgoth or his servant Sauron. The Middle Men, descendants of the ancestors of the Númenóreans, were not regarded as evil nor inevitable enemies of Gondor. Nothing is recorded of their religion or religious practices before they came in contact with the Númenóreans,[§] and those who became associated or fused with the Númenóreans adopted their customs and beliefs (included in the "lore" which Faramir speaks of as being learned by the Rohirrim). The "ancient monument" can thus not have been made by the Rohirrim, or honoured by them as sacred, since they had not yet

---

[*] That would have been regarded as sacrilegious.

[†] And, as was generally believed by their rulers, all who accepted their leadership and received their instruction. See next note.

[‡] For the Númenórean view of the previous inhabitants see Faramir's conversation with Frodo, especially II 287 [i.e. LR:678–9]. The Rohirrim were according to his classification *Middle Men*, and their importance to Gondor in his time is chiefly in mind and modifies his account; the description of the various men of the southern "fiefs" of Gondor, who were mainly of non-Númenórean descent, shows that other kinds of Middle Men, descended from others of the Three Houses of the Edain, lingered in the West, in Eriador (as the Men of Bree), or further south — notably the people of Dor-en-Ernil (Dol Amroth).

[§] Because such matters had little interest for the Gondorian chroniclers; and also because it was assumed that they had in general remained faithful to the monotheism of the Dúnedain, allies and pupils of the Eldar. Before the removal of most of the survivors of these "Three Houses of Men" to Númenor, there is no mention of the reservation of a high place for worship of the One and the ban on all temples built by hand, which was characteristic of the Númenóreans until their rebellion, and which among the Faithful (of whom Elendil was the leader) after the Downfall and the loss of the Meneltarma became a ban on all places of worship.

established themselves in Rohan at the time of the Oath (soon after the Battle of the Field of Celebrant), and such structures in high places as places of religious worship was no part of the customs of Men, good or evil.* [28] It may however have been a tomb.

At the words "It may however have been a tomb", Tolkien abandoned this text, and (no doubt immediately) marked the entire account of the Halifirien for deletion.

Christopher Tolkien writes: "These last words may well signify the precise moment at which the tomb of Elendil on Halifirien [cf. UT:304] entered the history; and it is interesting to observe the mode of its emergence. The original 'Firien' was the 'black hill' in which were the caverns of Dunharrow (VIII:251); it was also called 'the Halifirien' (VIII:257, 262), and Dunharrow was 'said to be a *haliern*' (Old English *hálig-ern* 'holy place, sanctuary') 'and to contain some ancient relic of old days before the Dark'; while *Dunharrow*, in my father's later words, is 'a modernisation of Rohan *Dūnhaerg* "the heathen fane on the hillside", so-called because this refuge of the Rohirrim … was on the site of a sacred place of the old inhabitants' (VIII:267 n.35). The name *Halifirien* was soon transferred to become the last of the beacon-hills of Gondor, at the western end of the chain (VIII:257), which had been first named *Mindor Uilas* (VIII:233); but there is no indication at all of what my father had in mind, with respect to the very express meaning of the name *Halifirien*, when he made this transference. The account given above, written so late in his life, seems to be the first statement on the subject; and here he assumed without question that (while the hill had earlier borne the Sindarin name *Fornarthan* 'North Beacon') it was the Rohirrim who called it 'the Holy Mountain': and they called it so, 'according to their traditions at the time of the War of the Ring', because of the profound gravity and solemnity of the oath of Cirion and Eorl taken on its summit, in which the name of Eru was invoked. He refers to a record in the 'annals' that 'an ancient

---

* The Men of Darkness built temples, some of great size, usually surrounded by dark trees, often in caverns (natural or delved) in secret valleys of mountain-regions; such as the dreadful halls and passages under the Haunted Mountain beyond the Dark Door (Gate of the Dead) in Dunharrow. The special horror of the closed door before which the skeleton of Baldor was found was probably due to the fact that the door was the entrance to an evil temple hall to which Baldor had come, probably without opposition up to that point. But the door was shut in his face, and enemies that had followed him silently came up and broke his legs and left him to die in the darkness, unable to find any way out.

monument of rough stones nearly man-high with a flat top' stood on the summit of the Halifirien – but he at once proceeds to argue strongly that its presence can be 'no support to the view that the mountain was in some sense "hallowed" before its use in the oath-taking', since any such ancient object of 'religious' significance 'could only have been erected by the Men of Darkness, corrupted by Morgoth or his servant Sauron.' But: 'It may however have been a tomb.'

"And thus the 'hallowing' of the hill (anciently named Eilenaer) was carried back two and a half thousand years before the Rohirrim settled in Calenardhon: already at the beginning of the Third Age it was the Hill of Awe, Amon Anwar of the Númenóreans, on account of that tomb on its summit. I have no doubt that the account of the Oath of Cirion and Eorl given, with the closely related texts, in *Unfinished Tales*, followed very shortly and perhaps with no interval at all the abandonment of this essay on the names of the rivers and beacon-hills of Gondor.

"It is thus seen that not only the present work but all the history of the Halifirien and Elendil's tomb arose from Mr. Bibire's brief query.

"This is a convenient place to notice a stage in the development of the story of Elendil's tomb that was not mentioned in *Unfinished Tales*. There is a rejected draft page for the passage recounting the definition of the bounds of Gondor and Rohan by Cirion and Eorl, which scarcely differs from the text printed in *Unfinished Tales* until the paragraph beginning: 'By this pact only a small part of the Wood of Anwar...' (UT:306). Here the rejected text reads:

By this agreement originally only a small part of the Wood west of the Mering Stream was included in Rohan; but the Hill of Anwar was declared by Cirion to be now a hallowed place of both peoples, and any of them might now ascend to its summit with the leave of the King of the Éothéod or the Steward of Gondor.

For the following day after the taking of the oaths Cirion and Eorl with twelve men ascended the Hill again; and Cirion let open the tomb. "It is fitting now at last," he said, "that the remains of the father of kings should be brought to safe-keeping in the hallows of Minas Tirith. Doubtless had he come back from the war his tomb would have been far away in the North, but Arnor has withered, and Fornost is desolate, and the heirs of Isildur have gone into the shadows, and no word of them has come to us for many lives of men."

"Here my father stopped, and taking a new page wrote the text as it stands in *Unfinished Tales*, postponing the opening of the tomb and the removal of the remains of Elendil to Minas Tirith to a later point in the story (UT:310)."

NOTES

1 That it was two lines from a poem attributed to Cynewulf, the *Crist*, that inspired Tolkien to create his mythology (cf. L:385, and Carpenter's *Biography*, pp. 72, 79), is an irony that no doubt keenly sharpened Tolkien's lament.

2 I.e., LR:1039.

3 No such corrected edition appeared in 1969, or during the remainder of Tolkien's life. For the corrected map that Tolkien refers to, and its fate, cf. UT:261–2 footnote, and 265.

4 I.e., LR:984.

5 I.e., LR:1114, entry for PH.

6 Cf. L:425: "Q. permitted, indeed favoured, the 'dentals' *n, l, r, s, t* as final consonants: no other final consonants appear in the Q. lists." Tolkien's list here omits *s*, no doubt unintentionally.

7 My thanks to Mr. Bibire for providing me with a photocopy of this letter.

8 Tolkien fell down stairs and injured his leg on June 17, 1968, while he and his wife Edith were preparing to move house from Oxford to Bournemouth. Cf. L:391ff., and Humphrey Carpenter's *Biography*, p. 251.

9 I.e., LR:274, 374.

10 The typescript actually reads *Gwathlo* here, though, as Christopher Tolkien notes, the Isen (Angren) river must be intended.

11 I.e., LR:1065; cf. also 1069. The name *Adorn* is given to this short river on Pauline Baynes's 1970 poster-map of Middle-earth, which is reproduced on p. 385 of the catalogue of the recent Bodleian exhibition *Tolkien: Maker of Middle-earth* (Catherine McIlwaine, 2018). The annotated map that Tolkien provided to Pauline Baynes, by which this name was apparently communicated, is likewise reproduced in the same catalogue, on p. 383.

12 Cf. UT:416 s.v. *Adorn*.

13 Pauline Baynes's "decorated map of Middle-earth" is the 1970 poster map just mentioned; and it indeed gives the name of the cape as *Andrast*, as does the annotated map also just mentioned.

14 The map of Middle-earth actually read *Hithaiglin*, prior to Christopher Tolkien's correction of the name to *Hithaeglir* when he redrew the map for *Unfinished Tales*. On the variation *Aiglos* vs. *Aeglos* (of the name of the spear of

Gil-galad, LR:243), Christopher Tolkien notes that he substituted the latter for the former in *Of the Rings of Power* (S:294).

15 I.e., LR:227.

16 Cf. LR:1113, entry for F.

17 In other words, the name is pronounced *Levnui*, with the sound of English v, but is best spelt *Lefnui* in an English context.

18 This not uncommon phenomenon of place names is exemplified further in *The Lord of the Rings* by such forms as *Bree-hill, bree* being an Anglicization of British *briga* (> Welsh *bre* 'hill'); and *Chetwood*, containing an Anglicization of British *kaito* (> Welsh *coed* 'wood, forest'). Cf. XII:39 fn., 81.

19 This was originally written as "Elvish settlement".

20 Tolkien provides a similar explanation for the initial element of the name *Gondor* itself: *gond* 'stone'; cf. L:409–10. Tolkien (appropriately) adopted this element into his Elvish languages from *ond, onn* 'stone', one of a very few words thought to have survived from the pre-Celtic languages of Britain; cf. L:410, VT30:10–14.

21 Tolkien here deleted a parenthetical note that read: "(Many of those who actually gave the names were mariners and settlers [*deleted*: who did not speak Sindarin fluently >] who had only small knowledge of Quenya and whose Sindarin was imperfect.)"

22 The words from "and Enedhwaith" to the end of this sentence entered as a handwritten note in the top margin. Cf. XII:328–9 n.66.

23 *Sward* originally meant, and can still be used to mean, the skin of the body (esp. hair-covered skin, such as the scalp), or the rind of pork or bacon.

24 The reference is to Gandalf's words while placing the White Crown upon Aragorn's head, LR:968: "Now come the days of the King, and may they be blessed while the thrones of the Valar endure!"

25 Tolkien did in fact go on to devise and record Cirion's "exact words": cf. UT:305.

26 Cf. LR:676.

27 See also XII:312–14.

28 In this footnote the name *Baldor* is (twice) an editorial replacement for *Brego* in the original. Tolkien has confused Brego, who completed the building of Meduseld, with his son Baldor, who passed beyond the Door of Dunharrow. See VIII:407, LR:787, 797–8; 1068, entry for 2512–70; and 1087, entry for 2570.

APPENDICES

I

METAPHYSICAL AND
THEOLOGICAL THEMES

"*The Lord of the Rings* is of course a fundamentally religious and Catholic work; unconsciously so at first, but consciously in the revision. That is why I have not put in, or have cut out, practically all references to anything like 'religion', to cults or practices, in the imaginary world. For the religious element is absorbed into the story and the symbolism." (L:172)

"Among the exiles, remnants of the Faithful who had not adopted the false religion nor taken part in the rebellion, religion as divine worship (though perhaps not as philosophy and metaphysics) seems to have played a small part...." (L:194 fn.)

"But since I have deliberately written a tale, which is built on or out of certain 'religious' ideas, but is *not* an allegory of them (or anything else), and does not mention them overtly, still less preach them, I will not now depart from that mode...." (L:283–4)

As stated in my introduction to part two of this book, Tolkien's claim that "*The Lord of the Rings* is of course a fundamentally religious and Catholic work" has puzzled many critics, because both *The Lord of the Rings* and Tolkien's wider *legendarium* are all but devoid of references to any religious *cultus* (let alone a *Catholic* system of rites and worship). And as I suggest, I think this claim puzzles many critics because they have overlooked what I believe is the most important word in the claim: sc. *fundamentally*. I take this word quite literally, and not merely as a throwaway rhetorical intensifier; that is, I take it that Tolkien is saying that *The Lord of the Rings* and, by extension, his broader *legendarium* (of which the *LR* is a deliberate part, and its lengthy coda), is *at its core and foundation*, or as one might say *in its essential nature*, based on religious, and specifically Catholic, beliefs and thought. Tolkien says as much in the third (seldom quoted) passage from *Letters* given above: "a tale, which is *built on or out of* certain 'religious' ideas" (emphasis added).

As I also stated there, it is my hope that the writings collected in this volume will support this. For some with knowledge of the Catholic faith – which in addition to a set of dogmas and religious rites entails a worldview encompassing *inter alia* a distinctive theology, metaphysics, cosmogony, and anthropology – many of the Catholic elements and themes highlighted and briefly explored here will have already been noted. But these will be opaque to many readers, and so I provide this concise guide for those readers who wish to know to what I believe Tolkien is apparently alluding or referring at various points that may otherwise only perplex or seem thoroughly abstruse.

AGES OF THE WORLD

p. 39: "we being in 1960 of the 7th Age...."

While many are familiar with the concept of named Ages of the World as found in classical mythology, e.g. the Golden Age, the Silver Age, etc., it is far less well known that the Catholic Church has long espoused a system of *numbered* Ages of the World, extending through at least a Sixth Age. Throughout Tolkien's life the Proclamation of the Birth of Christ, just before the start of the Christmas Vigil Mass, flatly stated that Christ was born "in the sixth age of the world". The text of the proclamation comes from the *Martyrologium Romanum* (Roman Martyrology), the Roman Rite Catholic Church's official list of martyrs and saints, with associated calendrical information. It reads in part (emphasis added):

... anno Imperii Octaviani Augusti quadragesimo secundo, toto Orbe in pace composito, *sexta mundi ætate,* Jesus Christus, æternus Deus æternique Patris Filius, mundum volens adventu suo piissimo consecrare, de Spiritu Sancto conceptus, novemque post conceptionem decursis mensibus, in Bethlehem Judæ nascitur ex Maria Virgine factus Homo.

... in the forty-second year of the empire of Octavian Augustus, when the whole world was at peace, *in the sixth age of the world,* Jesus Christ, eternal God and Son of the eternal Father, desiring to sanctify the world by His most merciful coming, having been conceived of the Holy Ghost, and nine months having elapsed since His conception, is born in Bethlehem of Judea, having become Man of the Virgin Mary.

BODY AND SPIRIT

p. 18: "their being was incarnate and consisted naturally of the union of a *fëa* ['spirit'] and a *hröa* ['body']"

p. 90: "'persons' – in whole being, *fëa* and *hröa*"

p. 237 fn.: "They say that the *fëa* or spirit 'remembers' its body (which it has inhabited in every part equally)"

pp. 247–8: "though those *fëar* that obeyed their summons were safe from the Darkness, to be naked was against their nature."

p. 272: "For the function of the body of one of the Incarnate is to house a *fëa,* the absence of which is unnatural to it; so that such a body is not ever in precisely the like case with a body that has never possessed a *fëa:* it has suffered loss. Moreover while the *fëa* was with it, the *fëa* inhabited it in every part or portion, less or greater, higher or lower."

Since the Enlightenment, and particularly stemming from the hugely influential theory of mind-body dualism espoused by seventeenth-century century philosopher, mathematician, and scientist René Descartes, it has become commonplace, even among many Christians, to regard the human person as a spirit (soul) that *inhabits* and *uses* a body, which however is of no particular importance to the nature or integrity of the human person. In this view, a human person is in no essential way incomplete when a soul leaves their body; in fact, for many the departure of a soul is actually regarded as liberating, as it frees the human person from material needs and burdens.

Though most who have adopted this view (in considered fashion or not) will be unaware of it, this dualist anthropology is in fact a revival of the ancient Platonic/Gnostic/Manichaean belief in the superiority of the spiritual to the material; and in their extremes, the belief that the material world, including the body, is inherently evil, a trap for the human soul, whose primary goal is, or ought to be, to free itself from the body and the material world.

In Catholic anthropology, on the other hand, the nature of the human person, and the relation of body and spirit in the human person, is precisely that which Tolkien ascribes to Incarnates, here and elsewhere, repeatedly and forcefully. That is, it is the nature of incarnate persons, both Elves and Men, to be a unity of body and spirit, such that if either is lost or separated, the incarnate person is incomplete, and has suffered a grievous loss and disruption to its nature. Neither the body nor the material world are inherently inferior to spirit, or something that a spirit has a duty to seek to escape.

p. 21 fn.: "by the birth of Lúthien [Melian] became enmeshed in 'incarnation', unable to lay it aside while husband and child remained in Arda alive, and her powers of mind (especially foresight) became clouded by the body through which it must now always work."

p. 210: "Pengolodh also cites the opinion that if a 'spirit' (that is, one of those not embodied by creation) uses a *hröa* for the further-ance of its personal purposes, or (still more) for the enjoyment of bodily faculties, it finds it increasingly difficult to operate without the *hröa*. The things that are most binding are those that in the Incarnate have to do with the life of the *hröa* itself, its sustenance and its prop-agation. Thus eating and drinking are binding, but not the delight in beauty of sound or form. Most binding is begetting or conceiving."

In marked contrast with that of Incarnates, the situation with spirits like the Valar and Maiar that are not incarnate by nature, but instead fashion bodies for themselves in order to more easily interact with Incarnates and the material world, turns out in one important aspect to be Platonic, as shown by this passage in Plato's *Phaedo* (*Plato: Complete Works*, Hackett, 1997, p. 73):

"The soul of the true philosopher thinks that this deliverance [from the body and the senses] must not be opposed and so keeps away from pleasures and desires and pains as far as he can; he reflects that violent pleasure or pain or passion does not cause merely such evils as one might expect, such as one suffers when one has been sick or extravagant through desire, but the greatest and most extreme evil, though one does not reflect on this.

What is that, Socrates? asked Cebes.

That the soul of every man, when it feels violent pleasure or pain in connection with some object, inevitably believes at the same time that what causes such feelings must be very clear and very true, which it is not. Such objects are mostly visible, are they not?

Certainly.

And doesn't such an experience tie the soul to the body most completely?

How so?

Because every pleasure or pain provides, as it were, another nail to rivet the soul to the body and to weld them together. It makes the soul corporeal.... As it shares the beliefs and delights of the body, I think it inevitably comes to share its ways and manner of life...."

EXISTENCE, CONTINGENCY OF

p. 289: "He [Eru] is outside Eä but holds the whole of Eä in thought (by which it coheres)."

In Catholic metaphysics, the existence of the material universe and all that is in it, is *contingent*: both in the sense that it does not exist by necessity but rather by a gratuitous act of Divine creation, and in the sense that its continued existence, in all its parts down to the most minute particle, and at all moments, is due to God's continuous (from a temporal view) willing of its existence. Its Catholic formulation (as so much else of Catholic metaphysics) is due to St. Thomas Aquinas, who greatly elaborated and expanded upon the contingency of existence.

Tolkien's particular statement here, that the whole of material and temporal existence (Eä, "the World that Is") "coheres" (< Latin *co-haerere*, literally 'stick together') in Eru's thought, also clearly echoes Scripture, in particular Col. 1:17: "He [Christ] is before all things, and in Him all things hold together". The ongoing contingency of existence is also reflected in Acts 17:28, where St. Paul, quoting (ultimately) Epimenides (who however had Zeus in mind), says to the gathered Athenians: "For 'In him we live and move and have our being,' as even some of your poets have said".

EVIL (AS LACK OF PERFECTION)

p. 173: " √*man* 'good'. This implies that a person/thing is (relatively or absolutely) 'unmarred': that is in Elvish thought unaffected by the disorders introduced into Arda by Morgoth: and therefore is true to its nature and function."

p. 250: "'Best', but not perfectly: that is, not in any case exactly according to the conceived and unrealized pattern. But such 'imperfection' is not an evil, necessarily."

Aquinas, like Augustine and Plato before him, held that evil has no independent existence. Certainly, rational beings can *do* evil things, but evil itself has no "being". Rather, in much the same way that dark has no independent existence, but is rather merely a lack or absence of light, evil for Aquinas is likewise some deficiency or lack of the good in/for created things. In Thomistic terms, this is held to mean a lack in a thing's *perfection of form*: that is, a failure or prevention of a thing to fully be or become that which by its nature it ought to be, in all its essentials. Hence it is in this sense evil if, say, a squirrel, which has the *form* (in Tolkien's parlance, *pattern*) of a quadrupedal tree-dwelling rodent with a bushy tail that typically feeds on nuts and seeds, either lacks or is deprived of one or more limbs: it does not fully realize, or no longer fully realizes, its form. This of course does not mean that such a squirrel is itself *evil*, only that it has suffered an evil (in this Thomistic sense). Obviously, too, there are degrees of such evil: if, losing one or more limbs, a squirrel is no longer able to dwell in trees or even obtain food for itself, then it suffers more of an evil than if, say, it lacked/lost part of its tail.

Even so, the Elvish definition of good, and of impairments to the good, hinges on the degree to which a thing or being realizes, or fails or is impeded from realizing, its particular *pattern*; that is, on the degree to which a thing or being is "unmarred". The unmarred state of Arda and its beings was perfectly "true to its nature and function"; but this perfection of all things was impaired by Morgoth, so that every thing in Arda has been subjected to an evil, and every being in Arda is in turn susceptible to an inclination to do evil.

EVOLUTION (THEISTIC)

p. 251: "This the Valar say is how the variety of Arda was indeed achieved: beginning with a few patterns, and varying these or blending pattern with pattern."

p. 288: "For it is clear in such lore as we have received from the Valar that they set in motion the unfolding of different living patterns at many different points in the *Ainulindalë*, and therefore this was repeated in Eä. Within Eä we have then not one single *Ermenië* or Great Pattern, but a number of early or Major Patterns (*Arkantïer*)."

p. 288–9: "... these 'major patterns' (*arkantïer*) developing in Arda will diverge whether by the design of their beginners, or by the varieties caused by the stuff of Arda which they must use, into different but similar groups of descendants."

A long-standing feature of what has come to be known as "young-Earth creationism" is the belief in "special creation": that is, that the first living things in all their species were created, if not "at once", nonetheless within a short period of time. This belief was (is) rooted in a literal interpretation of the creation account of Genesis, such that all varieties of life were created within a span of four days. Coupled with commitment to a theory of invariable, immutable forms (see HYLOMORPHISM below), there is no time or mechanism available for any sort of descent of species: all species must therefore have been directly created by God at the beginning of the world.

Tolkien's theory of *patterns* (forms) here, on the other hand, allows both for beginnings at different times of various species, from a variety of patterns (though always subordinate to and ultimately derived from Eru's own Great Pattern, and subject to the will of Eru), and even for their change, by blending or divergence, over time. (A time greatly lengthened by the alteration of the length of the Valian Year, though of course still nothing like geologic time.) It should be noted that this sort of theistic evolution is *not* the same as what is now commonly called "Intelligent Design", one form at least of which has God repeatedly intervening in time to shape and guide the development of species. Rather, the ability of patterns to blend and diverge over time is in a sense "built into" them. (Note that the term *evolve* itself, in origin and in this context, indicates a "rolling out" of some inherent potentiality already possessed by a living being, or in Tolkien's terminology, that "unfolds" over time.)

FALL OF MAN, THE

p. 222: "The Eldar thought that some disaster, perhaps even amounting to a 'change of the world' (sc. something that affected all its later history), had befallen Men which altered their nature, especially with regard to 'death'.... Andreth believed that death (and especially the fear of it) had come upon Men as a punishment or result of some disaster – rebellion against Eru the Eldar guessed."

In the Catholic view, the Fall of Man occurred when our "first parents", who are called Adam and Eve in the book of Genesis, transgressed against God's command that they not eat of the fruit of the Tree of the Knowledge of Good and Evil. Having done so at the instigation of Satan in the form of a serpent, they separated themselves from God's grace, and were expelled from the earthly paradise of the Garden of Eden. And because they were the first parents of all mankind, the consequence of their sin, called "original sin", was passed on to their children and so to all subsequent generations of the human race. It is for this reason that all of mankind is subject to toil, hardship, evil desires, and (at least bodily) death.

p. 88: "The Quendi never 'fell' as a race – not in the sense in which they and Men themselves believed that the Second Children had 'fallen'. Being 'tainted' with the Marring (which affected all the 'flesh of Arda' from which their *hröar* were derived and were nourished), and having also come under the Shadow of Melkor before their Finding and rescue, they could *individually* do wrong. But they *never* (not even the wrong-doers) rejected Eru, nor worshipped either Melkor or Sauron as a god – neither individually or as a whole people. Their lives, therefore, came under no general curse or diminishment; and their primeval and natural life-span, as a race, by 'doom' co-extensive with the remainder of the Life of Arda, remained unchanged in all their varieties."

Unlike Men, Elves did not fall corporately. They are thus in many ways a portrait of what Tolkien imagined unfallen Men could have been.

p. 23: "childbirth is not among the Eldar accompanied by pain"

Genesis 3:16 states that painful childbirth is one of the consequences of the Fall: "in pain you shall bring forth children". The Eldar, being unfallen, do not experience pain in childbirth. Moreover, since the Catholic Church teaches that the Virgin Mary was, as Tolkien says "the only *unfallen* [purely human] person" (L:286 fn.), i.e., preserved from original sin by an act of Christ's prevenient grace (the actual meaning of the Immaculate Conception), it likewise teaches that she did not experience pain during Jesus' birth.

p. 321: "The Númenóreans, or Dúnedain, were still in our terms 'fallen Men'; but they were descendants of ancestors who were in general wholly repentant, detesting all the corruptions of the 'Shadow'; and they were specially graced. In general they had little inclination to, and a conscious detestation of lust, greed, hate and cruelty, and tyranny."

Again, the early Númenóreans, though being fallen, by a special grace generally approach nearest to the unfallen Quendi, particularly in their right relations to God, to incarnate existence and self-mastery, to the natural world, and in their interests and arts.

HYLOMORPHISM

p. 249 fn.: "In the first shapings this primary substance or *erma* became varied and divided into many secondary materials or *nassi*, which have within themselves various patterns, whereby they differ one from another inwardly, and outwardly have different virtues and effects."

The Aristotelean-Thomistic metaphysic of *hylomorphism* (from Greek ὕλη, *hylē*, 'wood, matter', and μορφή, *morphē*, 'form'), holds that all material things (including human beings and all other things, living and unliving) are comprised of *matter* (ultimately derived from PRIME MATTER, q.v. below) and *form*, that is, a Divinely-willed organizing principle that shapes prime matter into the thing that it is. In a living being, its *form* is its *spirit*; in a human being (any Child of Eru) its *form* is its soul. In Tolkien's terms, living beings comprise *erma* 'prime substance' and an ultimately Divinely-willed *arkantië* 'great pattern'. A Tolkienian distinctive is that the *arkantiër* were developed in response to the Great Pattern, *Erkantië*, of Eru, and so represented a subcreative act; and yet were both permitted and willed by Eru. Another distinctive is that the nature of Incarnates consists of an unity of both body (in Tolkien's terms a *hröa*) and, as its pattern, a soul (in Tolkien's terms, a *fëa*).

INCORRUPTIBILITY OF SAINTS

p. 273 fn.: "Men report that the bodies of some of their Dead long maintain their coherence, and even sometimes endure in fair form as if they slept only. That this is true the Elves know by proof; but the purpose or reason is not to them clear. Men say that it is the bodies of the holy that sometimes remain long incorrupt: meaning those of whom the *fëar* were strong and yet were turned ever towards Eru in love and hope."

The Catholic Church recognizes as *incorruptible* a body that, without having been embalmed or otherwise artificially preserved, nonetheless shows little or no sign of decomposition even long after death. Incorruptibility is most often associated with saints, and among the laity at least incorruptibility is considered evidence that the deceased is a saint, whether (yet) canonized or not. Some incorruptible bodies are further said to exude the ODOUR OF SANCTITY (q.v.).

MARRIAGE

p. 20 fn.: "The 'desire' for marriage and bodily union was represented by √*yer*; but this never in the uncorrupted occurred without 'love' √*mel*, nor without the desire for children."

p. 155: "Elves married in *perpetuity* and as long as a first mate was alive and incarnate they had no thought of other marriage. In Aman the only case of a breach was Míriel/Finwë.... If a wife was left widowed (or vice versa) forever remarriage was permissible, but seldom occurred."

Two distinctives of the Catholic view of sex and marriage are 1) that sex has two natural and inseparable ends, sc. spousal unity and procreation; and 2) that marriage is permanent while both spouses are alive, and so indissoluble save by and at the death of one or the other of the spouses. (It is this latter fact that presented Tolkien with a conundrum when considering the case of Finwë and Míriel, as well as when considering the phenomenon of Elvish reincarnation.)

p. 318: "Marriage was regarded [by Númenóreans] as natural for all, and once entered into was permanent."

As highlighted above (THE FALL OF MAN), while the Númenóreans were nonetheless fallen, like all mankind, they were (initially, and for long) granted a special grace to return to a state nearer to that of unfallen Man (and thus nearer to that of the Eldar). This state is exemplified not only in their increased lifespan, but in their moral character, including their attitudes and behaviours concerning marriage, which in these matters is the same as that of the (corporately) unfallen Eldar.

ODOUR OF SANCTITY

p. 242: "the Maiar were usually invisible unclad, but their presence was revealed by their fragrance.... This applied only to those uncorrupted."

Writing in the fourth century, St. Cyril of Jerusalem taught: "In each person, Scripture says, the Spirit reveals his presence in a particular way for the common good. The [Holy] Spirit comes gently and makes himself known by his fragrance." (Catechetical Lecture 16, *De Spiritu Sancto*)

The bodies of holy people are also reported to emit a fragrance, often compared to flowers, known as the *odor sanctitatis*, 'odour of sanctity', while alive and, more often, at and after the moment of death. The incorruptible bodies of saints have also been reported to emit the *odor sanctitatis* even long after their death.

PRIME MATTER

p. 249 fn.: "Some of the loremasters hold that the substance of Arda (or indeed of all Eä) was in the beginning one thing, the *erma* ['prime substance']".

p. 256: "the matters of Eä proceed from a single *erma*"

p. 287: "Arda began with the *Erma* ['prime substance'] and then the *nassi* ['materials'], before the entry of the living things"

p. 292–3: "[The Valar] had assisted in the general design of Eä, and severally, in different degrees and modes, in the production from the *erma* (or prime substance) of things of many kinds.... Neither they nor the Incarnate could make things utterly new; they could not "create" after the manner of Eru, but could only make things out of what already existed, the *erma*, or its later variations and combinations."

In Aristotelean-Thomistic metaphysics, "prime matter" (*prima materia*) is the fundamental, created, but undifferentiated matter from which all material things are made, through the agency of ultimately Divinely-willed forms, that organize and shape a portion of prime matter into the thing that it is. In Tolkienian terms, it is the *erma* 'prime substance', from which all *nassi* 'materials' derive, by the agency of *kantiër* 'patterns' that derive mediately from the Valar, but ultimately from Eru.

Cf. HYLOMORPHISM above.

II

GLOSSARY AND INDEX OF QUENYA TERMS

This glossary and index is not intended to be exhaustive, but only to provide ready glosses and locations of Quenya terms that are important for understanding Tolkien's texts and their interrelatedness. Terms that are chiefly used as proper names (e.g. *Arda*) are indexed only as to locations where Tolkien offers a pertinent gloss or other qualification of meaning.

Aman 'Unmarred State', the Blessed Realm 173.
Ambar 'world': for the full meaning see 227; also 228, 230, 231 n. 5, 300–1.
Arda "the Earth" (lit. 'realm') 227, 245, 282, 285 n.6, 301.
arkantiër 'Major Patterns' (cf. HYLOMORPHISM in App. I.) 256, 288.
axan, pl. *axani* 'law' 210–13.
coimen, pl. *coimendi* 'life-year' (= 144 *löar*) 84–6, 88, 91, 105, 120, 121–2, 124, 143 n.4.
coivië 'living' (as a process) 84, 89, 92 n. 9, 119.
Cuiviénen (also *Kuiviénen*) 'Water of Awak(en)ing' 62, 63 n.10, 283.
Cuivienyarna 'Legend of the Awakening' 13, 55, 85 fn., 296.
Endor 'Middle-earth' (lit. 'Middle-land') 39, 94–9, 282.
Erkantië 'Great Pattern' (cf. *Arkantiër* above) 256, 288, 290 n.1.
erma 'prime substance' (cf. PRIME MATTER in App. I.) 14, 17 n.1, 172, 249 fn., 250, 256, 265 n.6, 286–7, 292–3, 294 n.2.

Ermenië 'Device of Eru' 256, 287–8, 290 n.7, 291 n.9.

fana, pl. *fanar*   visible 'raiment' of the Valar and Maiar 198, 233, 241–5.

fëa, pl. *fëar*   'spirit' 14–16, 18–21, 23–4, 25 n.6, 26 n.20, 27 n.21, 28–30, 54, 58 n.24, 66, 84, 86–7, 89–90, 119, 147, 155, 159, 171, 201–2, 204 n.6, 208, 213 fn., 217 n.3, 222–3, 225 n.14, 234, 236–8, 247–9, 253–64, 265 n.2, n.3; 266 n.13, 268, 271–3, 287, 290, 291 n.19, 344.

hröa, pl. *hröar*   'body' 14–16, 18–20, 23; 24 n.2, n.3; 25 n.6, 26 n.20, 28–9, 44, 54, 58 n.24, 59–60, 67, 70, 73, 77, 83–4, 86–90, 119, 121, 143 n.3, 147, 155 fn., 171, 204 n.8, 206, 208–10, 211 fn., 213 fn., 217 n.3, 222–3, 235–6, 260, 262 fn., 265 n.3, 266 n.13, 269, 271, 344.

hröambari   'incarnates' (lit. 'body-dwellers') 14.

hröangolmë   'lore of the body' 322.

hrondo, pl. *hrondor*   'body' 202, 204 n.8, 235–8, 269.

indemmar   'mind-pictures' 198–9, 237 fn., 240 n.3, 244 fn., 245 n.7, 266 n.12.

indo   'mind' 198 fn.; 'state [of mind]' 207; 'will' 221–3, 224 n.7; 'heart' 239.

kenta   'enquiry' 206.

köa, pl. *köar*   'body' (lit. 'shelter') 244, 302.

lambë   'speech' 208–9, 217 n.3.

löa, pl. *löar*   'solar year' (lit. '[period of] growth') 7, 10, 12, 22, 25 n.12, 26 n.21, 29–31, 34–5, 37, 40 n.1, 44–9, 51–2, 55 n.1, 56 n.13, 69 n.16, 84–5, 87–8, 91, 94, 101, 102 n.1, 103 n.13, 105, 107, 110 n.3, 111 n.2, 119–20, 121–3, 129, 143 n.2, n.7, 146–50.

nassë, pl. *nassi*   'material' (cf. *erma* above) 249–51, 255, 265 n.6, 286–7, 290 n.3.

olmen, pl. *olmendi*   'growth-year' (= 12 löar) 84–7, 91, 120.

olmië   'growth' from conception to maturity 84, 89, 92 n.9, 119.

Onnalúmë (*Ontalúmë*)   'Time of the Children' 22, 25 n.15, 26 n.15, 31, 87–8, 114, 116–17, 122, 125–7, 131, 143 n.11.

ontavalië   'puberty' 120, 121, 131.

órë   'inner(most) mind'; (pre)monition 176, 219–20, 222–3.

ósanwe   'interchange of thought' 206, 208–9.

quantolië   'maturity (lit. 'full growth') 91, 122.

sáma, pl. *sámar*   'mind' 207–8, 211–14.

sanar   'mind' 221–3.

sanwe   'thought' 208, 211, 213, 221.

tengwesta   'language' 206, 208–9, 217 n.3.

INDEX

This index aims to be comprehensive, but large entries such as *Elves* and *Time* are divided into subtopics. It covers the main text excluding the appendices (though reference is occasionally given to the glossary in Appendix II). Because of the large number of cross-references in this book, the titles of texts published within it are omitted (they can be found in the Contents), and so are those of *Unfinished Tales* and volumes in *The History of Middle-earth*.